YOUR WINGS
BOOK 1
SARAH CUADRA

Book Cover by Birdy Everhart — birdy.everhart@gmail.com

Published by Denvia's Archive

First edition: 2025

About the Author

Sarah Cuadra has been writing since she was a young child but mainly participated in telling verbal stories based on dreams or reconfigurations of other stories she had heard from others. She often felt overshadowed by others in her community who had access to proper resources and education. It was difficult for her to get others to read her stories due to the lack of grammar skills, but by the time she was a teen, she began writing for her friends who happily read a new chapter a day by email, for they were unbothered by all the mistakes and could focus on the concepts of the story.

A literature class with two other students also gave Sarah a door of opportunity outside of her limited world, and she began consuming works of old that helped her fall in love with writing from a different perspective than just what was accessible in the environment that she was contained within. However, due to the rigid system, Sarah would begin writing stories, only to abandon the concepts in fear that it wasn't good enough or, simply, not upheld by the standards that were only a cage keeping her from evolving into the writer she desired to be.

After decades of traveling through a journey of self-discovery, Sarah began to break the mental chains and, thus, Your Wings was written in a matter of months and started out with only half the word count. Sarah's partner was the first to read it, and encouraged her to polish it, share it, and keep going since it was only the beginning. Within the records of Sarah's abandoned stories, she discovered several ideas and drawings consisting of the early concepts of the Teraganes, giving hope that the stories we want to tell may take time before they are ready to be heard by others.

Sarah's journey is one of hope—a theme she wishes to convey through the trials and hardships in which the world consists. Stories are part of us, for we each have our own tale, and we never know when it may finally come full circle.

This story is dedicated to those who struggle to find their way in life

To those who seek answers when there is only silence

To the survivors of a cruel world that doesn't make sense

And to anyone who intuitively knows there is more in life than the basic path set before them

May you feel inspired and seen through the eyes of our dear character

May you find your wings to soar upon the winds brought by great storms

CONTENTS

CHAPTER ONE
WHEN CURIOSITY IS FOUND WITHIN A MEADOW

It was a particularly hot day that summer when I first met Lillie. As a young Teragane, I never thought much about the weather. My only concerns about the matter were when it was unpleasant to fly in, whether that was freezing temperatures from blizzards, fierce rainstorms with lightning, or the dreadful rays of a strong summer sun. When I felt the scorching heat hit the back of my wings, I looked for a place to escape from the unpleasant flying conditions.

As I made my daily routine flying path, I passed over a cliffside meadow I had seen many times before. The clearing enticed my overheating body to rest a moment, escaping the heat of the day before embarking back up the mountain. I had my sufficient nourishment for the day, hydration from fresh river water, and was ready to return home when the heat hit particularly harsh. Typically, my routine consisted of flying down from my mountain residence in the beginning of the day, and then heading back up before the rays of the sun were at their strongest. Most days, I would completely avoid flying midday.

Why did I that day? I have not the faintest idea, only the satisfaction of knowing that my world would become greater after stopping on that cliffside meadow.

I landed in the clearing, and the long shadows cast from the cedar trees cooled me instantly. The trees covered most of the mountain terrain, except towards the summits, where the steep ridges of rocky turf made it impossible for nature to grow. The small meadow, clear and surrounded by the giant trees, felt restorative from the scorching sun.

I sat next to a large boulder, folded my dark wings behind me, and stretched my legs along the cooling ground. The grass swayed as the wind rolled through, causing small pink and yellow blossoms of summer flowers to dance. Bees and little white butterflies bounced from each flower in harmony with the summer blooms and breeze. I rested while sitting in the grass, but only for a short while.

After feeling rejuvenated, I stood up to gaze over the cliffside. The mountain range extended far into the region with various peak heights, some higher elevations still covered in snow, and other lower ridges barren from the heat of the summer season. My eyes followed the highlands that descended into the valleys below, the glistening water of different rivers running through groups of trees. My still position at that moment was a rare sight for myself. My observation of the lay of the land was always from above while I ventured over the province every day, flying in the sky.

From my standing position on the edge of the cliff, I examined the area with a new perspective. The forest, the mountains, and the valley below—it all seemed so different and interesting from this new vantage point. I looked behind me, facing the cedar forest, and observed the mountain behind it. Its steep, sloping sides extended high with sharp ridges, and the summit was completely hidden by clouds.

The heat is no longer unbearable. I really shouldn't fly midday during the summer.

I observed the sun beginning to make its way between my home mountain and its neighboring ridge, and I prepared myself to take flight and return home above the clouds. A rustling sound alerted me as a strange young girl appeared from the forest.

"Hey there!" her friendly voice called out. I hesitated as she continued to walk towards me.

"I've never seen you before!" she exclaimed. Her smile beamed as she tilted her head, and her rosy cheeks rounded. Confused and stricken by shock, I only stared, for I was unaccustomed to meeting strangers.

"You found my meadow," she said, her voice soft yet invigorating.

"Your meadow?" I questioned curiously. I lowered my wings, folding them behind me.

"Okay, well, it's not *my* meadow, but it's my favorite spot. And no one else knows about it. Except you, I guess. I'm Lillie—what's your name?"

"Sable," I replied while standing stiff as a tree. I felt shocked, unable to fully understand the situation, yet tantalized by the sudden appearance of a friendly stranger. She approached me with a warm aura, like a soft summer breeze gracefully flowing through the tall grass.

She gazed upon me attentively, then began circling me. Feeling alarmed, I followed her movements, circling in place and keeping her from going behind me. She stopped, upon realizing I wouldn't let her fully examine my stature. Although my entire body was alert to the strange girl, I couldn't bring myself to fly away from such a new, exciting event.

"Nice to meet you, Sable," she said while standing very close and with eyes wide. "Are you a gremlin or a demon?"

"Neither," I replied. I had never heard of such creatures before, yet neither had I expected to meet someone different than me wandering out from the forest.

"Oh good—I wouldn't want you to pull out my hair or eat my soul!" she shouted, and I furrowed my brows. "You must be a Teragane since you have big black wings." I nodded in response while shifting my wings behind me.

"Cool! Must be fun to fly wherever you want. I've never met someone like you before."

"Nor I a—" I did not know how to respectfully respond. Her features were different from those of my own kind. She had no wings, and her skin was a stormy gray color with cool undertones, unlike my light brown complexion.

I did not mingle with others outside of my mountain colony, although I did know vaguely of other people who resided in the valleys and forests. I knew of their existence throughout the province as I was educated by my early guides, specifically to avoid interaction and respect their ways of life. I was taught that the Teragane do not engage with others outside of our own colony.

However, Lillie's unthreatening presence stirred curiosities within my mind, enticing me to ignore those original teachings. Although she was different from me, something fluttered in my heart as I anticipated further interactions with the strange young girl—a feeling I desired exploring.

"I'm from the forest," she said, and her pointed ears perked up. She did not elaborate, but it did not pique my interest or concern. I accepted this answer as satisfactory and anticipated her next movement, completely enamored by her presence and a strange feeling within my own heart.

"You live on the mountain?" she asked, then turned to point at a mountain peak from a further distance. "Like, way over there?"

"Actually, that one," I said, and pointed my finger to the mountain directly behind the cedar forest. As Lillie's green eyes followed the direction in which I pointed, the voices of my teachers rang in my head.

Do not speak to others nor give them any information about the Teragane people. We live our lives separately; do not partake in the imbalances of life.

"Whoa, you live pretty close to the forest," she said as she slightly bounced on her feet. "Can you see my house from up there?"

"I—uh, I didn't know there were houses in the forest," I replied, and I narrowed my eyes, trying to see through the woods, but the density of the trees and their immense trunks made it impossible to see beyond the initial tree-line against the meadow.

"Oh, yeah, there are lots of houses in the forest. Hey, is it super cold up there, like with snow?"

"Mostly." I began to feel nervous about how many questions Lillie was asking. My enticing curiosities turned into anxiety as I realized how much I was revealing to her as an outsider. The thrill of rebellion suddenly lost its allure as discomfort rose within my chest.

"Cool! I like snow. Hey! I wanted to eat my honey and bread. Would you like some?"

Lillie did not wait for my answer but instead turned around, walked to where a boulder sat, and settled herself on the grassy ground. Feeling relieved, I sighed as my instincts prompted me to leave the area. However, once again, my curiosity about Lillie stopped me as I watched her move around.

She ripped off her leather shoes and stretched her feet onto the grass. She removed a satchel she was carrying, unraveled a napkin holding something brown, and began spreading honey from a glass jar. A scent of something delicious enticed me to follow her, and I continued ignoring the teachings of my own kind.

Allowing myself to indulge in childish inquiries, I sat on my knees with my wings folded behind me and observed Lillie spreading honey on bread. I had never eaten bread before. I remembered eating honey when I was a younger child, when my mother would bring me something to eat. Since she no longer fed me, I had never bothered to gather any for myself. Bread was something completely foreign to my taste buds. It seemed odd at first, but, after taking my first bite, the complimentary flavors of the sweet honey and neutral, yeasty essence compelled me to try more.

"My mother made this fresh today, which is best," Lillie said. "Second-day bread, if it lasts, is usually best for sandwiches."

"What is a sandwich?" I asked while looking at Lillie. Without hesitation, she began explaining to me that a sandwich consisted of placing meat and other types of food between two slices of bread. When I asked more about this concept, she continued to explain the difference between the kinds of breads her village made, some methods of grinding grain, and different types of flour. Her life sounded advanced and artistic in its meal-making—something absolutely foreign to my own experiences as a Teragane who simply gathered food for survival.

I did not understand such concepts, but, as she talked, I felt relaxed and comfortable, and I enjoyed watching her as she moved her hands around and continuously shifted her sitting position while speaking.

"Sometimes we use the old bread that is too gross to eat as bait for the rats," Lillie explained while twisting her loose, brown hair with her fingers. "I don't think it's fair to trap the rats. But father says the rats will poison our food; that is why we kill the rats. I don't want poisoned flour. Then we can't eat our bread!"

"Rats are not poisonous," I said while furrowing my eyebrows.

"Yeah? Well, that's what my father said. Maybe rats in the cedar forest are different from where you are from."

"Perhaps."

"Maybe they become poisonous if they eat flour."

"Sure."

"Maybe! I once heard about this man from the north bringing an animal that hunts rats. Maybe we should get one of those to keep the rats out of the flour."

Even though I could not fully relate to what Lillie talked about, her voice and stories were interesting, and her explanations captivated my attention. I had never thought about animals being different depending on their area or what they ate.

I thought about my early teachings of hunting wild animals, which ones to avoid, like the boars or wolves that could cause me harm, and how quickly the smaller creatures were supposed to be consumed due to being inedible after a certain time. I was taught to use salt to preserve fish over winter, and that was the only adequate source of sustenance to be consumed through the isolation months. I remembered asking my teachers *why*, receiving thorough answers, but never did I think beyond what other methods of eating and cooking could be explored. For that was not the way of the Teragane.

My mind enjoyed the new concepts, and I rested against the boulder, leisurely adjusting my wings while I listened to Lillie. My nervousness subsided as I convinced myself that there was no harm in listening to the girl from the forest explain *her* culture.

Between the great shadows of the cedar trees and the cool summer breeze, it was the perfect relaxing summer afternoon for my younger self. I was surprised at how comfortable I felt with Lillie's amiable personality and how friendly she conducted herself. Perhaps she was just as captivated by me as I was by her.

Even though I already had my daily nourishment, the bread and honey filled my stomach with a new sensation of satisfaction and warmth. As I casually rested, listening to Lillie's soft voice, I noticed the setting of the sun as the shadows of the trees completely covered the meadow.

"The sun is nearly set," I said while sitting up from my position. "It is time for me to—"

"Oh!" Lillie shouted, startling me. "I need to go home. My parents will kill me!" She hurriedly grabbed her items, stuffing the napkin into her satchel, and put her footwear back on her feet.

"They will kill you?" I asked as I widened my eyes, suddenly feeling unnerved at what kind of people would kill their own child.

"No, not really," she quickly replied. "But they'll be mad. I gotta go!" She shot up and started running towards the cedar forest.

"It was nice meeting you!" she yelled as she ran back to the woods. I watched her small figure race into the forest, disappearing into the darkness.

I stood up, feeling enamored by my summer afternoon with Lillie. I was curious about her and whether I would ever see her again. My stomach was satisfied, and my heart was warm. As my mind felt captivated by new sensations, a desire to see Lillie again grew strong.

Maybe if I come back tomorrow, I can see her again.

CHAPTER TWO

WHEN FRIENDSHIP AND FLOWERS BLOOM

I returned to the meadow around midday, like the day before, despite the strong summer heat. I had hunted for my nourishment during the morning, as usual, and stopped at the cliffside clearing in hopes of seeing Lillie again. She was strolling around the grass, humming a song as she was filling her satchel with plants. I landed nearby, and her sun-kissed cheeks rounded upon discovering my return.

"Sable!" she shouted and ran towards me. "Look what I found!" She widened the opening of her satchel, revealing heaps of pink and yellow colors.

"Flowers?" I asked as I peered into her satchel.

"I will bring them back home," she said. "Maybe my mother can do something nice with them. I hope she likes them. Do you like flowers? Anyway, would you like something to eat?" Lillie, like once before, did not wait for me to answer any of her questions. She pulled a cloth out of her green skirt pocket and unfolded it, revealing a single slice of bread. I took it and munched happily, intently watching as she pulled out berries from another pocket.

"Try these," she said. I recognized the little black berries and happily ate them, enjoying the mixture of berries with the yeasty flavors of bread. "I just found a *ginormous* bush with lots of these."

"I've eaten them before," I replied as I licked the remnants of the berry juices from the palm of my hand.

"Ah, that's why you trusted me," she said with a changed tone of voice. As I looked at her with a raised brow, she grinned, her rosy cheeks rounding, and her long, pointed ears perked up.

"What do you mean?"

"Gotta be careful, Sable. I could have given you poisonous berries." Lillie suddenly laughed while pointing a finger at me. I felt my lips curl in amusement at her interesting behavior, thinking she was silly for saying such a thing. Yet the idea of her feeding me poisonous food suddenly overcame my mind. I was trusting of Lillie; I ate her food and answered her questions. Perhaps too trusting?

The forest dwellers live primitive lives in the valleys, I remembered my mother telling me while we stumbled upon a hunting camp during my early days of training. *We do not interfere with their lives, they not with us. We live separately to keep peace and balance.*

Why? Was interacting with Lillie a threat to myself? Her demeanor felt safe and friendly, she was by no means a vicious hunter or territorial bear protecting her cubs. She really had no reason to poison or cause me harm. I saw no logical reason for her to feed me indigestible food, and, if she were, why would she eat the same food if she was attempting to hurt me? Perhaps her remark was purely motivated by amusement; her change of tone enamored me, and a new feeling of audaciousness rose within my chest.

"I think if you wanted to poison me, you would have given me bread made from rat-flour," I finally said, sensing my cheeks turning warm. "That would have been difficult for me to detect."

"Hey!" Lillie bantered. "That's a good idea. I'll remember that next time I want to poison someone!" A chuckle escaped my mouth. Lillie's humor was entertaining, something unfamiliar to me, yet I thoroughly enjoyed partaking in such a sarcastic form of communication, relishing the playful sensation within my heart.

"How old are you, anyway?" she blurted out while wiping her stained, but smooth hands on her green skirt.

"I am in my twelfth year," I answered, still feeling the warmth in my face. I looked down at my hands, observing the dark stains also on my skin.

"So, you're twelve? Hey! So am I. That's why we are the same height." Lillie stood close to me, placing her hand near her forehead, and extended it to mine. She moved her stained hand from her head to mine in repetition, scrunching her nose as she measured our heights.

"I'm not sure that's how it works," I said, and took a step back from her close figure.

"I'm taller than the other kids my age. Nice to see another kid my size." I examined Lillie. She was, in fact, my height. However, she was quite different from me in her other features. Her deep gray skin revealed cool undertones, similar to a sky before a storm. Her green eyes sparkled in the sunlight, and her cheeks, nose, and the tips of her pointed ears were rose-colored.

My ears were pointed, but hers were slightly thinner and longer than mine. She wore a cream-colored blouse and an earthy green skirt that went just below her knees. Her brown leather shoes, tossed somewhere in the grass, were similar in color to her chestnut-brown hair.

Lillie resembled earthy, neutral tones, while I with my black wings and dark clothes felt the opposite. She was like a blossoming tree of nature while I cast a shadow behind with my dark figure.

"Are kids in your neighborhood the same height as you?" she asked while still observing the top of my head and our similar height.

"What is a neighborhood?" I questioned.

"Other people's houses, of course. People who live near you and stuff like that. You know? It doesn't have to be right next to you. I have a big neighborhood. Lots of kids live near me, although I don't think of all of them as my neighbors."

"Oh, okay."

"So, yeah, are kids in *your* neighborhood as tall as you?"

"Yes."

"Cool! I'm the same height as the Teragane kids!" Lillie ran off laughing, doing cartwheels in the open grassy area. I smiled while shaking my head. I thought she was childish yet entertaining. Her easily amused attitude was enjoyable to observe. Her answers to my questions were intriguing, causing me to think more about the world around me.

I jumped onto the boulder nearby and lowered myself into a crouched position. I watched Lillie continue to cartwheel around the meadow while grabbing little yellow flowers in between her movements. She hummed a tune like a bird singing in the morning light, and twirled her green skirt like the blossoming flowers spreading their leaves, smiling as she occasionally glanced at me.

I thought about my clever banter with her sarcastic comments, thoroughly relishing my witty participation. We may had been different in personality and physical features, yet I admired our differences. Then, I wondered about the concept of a neighborhood, thinking about the other Teragane kids who lived near me on the mountain. I questioned if *neighborhood* was the right word to describe my colony.

By force of habit, I started to establish my stop at the cliffside meadow as a midday ritual. After making my morning hunting trip down to the rivers, I would then fly to the meadow and wait for Lillie. Sometimes she was already there, singing to herself while walking around barefoot, and always overly expressive when she saw me. The other times when she had not yet arrived, I waited while the sun moved above in the sky. But, always, even if inconsistent in her timing, she would come with a beaming smile whenever she saw me.

Lillie also brought something to eat every day. Sometimes it was delicious; other times it was a strange experience. Her life was unpredictable but curious for me to observe, just like the food she shared with me. Often, she would explain the creative process of her food, sometimes with humorous details, but other times it was rather depressing, for life within the forest seemed difficult to obtain sustenance.

I did not always understand everything she talked about, particularly how her culture functioned. Her life seemed advanced in comparison to mine, mysterious at times. But, for my younger self, it was an interesting experience every time Lillie spoke. I always looked forward to listening to her stories, anticipating the new concepts to think about, and impetuously awaited the opportunity to banter with her sarcastic remarks.

"I had to fight for the stalks of corn today," she said one afternoon while we sat together.

"Why?" I asked while munching on the cornbread she had given me. I enjoyed the mix of grainy texture and honey, despite that Lillie had said it was incomplete without butter, which apparently was difficult to obtain.

"There was a shortage, as usual, and that darn Thabias stole my share. Mother told me to do what is absolutely necessary to retrieve our share of stalks. Don't let that dirty, stupid Thabias take our food."

"Why would he take your food?"

"Because he is stupid." Lillie crossed her arms and pouted her lips. She seemed quite furious as she sighed deeply and then took a vicious bite of the cornbread, causing bits of crumbs to linger in the corners of her mouth. Her thin brows were furrowed, and I noticed her rosy nose and cheeks deepen into a red crimson color, and her usual sparkling green eyes dimmed. It was my first time seeing Lillie angry, unlike her usual happy self. Thabias was a young boy living in her neighborhood, someone who I knew that she didn't like, so, naturally, I didn't care for him either, especially after hearing Lillie's opinion on his intelligence.

"Did you fight him?" I asked as I adjusted to my side in a laying position. I felt the wind rustle my black hair and slightly brushed my fingers through while my wings twitched as I folded them.

"Of course I did!" she shouted. I laughed, imagining Lillie attacking a child for taking her corn, defending what was rightfully hers. As a Teragane, I learned how to defend myself and was encouraged to play-fight with the others in my colony while we were young. Perhaps Lillie also learned how to fight with the children in her *neighborhood*. Were our cultures really that different? Were my teachers wrong about the forest dwellers?

My laughter started deep within—my first deep belly laugh, and I placed my hand on my side.

"What?" Lillie retorted, and rose to a standing position, anger still obvious upon her cheeks. "He deserved it! He thinks he is *so* much stronger than me—and better. I had to prove him wrong."

"He is stupid for thinking he can steal food from you." I continued to chuckle. Lillie's smile returned, and she began laughing while placing her hands proudly upon her hips and puffing out her chest.

"Yeah, exactly! An actual tree stump!"

"Sounds like he deserved every bit of your wrath." I hoped to only continue riling her up, for, I rather liked this side of Lillie. Her green eyes widened, and her cheeks further reddened with intensity. Often her face would redden with excitement, but this red was much stronger, like a fire turning into a blaze beneath her gray skin. I thought her skin to be enchanting, like a glorious cloudy sky before an intense storm with hues of purple and blue. I liked seeing her full of fury and defensiveness, for the scarcity of food was the pinnacle of her livelihood.

I was accustomed to the others in my colony having similar defensive reactions to situations of survival, yet, mostly, it was animalistic, bearing similarities to eagles fighting over a fresh kill or wolves snapping their jaws to keep their pack in order. Lillie, on the other hand, seemed more advanced, witty, and I enjoyed her behavior as one to challenge another's intelligence. Perhaps I could also do the same, at least, next time someone attempted to steal my food—if that even were to ever happen.

Suddenly, Lillie began punching the air where she stood, then cartwheeled around me, displaying her full wrath. As a rather thin 12-year-old, it wasn't much, but for me, as a young boy swirling with thoughts and new ideas, it was exciting, and I stood up and began cheering her on.

"A punch here." She jabbed, then wheeled away, then stood up and extended her bare foot rather high. "A kick here."

"A true defender of the corn stalks. No one shall steal from you ever again!" She punched, and I cheered; she cartwheeled, and I clapped.

It was glorious, impressive—well, at least for children in their twelfth years.

After several more cartwheels, punches, and dramatic kicks, she grew tired and plopped onto the ground. I followed along, and we laughed until our bellies ached and tears of joy ran down our faces. As her anger subsided, her cheeks and nose returned to their rosy complexions, but her eyes stayed glimmering with brilliant energy, and my stomach felt queasy. But, not one out of discomfort, but rather a lovely sensation of deep joy that I hardly expected to experience for I had never been taught such an expression could be attained.

I did not often think too much of Lillie's life inside the forest, other than imagining how she lived in parallel concepts of my own life. Her stories were entertaining, but rarely did I fully comprehend everything that happened within its components. I could only use my own personal experiences in relation, otherwise, I just enjoyed her narratives as something intriguing.

I thought of her as a friend, someone to spend my afternoons with, entertaining my curiosities and humoring me with playful teasing. She had her culture, I had mine, and being with her—being friends with her—was already against what I had been taught. Perhaps I didn't want to risk exploring my curiosities past the tree-line of the cedars, feeling content with what I had, for, it was very enjoyable. Why risk my rebellion further?

Looking back, I think Lillie was quite curious about my life on the mountain. Naturally, she was intrigued about many things, an attribute we shared, although I kept my thoughts mostly to myself. I never thought of it being interesting; her life seemed much more amusing, yet I rarely asked questions, perhaps to conserve my status. I was unaccustomed to partake in inquisitive interviews with others in general, for, the Teragane did not reveal information to others—not unless necessary.

"Why do you hunt by yourself?" Lillie asked me once.

"Because everyone hunts by themselves," I replied while lying against a boulder where we often settled, chewing on a stalk of something that Lillie had brought me. It was sweet, yet stringy, unlike the bones I had chewed on during my early developing years. I found the sweet stalk rather relaxing to chew on, causing my eyes to slowly close as I drifted into a sleepy daze with my arms behind my head, and my feet bounced as I crossed my outstretched legs.

The weather was turning cold as winter approached, but the meadow was still a relaxing spot for both of us. My woolen clothes were adequate for warmth, my leather, pliable boots suitable, but Lillie eventually brought a blanket for us to sit on, soon followed by her bringing a blanket to cover ourselves when the breeze turned colder. It was cozy, as she had described, and I enjoyed the advanced idea of covering with a blanket designated for the act of staying warm. Typically, I wore a cloak during the colder seasons, but, if needed, my wings could cover me adequately as a *blanket*.

"Why does everyone hunt by themselves?" Lillie asked. The sound of clinking wood resounded as her hands systematically maneuvered two wooden needles wrapped in material. Knitting, she called it, and she could make all kinds of other objects to wear.

"Because that is how we are taught," I sleepily replied.

"Who teaches you?"

"Our parents."

"Why don't you continue to hunt with your parents?"

"Because our parents stop hunting with us as children. They teach us to hunt by ourselves for our own survival."

"Your parents don't cook for you?" I stopped chewing for a moment, and my eyes widened from my sleepy haze. It was the first time I realized how contrasting our worlds were. Obviously, Lillie and I lived in very different environments; however, the conversation made me fully conceptualize the blatant contrast of those worlds.

I turned and faced her. She sat cross-legged, her bare feet wiggling underneath her. She was working with some type of material, making a scarf or hat—whatever it was. She was always working on something with her hands. I often listened to the sound of the clinking wooden needles, or the subtle rustling of her weaving dried grass. It was relaxing to listen to, as was her voice.

"No. No one cooks," I stated firmly.

"You eat fish raw? Is that why you like the food I bring?" she asked. As she tilted her head, her braided brown hair swayed to the side.

"Probably." I returned to my relaxed position, placing my hands above my head, and I continued chewing the sweet plant stalk.

It was true. I did love her food; even the strange food was enough of a captivating experience to satisfy me. Looking back, the weird food was not bad in taste; it was only an unfamiliar experience that created new sensations throughout my mouth. The worst was when it was painful—spicy, as she called it. Spicy *felt* horrendous, yet exciting.

"Do you share meals with others?" Lillie asked. I could sense she would only continue to bombard me with ongoing questions, so I decided to explain more of my culture, ignoring the pang of guilt rising from the reminders of my teachers.

"No. I do not share meals with others," I started, and I adjusted up from my relaxed position, leaning forward and taking the sweet grass out of my mouth. "Children are taught to be independent of their parents and others, hence why we do not share meals together. There's really no reason to do so. We are cared for as younglings, but only with the dedication of teaching us how to survive on our own. By age eight, sometimes later, we are nearly independent of our parents. Most of the time, the younglings are completely independent by age ten. Then our parents leave us. And we live on our own."

"Ten? You've been living alone since you were ten years old?"

"Yes."

"Do you at least live near others? Like, a neighborhood?" The clinking wooden needles stopped as she paused her working hands.

"Yes, there is a colony. Our parents find homes for us younglings before we are born, usually with other parents nearby and their children. Then, when the time is right, they leave and return to their original homes. So, yes, I live near others—some type of neighborhood—but we call it a colony."

"Do your parents visit you?"

"No. There are some Elder-Rituals, but not very often. I have only attended one gathering before. Maybe some other gatherings are required after certain years, but I often forget. There are Sages who keep track of that sort of stuff. They would inform me if there was a call for a gathering."

"Do you live *with* the others?"

"No, I live alone."

"Oh." Lillie grew quiet, and her facial expression appeared saddened, and an uncomfortable feeling rose within my chest. Not one of guilt of speaking about my culture, but rather causing Lillie to feel sad about my life.

"It's okay," I quickly said. "I like living alone. It is normal for me."

"It sounds terribly lonely to me," she said while blinking rapidly. "I could never imagine living alone."

"Well, that's not how *your* world works." Silence fell between us, and I leaned back against the boulder while Lillie continued to knit with the wooden needles. I did not think much of the matter until I later realized that it was the first time I had shared deeply about my life on the mountain. She often talked about her family, neighbors, and the people she interacted with every day, yet I never had stories to tell. My life probably seemed so desolate compared to hers. Her whole world revolved around other people in her life.

As the sun made its way behind the mountains, Lillie began packing her items—the blanket, the small materials for her project, and the napkins that held only food crumbs. She gently placed the items in her basket then hauled the wicker onto her back, fastening the leather straps around her shoulders.

"Unfortunately, I can't come every day anymore," Lillie said while looking at the ground.

"Okay," I replied as I stood near her.

"I can come every other day."

"Okay." She quickly approached me and swung her arms around me to give me a hug. Her warm embrace caused me to stiffen into an awkward position. I simply patted her back, feeling strange about the sudden burst of affection. She let me go, smiled, and then walked towards the forest, disappearing within the trees.

I took off into the sky, flying towards my home near the mountain peak, and I thought about her hug, particularly being near her. I thoroughly enjoyed her friendship and how our contrasting worlds collided, yet my mind began to ponder how things would evolve.

Was our friendship sustainable? Was it practical for my survival? Did it create an imbalance in my life?

No—at least, I didn't think as the seasons went by and Lillie and I grew older, living our separate lives in the environments we were born into. Her freedom to visit the meadow lessened as her obligations grew.

During the winter months, due to the freezing temperatures, I did not leave my mountain residence. Lillie also resided only within the comfort of her home during the colder season. By our teen years, we agreed to visit every two weeks, specifically during the days of a half-moon and the full-moon, and I was grateful for our blossoming friendship and continuous meetings through our growing years.

I spent my adolescence abiding by the rules and survivalist methods of my people, and Lillie followed the livelihood of her own people within the forest. She told me about her reading and writing lessons, learning about plants, various people she interacted with, filling her time with endless interactions of finding her way through her elaborate life, far from anything considered primitive.

I began to question the teachings of the Sage and my parents, specifically about their understanding of people like Lillie. Yet, I wasn't quite ready to challenge it and kept my meetings a secret from the others of the colony. Well, our natural isolation allowed me to never run into problems of my rebellion being exposed during those years.

As Lillie continued to pursue varying interests and survival with her own people, my life stayed consistently simple. I appreciated our time together in the meadow, but as her interactions with others increased, I began to feel a new sensation whenever I left after visiting Lillie in the meadow. My mind would ponder friendship and life within the mountain as an isolated Teragane every time I left the meadow.

I entered my room. A solitary residence. A cave carved into the mountainside.

When such sensations overwhelmed my mind and plagued my heart, I would acknowledge the word to describe my emotions: lonely.

CHAPTER THREE

WHEN THE MOUNTAIN IS ETCHED WITH INK

"**M**y father wants me to start working," Lillie said to me one day while we were sitting in the meadow. She was sewing a pair of trousers with a small needle, and a pile of various clothes lay next to her. I noticed her hands worked fast and efficiently as she mended the torn trousers, often mesmerized at how quickly she could move the pointed thin object through the thick material.

"Okay," I replied. I truly had no concept of the idea, only that I thought Lillie already did so much work in her daily life. I did not understand jobs or the need for such things since it was completely foreign to the way my culture existed, so, naturally, I sleepily listened to Lillie's words as she continued.

"I've been studying so hard; I just wish he would give me more time and space," she rambled.

"More time for what?" I asked while yawning, and switched my extended crossed legs, bouncing my right boot.

"More time to learn, of course! Like with my reading and writing lessons. I feel like I'm expected to be perfect at everything I set out to learn. I just wish they would give me more space. I wish I had more time to read and write."

"Then ask."

"Ha! You don't know what you're talking about." Lillie scoffed, and dramatically rolled her eyes.

"Okay." I shrugged, for I did not understand her situation, nor did I fully comprehend why she could not just ask for more time—and space—from her father. As I watched her hands swiftly repair the trousers, I noticed her demeanor turn sour, and I began to feel uncomfortable and slightly helpless as Lillie grew angrier.

"Ouch!" Lillie exclaimed and waved her finger around after pricking herself with the needle. "Stupid trousers." She threw the item away from her, then held her finger close to her chest. Lillie breathed heavily, trying to restore her composure.

I stood up from my relaxed position and walked over to the pants lying in the long, swaying grass. I grabbed it, looking intently at the pair of trousers. Large, made of brown pliable leather, I assumed were her fathers since I had never seen Lillie in trousers before.

I looked down at my own pants made of black wool, comparing the two different types of material. The leather pants were thick and heavy; mine were lightweight and flexible. Placing the trousers in front of me, I turned around and faced Lillie. Her green eyes widened, and a smile crossed her face.

"I think they look great," I said while striking a pose.

"Give them back," Lillie said and extended her hand with a flick. "Those are too big for you." I returned to her side and handed the item to Lillie. She continued her mending quietly, still smiling, but the pile of clothes next to her still heavily weighed upon her already burdened shoulders.

I wanted to help lighten her load. Regardless of not knowing how to use a needle or thread, I scanned the ominous pile of items, wondering if simply speaking about things would suffice. I may not have been able to help with the mending, but at least I knew that Lillie liked explaining about the process of her work.

"Tell me about these clothes," I said, and sat on my knees next to Lillie, and began sifting through the stack of textiles. The clothes were mainly large leather trousers, covered in dirt and extensive tears. The dirty items wafted a strange earthy smell, something I did not recognize—small details that could have helped me immensely in my future endeavors—if only I had thought to ask.

"Tell me about yours first," she said, and she peered at my torso with a curious expression.

"Mine?"

"Why are your sleeves unattached to your tunic?" Lillie pointed at my arms, and I followed her gaze. I had never given much thought to the structure of my clothes except when to clean them in the river and change into the other items I had been given by the Sage. However, upon observing the difference in the clothes Lillie worked on and my own personal items, I began to wonder about the differences too.

"The sleeves are easily removable for the Aging-Ritual," I said. My arms were covered in a pair of dark gray, thin sleeves that came over my shoulders, tied together with a thick, braided cord at the front of my chest. For my upper body, I wore a black, high-neck, sleeveless tunic that opened in the back for my wings with bone buttons that secured the wool material from the back.

Each item had been given to me by the Sage. I could only assume that it was the spiritual leaders of the Teragane who made the clothing—would I eventually also learn how to make my own clothes?

"Aging-Ritual?" she asked as she tilted her head. Her hands stopped moving and she tucked a few loose strands of hair behind her ear.

"Every year, a Teragane receives a new tattoo on their arm."

"Tattoos? You? You have tattoos?"

"Yeah, look." I hurriedly untied the cord securing my sleeves. I pulled down the left sleeve, revealing the markings on my arm. The tattoos were simple triangles with a horizontal line drawn across the upper point. Lillie leaned close to me, her green eyes widening and pointed ears perking up with great interest.

"They look like little mountains!" she exclaimed, then her eyes lifted, meeting mine. "But, why?"

"Each marking represents the year I passed over the mountain," I explained. "Each year signifies my return to my home on the mountain peak. I think, at least, that is what the Sage tell me. Each year, they always say: *Sable von Hira, remember to always return to the mountain*. And—uh—something else, depending on what is expected for the new year." Lillie counted my tattoos, her finger slightly touching my skin, causing a slight shiver to run down my spine.

"Fifteen!" she exclaimed.

"Yeah, but in winter I will receive another." I felt a sense of pride overcome my heart. I hadn't given much thought about the rituals, only the expected obligation to present myself to the Sage each year. Lillie's interest sparked a new sensation deep within my heart. Perhaps the tattoos were more than just a mere resemblance of my age. Perhaps the way of the Teragane *was* rather interesting.

"Cool. What an interesting way to keep track of your age. Does it hurt?" Lillie looked up at me, but her finger still lingered upon my skin, causing a new fluttering in my heart, especially as her green eyes continued to glisten.

"No, they heal quickly."

"No, silly, the tattooing process?"

"Oh, yeah. Maybe a little. But I'm used to it now. Nothing worse than that prick on your finger"—I pointed to her needle—"Just imagine that a thousand times in a row."

"Doesn't sound very pleasant."

"Yeah, well, that's just part of the process." Lillie finally removed her hand from my arm, and I pulled up my loose sleeves, tying the cord once again across my chest.

I realized that I had never thought about showing Lillie my markings. It was part of my culture—something sacred and diligently upheld every year. Yet, I only thought about it once a year, during the winter, when I was required to attend the ritual. My mind began to swirl with new concepts about the importance. But, also, a sense of guilt for revealing the traditions of my people to a forest-dweller caused my neck to slightly tense. Was I revealing too much?

"Thanks for showing me your tattoos," Lillie said as she returned to mending the trousers while smiling, her demeanor once again at peace. "Thanks for trusting me."

Perhaps it wasn't too much. What harm could it cause, anyway?

Maybe the Sage were wrong about the forest dwellers.

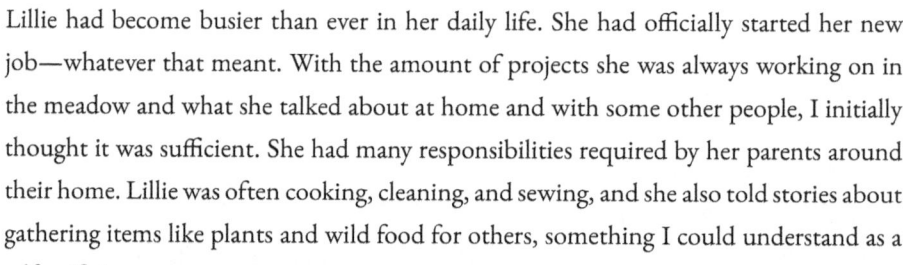

Lillie had become busier than ever in her daily life. She had officially started her new job—whatever that meant. With the amount of projects she was always working on in the meadow and what she talked about at home and with some other people, I initially thought it was sufficient. She had many responsibilities required by her parents around their home. Lillie was often cooking, cleaning, and sewing, and she also told stories about gathering items like plants and wild food for others, something I could understand as a self-sufficient person.

She liked to read and write, but often complained that she had no time to do such things anymore—yet, I knew the truth was that her parents hardly allowed her the *time and space*. However, she told me that she started an "official job," working with her father. She did not elaborate, nor would I have been able to understand if she did tell me—or perhaps she did?

Winter was fast approaching. We would both be entering our 16th year. I did not necessarily know how her new obligations would affect our friendship, and only assumed that we would continue to meet once a fortnight, which was sufficient for me. Lillie's life was still foreign in my mind and seemed to only consist of ceaseless work and infinite problems. I noticed her struggle to enjoy the pleasures in life while balancing all the responsibilities required of her.

Lillie's life confused me most of the time with its complexities and never-ending demands, allowing me to appreciate the simplicity of my life, regardless of its loneliness. If living in a busy village with many people only caused endless work, perhaps the limited interaction with others wasn't so bad. However, I accepted Lillie as she was and only anticipated our next meeting in the upcoming spring season, regardless of the ongoing complaints that never seemed to have any suitable solution. Perhaps it was the sense of helplessness that caused me to wonder only to myself. For, what reason would I have to criticize her way of life?

I had my established routine during the winter: plenty of stored foods, the warmth of the eternal fire, and the anticipated visit from the Sage, who would grant me my aging tattoo. I had survived many winters before; however, when the final goodbyes of the valleys below became official and the freezing temperatures arrived, I found that winter to be *quite* different.

During the solitary days of winter on the mountain summit, new impenitent emotions overcame me. I missed Lillie's smile, her silly stories, and, most of all, her willingness to share her time with me. I knew that her time was valuable, often stretched thin amongst her daily responsibilities, which only made it feel more special that she would still meet with me after four summers had already passed.

When I was visited by the Sage, who would do my ritual tattoo, symbolizing the start of my 16th year in the province, I remembered Lillie's curiosity of my markings and I became curious, driven by boredom and loneliness.

"Could I get another type of tattoo?" I asked the Sage when they were nearly finished.

"Quiet, fool," they hissed, and continued to mark my left arm, shifting the pressure into more malicious movements. I slightly twisted my neck towards them in an attempt to watch the process.

"Look forward," they once again demanded in a snake-like voice. I turned my head in obedience, wincing at their increased pressure, noticing their voice sounding unusually irritated that winter. I knew that they were attending the others in the colony for their rituals and wondered if they saw the ritual as an annoyance. Or was I simply stepping out of line of expectation?

Upon finishing the ritual, the Sage left my home with a traditional reminder to always return to the mountain and remember the ways of our people. The Sage were mysterious and rarely spoke, only when required for passing information or instructions.

They wore a bone mask shaped like an owl, hiding their identity and any defining features. They wore a black robe with wide sleeves over a tunic and trousers like my own traditional clothing, but their black leather waist belt held many strange ornaments and pouches, most likely filled with their tools and the source of the strong herbal scents permeating from their figure. In the winter, they also wore woolen cloaks with many layers that draped evenly over their shoulders and between their wing-blades, giving their figure a rather bulky appearance. They were obviously adults, referred to as elders, at times, and, besides the parents of the others in the colony from our early years of training, the only other adults who would occasionally visit Mt. Hira.

Although I interacted with them for the purpose of the ritual or occasionally in passing after they would come with new clothes and boots as I was growing, one of the colony members was training to become a Sage, which meant sometimes the Sage could be seen in the valley during his training. His name was Cami, someone who I had considered a neighbor-friend, if I were to use the term I had learned from Lillie.

After the Sage had left my home, I visited my friend, who had also received his 16th marking, in hopes to drive away the boredom and explore some new curiosities welling within my heart.

"Would you be willing to mark me with a different type of tattoo?" I asked upon arrival at Cami's residence.

Cami was chosen to become a new Sage at a young age, and he was often required to observe and learn how to properly conduct the ritual during his training, and had shadowed the Sage last year for the first time during my ritual. His life was just as mysterious as the Sage themselves. But he was the only one from the colony who I could even call a friend. Perhaps it was because he was the only one willing to speak with me longer than a single sentence.

"That is not the way," he said, and raised his dark brown eyebrows.

"I know, but it could be interesting," I said. My heart felt excited as I waited for his response, and I held my breath as Cami pondered for a moment.

"I find this to be foolish behavior," Cami said as he stroked his narrow chin. "Why are you asking me?"

"I thought it interesting, like I said already, yet possibly useful for your training. I want to understand more about the process of the ritual and basic tattooing."

"Hmm." Cami's brown eyes darted as he continued to ponder. The reflection of the blue light from the eternal fire bounced on his brown skin as he deeply thought about my request, and he began to systematically adjust his curly brown hair.

Although I was motivated purely by my selfish curiosities, I was, in fact, interested in the process. I did not intentionally want to disturb the balance of our way of life, as some may claim. However, that day, I felt bored and curiously wanted to try something different from the habitual status of life. The Sage were quiet and expected silent compliance. At least, with Cami, I could watch without being told to look away, and, as he pondered, I eyed the tools lingering upon a wooden shelf near the neatly folded robes of a Sage.

"Okay, but nothing obvious," he finally said. "It would be good practice before my final conversion and good education for you. Then you won't annoy the Sage again with your silly requests."

I rolled my eyes while Cami drifted towards the wooden shelf I stood by, and he began preparing the small tools used for traditional tattooing: a bone-needle attached to a stick, a smooth rock, and a stone-bowl filled with a dark powdered substance heavily scented of ash. He began preparing the powder to make ink, and eventually ignited a bundle of herbs he called a smudge, allowing the strong aromas of herbs to fill the air with its earthy fragrance. Then, he wrapped the dark robe of a Sage around his body and maneuvered his slim hands into black gloves.

"Oh—where should I mark?" Cami asked while turning towards me and he motioned with his gloved hand for me to sit down.

"I want a tattoo—uh—here." I pointed to my neck, just below my right ear. The thought of Lillie seeing it immediately when we would meet again caused a fluttering sensation to fill my stomach, and I grinned, yet Cami only scowled.

"No! Anyone can see that," he retorted, causing the fantasy to enhance even more in my mind. "I said nothing presumptuous."

"Fine, the back of my neck."

"No, that can be problematic when you become older. I don't want the Sage to be angry with you—or with me. Are you trying to make your silly antics obvious to the Sage?"

"Okay, where would it not be a problem?" Regardless of the exciting idea of impressing Lillie, while Cami examined my figure intensely with his narrowed eyes and grimacing expression, I knew that we were already partaking in something against expectations, something possibly needing to conceal from the eyes of our teachers.

The older Teraganes often had tattoos covering their arms and backs, encircling their shoulders and wing-blades. Sometimes the older generation even had their chests covered. I didn't remember my own parent's having extensive tattoos, but I did recall a parent of another colony member having impressive trailing markings along their body.

However, Teraganes did not often showcase their bare skin to others; only during rituals performed by the Sage did they reveal their markings or when bathing in the rivers. Yet, even that was more private and only something I had been exposed to in passing. Although I was still young, Cami's concern for my future was evidently to prevent problematic situations to arise if a Sage were to ever discover something as unnecessary as a tattoo for fun. Cami brutally reminded me that I still had the future to think about even if I was obviously ignoring it.

"Your leg?" he finally suggested while darting his eyes.

"Perfect," I replied, and I sat down on his stone bed, folding my wings behind, and situated my leg, lifting my black trousers to expose my calf after taking off my leather boot. Then, I pointed to my leg. "The ankle, right on the side."

Smiling, excitement filled my heart again now that my friend finally accepted my request, and Cami kneeled between my legs and began tapping the inked bone needle with a stone hammer. However, the excruciating pain of the needle piercing through the skin on my ankle caused me to instantly regret my decision. This pain was vastly different from that in the upper arm area, and I felt my curling toes tighten at each tap.

He studiously focused on the process like a true Sage while I struggled to keep my expressions from revealing my obvious pain, afraid to disappoint him after I had convinced him to partake in what he could call *silly antics*. After the session, I decided to never ask for another random tattoo.

That day, I discovered that not all curiosities should be explored.

The winter months passed, and, at the end, I sensed the change of the season. Normally, I only focused on the mere depletion of my winter food supply, considering my stock of food and when I would absolutely need to leave my mountain residence.

That year, however, was different. When I detected the change in temperature and sensed an improvement in air currents rushing through the feathers of my wings, I grew excited but anxious to return to the meadow. In the past, I had previously revisited the meadow to see Lillie during the beginning of the spring season. Sometimes I had to delay my initial departure due to late winter storms—or just pure laziness for flying in the cold for long periods of time was rather unenjoyable. Often, I did not care if I had to wait due to my unwillingness to fly during the freezing temperatures. I was always excited to eventually spend my time with Lillie in the meadow; however, for some reason, that year was *different*.

"I must be excited to show her my ankle tattoo," I said out loud to myself. I chuckled, imagining her face lighting up upon revealing to her my new marking.

Although I still had plenty of food in my storage, I felt the shift in weather as well as a slight change in my own demeanor. The smell of melting snow traveled through the air currents, and the muscles in my wings did not freeze up, nor did the wind pierce my ear with excruciating power.

When the moment had finally come, I flew down from the mountain summit directly to the meadow, full of hope and excitement, now that the winter isolation was over. The snow was patchy, the short green grass was visible, and small white and purple flowers were beginning to emerge from the ground. I waited all afternoon in the clearing, slightly shivering and tucking my hands under the layers of my cloak, but Lillie never debuted from the woods that day.

It is just the beginning of spring. No need to worry.

I visited the meadow every day, checking for signs of her anticipated appearance. On one of those fateful spring days, she arrived, happy to see me, but I noticed some things were different about her. Her lavish brown hair was fading into a lighter color, and her stormy gray skin looked paler and did not shimmer with cool undertones as vibrant as it once did. However, her cheeks still had their rosy complexion, and her spirit was lively as ever.

She carried her basket, storing her blanket, snacks, and projects to work on, reminding me of all the things I enjoyed observing from the complexities of her life within the forest.

However, for once, I had my own exciting occurrence that winter, and I eagerly told her about my Aging-Ritual with the Sage, the tattoo I received, and, most importantly, the spontaneous adventure of receiving a tattoo on my ankle per my request.

"Really?" she said. "You did something totally random?"

"Yes!" I uttered. "Look!" I pulled up the leg of my trouser, removed my leather boot, and exposed my ankle.

"It's a little clover!" Lillie exclaimed while clasping her hands together.

"Yes!"

"It's so cute. But"—she looked up at me—"why a flower?"

"I—uh."

Yeah, why did I ask for a flower?

When Cami had asked what I wanted, I just blurted out a flower. He never asked why or what kind of flower, only slightly raised his brow and cast his usual disapproving expression, and then began the tattooing process.

It was a simple clover, one seen growing anywhere in the mountains—a flower I often observed bouncing in the grass as the winds blew around during the warmer months. A pink flower with sharp edges found along the grassy lands in the valleys. Perhaps it resembled something deep within my heart: my deep loneliness amidst the top of the mountain, and my yearning for the meadow—my yearning to be with Lillie. But why did Cami choose a clover? Did it mean something to him?

Perhaps simply part of his Sage training.

"I don't know," I replied. I did not want to admit that I was simply bored and begged my friend to entertain my idle behavior, nor could I begin to think of a way to explain the procedure of Cami's training when I hardly understood it myself. I was curious, yes, provoked by appeasing my boredom at random. Or was it something deeper?

"I think it is brilliant," Lillie said and began bouncing up and down. "I think it is wonderful!" Her excitement caused a rush of emotions to fill my heart as I watched her fading brown hair bounce with her movements.

The initial fantasy of her seeing a new tattoo was nothing compared to living it. She had been impressed by the ritual tattoos the year before, but the simple clover now stained within the skin of my ankle evidently brought true joy into her heart. Her simple happiness became my happiness.

I had not realized how cold and lonely the winter was until I felt the warmth from Lillie's smile, and her sweet gestures filled my heart. The fascination of her seeing something new on my skin seemed like a silly fantasy during winter. Yet, in that moment, the reality of her joy ignited a new fire within. I became proud of myself for asking Cami to create a tattoo on my ankle, even though it was extremely painful. I experienced an overwhelming sense of achievement by pursuing something random that I had thought about all on my own.

CHAPTER FOUR
WHEN A FRIEND IS DOWN

"I wish to live in the trees," Lillie said while she stared at the giant cedars. We were sitting together in the meadow, relaxing on the blanket as usual. The cloth napkins lay nearby, left with only a few crumbs within the folds; our shoes sat idle near Lillie's basket. There was a drizzle of rain before I had arrived, filling the spring air with freshness that felt rejuvenating. Lillie's blanket was woven with thick wool, sufficiently protecting us from the dewy grass.

I noticed she had not brought any projects or books that day; she only brought food to share with me. I glanced at her hands, empty for the first time, but appeared rough and scarred as she simply rested them on her lap.

"Why? What is in the trees?" I asked and lifted my eyes to gaze towards the forest.

"It is not what is in the trees, but rather the view I long for from up in the trees," she replied, then turned to look over the cliffside. Her eyes and mind seemed far from where we were, unusual for her since she usually spoke clearly and kept her eye contact very direct.

"This is a great view," I said, and turned to face the cliffside as well. There was a steep drop from the edge, overlooking the ongoing forests and valleys below where I often flew high above in the skies and dove down to hunt in the rivers.

There were no settlements of forest dwellers anywhere past the cliffside, only some farms on the other side of the mountain where I usually avoided flying. As a Teragane, I kept my distance from Lillie's kind, as instructed. But, frankly, I didn't have a desire to meet anyone else—especially after hearing all the depressing stories of how harsh the people were and the struggles they had in life.

The mountain range beyond the cliffside was covered in white summits, and the greenery across the landscape was blossoming in its spring glory. The soft white and purple colors of spring and the misty air created a sense of tranquility. I had flown over the area countless times, often in awe of the natural beauty of the landscape. However, my view from the meadow was by far my favorite.

A place for only Lillie and me.

"It is all so far away. The trees are here," Lillie said, and moved her head again to look at the looming trees. Then, she stood up and walked towards the giant cedar forest and I followed her, curious at what brought her attention suddenly to the trees. She walked solemnly, unlike her usual self, as if she were stuck in a dream-like state that I could only observe as an outsider.

As we approached the forest, the immense size of the trees dawned on me. I began to feel small and miniscule. Still, we continued to walk towards the giants of nature. It was our first time talking about trees; she never seemed to be interested before. She was very different this year.

Lillie stopped at the base of a cedar. The hue of red was a strong contrast against the green grass, but the dark, green color of the pine needles complimented the grassy area of the meadow. Lillie's paling complexion and lack of vibrant undertones became noticeably stronger as I watched her look up at the massive trunk grounded before her.

"Look how amazing this tree is!" Lillie exclaimed. The enthusiasm in her voice returned as she attempted to wrap her arms around the trunk of the tree. The base, being larger in proportion, made her look tiny in comparison. I came closer to her, curiously observing her behavior, wondering if she was in her own dream and had nearly forgotten I was standing nearby. She was resting her head on the tree, closing her eyes, and smiling, her arms completely spread across the girth of the trunk. I placed my hand on the tree, near her hand, and looked at the bark intently, finding it simply part of nature and nothing of interest.

"It just fills me with happiness," Lillie continued, and I slightly narrowed my brows. "I can almost imagine the tree having a heartbeat. I can nearly hear it."

"You're so silly," I replied, using a phrase she often had said to me. I looked down at her, expecting her to laugh or scoff, but, instead, she spun around instantly, huffing her chest, and her eyes no longer resembled one stuck in a dream.

"Why? Why is it silly for me to be happy hugging a tree?" Her cheeks and pointed ears were vibrantly red as she scowled. I could feel my own cheeks and ears feeling warm, not out of anger, like Lillie, but out of embarrassment and bewilderment. She looked up at me with her fiery spirit, startling me as she was very much present in reality. I took notice of the fact I had grown taller than her, yet her shorter stature did not stop her from intimidating me as ferocity of emotions arose within her voice, especially as I stepped backwards and moved my hands to my side.

"It's just a tree," I said, and I darted my eyes away from Lillie's angry glare.

"Yeah? And?" She huffed, tilting her head in aggravation. "It's just a meadow. It's just a mountain. It's just *another* thing in our world that exists!"

For the first time, Lillie was angry with me, leaving me defenseless of how to respond. I had seen her angry before, but this time her heightened emotion was directed at me. My flushed cheeks grew hot, and my heart beat fast as I felt Lillie's eyes pierce through me, somewhat wishing she were still stuck in her dreamy state just moments before.

"Okay," I said, and stepped backwards again, feeling my wings twitch and I scratched my chin. Lillie looked back at the tree and huffed a deep snarl and started to climb.

"I just want to climb this tree and be happy!" she yelled. Her nimble fingers found holding spots in the crevasses of the red bark. She maneuvered her way up slowly, grumbling to herself. I helplessly watched, feeling bewildered by her attitude, changes in different emotions, and I slightly gaped my mouth as her figure continued upwards like a young squirrel first learning to climb.

As she ascended, I realized that if she fell, she could get hurt, unlike a young squirrel who had the dexterity to withstand such high impacts. I did not want Lillie to fall nor get hurt, and felt a sense of fear overwhelm my anxious heart. She was seething with anger, more disgruntled than I had ever seen her before. Why? I did not know at the time, nor was I certain how to find out.

When I was a younger child, I had learned to climb trees, but smaller types with lower branches. I learned, like many other children, to climb from limb to limb. It was customary for Teraganes to learn how to maneuver through the terrain of the forest, although we had wings. Hiding in trees was useful when it came to our survival.

These giant cedars, however, did not have lower branches to mount, only immense trunks and deep crevasses. If I were to ascend a cedar tree, I would need to jump up and use my wings to lift myself, and, if I fell, I could use my wings to decrease the impact of unseen forces of nature.

As I watched Lillie, the nervousness welling in my heart could not calculate how she could avoid getting hurt if she were to fall, and I could sense that she was running out of energy. Her rage was dwindling, and her arms began to shake. Her foot slipped, startling me, yet she kept her tight grip and continued to move upwards.

Instincts began to overtake my mind as my wings flinched and my knees bent, ready to take flight, despite usually avoiding flying around Lillie. When we were younger, I sometimes flew around when teasing her, holding a book from her reach—something menacingly obnoxious. But I always returned to the ground when I noticed she was no longer enjoying the childish behavior. As we grew older, I was growing taller and bigger than her. I knew that I had strengths and freedoms that she did not, and I put away my childish behaviors to respect Lillie and our differences.

"Lillie!" I shouted. "You're going to fall!"

"Shut up!" she responded, but her foot slipped again and her hands began to shake. Bark fell from underneath her unstable position, and I jumped off the ground, and flew up towards her.

"Lillie!" I called. "Let me help you down."

"Leave me alone," she growled, but another foot slipped, and she was unable to hold her position, falling backwards, right into my open arms.

However, the sudden impact stunned me, and we both slowly fell to the ground as I vigorously pumped my wings to no avail. I fell to the ground, Lillie right on top of me, and her miscalculated extra weight caused me to gasp for air.

"Sable!" Lillie cried and spun off me. "I'm sorry. I'm sorry!" Lillie leaned over me, stroking my face as I tried to breathe. Tears welled in her eyes as she continued to apologize.

"I'm fine," I grunted and leaned forward, wincing in pain and heavily breathing through my clenched teeth. My torso felt heavy, my wings felt bruised, and my lungs ached for air. As Lillie held my neck while I sat up, she kept apologizing, seemingly scared as she looked at my disoriented self.

"You don't look fine. Oh! I'm so sorry," she muttered.

"I'm fine, really," I said, and I loosened my jaw as I slowly regained control over my breathing. The pain began to subside, and I stood up as carefully as I could. I shook off the feeling, allowing my dark feathers to ruffle.

Lillie wiped her teary eyes, attempting to keep herself from fully crying. She combed through my wings and dusted me off, pulling sticks and pine needles off me. Her fingers were gentle against the feathers, only slightly pulling where sticks had been lodged in between, and a shiver ran down my spine, which triggered more pain to surge through my muscles.

I hadn't fallen like that since I was a youngling, nor roughly played with another Teragane, and although the pain felt familiar during my early years of training, the pain in my heart was completely foreign and much worse than any sore muscle.

"Sable, I'm sorry. I shouldn't be so stupid."

"Hey, it's okay. You're not being stupid. I'm fine. It's not my first time falling like that. Nothing is broken." Lillie continued to brush me off, sniffling abruptly and rubbing her reddened nose.

Although my body felt horrible, my heart felt worse. Lillie was in more pain than me, and I didn't know how to fix it. Normally, I could just say something silly or ask her a question to get her mind off her troubles. I wanted her to be happy again; I didn't want her to be angry or sad. But it didn't appear that anything I would say could erase whatever misery she was enduring within the dream she seemed to be caught up in.

I just wish she could escape her miserable life already. That seems to be her main source of pain.

After Lillie was satisfied that I was, in fact, fine, we sat down together again on our blanket spot and for a very long time we sat in silence.

Summer was coming as the air was shifting into the warmer season. The soft white and purple colors of the spring flowers were fading, while the yellow and pink summer flowers began to bloom with vibrance. The grass was getting taller, and the bees were becoming more numerous. But, for the first time, Lillie stayed unhappy, regardless of my reassurances or efforts to cheer her up, and her sadness was overwhelming.

I knew that ever since she had started her job before last winter, her demeanor had drastically changed. Although I understood basic concepts of survival and sustaining oneself through life, I knew that her culture had a very different way of providing security, hence why working was important to her. Or so I theorized. But, why did it have to cause so much misery? That was impossible for me to understand.

"I think you deserve to be happy," I finally said as a soft breeze blew through my hair. Lillie forced a weak smile while looking at her scarred hands. "If living in a tree would make you happy, then I would visit you in the trees."

A small tear ran down Lillie's round cheek, but she did not respond. I felt a prick of pain on my neck, sending a shiver down my spine, even though the breeze blowing through the grass was warm and the air was humid from the previous rain.

For once, I felt uncomfortable in Lillie's presence. Her silence felt unnerving, and I shifted into sitting with my legs crossed as my hands began to twitch. I tugged on the ends of my sleeves, hoping to settle my nervousness, but my wings fluttered, and pain lingered through the aching muscles.

She stayed silent as she began packing up her supplies, folding the blanket, and stuffing the napkins into her basket, and I knew that it was time to say goodbye. She would return to the forest, and I would return home on the mountain peak. For the first time, I realized that I did not want to say goodbye—not while Lillie sulked with unknown reasons of sadness. I didn't want her to leave like this—no, not like this.

But I did not know what to do. I was clueless. I felt powerless, and my eyes darted as I helplessly watched Lillie secure her basket onto her back. I thought about asking her about the object in which she brought every time, curious to know if she had made it. It was sturdy in form, wide, and had leather straps that she wore over her shoulders, and a lid that could open and close, securing all her items that she could easily carry. I had seen her weave baskets before, and I wanted to cheer her up by asking about this one in particular, especially since the linen satchel I used to carry my supplies was strapped to a waist belt, as well to another across my thigh that secured the fish I often carried to the mountain.

Lillie likes pointing out the differences in our objects. Maybe she—

"Sable," Lillie said while looking down at her shoes that appeared to be too small for her.

"Yes?" I responded, anxious about what she would say next as my mind thought about her basket, now her shoes.

"I cannot meet so often again. But I will come to the meadow every full moon."

What? Is it something I did? Is she angry with me?

"I have too much work, but I still want to come," she said, as if she could read my mind. Lillie lifted her chin, but her green eyes did not sparkle, not even while the sun cast its glorious rays against her face. Her once chestnut-brown hair was becoming whiter every time I saw her. As her sadness overtook her demeanor, her skin was a stagnant gray, void of its stormy hues of cool undertones. Lillie's rosy complexion was hardly noticeable without any exertion of her playful emotions.

"Then I will see you every full moon," I replied.

"See you then," she said while turning around to leave, slowly lowering her head and her fading, loose hair drifted over her face.

I reached out and grabbed her arm, causing her to pause. I moved close to her and wrapped my arms around her waist, hugging her with a stiff embrace. She melted into my arms, wrapping hers tightly around my torso, her head resting against my chest. Her warm embrace eased my rigid composure. The warmth of her body felt comforting, yet her sorrow felt excruciating.

Subjects of baskets and linen satchels escaped my mind as I let my heart ache for Lillie and her sadness. As the grief overwhelmed my beating heart, tears began to form within my eyes—unusual, since I never cried over anyone before.

I remembered the moment my parents left me the winter I entered my tenth year. They said goodbye and took off into the cloudy sky as spring slowly emerged, and yet, even then, I didn't shed a single tear.

However, with Lillie, the natural sensation of grief being shared flushed my skin, and the warm tears streaming down my cheeks felt odd but comforting to know that I wasn't completely heartless. I only wanted to take away her pain and her sorrow for I hated seeing her fade away. The young girl I had formed a deep connection with suddenly caused my heart to flutter in ways I had never thought possible. Yet, the grief was nearly unbearable while I held her in my arms.

As always, like the fading sun over the mountain range, we parted ways. Like the mysterious location of where the sun goes while the darkness shadows the lands, I stood in the meadow and watched Lillie's figure slowly disappear into the forest. Over the years, I never paid much attention to her departure or thought about the sorrow of her goodbyes or our separation.

That day was different.

As the tears rolled down my face, my heart ached, and my chest felt heavy. The pain from the fall had subsided, but the pain from Lillie's sadness felt agonizingly worse. I did not want to see her leave unhappy. I did not want to wait until a full moon for our next visit. I wanted to see her happy, see her often, and watch her laugh and share her food. I wanted to ask her about her basket, consequently leading her to asking about my satchel.

I wanted all these things, but I had no idea how to achieve these desires while the changes in Lillie were ever so confusing. It felt as if subjects of basket weaving or clothing were no longer enough to bring joy upon her face. If discussions of trees were detrimental, what other hidden pains could evolve with such simple subjects?

I had no idea how, but I wanted to help bring back Lillie' happiness and her fiery spirit to return to its full glory.

"I will help her climb the trees so that she can live there happily," I said out loud while standing in the shadows of the cedars.

I will help her find her joy again, whatever that looks like within these new changes.

CHAPTER FIVE

WHEN FOOLISH BEHAVIOR AND COMPASSION COLLIDE

"Why can't I help the little rabbit?" I had asked my father when I was a youngling. I watched helplessly as a little brown rabbit struggled to free itself from a hunting trap. Its leg was bleeding, broken from the immense pressure of the metal trap ensnaring its limb.

"The rabbit will be someone's meal," my father had said. "We do not interfere."

"But, please, it looks so helpless," I pleaded. "It's in pain!"

"Quiet, Sable. That is foolish talk."

I remember tears welling in my eyes and the intensity of my father's scowl as he pulled me away from the scene that we had stumbled upon during one of our training sessions in the forest.

"You need to learn to accept the natural ways of this life," he had lectured while we flew away from the forest ground. "Don't dwell on such thoughts. It is okay to have compassion, but you must not let your emotions guide your actions. You need to rely on your instincts and your training for guidance. You must accept that this world is full of death, one animal feeding the next, and in that suffering, life is sustained. Too much compassion can disrupt patterns of life. If you saved that rabbit, you may starve the hunter. What if that same hunter prevented you from gathering your own food? Say what, then?"

"I think I understand," I had replied while wiping my tears away. My father grumbled about no longer training in the area where forest dwellers hunted, but then looked back at me with a scowling expression while we glided over the treetops.

"Don't allow imprudent behavior to dictate your actions. Help is only a mere disturbance in the patterns of life."

I distinctly remember the pain in my heart as I thought about the struggling rabbit. I remember the sensation of salty tears dripping down my cheeks and some resting on my lips. I hadn't often cried as a youngling, so why was I crying over a little rabbit in the forest?

I was a Teragane. I hunted animals, ate their flesh, and slept on pelts of larger beasts. It was the way of life, as my father and mother had taught. We were part of a life cycle that functioned according to survival. Bigger predators hunted smaller ones. Some lived in packs, like wolves, and others were territorial like bears. The forest dwellers hunted with sharp traps and weapons; I and those alike hunted with our hands. Food was necessary for me, and I was taught to capture fish and smaller animals to sustain myself.

So, then, why did I care so much?

As I pondered my desire to help Lillie, my memories of my father's teachings troubled my mind. I knew in my heart that I was not purposely disrupting life, and my desire to help Lillie came from my compassion for her as a friend. Yet the feeling of contriteness lingered in my mind.

I had already created a friendship outside of my own colony, against the early teachings of the Sage and my caregivers. I had accepted my defiant behavior as a natural part of my life, although I preferred to think less about its being a purposeful act of rebellion.

Yet, at that moment, as I thought about my desire to help Lillie, my thoughts swirled about my actions and how they affected my life. If I helped teach her to climb the cedar trees, that would not necessarily disrupt the balance of life, right? In addition, it could bring back her happiness and enhance her daily life.

It wasn't affecting my survival. Or was it?

"If I can teach Lillie how to climb the cedar trees," I said out loud, "then maybe she will be happy again!"

Wait—Me? A Teragane teaching a forest-dweller how to climb trees? Not any tree—a giant tree! Am I a fool for thinking like this?

I did not know how I could help Lillie learn to climb trees. In fact, would climbing a tree really help her? It seemed silly after a few days of contemplation. The trees were nearly impossible to climb due to their massive girth and high branches—well, at least for someone without wings.

Then again, why was I thinking this way? I am a Teragane! I fly above the trees, up to the highest peaks, and down to the lowest of valleys within a single day! I am a solitary being who depends on only myself.

Perhaps it was an absurd concept that I should teach Lillie to climb the giant cedar trees. How, in logical aspects, would it even help Lillie other than give her the happiness she seems to seek out from up in the forest canopy? For, how long could it even last?

Wait—what if I could fly Lillie up into the trees?

I cherished my time with Lillie and wanted to help secure her lifelong happiness that was dwindling due to her miserable life in the forest. I wanted to drive out the sadness and bring back Lillie's exuberance, like the sun arriving after a cold, harsh winter.

Perhaps her village on the ground kept her miserable, and the chance of being up in the trees would give her an escape from her reality. Yes—I could help her establish those desires by using my differences to help her!

You must not let your emotions guide your actions, I remembered my father saying.

And why not? What good are emotions if not to allow me to feel and act upon them? Wasn't that what made me different from the beasts of the forest and other creatures of the sky?

I shook my head with disdain. I knew that my compassion for Lillie was not imprudent. In fact, I thought perhaps it was more than just childish affection. Perhaps it was growing into love.

I think—I think I love Lillie.

Love? What is love? A stronger emotion, a bond with another? Could I even understand such deep emotions without guidance?

At the sudden revelation, I nearly jumped out of my mountain home to return to the meadow, my heart pounding and my head spinning, but I stopped in my impulsive tracks.

First, I remembered I had to wait until the full moon before meeting with her again. Then, I remembered the incident in which Lillie fell from the tree and crashed on top of me. I could not hold her above the ground, let alone fly her around.

You dullard! You are weak! You can't even hold Lillie up. You let her fall to the ground. You could not even breathe after she fell on top of you!

I began pacing my room, pounding my hands on my head, trying to get my mind to think clearly. It was the most thoughts I had all at once in my entire life. My mind was filled with contriteness, swirling with personal insults and feelings of inadequacy.

I could never talk to anyone else about my thoughts. I thought for a moment about Cami and the others living in the colony of Hira. We all lived our private lives, independent of each other and separated by any need for companionship, at least while we were young. It also reminded me of the inevitable response they would have.

"It is absurd to have compassion for others outside of our way of life," they would say. "How could you ever get yourself into a contradicting practice of a bond with a forest dweller? Have you no shame?" Immediately, I dismissed the idea of seeking their counsel. I had no desire to feel even more inadequate.

I looked around my home. There was a shallow, carved fireplace with a simple iron cauldron where an eternal fire rested within, in which was brought by the Sage. The glowing blue light heated my cave-like home, keeping me comfortable even in the freezing winters up in the mountains. The eternal fire did not cast smoke, but only warmth and light. I didn't even know where this eternal fire came from or why it never went out, not like the orange fires I had seen used by hunters. I never questioned it nor even cared. It was just part of the Teragane world guided by the Sage.

I had a storage area built into the ground, enclosed by a wooden trapdoor, where I could preserve food and water during the winter months. A linen bag with salt remained inside as well as a metal cauldron used for water conservation. The basics of survival was all I needed—at least, that was what I was taught.

During the warmer months, I did not even eat in my own home, sometimes while flying but mainly right after my hunt. I thought about my home and how it was set up. Everything was given to me either by a Sage or from my parents when they first brought me into the world.

Even my clothes were given to me. Where did they come from and who made them?

Lillie wore different clothes and accessories; she even sometimes wore wooden beads in her hair. I had nothing like this. I wore simple black woolen trousers and a tunic with detachable sleeves. During winter, I had a lightweight woolen cloak, designed specifically with detached layers that can be draped over my head, splitting in the back to adjust for my wings. The poncho-like cloak sat mid-thigh, and I could fasten it around my waist with a leather belt, securing the loose material for flight efficiency yet still sufficiently keeping me warm and dry during the cold and wet months.

My black hair did not grow past my shoulders, was jagged and always unkept. I saw no point in combing or taking care of my hair since the wind and weather would ruffle any effort. Then again, I did not have a reflection glass nor cared to even have one like I had seen Cami use before. Yet he often stayed in the mountain; rarely did I see him outside, not like me. My life was in the sky, near the lakes and rivers, in the mountains, or in the meadow with Lillie.

With Lillie—

For the first time, I realized I didn't even know what she thought of me.

Did she think my brown skin was beautiful like I thought her gray stormy complexion was?

Did she marvel at my black hair like I did with her brown, yet whitening hair?

Did she ever notice the color of my eyes? Oh, I remember her eyes when I first met her; they were sparkling green, like the lakes shimmering in the summer.

Wait, what is the color of my eyes?

My head was spinning from thinking about my life and all the questions I asked. All the thinking and observation of my life and Lillie's sudden sadness drove me frantically out of my home, and I descended below the summit.

I flew to a forest where I knew bears lived. I liked watching them catch fish in the river. When I arrived, there were no bears, and I leaned over the edge of the riverbank, looking at my reflection on the surface of the water. I saw my dark, large figure looming, and I bent closer to examine myself, hoping to catch the color of my eyes, but the quickly moving water made it impossible to see a clear reflection.

Brown, maybe? But not quite. Maybe I can ask—

The noise of approaching creatures alerted me, and I retreated away from the river, and I flew up into a nearby oak tree. I settled upon a sturdy branch and waited. The small group of bears arrived to hunt their meal from the river. Summer was a casual eating time for bears, not too rushed like in autumn, which is before winter hibernation. Spring was a vicious bloodbath of desperation for food after a long winter sleep. No—the beginning of summer was perfect for relaxing and eating.

Although brown bears often lived solitary lives, like the Teragane, the mothers would raise their cubs for a couple years, training them to survive on their own before eventually parting ways. Occasionally, depending on the time or location, the bears may congregate. They were no different than the Teragane in their natural way of life, often giving me a slight sense of comfort as I watched the two-year old cubs playfully splash around the water. My father had taught me to learn from the bears, and my mother pointed out the similarities to our own people. Ultimately, they taught me how to safely observe the predators of the valleys, for they knew where the fish were plentiful.

"Never feed before the bears, only after," my father had told me. "Otherwise, they will hunt you next for taking their food supply."

Not only were the beasts similar to my own kind, they were also exceptionally strong—something I desperately wanted.

I could wrestle—again.

No—I had no one to wrestle with. As a youngling, I often wrestled with the other colony members, similar to the bears. But, by my ninth-year, I was taught to disregard primitive-instincts, due to it being heedless behavior that could cause harm.

I remembered once attacking Cami, who hit his head on sharp rocks in the river, spilling blood all over. After the incident, my mother had thoroughly taught me to withhold myself from ever attacking unnecessarily. There was another young member from my colony who I had often wrestled with, building our strength together. I had enjoyed wrestling Mika, but I had not seen him since we were quite young, since we were taught to no longer participate in the primitive behavior of strength training. Even if I were to seek Mika out for the sake of wrestling, what kind of harm could I cause to the colony members?

Cami was already dismissive of any of my other ideas. Mika? I had no idea, nor whether it was worth the risk seeking him out since he had often displayed rather vicious tendencies when we were younger.

Instead, I chuckled at the idea of wrestling with an animal similar to my size. Maybe a black bear. When standing upright, a black bear was the same height as me, but I did not know of their residence in the area. Since the brown bears congregated in recent years, the black bears I saw before were long gone. The brown bears were much bigger and deadlier, hardly suitable for me to challenge in terms of strength building.

My colony on the mountain would laugh at the idea. Other Teraganes would shame me for participating in reckless behavior, deeming it unnecessary and childish—something expected for me to have already outgrown.

Suddenly, a bear grabbed its brother, picked it up, and slammed it down onto its back, splashing water everywhere. It snarled its deadly teeth, and its massive arms shook with a thundering effect. I admired the raw strength of the bear, feeling amazed at how easily it picked up the other.

That's it! I need to lift heavy things to get stronger!

The thought of strength training seemed outrageous at first, but it was the only solution that made sense in my mind. Lifting heavy things would not be dangerous to my wellbeing—unlike wrestling with bears or seeking out other strong Teraganes to fight.

If I were stronger, then I could carry Lillie, and she would not be sad anymore. If I could fly while holding Lillie, I could take her up into the trees. Actually, why stop there? She wanted to be up in the trees to have a better view.

If it's a better view she longs for, then I can just fly her anywhere she wants!

This inspiring curiosity motivated me, and I flew away from my perched position within the tree branches of the oak tree. I began my strength training as a clueless beginner. I looked around for heavy rocks and simply began lifting in repetition or throwing the rock over my shoulders.

Naturally, this hurt my back after a while and made me feel ridiculous as if I were a child looking for salamanders under rocks. So, I began to think of better methods. I still had some days before the next full moon, so I began pondering different ideas on how to build my strength, basing my concept of time on the phases of the moon. Over the days, I tried different methods, often finding them embarrassingly childish.

I decided to return to the river and learn more from the bears. I watched the beasts closely, this time at their wrestling matches, exhibiting their muscularity, stamina, and power, and I took notice of their food consumption. According to my early teachings, I only ate enough to keep hunger at bay—enough to meet my basic survival needs.

Maybe I need to eat bigger quantities like the bears? Perhaps this will give me strength, more muscles, and more power.

Instead of one fish, I began eating two. It was hard at first, for I was not accustomed to eating so much in one sitting. I ate small amounts of food with Lillie, but at my leisure while relaxing. This time, I ate to fuel my stamina and enhance my power.

The brown bears also ate other foods, like berries, honey, and even mushrooms. I followed them, watched, and learned from the great beasts of the forest. I kept all this to myself, and I dared not to tell the others in the colony, and I watched over my shoulder carefully to not be seen by any Sage or member flying over the vicinity.

Over the years of solitary living, we had claimed territories, enclaves often called, but, still, the lingering anxiety of a Sage discovering me kept me vigilant within my enclave. I knew there was a possibility of them scolding me or deterring me away from my goals—perhaps even claiming that I had gone crazy.

Perhaps I was crazy. I was doing all this work for someone else. I was planning and adjusting my life according to someone's survival and their happiness. That was not the way of the Teragane people.

Our culture was independent; we were lone survivalists. We were magnificent avians beyond the vultures or eagles that resided within the skies as well, but secretive and mysterious, and we always kept our private lives simple. I did not want to do away completely with my culture, but I did know that my love for Lillie motivated me to become something more than what I was taught. Her happiness, her companionship, and our time together meant everything to me. I wanted to preserve that more than anything. I wanted Lillie, within the complexities of her life, to have some sort of security—with me.

Was it all absurd? No—I was in love, or at least love was blossoming within my heart. And I wanted it to continue to grow! I wanted to accomplish all these things for Lillie and even for myself.

Motivated by my love for Lillie and inspiration to grow my strength, I observed other animals in the forest. Some were clever, like the foxes. The boars of the valley were fierce and relied heavily on their colony. Squirrels were creative when it came to finding food and how they made their way around in the trees. I thought of Lillie and amused myself with the imagination of her learning to maneuver high in the trees on the branches like a squirrel. If I could fly her up in the trees, how easy would it be for her to learn how to jump from the high branches? I always relied on my wings to carry me where I needed to go, so the thought of being without caused me to worry about the sustainability of Lillie staying in the trees. Was that enough for her to be happy?

As I observed a group of squirrels and their creative process of moving freely around, a new problem developed in my mind.

It's not enough to be strong—I need to train the strength of my wings. But, how?

I had the endurance to take long flights like the large eagles crossing over the valleys with simple strides. I could glide with ease, dive when necessary, and even balance in mid-air. With each downward stroke, my wings would displace the air, allowing me to ascend with great power and precision. My flight abilities were instinctual, well established after so many years. As each new year passed, my body grew, and so did my wings. My wings were strong, but only enough to carry my weight.

I began experimenting with picking up heavy rocks again. This time, I took to the sky and flew in small sprints while carrying the extra weight. My wings felt shaky and weakened by the extra burden, but I continued to push myself in small increments.

I spent my days eating large quantities of food and carrying weighty objects while flying. The muscles in my legs felt achy when lifting from the ground, and my arms were sore when I pulled myself up from tree branches in a repetitive manner.

Whatever I saw in my environment, I thought of ways to utilize it for strength training, but only once did I overstep into another's enclave.

"What are you doing here?" Polcha asked as I dropped a large rock near my foot, and it tumbled away, eventually splashing into the river.

"Oh—my apologies," I uttered while I bent down to pick up the rock again, finding it too perfect to leave behind even though I had stumbled into a different area by accident. "I was following the stream and I—"

Water dripped from the ends of Polcha's dark, short hair as she wrung out the ends, obviously finishing up bathing in the river, for her extra pair of clothes were drying in the sun, and she only wore a tunic that sat mid-thigh. I darted my eyes, focusing on the rock I pulled out from the river, but felt Polcha's piercing eyes upon my back.

"What is so special about that rock that you lose your way into my enclave?" she asked, and I heard her shuffle next to me. She sat down onto the riverbank, allowing her bare legs to hang over, dipping her feet into the cold waters as the summer rays beat upon us. I hadn't interacted with Polcha since we were younglings, and I nervously stood up while she kicked her long legs and peered up at me with a curious grin. She had changed a lot—but, similar to Mika, caused a sense of apprehension whenever I was near her. Was it the guidance of being solitary? Or, was it stumbling into her enclave after she had just bathed?

"The rock is helping me with—uh, something," I replied, and extended my wings to leave while holding the rock, but Polcha grabbed my ankle.

"Like what?" she asked, and I looked down at her. Her brown eyes glowed in the sunlight, but her rounded cheeks from the mischievous grin caused my throat to feel weird.

"I'm just—just trying to get stronger."

"That's good—being strong will do well for you in the future." She tugged on the hem of my trousers, and I stepped away, and she released her hand after quietly giggling while eying me. My heart raced at her strange comment, and I bowed my head, desiring to leave.

"Sorry for disrupting you. It won't happen again."

"Oh, I don't mind."

I quickly extended my wings and flew off while carrying the rock, ignoring the racing of my heart and the weird sensation rising within my throat. However, as I carried the rock back to my enclave, I thought about my interaction with the colony member. I had partially assumed that she would have been critical, possibly scolding me for crossing into her territory.

Then again, maybe that was simply because that was how Cami had reacted during our early years of territorial foundations.

Maybe being around the others wasn't so bad after all.

CHAPTER SIX

WHEN MEMORIES FORM IN WATER

Although it was still midday, I could easily detect the round shape looming in the sky in broad daylight. The full moon came, and I made my way to the meadow. Feeling inspired by my change of mindset, I began looking around the area for things I had perhaps never noticed before.

I observed the forest tree-line; there was a small opening, usually where Lillie came from. It was dark, ambiguous, and intimidating. I preferred open areas, not dark spaces, unless it was the familiar cave of my home on the mountain or the other caves where my peers lived. I knew that she lived somewhere in the forest, but I began to imagine the type of home she would have. Was it carved in the trunks of the trees? Did she live in a cave, like me?

While I stared at the dark forest in a perched position on a rock, I noticed Lillie emerge. It had been an entire moon phase since I had last seen her. Her stormy complexion had diminished into a stagnant gray, something similar to a river during a lethargic drizzle. Her brown hair faded from its chestnut color, turning nearly all white.

When she saw me, she began to run, causing my heart to flutter. I rose up and jumped off the rock and opened my arms wide, and she embraced me. Her head upon my chest felt wonderful, and I sighed deeply as the anticipation of finally seeing her again began to subside.

"I missed you," she said, her breath casting further warmth upon my body.

"I missed you, too," I replied. My throat felt weird, and I almost choked up attempting to speak, and I quickly grunted as I moved my arms to my side.

"Come, let's rest and eat." She smiled as she looked up at me with a tilted head, but then quickly turned as she removed the basket from her back.

As usual, Lillie laid out the blanket, but I grabbed one end and helped her lay it onto the dewy grass. The natural-colored woven fibers were fading after being used so many

46

times throughout the years. I sat down next to Lillie and stroked the material, curious to know if she had made it and where she had obtained the material. I asked her, and, while she prepared some slices of bread and bits of meat, making us sandwiches, she explained the process of blanket weaving.

As she spoke, I watched her hair dance in the cool breeze while small wooden beads woven into thin braids clinked together as her hair shifted. I noticed Lillie's hair had grown long over the seasons and sat halfway down her back. Once she finished explaining blanket weaving, I asked her about the wooden beads braided into her hair, and she explained the process of bead-making, something she learned as a young child. She often moved her hands while speaking, but upon resting her hand on her earthy green skirt, I noticed her hands appeared cut up and her nails were brittle. I grabbed her hand and intently observed the deep grooves, then I looked up, sensing her surprise at my sudden physical movement.

"Lillie," I said while staring deeply into her eyes, "has someone hurt you?" She abruptly pulled her hand away from me, then began nervously adjusting the brown scarf around her neck.

"No," she mumbled. "It's just from work. I use my hands all the time. It just happens." Lillie quickly changed the subject, avoiding making eye contact. She started talking about the food shortages, the different kinds of soup her mother was making, and the plant seeds that she had gathered from the forest to grind into flour. I listened as usual but purposely refocused my observations on Lillie's life and the problems she faced every day. Lillie, possibly discerning my attention, changed the subject once again.

"And how is mountain life treating you?" she asked while stroking the fibers of her scarf.

"Normal, as usual," I replied as I intently watched her hands move along her scarf, then I looked up at her face. "Actually."

As her long, pointed ears perked, her eyes finally drifted, making eye contact, and I felt my throat grow suddenly very dry. I wanted to tell her about my plan to carry her up into the trees, about my strength training, and all the different methods I had created to achieve my goals. However, as the dryness in my throat increased, an intuitive judgement forced me to hold my tongue. Was it my fear of disappointing her? Or, did I desire to surprise her after I was finally ready to carry out my efforts?

Did I fear providing a false sense of hope, only contributing to her misery?

"Actually, I gathered my own honey for the first time," I said, holding back the truth. I could feel the tips of my ears grow warm, my cheeks felt hot, and my throat was still very dry. I darted my eyes away and looked down at my woolen trousers and noticed a little butterfly land upon my knee.

"You did?" she gasped and leaned towards me, her hand resting near my leg, causing the butterfly to flutter away. "You, Sable, gathered something other than basic food for survival?"

"Hey, perhaps I need it for survival," I said with a shrug, and suddenly Lillie pushed me with her arm. We began to chuckle in unison. She kept eyeing me while shaking her head, causing her hair to sway and the beads to clink against the other small braids.

Her giggles increased, consequently leading into an outburst of laughter. I followed, our eyes meeting each other. Her laughter grew hysterical, and she slowly lowered herself backwards onto the ground. Tears ran down her cheeks and her chest heaved as she clasped her hands to her heart, then reached up to loosen the scarf around her neck. My heart pounded within my chest as I observed her, and I reached across the blanket and pulled out some grass and tossed it at her face.

Her eyes dilated as she lifted herself up, and she pursed her lips while her rosy cheeks deepened in color. She grabbed a handful of grass and threw it at me while rising to her knees. Still laughing, I grabbed a napkin and shot it at her, and she quickly stood up, ripped off her brown scarf from her neck, and aimed it at me. I easily caught it, then tossed it in her direction while I faltered backwards onto my rear.

In rage, she lunged forward, attempting to tackle me, and I grabbed her waist, and flipped her over onto her back, allowing my wings to flutter behind me. I was gentle, unlike the bears I watched, or when I was younger and wrestled the younglings from my colony. I could sense her smaller stature was hardly one to be abrasive with. But something new stirred inside my heart—unlike the bears, I'm sure.

I stared down at her as she lay flat on her back in the grass, and my hand was still around her waist, the other balancing me while resting on the ground as I kneeled over her. Her little nose wrinkled as she giggled, her smile rounding her cheeks, and the tips of her pointed ears reddened. She opened her eyes and stared back, and her smile began to slowly lower. The meadow grass bounced around her face, her fading hair intertwining around the grass. My heart fluttered as I noticed her lips for the first time.

Why do they look so delicious?

Scared of my new overwhelming thoughts, I plucked a clover nearby and tickled her nose with its jagged petals. Lillie squinted, giggled, and then bent her knees as she moved her feet upon my stomach to push me off. I was bigger and heavier than her, but I noticed her legs were rather strong, and I rolled over as she quickly sat up, heavily panting. I did not dare make eye contact until I steadied my breathing, regardless of the impossible feat of slowing the rate in which my heart was beating. The overwhelming sensations filled my body, and I sat contemplating how pleasant it all felt.

I looked over and saw her scarf laying on the ground, but Lillie quickly moved over to it and grabbed it, then wrapped it around her neck. Her eyes darted as she looked at me—yet I couldn't stop staring at her lips. Why did I feel so drawn in?

"What?" she suddenly asked as she adjusted the scarf, and I lifted my eyes. "What is so—what are you staring at?"

"Nothing," I replied, and turned to look away, ignoring the racing of my heart. "I'm just really happy you're here."

"I'm happy to be here, too," she said. "Although you did mess up my hair."

"Sorry."

"Don't be."

"Okay."

Was she always this intriguing?

Keeping my goals a secret from Lillie was uncomplicated. My strength training was slow and non-impressive. I learned to intentionally add new practices and methods to help achieve my desired outcome. Originally, the catalyst for my idea was emotionally driven. Now, I could adjust my rational mind and instincts to build a new routine for myself. Guided by traditions and intuition, I could add my personal desires to my ritualistic lifestyle. With my constant physical activities, I felt less bored and more in control of my rampant thoughts, especially now that something new was stirring in my heart. I felt energized to direct myself and had a slight sense of freedom to make my own decisions. At least, in secret—for now.

"You must learn to be independent of the others on the mountain for survival," my mother had said to me as a youngling. "But you also should not neglect your colony. Remember your training from me, your father, and the Sage. Look to the others as a reminder that you are not alone in this world. Like the bears, we live separately, but remember those who taught us and respect those around us, taking only what we need."

I didn't quite understand my mother's directive, but, over the years of my upbringing, I did feel a sense of community with the others—*at times*. Lillie's friendship was drastically different, but she was also raised in an obviously connected environment. I did not interact with the other Teraganes on the summit very often, except for Cami, but even that was seldom and only initiated by my loneliness and curiosities. I had stumbled upon Mika once during our early years of solitude, but the memory was rather formidable, since it appeared he had recently made a large kill and was covered in blood. I also didn't appreciate the way I felt being around Polcha, but I was curious about the others in my colony, and I decided to extend an open invitation in efforts to connect with the other Teraganes.

"I hope you invited us because you found a plethora of fish," Cami stated upon his arrival with the others. We met at my home on the mountain, and Cami was just as disgruntled as usual. However, the other two seemed apprehensive, but also interested in meeting with me after I had found them both in their separate homes upon the mountain.

"Not entirely," I replied. "I wanted to show you all something." I had originally tried inviting all the members of the colony of Hira, but I couldn't find the others in their homes, nor did I desire to seek them out elsewhere. So, I was grateful that at least Cami, Deruk, and Kora had arrived, even though they were obviously skeptical about the idea of meeting all together. Yet, they did come, after all, providing assurance that they must have similar curiosities as me—at least.

"Follow me," I said, then took off in flight from the edge of the tunnel entrance. The other three followed, and we created a V-flying formation, descending from the mountain. The air currents were favorable, and the sky had cleared once past the summit. The sun was hot, but, as we descended, it felt tolerable as the wind blew through my hair and wing feathers.

The landscape below was blooming with life during the summer, scattering the scenery with vibrant colors of green and yellow. I directed our flying party to the river where the bears hunted. I landed at a far distance from the river itself, with the others directly behind me, and I led our group of four through the trees towards the river. I pushed my finger to my lips, signaling to be quiet. The others expressed skepticism, darting their eyes at each other, but obeyed as we continued along stealthily. I could hear the bears splashing in the distance, one giving a loud roar.

"What?" Deruk whispered as he darted behind a tree.

"He's leading us to a group of bears," Kora quietly exclaimed. "What's wrong with you?"

"Shhh," I beckoned, noticing Cami slightly flinch while the other two hesitated. "It will be alright." I motioned for them to continue to follow. They crouched closer to the ground, dark wings folded, arms ready for attack or a quick escape. Yet, they still followed me.

When we reached the riverbank, we were concealed by trees and thick brush, and I jumped into a large oak tree and the others followed. In a staggered formation along the thick branches, we sat comfortably in the large tree. For some time, we perched silently, watching the bears play-fight, consume fish, and do as they wish.

Teraganes are silent observers. We could often sit for hours without ever speaking or even needing to move much. Apart from younglings in training with their parents, we are solo observers. It was a rare occasion to be gathered like we were at that moment in the tree—our dark figures lining the thick branches of the oak tree. It was not much, but it made my heart feel warm and happy. I did not dare break the silence; I only made side glances to observe my peers.

Cami was slightly expressive, furrowing his thick brows as the bear cubs displayed vicious tendencies. Deruk looked anxious; his black eyes darted, scanning the area, and tensing his jaw. He sat in a ready-to-flee position, hands gripping tightly to a branch. Kora was the only one who I could suspect was amused by the scene. Her position was leaned forward, intently observing the activities of the bears, with a slight curl in the corner of her lips. I smiled to myself as I inspected the others.

It's been a long time since I was with the others like this. I wonder what they do most days...

When the bears eventually left and I was certain that there was no danger, I flew down to the river, and the other three followed. With my bare hands, I snatched unsuspecting fish from the running water, gathering a few for myself while the others also plucked out fish for a quick meal. Kora even found some crayfish, and shared it with me, and I crunched down upon the small creatures with pleasure.

The rays of the summer sun were strong, and the heat was almost unbearable at that point in the day. When I returned to the grassy riverbank, I removed my boots, and rolled up my trousers. I smiled at my ankle tattoo as I removed my sleeves, tossing them onto my boots. I only exposed myself for bathing, which was never done around others, but the sunshine on my skin felt invigorating, the side glances from the others exciting.

I then walked into the shallow waters of the river and scooped up a handful of water to drink. Without a word but plenty of observational glances, Cami followed me, although he only removed his boots and tucked the trousers above his knees. Then Kora and finally Deruk made their way into the shallow waters without their footwear, but rolled up their sleeves as Kora continued searching for more crayfish with Deruk following.

It reminded me of our years as younglings, when our mothers would bring us to the different rivers to drink water and cool off in the summer heat. During those summers, for a few moments, our mothers allowed us to play together in the water. I had wrestled with other younglings too, but I was brutally reminded how after our tenth years, we were no longer encouraged to play in the rivers together—or anything, in fact. Yet, in our sixteenth years, living without parents, we were all gathered again, and a sense of community overwhelmed me as I gazed at Kora.

"Hey Kora," I snickered as she lazily patted water on her neck causing droplets to form upon her dark high-neck tunic. She looked at me curiously, her brown eyes widening. With one strong swoop, I swung my arm across the water surface, sending a splash of cold water onto her.

"Hey!" she yelled, then returned an even bigger splash. Deruk threw aside a few crayfish as he ran towards us, sending an alarming amount of water onto me. Cami came to my defense, and the four of us created a chaotic scene of water explosions using our arms, legs, and even wings. The river water extended high into the air as our dark wings and figures swung ferociously in a playful manner.

"Okay, okay!" Cami shouted as he stumbled backwards. "Stop! I'm soaking!" I halted the splashing yet still chuckled while breathing heavily. The freezing water sent a shiver down my spine, but it felt refreshing after standing in the sun for so long. Kora and Deruk stopped their attacks as well, and the four of us stood sopping wet and heavily breathing.

"That was fun," Kora said with a smile and pushed her black hair out of her face. Deruk looked at her, then smiled as well as his sharp teeth glistened in the sunlight.

"Yeah," he said as he also combed his dark hair back. "A little crazy, though."

"It will take forever to dry now," Cami complained as he marched out of the river. He spread his wings, vibrating them vigorously, sending droplets onto the grass. I followed Cami on to the grassy bank, also shaking myself dry. Although my clothes were made of lightweight wool, the water-play drenched them significantly. I completely removed my tunic by unfastening the bone buttons from the back, and then twisted my shirt, removing the water. Cami, who had only removed his sleeves, looked quickly at my bare torso.

"It's easier to dry this way," I said after noticing Cami's widening eyes of surprise. He quickly slid his sleeves back on and began wringing out his trousers, turning his back to me. I looked down at my torso, noticing the curves of muscles starting to form. I put my partially dry tunic back on, feeling elated at the progress of my strength training.

I glanced over at Kora and Deruk, noticing that they were quietly conversing while still standing in the river as Deruk snatched more crayfish, presenting each to Kora who would either shake her head until he presented one more suitable to her liking. In which, she would then twist the end of her hair while crunching down loudly as she watched him, again, seek out more for her as he spoke animatedly.

The way she gazed upon Deruk was similar to how Polcha smiled at me—but, the twisting of the ends of her hair reminded me of Lillie, causing me to wonder if such interactions was caused by attraction.

Hmmm. Interesting.

"Hey, you two love birds!" I called out to them while waving dramatically. Deruk glared at me, and Kora blushed, tucking the hair behind her ear, only enhancing my theories.

"Sable," Cami muttered as he spun around towards me. "Stop being so idiotic. Leave them alone."

"I'm just teasing," I said, and grinned widely at Cami.

"I think you've been in the sun for too long," he huffed. Smelling strongly of crayfish, Kora and Deruk joined us on the grass, and the four of us continued wringing out our clothes. Deruk also pulled out another fish to eat. His long, sharp canine teeth sunk into the flesh and tore it apart, and Kora contently picked at her teeth while sitting directly in a sunny spot, allowing the heat to further dry her.

"I thought about making a fire," I said after sighing happily. "Then we could dry faster—maybe even cook our fish." The three others stayed motionless, staring widely at me. Water and fish flesh dripped from Deruk's chin and only the sound of the rushing river filled the stunned silence.

"First bear watching, now fire-making?" Cami announced loudly with his usual judgmental tone. I shrugged my shoulders. I knew it was a new idea for them. We were having fun together, something we had not done since we were younglings. I was curious if they were open to trying something new altogether. I had hoped to make the afternoon even more memorable for myself and the others. However, I knew that this was an unexpected idea for us to participate in as growing Teraganes, but I didn't quite care enough since it felt natural and fun. I was enticed to try something new with the people who lived near me. The only people who I could call my friends—maybe even a family—besides Lillie, of course.

"I've had my fill for the day," Deruk said with a hint of annoyance. "Thanks for the invite." He threw the half-eaten fish back into the river and took off into the sky, leaving a trail of mist behind. Kora watched him leave, then looked at me with an expression of conflict, but yearning.

"Yeah, thanks," she said, then also shot off, seemingly following Deruk. Cami straightened up after brushing off his trousers and watched the others disappear. He continued to adjust his clothing, perfectly aligning the ends and folds, and ignored my remark.

I waited patiently for his answer, holding my breath. I didn't even know how to start a fire or how to cook fish; the idea spontaneously appeared in my head. Perhaps it was a random thought motivated by Lillie's stories of the many meals she cooked over an open fire. I wanted to try it and perhaps see if my friends could witness the experience of trying new ideas. We didn't need fire to cook our food, but, I liked the idea, especially watching Kora share the crayfish with us. Maybe it was simply natural for females to share food with males and had nothing to do with attraction.

Then again...

"It sounds interesting, but I think I've had enough interesting events for one day," Cami finally said. He straightened out his clothes one last time, satisfied with his efforts. "In addition, neither of us are Mages and cannot procure the eternal flame."

"I was thinking of an orange fire—like the ones the, uh, hunters use to cook." Cami narrowed his eyes as he paused his hand upon the folds of his tunic, tapping nervously.

"The fire of the forest-dwellers is uncontrollable—it is primitive and dangerous. You shouldn't play around with foolish ideas."

"Well, like you said, neither of us can produce the blue flame of the Sage. So, what other kind of fire could I create?"

"None, obviously." His words were cold—expected from a Sage in training. All the more reason for me to keep my interests to myself and far from his knowledge. Perhaps it was foolish to speak of my curiosities to him after all.

A moment of silence drifted between us as I sat on the riverbank, shoeless, and I watched the stream of water rush by and felt the crawling of an ant over my toes.

"Thanks for showing me the bears," Cami suddenly said, and I looked over at him, noticing a slight change of demeanor. "I have not observed bears since I was a young child, nor played in the river since—"

"With our mothers," I said, finishing his sentence, recalling the memories I had swirling through my mind all day.

"Yeah, that was a long time ago," he said and began brushing his fingers through his curly brown hair. "But those days are in the past. We are not younglings anymore."

"Doesn't mean we can't cool off in the river, or watch the bears."

"Yes, but we must still observe in solitude. We shouldn't be together in the open like this."

"Why?"

"Don't be absurd by asking such things. You already know why."

"But, why can't we also participate—"

"Sable!" Cami shouted, his voice returning to one of disdain. His voice echoed as he moved his hair around in frustration. He looked troubled and choked up while trying to swallow. He knew the importance of abiding by rituals, traditions, and unspoken rules. He knew better than any of us, or, so I assumed.

"Your father and mother in their wisdom have taught you the natural ways of life," he lectured while still combing through his hair. "Perhaps you should be wise and remember who you are." He walked next to my side, staring at me with his intense brown eyes and grimacing expression. The sun beamed behind him, and his dark figure stood tall and regal. He stopped brushing through his curls, finally satisfied, then he eyed my tangled locks.

"You really should comb your hair," Cami said.

"It will only get messy again," I replied, causing him to scoff. He extended his wings, took a step back, then shot off into the sky in a shadowy blur. He left me like the others, and I could only assume that they all went their separate ways, abiding by the rituals of solace. Their lingering absence reminded me of the reality of what it meant to be a Teragane.

I did not feel motivated to even attempt to make a fire—not after the warning—and only ate what fish I had left, caught more within the river, and foraged around for berries.

Although I felt immensely disappointed that Cami and the others were less intrigued by my idea of fun, I was at least satisfied with the idea that pursuing my own goals would allow me to create a better life for myself. Those moments of happiness, reliving pleasant memories from the past, gave me a sense of belonging—at least for a moment. Even if we were going against the taboo of gathering, they did come out when I had asked. Perhaps there would be more opportunities in the future.

I pushed myself to strength train that day. I brought my extra fish and berries back to my mountain residence and, by the evening, felt hungry again. I decided to continue making a habit of gathering a plethora of food during the day, eating as I wanted, and fueling when I exert energy. I thought about my time at the river with the others. I felt a sense of community, at least for a moment, when we played together in the water or when we sat in the oak tree, watching the bears.

However, the ending of our time together slightly disheartened me. I wished Cami would have relaxed more or at least considered the idea that life could be fun at times. He was always so serious. But, maybe that was due to his training with the Sage. Who knew the extent of his expectations—I surely did not. Regardless, I shook off his lecturing and instilled the happy memory of the four of us splashing in the river and eating crayfish. I relished the concept of sharing food with the others.

The idea of fire-making lingered in my mind, and I thought about asking Lillie to teach me to make a fire the next time I saw her. Cami was right—fire was dangerous, and the eternal flame within my home was controlled by the Sage, even if I did not understand how during those years living in the colony of Hira.

CHAPTER SEVEN
WHEN A FLAME BURNS HOT WITHIN

Lillie was quite overjoyed when I had asked her to teach me how to make a fire. Her explosive enthusiasm was as if she had waited her whole life for me to finally ask. She led me into the woods, instructing me to gather small sticks—kindle wood, she told me—and branches from the forest floor.

"Only gather dry wood," she said while holding up a damp stick covered in moss, then tilted it from side to side. "Wet sticks don't burn." She then tossed the stick aside. I nodded, and then I wandered around the area, looking for dry branches and kindle wood.

As I strained my eyes to see around the foliage, I realized that it was my first time entering the cedar forest. In the valley where I usually hunted or had trained with my caregivers, the forests consisted of oaks, pines, and some white birch trees. Walking through the pine forest never bothered me, and most forests in the valley of my enclave were sparse enough that I could easily move in and out without much thought. The giant cedars, by contrast, were overbearing and created a looming, frightening sensation in my body. A prickling tingle crept along my neck as I looked up and around, feeling uneasy about the dark canopy above and the massive trees blocking any clear view of the area.

"What's wrong?" Lillie asked me as I was staring up at the darkness overhead, then she followed my gaze.

"Pretty amazing, huh?" she said with a smile.

"No, it's too dark," I muttered while looking down at her, noticing her grin slowly disappear. "I don't like it." I then turned away, making my way out of the gloomy woods. We had not walked too far into the forest, and, within moments, the light beamed through the tree-line, and I could see the meadow.

Towards the clearing, the trees grew sparser despite their enormous size, and I extended my wings, flying swiftly out of the forest, leaving Lillie behind. When I exited the overbearing trees, a sense of relief passed over me, and my eyes adjusted to the bright light of the sun again. As my tense muscles relaxed, my breathing became easier, and I shook my head, allowing the tingling feeling to subside and release from my neck.

I felt somewhat guilty for leaving Lillie behind, but as I tossed the sticks onto the ground near her blanket, I justified my reasoning. She was a forest-dweller living within the climate of darkness. I was a resident of the sky, the open air, and the mountains. The density of the trees, the darkness of the canopy—it all felt terrifying, and I hardly wanted her to know how I truly felt.

She returned quietly with her arms full and began assembling the wood for a fire, and I crouched next to her, watching her every move. After establishing the correct formation, she showed me the primitive techniques: the use of friction with stones that caused sparks, igniting thinner twigs, and the careful attention to enhancing the fire through patience, a steady hand, and gentle fanning of the small flame.

"From now on, I'll just gather supplies if we want to build a fire together," Lillie finally said after the flame had matured into a larger fire. "But I do think it's good for you to learn how to gather the proper wood if you decide to make a fire on your own. I'm sure not all forests are as dark as this one."

"Yeah," I replied as I observed from my kneeling position. "Thanks."

"Why did you want to build a fire today in the first place?" she asked, then tilted her head. I pulled out from my satchel two of the four fish I had caught, and Lillie's eyes widened. "You want to cook your fish?" I smiled and nodded as I held two fish by the tail, and Lillie stood up while the fire blazed, and she crossed her arms while raising a brow.

"Hey, I thought Teraganes don't cook," she said while tapping her bicep and pursing her lips.

"I want to try something new," I replied as I still held the fish in my hands.

"Really?"

"Yeah—your food is cooked and always tastes good."

"Well, if you put it that way." Lillie's cheeks rounded and she looked over at the forest. "Alright. This will be fun. Wait here while I go fetch some more sticks. While I'm gone, you can gut the fish."

"Huh?" I grunted as I lowered the fish, and my eyes darted over to the fire.

"Like this," she said, then pulled out a knife from her skirt pocket. She held onto the wooden handle while unsheathing the sharp blade. My eyes widened as she skillfully moved the blade underneath the belly of the fish, spewing its insides from the opening. She grabbed the entrails and threw them in the fire, little by little.

"Like that, see?" she said after carefully moving her loose hair away from her face with her arm. Then, she rotated the handle of the knife in my direction, unfazed by the fish goop dripping from her hands.

"Never seen that before," I said as I grabbed the knife. "Why don't we eat that part?"

"Well, maybe your stomach can handle it, but mine can't." She raised her brows repetitively, then wiped her hands clean with a cloth napkin, then returned to the forest. I gutted the remaining three fish as Lillie instructed, feeling excited to follow her directions. I held the knife awkwardly at first, adjusting my grip as I learned how to use it properly. It was wide, slightly curved, and very sharp. I had never seen Lillie's knife before, and I felt shocked by the fact that she carried such a dangerous yet useful tool.

She's always surprising me.

I threw the entrails into the fire, noticing the flames engulfing the fleshy substance. The orange flames bounced and sizzled, and I wondered why the flame was orange instead of blue, like the flame eternally flickering in my home. Why were the fires so different? Even the smells were contrasting.

Lillie returned, carrying four long, narrow sticks. I watched as she kneeled next to me, and she grabbed a water canteen from her basket, pouring water on her hands and mine, and we wiped them dry with a cloth napkin. She took her knife and shaved the ends of the sticks to a point. Finally, she used the knife to pare off the scales on the skin of the fish, flicking them towards the fire.

"I didn't think there was so much to cooking," I said, causing a scoffing laugh to escape Lillie's mouth. Then, she handed me one of the fish and shaved sticks.

"This is nothing," she said. "I understand why Teraganes skip the whole thing if they can just gobble up a fish without any preparation. My life would be extensively easier if I didn't have to cook all the time. Now—do as I do." She adjusted the mouth of the fish, then inserted the pointed end inside the gap. I followed her movements but struggled with prying open the mouth of the fish. The teeth were jagged, surprising me for a moment. When consuming fish, I would avoid eating the skull, although I did enjoy the flavors of the eyes, but I did not expect the teeth to scrape my skin.

"Ouch, these things are sharp," I said while I carefully watched Lillie thrust the stick further down the fish into its tail, impaling it completely.

"Kind of like your teeth," Lillie said. I used my tongue to feel the edges of my teeth, crinkling my nose. My teeth were, in fact, quite sharp, the canine being the pointiest.

"Yeah, I guess so. Are your teeth sharp?" I leaned closer to her face, waiting for her to reveal her teeth. She opened her mouth, showcasing the smooth edges, some only slightly pointed.

"A little bit," I said encouragingly, causing Lillie to slightly giggle, and we continued skewering the other fish. Then Lillie stood up and walked towards the fire, and I followed while carrying one of the skewers. She shoved the bottom of the piece of wood into the dirt next to the flames, then grabbed her knife again, and used the wooden hilt to hammer the top of the stick, driving it deeper into the earth, and allowed it to sit at an angle, the raw fish precisely over the open flames.

"You try," she suggested with a beckoning hand, and she flipped her hair over her shoulder. With one powerful movement, I jammed the stick deep into the dirt at a perfect angle, catching Lillie by surprise. I looked up and pushed my hair out of my face.

"Alrighty—then you can do the rest," she said as her eyes darted, obviously observing my arm. At first, I did not intentionally want to show off, but Lillie's look of admiration encouraged me to impress her again. I took the other two skewered fish in each hand, and a sense of audaciousness overcame my body. I lifted both my arms high into the air and, again in one dramatic swoop, struck the ground, lodging the stalks firmly. Lillie giggled and I felt my cheeks grow hot, and my muscles tensed.

"Well—that's impressive," Lillie said while twirling the ends of her hair. "Now, we wait." She continued to stoke the fire with wood, keeping a steady flame, and pointed out the signs of which fish were cooking faster or the ones that needed a slight adjustment. I enjoyed learning from Lillie, and was ever so grateful that she obliged in my request of cooking and fire-making. Although she had said her life would be easier if she didn't need to cook, she seemed content working with me, and I thoroughly relished the aroma of the sizzling fish.

"I usually cook food prepared in a pot over an open fire, or in an oven in the kitchen, so this feels fun. Like camping after a hunt—or traveling to a new city," Lillie remarked as she examined each sizzling fish. She looked over at me while I observed from over her shoulder with my hands folded behind my back. "You still don't cook, do you?"

"No," I said while shaking my head.

"And you've never made a fire?"

"Correct."

"Not even to stay warm?"

"I have a fire that never goes out." Lillie suddenly jolted, then slowly turned her head to view me again, and I blinked rapidly as my wings twitched.

"How is that possible?"

"I don't know." I shrugged, and she lifted a thin brow, and opened her mouth to speak, but the sound of a branch falling outside of the fire circle alarmed her, and she quickly adjusted it back into the burning flames. Then, she claimed that the fish were ready to eat.

We sat down upon the blanket near the fire, and we consumed the fish straight off the skewer and I found it rather delectable. I felt a sense of pride and goodness within myself. It was my first time bringing food to share with Lillie, and I had hoped that Lillie appreciated it. Well, it seemed that it did as her green eyes glistened in the sunlight—did her skin also reflect some hints of cooler tones again?

"Do you eat fish every day?" Lillie asked while licking her fingers.

"Mostly," I replied. The cooked fish was delicious. No—it was spectacular! I only consumed raw fish all my life, but this was different. It was good, it was amazing, and it was satisfying, not just for my stomach but for a deeper part of me that I didn't quite understand at the time.

"Well, if you bring fish next month," Lillie said while grabbing a water canteen and taking a sip, then wiped the drops from her lips. "I'll bring some salt, maybe some other spices, and we can make the fish even tastier."

"Tastier?" I asked and raised my brow while cleaning my teeth with my fingernail.

"Yeah, silly, this is just basic cooking. If I bring some other spices, I can make it even more delicious."

There she goes again, surprising me. I don't think there is anything she can't do.

"Actually," she continued, "there are many tastier ways of preparing food. Bring me anything, and I will make it better. Oh, this could be fun."

"Even honey?" I asked curiously, hoping to catch her off guard.

"Even honey! Honey on fish is a delicious meal in itself."

"You cannot be serious, can you? Honey on fish?" Lillie started laughing as she twisted the ends of her hair. I probably sounded like a foolish child to her at that moment. I was shocked that honey could be cooked on fish. Actually, I was surprised that anything

61

could taste better than cooked fish over the flames of the orange fire. Initially, when I first thought about it, I had a vague idea of how the cooked fish could turn out. After consuming it, my mind was swirling with astonishment, absolutely dumbfounded that something I consumed all my life actually could taste amazingly different.

"Oh, Sable," Lillie said as she still twirled the ends of her hair. "You are so funny sometimes." My cheeks flushed and I looked down at the empty skewer across my lap and began picking at the bark, feeling grateful to be near her again and suggesting something that she thought was interesting—something fun to do together.

"Thanks for teaching me how to make a fire and cook fish," I quietly said as I stripped the bark off the skewer. "I know you said your life would be easier without cooking, but this was really fun."

"You know what?" Lillie said, and my eyes glanced over at her. "It was fun. Let's do it again." I grinned as Lillie continued to speak about other combinations that we could create, and I told her about the foods I could collect from the valley. As the orange fire blazed its glorious flames, our conversations drifted, bouncing like the smoke. She talked about some new friends she had met, one of whom was particularly amusing. I listened, admiring the highs and lows of her voice and her animated features as she explained things.

I looked around, enjoying the cozy moment, until my eyes settled on the cedar trees. It still bothered me—those lurking shadows of the giant forest. A sudden shiver ran down my spine as I thought about those moments under the towering giants. I had never felt that way before. I recognized that terrifying sensation creeping over me again as my eyes lingered upon the dark forest. From my recollection, I was never afraid of anything. I knew how to defend myself; I always had an escape route if needed. This, however, felt different—something I was experiencing quite often as of late.

"You were really scared in the forest," Lillie said, and I assumed that she had noticed me staring at the trees. I could feel my heart begin to pound in my chest, and my face grew solemn. I did not want Lillie to think of me as a coward; I did not want her to think I—a powerful Teragane—was afraid of the cedar trees.

"Have you ever been inside these woods?" she asked. I shook my head, causing my black hair to bounce around my forehead. As discomfort overshadowed my demeanor, I could not find any words to defend or explain myself. I tossed the stripped skewer onto the grass as I continued to stare at the trees, and slightly leaned closer to Lillie.

"Well," she hummed, and I shifted my hands onto my lap while crossing my legs. Strangely, silence fell between us, and I could still feel my heart race within my chest as I thought about the forest in which Lillie lived within. I wondered if she was struggling to find appropriate words to speak or was attempting to formulate a joke about my cowardice. As sweat from anticipation and the fire nearby formed beads upon my forehead, I kept my eyes focused on my hands lingering on my lap, and I began picking at the bits of dirt and fish grease lingering on my fingertips.

To my surprise, Lillie slowly nudged closer to my side as she scooted across the blanket, and her thigh touched my side. Then, ever so slowly, her hand slid into mine, and I watched as our fingers intertwined. Her hand was rough, but warm, and I embraced the affection. She then moved my hand onto her lap, and my eyes darted as her fingers began to caress mine.

"It makes sense," she said while staring at the forest, and she leaned her shoulder against me.

"Why?" I asked while my eyes were still drawn to our hands clasped together, and my heart pounded and sweat continued to form upon my forehead.

"You're a Teragane, a creature of the sky," she started. "Your life is in the open air, high above the ground. The great forest is enclosed and overbearing. It can be a dangerous place. Predators can be lurking from any angle; the darkness can be terrifying and dangerous." She was right. Every ounce of my survival instinct was triggered, causing the unwanted emotional reactions. But why did that matter?

"Why is it not terrifying for you?" I asked, realizing how easily Lillie entered and emerged from the forest. She often seemed nonchalant and casual, and she acted as if the forest was a non-threatening environment for her. Oh—of course, she was a forest-dweller after all.

"Well, I guess it is just what I know. It is all I have ever known throughout my life. I was born and raised amongst the cedar trees."

"Like me living alone in the mountains."

"Yeah, exactly. I find that terribly frightening. For you, it is normal. The cedar forest is my normal."

"I guess that makes sense."

"I guess so, if we think about who we are as individuals and how we've been raised. The trees may be dark for you, but after living in the shadows all my life, you kind of forget there is light beyond the branches—you kind of just accept the lurking predators."

I squeezed her hand, feeling enamored by our affection, regardless of the subject—my fear began to wane as pleasant warmth cast throughout my body. Not one of the fire or the flushing sensation of fear, but of an embrace from someone I loved.

She looked at me, and I at her, and we exchanged loving smiles. She laid her head on my shoulder, gently caressing my hand with soft movements of her thumb, then I extended my right wing behind her, offering further intimacy.

I sighed with happiness as her acceptance of me, I of her, was a foundational reason why I loved being with Lillie. When I was with her, I felt accepted, understood, and wanted. I felt joy, excitement, and appreciation. I knew that my future goals were to help her escape from her dark, forest world—a world she just accepted, regardless of its predators, so to speak.

But, on this occasion, all I wanted was to sit by her side, her hand in mine. All I wanted was to know that we would always have each other. I only wanted to be accepted exactly as I was, and I think Lillie also wanted that from me.

As I continued to stare at our intertwining hands, I noticed the comparison of our skin colors, and my heart began to flutter. We were different, yes, but both seemed to care about each other immensely. Although my stomach was full of the cooked fish, my taste buds tingling, the overflowing of love within my heart enhanced the whole experience.

I knew that I loved Lillie, but at that moment, I knew that she also loved me. She may have never said it, but her actions were evidential to her feelings towards me. It was enough to solidify the very real fact simmering within my pounding heart of anticipation of being accepted by the one who I loved.

CHAPTER EIGHT

WHEN STRENGTH IS ACKNOWLEDGED

S ummer was at its end, and the autumn colors rolled through the landscape, causing the trees to change to orange and red, and the rains lingered longer, casting a hazy mist during the mornings while I explored the valleys. My efforts at strength training began to pay off as I felt stronger each passing day. I was able to eat larger portions of sustenance and more often. I filled my days with extensive hunts, lifting large rocks while soaring through the air, and learning from the creatures throughout the valleys. I explored new areas, avoiding the enclaves of the others, and used tree limbs to hang from, lifting myself either by arm strength, or I would hang from my legs and lift myself with a curling method.

While I became more proficient in my hunting skills and continued to increase my physical activities, I was in great competition with my personal goals. During my early years of training as a youngling, I was taught to only hunt twice my fill during the autumn months in preparation for the winter. Now, I had already made a drastic adjustment to my new routine and needed to realign my way of planning for the upcoming cold months. During the day, I was constantly changing the amount of food I consumed, depending on my mood, my energy levels, and what extra nourishment I could find in my adventures around the valleys of forests and rivers.

For the first time, I began to worry about how I would complete my goals and keep up my progress over the winter, as I would be isolated upon the summit. Unlike my earlier methods, I was no longer just focusing on sustaining myself for survival.

"The only times you must gather more food is for the winter months," my father had once said while in my younger years of life-training. "But, since you are not exerting so much energy, you do not need to eat so much. Only bring what will suffice your needs for survival."

"How will I know how much I need?" my younger self had asked.

"You will learn over time. As you grow up, you will need a little more than the year before. Just continue to remember how much you eat every day and add a little more each year. Allow your instincts to guide you."

Instincts. The real Sage of our culture. We lived on survival instincts. Anything else could prohibit us from learning from our internal teachers. Instincts and listening to the guidance of the Sage, which often reminded us to live only by such dispositions—anything else was irrelevant.

Now, I faced a new dilemma: I was allowing myself to be guided by emotions. I was following something completely different than I was ever taught and utterly against my original teachings. When I had first met Lillie, I simply thought there was no harm in meeting with her nor could I be swayed to change my life, necessarily.

Oh, how wrong I was.

My understanding of what would entail after meeting Lillie and where it could lead me was the acceptance of the pursuit of happiness and personal freedom. I had my instincts to survive; now I was being led by my heart to a whole new world no one had ever prepared me for. There were no Sage to guide me in tradition. I thought at times that perhaps I was crazy. However, all I had to do was think about Lillie, the warmth she brought me, and compare that to my cold, solitary life I was expected to live by forever. If I was insane for trying to live a different life than the others, then yes, I was crazy.

When I met Lillie four years ago, my life changed. I cannot fathom the idea of never knowing what I know now.

No one on the mountain ever made me feel excited, motivated, or desired. How could they? Sometimes, in passing, I'd see the others fly to their summit home and I would wave or attempt to greet them, and they would simply scoff or observe me in a way that only made me feel uncomfortable. The Teraganes in my colony were as cold as the snow piling on the ridges. On the other hand, Lillie's presence in my life created wonderful sensations. These feelings for Lillie were enough to embark on the crazy adventure of finding a new way of life for myself. I knew that it was different, that the others would not agree if I ever explained anything to them, but I truly did not care what others thought—not anymore.

My life on the mountain, even within my colony, was isolated, set apart from my peers—my people. I didn't even know anything about their lives outside of the expected traditional way of life, except for Cami—yet even that was severely limited.

With Lillie, I knew something far different, far grander than I could have ever experienced with my own people. I knew what real friendship felt like and what it looked like. I felt a true sense of warmth, comfort, and appreciation. I was not ready to lose that nor let it just fade away like the changing colors of the leaves.

If I could help restore Lillie's life outside of the forest and secure a happy future for her, then we could live the life we both wanted, far from our traditional ways of life that were set up by others and their old customs. We could do away with unsatisfactory outcomes and unpleasant experiences, and we could spend every day together.

Such an idea thrilled me—seeing Lillie every day. I wanted a life worthy of satisfaction. A life where I could enjoy every moment with excitement and curiosities and something I could look forward to every day, not just every full moon. Creating this life seemed easy for me to think about, but as I put the work into myself every day, it also became easier to create on my own.

But, most of all, I wanted to live my life with Lillie, either in the meadow, in the trees, or wherever she desired. I didn't know what would happen or how others would respond, but if I could establish a happy life, then why would it matter? I was responsible for myself, no one could make that choice for me.

Lillie was obviously distraught about her life and relied heavily on doing work for others to sustain herself in her advanced society. If I could allow her to break free from it all and provide for her, then I could free her from the burdens weighing her down. Cooking together was obviously something that she enjoyed, a chore she hated back in her village. If everything that she hated could be reversed when with me, then for certain I could provide her with a happy life that she deserved. That was all that mattered in those moments of childish innocence. How blissful one's innocence is when they have no concept outside of their small reality.

<hr/>

"What are you doing?" I heard a voice say. I was examining a large branch near the river, my common spot to fish and watch the bears. I had the idea of installing large, sturdy branches in my home to help with my training during my isolated time on the mountain. I twirled around, unaware that he was behind me. My friend Cami unexpectedly asked me the question. He was observing me, his thick brown eyebrows slightly raised while his arms were crossed.

"I am—" my voice broke, for, I had no desire to explain anything to him, causing us to stand in silence for a moment. Then, I grunted while asking, "What are you doing here?"

Cami's eyes darted as he began adjusting his curly hair, and I realized how unusual it was for him to visit me unexpectedly. If I wanted to seek out Cami, I usually would fly to his home where I would always find him studying or arranging herbs for training. Yet even that seemed less acceptable as I grew older and was often met with a disgruntled attitude for interrupting his studies. After inviting him and the others to watch the bears, I felt apprehensive to seek anyone else out again—especially him since all he did was scold me like the Sage he was becoming.

"I'm sorry," Cami replied as he stepped back. "I know this is your enclave."

"It's okay," I assured him, feeling intrigued by his unusual presence. "I'm happy to see you. Just surprised."

"I had remembered that day we watched the bears," Cami said while his eyes drifted behind me. "I thought about it and came here—spontaneously."

"Really?" Cami continued to look around, obviously uncomfortable with this new idea of being spontaneous. His curly brown hair bounced as the wind tossed it around. He kept it neatly groomed around his narrow face and slightly longer in the back, and I noticed his brown skin was lighter than my own. I spent more time in the sun, I assumed, causing my skin to deepen over the summer, whereas he often stayed on the summit. He wore a similar tunic and woolen trouser, like all the others, but he also wore also a Sage-ceremonial necklace made of bones and a red scarf. He was slightly taller than me, but very thin—had he gotten even thinner?

Most of us Teraganes were tall and had black hair, from what I could remember of the others. However, I noticed that Cami was the only one with brown hair, similar to Lillie's when I had first met her. He was looking around with his narrow brown eyes, but then glancing at me for a moment. I could only imagine his thoughts as he examined me. The last time I had seen Cami was earlier in the summer months, and I wondered if he had noticed my physical changes.

"Are you preparing well for the winter?" he finally asked while adjusting a crimson red scarf around his neck. I had never seen him wear it before, and for some reason it looked familiar, but I turned my attention away from my mysterious friend.

"Yes, in fact, I am preparing a lot more than usual," I replied, and picked up the branch and examined it once again. It was thick, sturdy, and could be useful for furthering my training.

"Why?"

"Because I want to get stronger."

"You look stronger."

"I guess I was inspired by the bears. I want to be strong like them." I smiled and put the thick stick down in a pile of other branches. Cami raised his eyebrows again. I sensed his curiosity being held back by his logical reasoning, yet, surprisingly, he did not lecture me nor scoff as usual.

"The fish are plenty," I said and beckoned for him to join me in the river. His eyes darted and he quickly looked over his shoulder and up in the sky. Then, accepting that there were no prying nor judgmental eyes to see us, he followed me up the river.

We caught some fish together and then returned to sit on the grassy riverbank to eat our fresh meal. Cami did not ask me any more questions nor lecture me, to my surprise. Maybe he was curious—maybe bored, I could hardly determine at the time. I enjoyed his presence, even if we sat quietly without speaking, and he expressed only a stoic expression, yet one of many internal thoughts. I gathered a satchel full of fish to carry back home up to the mountain and picked a few red berries from a bush near the river, handing him some, although he hesitated to eat until after I popped a few into my mouth.

"Who told you that these are safe to eat?" he asked after wiping his hand upon his pant leg.

"The bears," I cheekily said, causing Cami to grimace, and I waited for his disdainful remark.

"Bears are far from adequate teachers, you know? They can eat poisonous mushrooms, or withstand bites from insects that can cause you harm."

"I know."

"Then—don't give me any more food if you're relying on bears to guide you. I don't feel like dying from toxic plants."

"Okay. But, these are safe. I have been eating them all summer." Cami grumbled in response, rolling his eyes, but he still stood next to me as I picked a few more berries, and munched happily knowing that I relied heavily on Lillie more than the bears to understand the wild foods of the lands. However, as I handed a few more sweet fruits to

Cami, he quietly ate them without further complaints. Why was he so stubbornly difficult to interpret?

"During the winter months, would you like to visit me?" I asked Cami before we departed our separate ways. Our homes were in proximity—in the same *neighborhood*—and the flight path was passable, if the winter weather conditions were decent.

"I—uh. I'm not sure that's..." Cami's voice trailed as he looked off into the distance with slow moving eyes. Again, he looked over his shoulder, then up in the sky, then focused on the trees again, and his wings twitched nervously.

"Well, I know that you fly with the Sage during the rituals, visiting the others," I said. "I don't see much of a difference if you just came to visit when the weather permitted. Would be nice to have some company. You can think about it first. I just wanted to give you an open invitation if you get bored."

"Life can never be boring for you, can it?" Cami said while shaking his head, and his wings seemed to relax. He looked back at me, the wind rustling his curly hair around his face. He brushed through his hair with his slender fingers, keeping it from becoming too tangled, and I noticed that his crimson scarf wrapped loosely around his neck reflected a warm complexion on his face. "I'll think about it."

"Okay." I grinned, then began gathering my items to carry back home. Cami sat perched on the riverbank, contemplating my invitation and, obviously, reasonable request. He stared at the moving water of the river, and his eyes darted back and forth as he continued combing through his hair while in deep thought. Although we spoke very little together, or even met outside of purposeful intentions, I was intrigued by Cami's friendship over the years, thankful to have at least one friend from my colony.

"Have a successful preparation for winter," I said before leaving Cami alone with his thoughts and pointless grooming.

———◆◇◆———

As the winds began to plummet in temperature, so did that agonizing sinking feeling in my heart. Winter was approaching, which meant the unbearable isolation in the mountain and the halted visitations with Lillie in the meadow. I began to fantasize about flying from the mountain during blizzards to the meadow, just to be with Lillie. But I knew it was all just reckless ideas—even deadly.

On the day of the full moon, I felt too anxious to wait until midday, as usual, to venture out to the meadow. I arrived early in the day, not caring if I waited half my time alone before Lillie would arrive. I would rather wait in the comfort of knowing that she could emerge from the dark forest at any moment than suffer in anticipation in my mountaintop home.

The grass was tall, but the flowers had all gone to seed, and I began picking at the seeds, throwing them around. I put some in my mouth, only to spit them as far as I could, and began targeting the rocks with the grains. I began making a challenge for myself, extending my shots to further placed rocks, and ended up spitting as far as a large boulder located near the edge of the cliff, which helped ease the anxiety—for a short time, at least.

When I couldn't stand the bad taste of the seeds any longer, I shot over to the boulder and pushed it. It was massive and too heavy for me to carry, but I pushed regardless. My wings flapped, giving me extra strength, and I could feel the tension in my legs as I braced myself securely, and the boulder began to budge. I angled myself better and gave a stronger push, this time moving it significantly. I could feel my nerves tingle with excitement. Energy rushed through my veins, and my head began to feel hot. I grunted, then shouted as I pushed harder.

The circular boulder began to roll, and I could feel it catching speed. I pushed, and pushed, and pushed, blinded by adrenaline and fueled by power.

The ground gave way, and I caught myself in the air, and the boulder plunged over the cliffside. I watched it roll down as far as I could see, until it disappeared into the forest far below. I heard the crashing of trees and snapping branches, the flight of unsuspecting birds, and the fading of rustling sounds as I imagined the boulder rolling through the forest below.

I slowly landed myself on the edge of the cliff, heavily breathing and sweat dripping along my skin. I felt a tantalizing sense of power as I lifted my hands and noticed the bulging veins running along the back of my hand as my fingers flexed.

"That was intense," I heard Lillie's voice say. I whipped around, angling my wings, causing a rush of air to wave through the tall grass. Lillie was standing nearby with a smirk on her face, and she raised her brows in repetition.

"I uh—" I uttered, still heavily breathing.

71

"What did that rock ever do to you?" she teased as she tucked a long, white strand of hair behind her pointed ear.

"I definitely did not like what it said about you," I bantered back and wiped my sweaty forehead with my sleeve.

"Oh? So, you're defending my honor?"

"Yes, exactly."

"Then the boulder deserved such a fate, served by none other than my honorable winged hero."

"And I would do it again if it ever returned to slander your name." I bowed dramatically, causing Lillie to giggle and she bowed as well. She then turned around, whipping her loose, white hair, and she walked to the middle of the meadow. She had dropped her supplies in our usual spot but now returned to set up the blanket. Again, I wiped the sweat from my forehead and felt my rushing heart begin to settle. The cold air was pleasant on my face, but my exertion still profoundly affected my perspiration. It felt good. I felt powerful and quite happy that Lillie saw my act of strength. My cheeks felt warm, but not from my exertion but rather from a feeling of delight.

I'm so glad she saw how strong I am. It will make it easier to convince her that I'm strong enough to protect her when I ask her to leave her home to be with me.

Because, yes, that was all I needed to be for her—or so my little innocent heart believed.

CHAPTER NINE

WHEN BREAD IS TASTIER WITH JAM

Like the dying fire used for cooking, red and orange colors of autumn were slowly disappearing along the valley as the season approached its end. White snow peaks spread across the mountain range, disappearing into the cloudy skies. The forest of cedars deepened its green, but the flowers of the meadow were gone. The bees had left, the sun would set earlier, and the crispness of the air had sharpened, forcing me to begin wearing my cloak and stuff animal fur into my boots.

"Winter is nearly here," Lillie said. The wind was blowing harshly, causing both of us to move closer to the fire we had created. After many failed attempts and eventual successes, I was able to feel accomplished with my fire starting skills, with the help of Lillie's material gathering and watchful eye. We gathered stones to create a designated circular fire-pit, a place where we officially knew that we would come together. I continued to bring fish, and Lillie brought minerals and other spices to enhance the flavors, astounding me each time. We arranged the sticks used for skewering the fish next to the rocks after each use. On this particular cold autumn afternoon, Lillie had a surprise for me.

"It's bread dough," she said after revealing a wooden bowl filled with a creamy, round substance. A waft of yeasty aroma filled my nostrils as I peered over it, and I moved my finger upon the surface, feeling the soft but cold dough.

"What are we supposed to do with that?" I asked while glancing up and removing my hand.

"We roast it over the fire, silly," she replied and set the bowl down on one of the stones. "Watch this." She grabbed one of the skewers and let it slightly heat over the fire, causing the grease from the previously cooked fish to sizzle. Then she waved it, cooling it from the heat, and handed me the thick stick. Lillie began rolling out the dough into snake-like shapes upon a smooth rock she had found in the forest. She rolled four snakes, then wrapped one in a spiral around the end of the long stick.

"Try it," she said, and I grabbed the dough. It was soft, squishy, and slightly warmer after being worked through by Lillie's hands. As I twirled it around the skewer, it began to stretch.

"Quickly, before it loosens up too much," Lillie encouraged, and I wrapped faster, which caused the dough to stretch even more. I looked at Lillie's. It was a perfect spiral, the dough even throughout. Mine was uneven, stretched out, and widely spaced. I frowned with disappointment in myself, but Lillie patted my arm with a gentle hand.

"Looks great," she said with a grin, then proceeded to roast the bread-dough over the fire.

"It looks nothing like yours," I grumbled while grimacing as I looked at the ugly bread dough on my stick.

"What did you expect on your first try?"

"I didn't think it would be so complicated."

"It's not. It's just your first time handling dough—I assume." I watched Lillie slowly rotate her dough over the open flames. The spiraling dough began turning brown as it roasted. "Come on, cook your bread."

I stepped closer to the fire, held the stick over the flames, and copied Lillie's careful rotation. My hands grew warm from standing close to the fire, and my cheeks felt flushed, but the cold wind against the back of my wings caused me to slightly shiver.

"You don't want to cook it too fast; otherwise, the dough will be gooey in the middle and hard on the surface," Lillie said while bringing the dough close for both of us to examine. "It needs a slow rotation in order to evenly cook."

I nodded, feeling grateful how much Lillie was willing to teach me, even if it were simple tasks she probably had learned long ago. She stood close to me, and I stole glances at her efforts—occasionally looking at her face, specifically her lips, wondering if feeling drawn to her was also part of the natural instincts of emotions and attraction.

As our bread slowly roasted, I listened to the sound of the crackling wood and enjoyed the pleasant aroma of bread and smoke. I was thoroughly enjoying the process of learning this new concept of eating and sharing meals, and cooking with Lillie became a new favorite pastime. She was kind, patient, and a helpful teacher. It became something I desired—a new passion that I felt burning in my heart. It was an experience worth waiting for each month. She always brought something interesting to try, and I began to feel inspired to bring other foods to experiment with.

Maybe mushrooms would taste good cooked. If Lillie and I lived here in the meadow together, what else could we make?

"Looks good!" Lillie exclaimed as she pointed to the bread at the end of my stick, and I removed it quickly from the skewer, nearly burning my fingers. My second attempt to spiral the dough came easier, although less beautiful than Lillie's, which, again, she only encouraged that my efforts would improve the more I practiced.

When all the bread had finished roasting, Lillie lifted two jars from her wicker basket and placed them in the middle of the blanket while I moved the cooked bread onto a napkin. While sitting, I watched as she opened the wooden lids of the jars, revealing a red color of a berry mixture and smooth honey. She then pulled apart the spiral bread, using smaller pieces to scoop out the berry mixture.

"Try it," she said and placed the bread into her mouth, huffing loudly as the bread was still rather warm. I followed her every step, and I savored every bite. It was sweet, warm, and comforting. My stomach, nearly full from consuming fish from earlier, felt warm and delighted to eat something so tantalizingly sweet. Not even the sun ripened berries from the riverbank tasted as amazing as whatever Lillie had brought.

"Did you make this berry mixture?" I asked while licking my fingers after my last bite of bread.

"My mother and I did. It's called marmalade," she answered while scraping out the last bits of it from the jar.

"Did you gather the berries from the forest?"

"I did. There are so many berry plants in the summer months. I usually gather them every year, and then I make marmalade with my mother. I really love the gathering part. I also like eating it. Not so much the making process, though." Lillie looked down and began fidgeting with her fingers, and I looked at her hands. As usual, they looked dull, rough, and had many scars.

"What's wrong with the making process?" I asked.

"Oh..." Lillie's voice lowered, and I waited patiently for her to finish. She continued to play with her fingers, scratching at different stains from the berries, and then eventually spoke again. "It's just my mother. She can be quite difficult to work with sometimes."

"How so?"

"Oh, she's just very critical. Seems like nothing I do is right by her." Lillie grew silent again. This time, she looked away, towards the cliffside. Her eyes were distant, and her mind was even further away. I could see that she was deeply agonized, although I did not entirely understand the complexities of her relationship with her mother.

My own caretakers—my parents—were stern with their teachings during my younger years. However, my relationship with them was clear and unproblematic, and I never doubted their ways. I knew that they abided by our traditions and ways of raising younglings. When I made mistakes, they allowed me to learn, but also how to progress and avoid making blundering choices. My parents taught me the rigid ways of survival of the Teragane people because they wanted me to thrive beyond their instructions. When my parents left in my tenth year, it was proof that they had fulfilled their obligation, providing me with everything I needed to live on my own. I never once doubted their methods, nor did I question their absence in my life.

It was obviously different from Lillie's, perhaps others from the forests, but I was confident that there was a greater purpose for the Teraganes to practice our particular traditions. However, what I couldn't understand was what Lillie's parents were attempting to accomplish by being so critical and rigid in their methods of teaching and raising her, specifically their lack of support in the things that she did.

She is successful in anything she does—why wouldn't her mother be able to see that?

The wind blew harshly, pushing my hair around in a tangled mess against my eyes, and I shifted closer to Lillie, feeling the need to comfort her. She still looked far off, lost in her own thoughts and unsaid pain. I enjoyed her marmalade, but I did not like the fact that it brought up a painful subject.

As I sat next to her, I looked down at her hands folded against her green skirt. My eyes trailed upwards, and I moved my hand and began softly rubbing her arm with the back of my fingers, feeling the thin material of the tan-colored blouse. I pushed my hand gently against her arm and felt the warmth of her skin, but her distant gaze seemed to preoccupy her to notice my affection.

"I think you always do right," I said, breaking the uncomfortable silence. "I wish your mother could see you the way I do."

"Yeah, and how is that?" she asked with a scoff. "A silly girl running through the woods to escape life's obligations?"

"A girl capable of accomplishing anything in spite of the burdens of her reality." Lillie's eyes widened, and she slowly turned her head, causing her white hair to fall over her shoulder, and the wind gently swayed the loose strands, causing the beads in small braids to clink together. Her cool hues had vanished, but, at times, I could see hints of the undertones in the light of the dancing fire. I gazed into her sorrowful eyes, but then glanced down at her berry-stained hands, feeling drawn to feel their warmth once again. So, I slid my hand into hers, intertwining our fingers, allowing the tantalizing feeling to overtake my body once more.

"I wish that I could see myself that way," Lillie whispered as she looked away, but her fingers tightened between mine. "Thanks, anyway."

"You are so much more than just the burdens you carry."

"Yeah? Good to know." As my heart raced within my chest and my fingers tingled in our embrace, I felt the urge to tell Lillie that she never had to return to her life in the forest and that she could be free from her parents' rigid obligations burdening her. I desperately wanted to pick her up with my arms and tell her that I would fly her away to my home, where she could live happily with me, never again bothered by a hard life. I wanted more than anything to inform her how much I cared about her and wanted to make her happy and that I would never force her to do anything that she didn't want to do.

But.

My instincts said otherwise. My *stupid* instincts told my beating heart to settle down. My ever so-prudent instincts told me that a forest-dweller could never survive in the mountains with me, let alone be happy in the cold, dark cave where the Sage of the Teragane could discover her and easily throw her out, perhaps threatening our friendship forever. What could I even offer her up there in the mountain? I had only enough food for me and had been living with only the bare essentials for my survival. Lillie could never be happy up in the mountains—no, she needed more, and I was not ready to give her what she deserved. I needed more time and more strength to be the man who could deliver on his promises.

"Winter is nearly here," Lillie said, and we moved closer to the fire, keeping our hands intertwined and ever so warm.

<hr />

On our last day together before winter officially swept the province with snow and ice, Lillie gifted me three jars of berry marmalade, honey, and fresh bread.

"I know it's not much, but perhaps you can enjoy it for a few weeks," she said while twisting the ends of her hair with her slim fingers.

"This is amazing," I said while examining the items she placed on the blanket. "Thank you for the kind thought. I brought you fish, too." I realized that it was our first time exchanging food to take back to our individual homes. Initially, I did not actually plan to give her anything. I brought the fish, as usual, to cook together during our time in the meadow. However, in that moment of her generosity and thoughtful consideration, I also wanted to participate in sharing something with her, allowing my emotional instincts to guide my heart.

"Oh, my parents will be shocked that I brought fish home," she said as I placed the items next to her basket.

"Why?" I asked and tilted my head.

"Well, we don't really have access to fish. Actually, most people in my neighborhood don't even know how to gather fish, and the allotment never has any. I don't think anyone is fast enough to catch the river fish or willing to take the long journey to the lake. Maybe some hunters—fishmongers."

"Then it will be something you can impress your parents with." I grinned and puffed up my chest.

"My parents are very difficult to impress." Lillie scoffed while rolling her eyes, causing my smile to fade and I slightly slouched. "If I bring home fish, they will only demand for me to continue. Can't really do that over winter, you know?"

"Then, don't share it with them. Keep it only for yourself, or share with your friends." My pounding heart felt achy, for I did not want to trouble Lillie or cause her more problems at home. I couldn't understand how something as simple as bringing certain foods home could be so problematic. As her eyes nervously darted while she fidgeted with her hands, I bit my lower lip, attempting to find a better solution.

"Don't worry, I'll think of something."

"Please, I don't want to cause you more problems."

"Oh, Sable, you don't cause me any problems."

"Okay, but please, if the fish will be problematic with your family, then let us just share it here, right now."

"It's fine, really. Don't worry about it." Lillie began shaking her head, then gestured ambiguously with her hands. "I'll think of something."

"Lillie, please." She stood up and began nervously brushing off her green skirt while sniffling as if she were about to cry, and I rose to my feet as well and grabbed one of her hands. Her eyes lifted as she finally looked at me. Her countenance was conflicted and on the brink of tears. I pulled her close to me, wrapping my arms around her shoulders, and I felt her arms around my waist. Her body began to tremble, and her breathing was abrupt as she whimpered. I held her as she expressed her sorrow, and I leaned my head closer to hers.

I did not know what it was like to have parents who were consistently critical or expecting consistent chores to be fulfilled, but I did begin to understand my own deeper pain. Lillie had her parents, friends, and neighbors in the village—I had no one but her and the cold existence of the other Teraganes of my colony. I knew the pain of isolation. I knew at that moment that this was my last chance, for a while, to be close to someone who cared about me. The harsh, freezing winter would leave me lonely, without Lillie, without tender love and kindness. I may not have had hundreds of chores or work to do, but perhaps the lack of those things is what made my life so miserable. Yet, she was also struggling—perhaps the life we could create together would be something in between—a life of balance.

Tears welled in my eyes as Lillie's sorrow collided with my own distressing emotions. Yet, holding her and feeling her warmth, regardless of the anxiety rising within my body, a sense of comfort began to settle in my heart. Bittersweet—yes, a bittersweet sensation overwhelmed me as we both endured our sorrow together.

"We'll be fine," Lillie eventually said and gently pushed me away. She wiped her dewy face with the end of her worn out cloak, and sniffled as she rubbed her nose. Her face was flushed, and her cheeks and nose were a deep crimson color. Her faded skin looked glossy, and her pointed ears alert, and her glistening green eyes darted as she avoided eye contact.

"Will we?" I asked while wiping tears that seemingly escaped my eyes.

"Oh, Sable," she said. "It'll be okay. I'll be alright."

"If you say so."

"But—" She looked down and twisted her shoe against the blanket. "Thanks for holding me." I came closer to her, placed my hand under her chin, and slowly lifted her head, and our eyes met.

"Always." She stared into my eyes for only a moment, then moved away from me, tucking her hair behind her ears as her face continued to beam its rosy complexion. She inhaled deeply, suggested that we create a fire and enjoy our last day before winter. I happily agreed, and only hoped to ignore the aching pain welling within my heart.

I helped build the fire, cook two of the four fish I had given Lillie, and we spoke about some spring mushrooms we could go looking for in the forest together. She told me what kinds of trees the fungi grow on or near, depending on the type, and I anticipated the idea of seeking out the mushrooms during the first signs of spring to bring on our next meeting.

"If I bring a pan, maybe we can cook some vegetables," Lillie said while munching on the bread she had brought, apparently from her friend. "Ever eaten a potato?"

"What's a potato?" I asked while crunching on the fish bones. Lillie laughed, then began describing a tuber that grows underground, stating that it's hard as an apple, but soft when cooked.

"We call it an earth apple—I think you'd like eating potatoes."

"I like eating anything—with you."

Lillie's cheeks flushed as she looked away, and I inched closer to her, allowing our sides to touch. I eyed her hands as she picked at certain tears of her faded green cloak, grumbling about needing a new one, reminding me of the complexities in which survival meant for both of us.

I moved my hand behind her back, resting my weight on my arm, and moved my nose slightly close to her head. I breathed in the lovely scents of smoke, earth, and aromatic herbs I could only assume that she used at home. Then, ever so slowly, I hovered my other hand over hers. But suddenly she leaned away, and began organizing the items she had brought me, and placed each one into my satchel.

We continued to speak about simple terms, expectations of another winter, and, once again, I held back my anticipating plans of creating a way for us to live outside of our miserable lives. As the sun slowly moved behind the mountain, we started preparing for our fateful goodbyes. Lillie stayed until dusk, which, normally, she left long before the sun had completely set, but on that day, she stayed for as long as possible, savoring our last day together before winter isolation. We cleared the fireplace, folded the blanket, packed our bags, and Lillie started walking towards the forest.

"Sable," she said after turning quickly back to me.

"Yes?" I replied. The wind was blowing hard, sending a shiver throughout my body and a sharp pain into my ears. My hair bounced across my face, and my wings began to ache. While Lillie's long hair twisted and twirled, her sorrowful green eyes glistened in the fading sunlight.

"I'll see you in spring?"

"When the air is warmer, the snow is melting, and the first snowdrops begin to bloom. I'll be here."

"You'll be alright, alone in the mountains?" She twisted her neck to view the mountain behind the cedar forest, but the cloudy sky made it impossible to even view the mountain range.

"Yes, I will be alright."

I wanted to stay with her. I wanted so much to beg her to come with me to the mountain. But I didn't—at least, not this time.

"Okay." Her voice was low and sorrowful, and she kept her eyes slowly drifting around the scenery, perhaps taking it all in before leaving for her dark world as well.

I hate winter. This is unbearable. Why must it be so dark and cold?

"And you?" I asked. "Will you be alright?"

"Of course. I'll be fine," she said with a forced smile, and her eyes lifted. "I always am. Since, you know, *I'm a girl capable of accomplishing anything in spite of the burdens of her reality.*" A grin crossed my face, but the cold wind rushing through the open area caused my whole body to rapidly shake.

"That you are." We stood in silence. Neither of us wanted to take the first step—neither wanted to leave.

"See you in spring," I finally said, holding back the choking feeling in my throat, for I really didn't want to cry again, not while my last moments with Lillie still lingered with the fading sun.

"When the first snowdrops bloom," she replied, and I nodded while my hands at my side shook, not from the cold air, but heightened emotions of saying goodbye.

"Yes, when the first snowdrops bloom." Then, without hesitation, Lillie walked up to me and wrapped her arms around my waist, this time, happily. I hugged her, sliding my arms around her back where her basket was secured, feeling the warmth of her body against my front. Her head came directly onto my chest, and I rested my head close to hers. I breathed in heavily, smelling her hair again, which permeated heavily with smoke and earth, and the strong herbs. Not like the Sage—no, these herbs smell floral—perhaps it was a type of flower grown within the forest.

I wanted to keep Lillie in my arms forever, allowing the mysterious floral scents to fill my nostrils, but the darkness was coming, and the cold wind was causing my bones and wings to shake. The pain in my ear increased as the winds shifted. I wanted to beg her to come with me, but my instincts told me otherwise. I wanted so much to ignore the impending future of being alone.

"Goodbye," Lillie whispered, and, once again, pushed herself away from me. She then turned and ran away, disappearing into the dark forest, leaving me once again alone, but this time, my heart ached with the unbearable sensation I was dreading most of the year. My heart ached more than I had ever experienced before as I stood in the cold, observing the dark, looming forest. I imagined it like a monster, a type of evil creature that engulfed the love of my life every time, menacingly laughing at me, the helpless fool.

Just wait...I will save Lillie. I will save her from this monster that mocks me and holds her hostage. I will save you, Lillie! Then, there will be no need to carry those burdens—we can run away from it all and not be bothered by the lurking woes. We will cook and eat together, never separate, and live happily—forever.

Just wait a little longer...

Chapter Ten

When a voice of concern vacates the premise

Winter came. That cold, freezing winter I dreaded so much. No power of my own could stop it. It came with all its unpleasant dreariness.

I had created an intricate branch system in my home to help distract me from my loneliness and continue my strength training. I brought heavy rocks to lift. I overstocked my cache, filling the small ground storage room to the brim with all the food I had gathered and what was given to me by Lillie. I tried cooking over the eternal fire, but it tasted horrible. Perhaps the enchanted fire was only meant to warm my home and not my stomach. I settled with my salt-preserved fish after that unpleasant experience.

I looked at the small jars of marmalade and honey with desire, savoring the memorable flavors in my mind, but withheld myself from enjoying any until the true depths of loneliness set in. I ate the bread immediately, as Lillie suggested, stating that it is best to be eaten within a few days. It filled my stomach, but the yeasty flavors brought some sadness. Usually, I was eating bread while sitting next to Lillie, listening to her stories, feeling the heat of the sun on my skin, and watching the bees buzz around the meadow. I closed my eyes, imagining myself in this setting. I could not feel the warmth of the sun, not while I sat on the stone floor. So, I stood up and sat on my bed while I munched on the flaky bread.

Still doesn't feel the same...

My bed was a stone platform covered in animal pelts. I had been given them by my parents when I was a youngling, at least, the pelts were already there from my recollection. It was enough to bring some cushion to the carved stone, enough to wrap myself for extra warmth if my wings were not sufficient.

At least, while eating bread, I could feel some sort of comfort, but nothing in comparison to the blanket I would lounge on next to Lillie in the meadow. It was nothing compared to the heat of the campfire we would make together or the delicious sensations of eating cooked fish that slowly roasted over the flames. As a Teragane, I could live in cold environments, to some extent. At least, that was how we lived, and I knew nothing else.

However, this coldness was different from what I was used to bearing through. The cold feeling of loneliness, the feeling of missing out on good times spent somewhere else, with someone who brought me warmth, with someone who brought me joy.

The beginning of the winter season of settling into my mountain home was torture. In the past, I had rarely thought of my future or my time of rest during the freezing months. In contrast, this winter was different, and I thought often about how I wished it would end.

I busied myself with my strength training and vigorously counted my food supplies to account for the proper sustenance for my gradual hunger needs. Normally, during the isolated time on the summit, I would sleep a lot or sit in deep, mindless thoughts of nothingness. Nothing particular, just lost in my own mind, which was quite stagnant most of my life. I could easily stare into the blue light of the eternal fire for who knows how long. During that winter, I had other ideas to think about, and I tried settling in front of the eternal fire, watching it bounce within the confines of the iron cauldron, and I examined the different shades of blue and white.

It reminds me of how enchanting Lillie's skin was just a year ago. Not necessarily blue, but I could definitely see some hues of cooler colors underneath the gray. Oh, especially when the sunlight kissed her skin. And now her hair is so white! I wonder what is making her change so much. Maybe that is normal for her kind? Hmm, I wonder why? I wish I could ask her right now!

I stood up and began pacing my home as I fought the restlessness and torturous thoughts. Looking at the blue fire only brought more questions and unpleasant feelings of anxiety. My mind raced as I wished to be near Lillie once again. I wanted to talk to her; I wanted to ask her questions.

I can't keep going like this. I will run a groove in the ground!

I jumped around my cave, flying towards the branches I had installed into the stone walls. I had found some bones in the woods that I used to create carved notches in the walls that could secure the large branch ends, wedging them between the narrow edges of the staggering walls and ceiling. It was hard work, but my efforts were rewarded. My cave-like home was small on the surface, but the ceiling was tall and narrow. I could easily fly up to the branches, hang from my legs, and slowly lift my body upwards in a curling method, similar to how I performed the action with tree branches in the valley. Sometimes I would even hold the heavy stones to add more weight, challenging the limitations of my body. The only way I could get out of my own head was to exercise, to strength train, and then think about Lillie and the life I would provide for her when I was ready.

I theorized my abilities to continue, my experience with pushing the giant boulder over the cliffside, and how I thought I would be strong enough by the next time I saw Lillie. I committed to utilizing that winter as my final form to become strong enough. By spring, by the time those snowdrops began blooming and the snow was melting, I would be flying Lillie up into the treetops.

Then, she will be so happy!

As I crouched in the exit tunnel leading out of my home to watch the grey sky grow dark, I imagined Lillie's smile and the warmth I would instantly feel. I fantasized about how I would heroically tell her that she never had to return to her hard life. I imagined her embracing me, crying with happiness, and how I would easily lift her from the ground and soar throughout the sky with her in my arms. I envisioned this dream until I fell asleep most nights, then I would dream about the beautiful scenario. When I woke, I would continue the fantasy—the fantasy of living a life with Lillie.

As I ate my cold food, I imagined myself bringing fish to Lillie, us cooking it over the fire in our hand built fireplace, Lillie tossing random spices and salts onto the fish, adding honey and berries she had gathered from the forest. I anticipated finding spring mushrooms, and even explored the thought of flying Lillie to the river to watch the bears snatch their first meals after a long hibernation. The grown cubs would soon separate from their mother, and this could be the last spring to see them congregate within the territory.

I imagined all these things and how our time together in the meadow would become a daily routine where we never left and happily lived. I even dreamed about what kind of home we could have—maybe we carved a shelter within a cedar tree—perhaps there was a cave nearby. I immersed myself in the fantasy of never saying goodbye to Lillie and imagined her skin returning to its original stormy hues, her hair turning brown again, and that lovely green sparkle returning to her eyes.

Oh, Lillie, wait until you know the future we will have together.

"Greetings, Sable," Cami said to me as I arrived at his home. Before winter started, Cami had finally agreed to visit, inviting me to his home first. For a moment, I thought about Kora and Deruk. However, after the bear-watching and river incident, they would act skittish around me. Sometimes I saw them flying down the mountain, only to watch them abruptly change their flight path in another direction, obviously avoiding me. I tried to disregard this on a personal level, fully understanding that they had every right to live their traditional, independent lives. Perhaps they did not appreciate me teasing them about their obvious affection. How could I know? I never did find out.

Feeling tortured from my endless thoughts, I noticed the winter storm had died down, allowing me to venture out to visit my friend. Cami's home was similar to mine in some ways: an eternal fire for warmth, a stone bed with animal pelts, and a small storage area for food. In contrast, he had a shelf full of ancient books written in a Teragane language, meant only for the Sage. He had a few other tools for tattoos, black powder for ink, and other ritual aspects. I noticed bones and other types of ornaments that I did not recognize. His home had a distinct smell of burning herbs, which he kept on a small wooden table. The mysteries behind the Sage were kept a secret, and I knew that it would be disrespectful to ask, but I was often too curious to not at least peer around his interesting items on the shelf.

"It feels good to stretch my wings," I said upon my arrival. "The weather finally changed for the better." Cami was bent over an ancient book, sitting at his small wooden table, his wings folded stiffly behind. As usual, he examined me, raising his eyebrows once again while noticing the changes in my body, and his judging expression turned into an obvious frown.

"Feels good to stretch my muscles, too," I said as I moved my arms from the layers of my cloak, flexing my biceps.

"Your strength training. It seems..." Cami's voice trailed off as he watched me remove my cloak. His eyes narrowed while I threw the damp cloak onto the ground near the fireplace.

"Seems what?" I asked, then shook my hair, casting more drops of melted snow onto the ground. Cami looked down at the small droplets, then his eyes wandered around my body. I could only assume that he was attempting to find the right words, perhaps a correct lecture—perhaps an insult. I hoped he would only admire my physique, but I anticipated his obvious disapproval.

"It seems like you are gaining weight," he said with a grimace, then returned his attention to his studies.

"Yes, I have been eating more, but my training is making me stronger. A lot of the extra weight is muscular, I assure you."

"But, why? For what purpose do you need extra muscles—extra weight? As an avian—as a Teragane—extra weight can put stress on your flight abilities. It can be dangerous for—" Cami paused and started rubbing his forehead as I stepped closer to the table he sat at. "You can be vulnerable in your condition."

"But how?" I asked and leaned against the table. "I am stronger. I can take on the extra weight and still be at my peak capacity. My wings grow strong every day. I am more powerful than ever!"

"The Sage will not approve. They will recognize your physical challenges as a threat to your survival."

"I don't care. It's not a challenge to my survival. I am surviving just fine. Actually, I'm thriving!"

"Thriving? What does that even mean to you?" Cami looked up at me with narrowed brows, and he closed the large book with a loud thud. He began to nervously tap his slim fingers on the leather back while his eyes focused on exemplifying his disapproval.

"I am doing alright," I replied with a firm voice but a gentle smile. "I like being strong. I like what I'm doing. It gives me happiness and allows me to do something when I'm bored. It gives me motivation. I promise you that my extra weight is not putting me in danger or at risk. Even the mighty Harpy Eagles or Bearded Vultures are more muscular than little songbirds."

"Sable, you are not a bird."

"Nor am I a bear, but that does not mean I cannot learn from them. You have your teachers, I have mine. I appreciate your concern, but you really don't need to express such apprehension towards me."

Cami stared at me as he rested his narrow chin in the palm of his hand, and I stared back while I leaned against the table. Only the sound of the crackling eternal fire echoed in the room as we continued the intensity of our fixation. The blue light danced on the stone walls and on Cami's light brown face. His skin seemed lighter than usual, as if he was barely in the sun during the warm seasons. In fact, I wondered how often he even left the mountain, especially with how many books and papers he had stacked on the shelves. His lecturing only made sense considering his devotion to the Sage.

Questioning our way—the way of the Teragane—was not customary in our culture, let alone openly discussed. Although there were no absolute rules against becoming stronger or gaining weight, the very mere fact that I was pursuing something outside of my basic survival instincts is what Cami felt concerned about, at least, I assumed. I was challenging the status quo of our natural way of life as a Teragane. What our parents taught and what a Sage claimed as tradition, is what decided our fates.

Our lives were independent, yet we silently lived by traditions passed on to us. We were encouraged to stay within our colony and observe our friendships from a distance, but only to remind us of our obligations as Teraganes. We were taught how to survive, take only what is necessary, and abide by the natural ways of this life. There were never any open discussions. There were never ideas freely expressed. However, I knew I no longer wanted to be normal. I wanted more in life. I wanted the life I was currently building and aiming for. A life of strength and warmth. A life with Lillie.

"Well, I guess happiness can be part of life, too," Cami finally said, then exhaled heavily. "I do not understand how this" —he gestured towards me— "can make you happy. But your cheerful demeanor is evident of your progress and I'm glad you can *finally* appease your boredom."

"Yes," I replied while grinning widely. "Sometimes happiness cannot be fully understood, but, over time, its comprehension reveals itself. May you also discover the true warmth of happiness." Cami examined me thoroughly, once again. This time, I finally sensed a glimpse of acceptance. The light of the blue flame revealed a change of demeanor as his brown eyes softened, and his lips curled into a smirk.

"Well, whatever happiness you are pursuing," he said, "it looks good. But don't say that I didn't warn you about the disapproval from the Sage during the upcoming visit. May you be prepared for their inevitable criticism."

"Don't worry so much," I teased, and straightened up from my leaning position. "I can handle the scrutiny of a Sage. I have been practicing with you all these years." He narrowed his eyes, and his grin vanished as he scowled. I couldn't help but chuckle, feeling presumptuous with my sarcasm, heedless of my friend's appreciation.

Cami eventually took an interest in my strength building routine, particularly after he openly expressed his concern. I was glad that he accompanied me when he felt brave enough to venture outside of his winter-isolation. I was happy to no longer be alone and have the company of a friend. We did not talk of the others, acknowledging the fact that spending time together during the winter was already impermissible. The previous year of my random ankle tattoo—and, perhaps, my presumptuous attitude—already helped Cami accept that I was obviously different from the others.

However, he was chosen as a Sage-in-training, indicating that his life would also be different and set apart from the rest of the colony. If all the Teragane people were isolated, the Sage were completely detached. They held onto nothing except their traditions. The books of the Sage were also passed down through the generations, reserved only for them, for they were the only ones able to read or write. As Teraganes, we only knew one rule: abide by the Sage's Word.

Why was Cami chosen? I couldn't say at the time. He did not even know, suggesting that he would only learn after his final conversion. So much of the secrecy was preserved by whatever concepts the early tribes indicated. Regardless, that winter spent with Cami visiting each other was pleasant, even if it was our last moments together on the mountain summit. For, we would never meet again on Hira.

We stayed in silence most of the time, meditating, thinking, or just quietly eating. Sometimes I would strength train while Cami would read a book or write lines on paper. He did not mind anymore whenever I removed my tunic while I exerted my stifled energy, although he often glanced whenever doing so, swiftly adjusting his crimson scarf whenever I caught him staring.

I knew that it was only a matter of time before his final conversion into the world of the Sage. I did not know what to expect, but, at the moment, I did not care to think about anything other than my own endeavors. Cami kept me company and was pleasant to be around, except for his occasional comments about my untamed hair. Regardless, he admired my abilities. I did not mind his quick glances or disdain for my grooming habits—or lack thereof. I admired his dedication to his studies, often overlooking his shoulder, attempting to read, although failing when only observing the squiggly lines that made no sense to me. This often made Cami laugh. For once, I felt seen and accepted by my own kind, even if he were far from one to be accepting if he only knew everything about me.

One afternoon, I decided to open a marmalade jar, which surprised Cami that I could even own such a delicacy. Intrigued to share something from my secret life with my one friend on the mountain, I revealed my precious jar of berry mixture in hopes to enlighten him just slightly about who I really was outside of the way of the Teragane.

"What have you done?" he exclaimed when I brought over the jar.

"Try it, don't ask," I said while pushing it near him. I dipped a single finger inside, then slurped it up. He followed, expressing utter confusion, but the emotion of great excitement covered his face as the sugars of the berries made their grand excursion onto his taste buds.

"Sable," he gasped while his brown eyes widened. "How? What?"

"From a friend," I said cheekily. We said nothing else about the matter, but perhaps that single jar of marmalade kept Cami's interest, which led to him asking for a small taste whenever he visited. Our times together became more frequent, and his taste buds continued to desire the sweet taste of marmalade. I was happy to share the sweetness of Lillie with someone else, even if Cami did not know it was directly from her.

Maybe, just maybe, Cami can meet Lillie this spring.

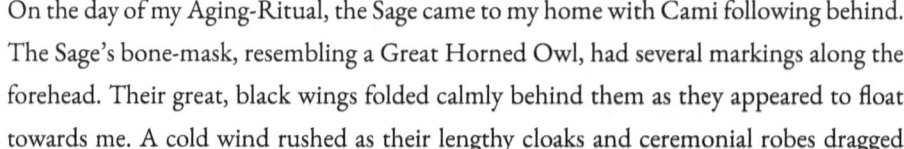

On the day of my Aging-Ritual, the Sage came to my home with Cami following behind. The Sage's bone-mask, resembling a Great Horned Owl, had several markings along the forehead. Their great, black wings folded calmly behind them as they appeared to float towards me. A cold wind rushed as their lengthy cloaks and ceremonial robes dragged across the floor. They wore many bone-ornamental necklaces, full-length gloves, and leather belts with various tools connected, and they smelled strongly of burning herbs.

"Sable von Hira," they said with a deep voice. "You have passed over the great mountains for the 17th year. It is time for your marking." I bowed, removed my sleeves, and sat on my knees in the middle of the floor, folding my wings. The chilly floor shot a shiver up my spine, but I refused to show any emotion or reaction, like expected. I was accustomed to pain, pushing my body to its limits, and the coldness of the mountain. I was in my 17th year, and I knew that I was closer to becoming "fully grown." There was no exception to acting in compliance with the Sage.

I could feel the coldness of the Sage pass by as their cryptic figure settled into marking my left arm. Cami silently watched from behind, observing with dedication while he wore his ceremonial robes and carried the bowl of ink and a bundle of smoking herbs he once explained was called a smudge. From the corner of my eye, I saw the Sage look around my home, observing the branches I had installed towards the ceiling. I shot a glance at Cami, who also followed the Sage's observation.

Sweat began to pile on my forehead, and I gripped my trousers at the thigh. My eyes wandered down to my arms and torso, and I noticed the bulging veins on my arms as my hands grasped at my clothes, and I quickly relaxed my hands in an attempt to hide my sudden nervousness. My body had changed drastically from the previous winter, and I was bigger and more muscular, obviously showcasing my dedication to my strength building. I sensed Cami's nervousness too. Suddenly, all my apathy towards potential criticism rose within my chest. Was it because of my physical changes? Or did I fear the Sage questioning my *reasons* for my strength training?

I thought of a simple response, one that did not evoke anything leading to the truth about my desire to be with Lillie. Perhaps my strength training was only for the necessary reasons of defending myself to prevent a bear attack since my enclave had such beasts residing in the forests.

Yes. I am just attempting to grow stronger to ward off bears—that is all.

"You must soon begin your understanding of the upcoming mating-ritual," the Sage suddenly said.

"What?" I exclaimed louder than I anticipated and sweat dripped down the side of my head. While my heart pounded, I gripped my trousers once again, and the Sage deeply sighed.

"Yes, 17th-year Teraganes seem surprised to start learning of their required obligations as a full-grown," they explained while still tapping the needle upon my left arm. "Even though the ritual does not happen until after you've reached the age of maturity, you must begin your learning of its nature. In spring, a Sage will visit. They will educate you about the mating-ritual, where you will be instructed about procreation with a designated mate."

"Okay," I answered with a steady voice, but I was fearful that the Sage could hear my own heartbeat as it drummed within my chest.

"Well done." With a final tap of the thinly carved bone piercing my arm, the Sage finished the tattoo. The scent of burning herbs and fresh ink filled the air, but the atmosphere was stifling as I continued to sweat. The Sage rose to their full stature while grunting, then moved past me, sending a whirl of their scents around as their cloaks drifted.

"Sable von Hira," I heard them say from behind me. "Until next winter. Always return to the mountain. Anticipate a colony-trainer in spring. In the meantime, remain vigilant in your previous training as you prepare for your next phase in life."

I heard them leave my cave with Cami following like a shadow. I sat motionless, feeling cold but numb from the overwhelming thoughts whirling in my head. I anticipated their strict criticism—perhaps even a long lecture about my muscular body being a threat to my survival, as Cami had warned. But this?

What? Next phase of life? Designated mate? Procreation??

I wanted to melt away. I had no intention of mating or reproducing with any of my own kind. I wanted to be with Lillie, living in the trees near the cliffside meadow. I had no space or thought for anything else. At that moment, I did not want any more tattoos nor anything else to do with my own kind. I was sad living this lonely life; I was done accepting the concepts and rules of the Sage that didn't even make sense at times. I did not want to always return to the mountain. I only wanted the life I lived in my imagination—my fantasies with Lillie.

Then, I thought of Cami. I was beginning to really enjoy his company. His openness to visit me and enjoy the marmalade enthralled me. His curiosity was awakening; perhaps he would continue to allow his mind to open up about different possibilities. He seemed accepting of me, finally. Perhaps there was still a life for me here on the mountain.

I'm still young, and the Sage said the ritual doesn't happen until later. So, there is no use worrying about it right now. Right?

The next day, I flew to Cami's home, and he greeted me with an unusually distant demeanor. I had brought the last of the marmalade and some fish to share, and he moved an animal pelt to the floor in front of the eternal-flame. I sprawled out, feeling annoyed by the ritual from before, but grateful at least to not hear any lectures from Cami about the disapproval of the Sage about my changes in life. However, as I bounced my foot, savoring the last bits of marmalade, Cami cleared his throat and stiffly adjusted his wings.

"I am leaving tomorrow," Cami said, and I twisted my neck with widened eyes.

"What?" I exclaimed, causing him to flinch, and I lowered my voice. "Leaving? Where?"

"You know I was chosen; I was chosen to become a Sage." Cami spoke in a pensive manner. He stared at the eternal fire while holding his notebook on his lap. He had been sketching a bone-mask, but, at that moment, his slim fingers sat idle.

"Yes, but not now—really, now?"

"Yes, tomorrow."

"You're so young; where will you go? And why so—"

"This is how it is done," Cami interrupted me with a cold, distant tone.

"But, why? I was just told about the mating ritual this upcoming spring! How? We are only in our 17th year. Why should we learn before we are even fully-grown? How can they choose you and take you away? Cami, please, how is this—"

"This is how it is done," he interrupted me again with his stoic voice. Cami's brown eyes stared widely at the blue fire. He seemed unnerved and did not even touch his hair, although I thought it was already perfectly placed. He swallowed as he clenched his jaw and hardly moved. His slim fingers pressed hard into the notebook that he gripped, causing the color to flush from the ends. I stared at the empty jar of marmalade sitting between us. Then, I looked at his notebook sketch of the bone-mask—it was the shape of a Barred Owl.

"At least tell me where you will go," I pleaded while grabbing his arm.

"I cannot," he replied as he placed his cold hand on my own. He gripped me tightly, still looking sternly ahead. "To be honest, I do not even know."

"Will I see you again?"

"No—at least, not as you know me."

"Why?"

"This is how it is done." Cami slowly moved his face to finally look at me, but only for a moment. He quickly turned his head away and removed his hand, and began combing through his hair, perfectly setting each wavy lock in place. "Promise me one thing?"

"What?" I asked after letting go of his stiff arm.

"Actually, two things," he said. "One: don't forget me. For I will never forget your friendship. I will never forget our childhood together on this mountain, nor the river, or the others."

"I will never forget you and all that you speak of—I promise."

93

"And secondly." He turned to look at me again, his grimacing face obviously displeased. "Please start combing your hair." Then, he turned away and began adjusting the crimson scarf around his neck. He stroked the fibers with his forefinger, and I began to wonder how he came into possession of something that looked familiar. I had never seen another Teragane wear a scarf, only Lillie.

Did he also make friends with a forest-dweller? Or was there someone else? No—probably the Sage. Cami is devoted to their practice. He would never, right?

We spent the rest of the evening in silence. I realized there was no arguing. Cami would leave, and then I would be alone again. He would go on to become a Sage, lost to my friendship, accepted into a world filled with rituals and rules. Cami would become one of them. He would wear the mask, and no one would know him by his first name ever again. He would become the cryptic Sage. He no longer would visit to eat with me, not even for a jar of Lillie's marmalade or to scold me about my lack of grooming.

Any hopes of him knowing me better suddenly vanished; any fantasy of my two friends meeting completely dissipated. Even though he went out of his way to visit me and openly enjoyed my company and food, he was still a Teragane who would follow rituals and traditions until his death. He would always abide by the Sage's rules, he would always do as they said, and he would always return to the mountains, only now as a devout Sage.

And he did. He left the next day, and I was alone once again.

Chapter Eleven
WHEN THOUGHTS RUN WILD

I never did promise to comb my hair. I couldn't find a reason for an extensive purpose to commit to such a grooming act. My parents never exemplified this behavior, and I found it absolutely unnecessary since it would only get messed up from the wind currents. I also had no desire to be constantly adjusting it, and Cami was no longer around to annoy me with his nagging reminders. But I did commit myself to always remember him and our friendship, no matter how cruel the fates were by separating us.

I spent the remainder of the winter season completely isolated. I focused solely on my training routines and motivated myself with future fantasies. For a moment, with Cami, I thought perhaps there could be more to life within the colony. He was beginning to show interest in something different from our normal way of life. Cautious—yes, but he had always been that way since he was a youngling. Perhaps that was his regarded attribute that caught the eye of the Sage. Regardless, his apprehension did not overshadow his curiosity, and, for a short time, I had a strong sense of hope that he could be open to having more pleasures in life. I realized that, in his absence, it was a false sense of hope.

Cami would become just like the others. The only thought I had left for my friend was the hope that he found the warmth of happiness in his new life, wherever that was. The mysteries behind the Sage and their rules seemed difficult to understand, but perhaps Cami would enjoy partaking in filling his days with more learning and enhancing his knowledge about our people. For, it seemed, at least, that was all he really cared about.

Cami, I hope you can stay true to yourself and find some sort of joy in your new life.

The rest of the winter season was spent physically alone, like a single stone cast into the icy waters of the mountain lake. But, mentally, I was hopeful with ideas of the future I would create. Cami's reassurance of my physical changes motivated me to continue my efforts. His recognition of my weight and muscles affirmed that my work was flourishing, which was obvious on a physical level. I felt strong; I could easily lift anything I wanted. I was still eating several times a day. Even in my isolation, I pushed myself to strength train until my muscles ached.

During the visit of the Sage, I was worried about their disapproval of my body changes and muscle gains. I half-expected to be scolded, like Cami warned, but they never said anything directly. They observed my home but did not lecture—poor Cami looked terribly nervous. Perhaps instead, the Sage saw me as a strong Teragane, fit to achieve the next steps in life.

I looked down at myself, examining my arms, my legs, and my abdomen. I liked what I saw; I felt good in my body. Feeling enthralled by my physical and muscular physique, I would fantasize about wrestling the bears, taking one by the arm, and slamming its body over itself.

Then I would be torn apart by its sharp teeth.

I laughed to myself at this humorous idea, fully knowing that the bears were literally twice my size. I allowed myself the pleasure of the fantasy of being capable of fighting and winning a wrestling match with a brown bear.

Between the rampant imaginations and physical exertion, I busied my waking hours with such distractions. I did not want to think about my loneliness nor Cami anymore. He was gone, far removed from my life—all was said and done with or without my opinion. Even if he were to visit me as a Sage, I would not be able to identify him, nor would he be able to reveal his identity. At least, that is what I assumed. Throughout the visits of the Sage, their identities were never revealed, nor did I believe the same one would visit. Or did they? How could I know? If Cami were to come to instruct me as a Sage, he would be cloaked in robes and covered with the bone mask of an owl. Would I ever be able to recognize him?

No...for, that is the purpose of the masks, isn't it?

I shook off the uncomfortable feeling of him visiting me and not granting me the pleasures of friendship. No—I removed such thoughts and regained control over my mind as I pushed myself to only focus on what I could control in my life, moving my body vigorously as I waited for the turn of the season.

As the winter season of my 17th year was coming to an end, I began observing the weather and flying conditions, waiting for the right time to take my first descent from the mountain of the new year. I gazed outside my little home while standing in the exit tunnel, examining the grey sky surrounding the summit, deciding by my instincts whether or not it was safe to take a long flight.

My home had been formed deep into the mountainside, carved by ancient peoples. The entrance was narrow but large enough for a fully-grown Teragane to enter and exit. The entrance was a tunnel that curved in and led upwards, where it would eventually open into the main living area. The curved and inclined tunnel kept the cold winds from entering my living space and allowed the eternal fire to retain its heat.

I stood on the edge of the entrance to my home, looking around, breathing in the air, and smelling for certain scents. The winds were light, and the air was crisp, yet I felt a sense of heavier humidity. The ice against the rocks glistened from light shining through the grey clouds, and I noticed the prolonged dark days were decreasing. The cold air did not instantly feel threatening or pierce my inner ears with sharpness, and the rise in humidity indicated that spring was coming.

It is time.

I dropped from the edge, forming a nosedive, and plummeted fast alongside the steep ridge covered in ice. Then, I felt the perfect air current and extended my wings, adjusting into a glide. My extended wings were three times my arm span to the furthest tips of the black feathers that separated like a raven's wing, but, in the open sky, I rarely had to think twice about their width at its fullest extent.

The clouds were always thick near the summit, but as I descended further south, the skies became clear, revealing the valleys below. Snow still covered the area, but small patches of green poked through, and shimmering lights reflected from the rivers, indicating that the ice was melting. It felt good to fly in the open sky again. I had only made quick trips to Cami's home, for the path was only a few moments of flight around the mountain ridge.

I wondered who would be sheltering in his now-vacant home. The traditional way of life among my people was never to disclose too much information, only on a need-to-know basis. I was positive that if I were to even ask, no one would tell me. Yet, at this point, who was there to ask? There was no opportunity for curiosity, questioning, or wonder, perhaps even no chance of friendship. So, why did Cami accept mine?

Is that why he was always lecturing me? Was I too assertive to stay friends all these years? Was he attempting to guide me, using me for his own training?

I thought of the red crimson scarf he wore, and how he stroked the fibers with a fondness, a desire of comfort, perhaps? Did he make it? Or did someone give it to him? I hardly could understand him, nor could I ever, now that he was gone.

As the dark cedar forest emerged from below, I strained my eyes, attempting to see through its dense canopy, always curious to know what kind of village lay deep within its protective branches. Then, as the concept of wonder and curiosity flooded my mind, I began to question how I even came upon these attributes after being raised by the traditions of the Sage. Then, I thought of Lillie. Because of her, these things were suddenly awakened in my mind. Perhaps, without Lillie, I would have never developed the ability to wonder.

Was that even possible? Does no one, not even the most isolated people, wonder just a little bit? Does one not instinctively wonder about the existence of one's own reality?

As a youngling, I was curious and often asked questions until my caregivers would exhaust their knowledge—yet, still, it never felt enough. Curiosity seemed like a threat to others. Yet, I never let my inquisitiveness be completely abolished through rigid teachings. When I was younger, I was not as inquisitive as Lillie, but she also took a liking to me because I did display such wonderings and was open to exploring curious things.

Granted, I was by no means as interesting and open-minded as Lillie was, but I could at least attribute to myself for exhibiting these curious tendencies. She did find me interesting enough to keep visiting and spending a great deal of time together. Or, perhaps, she just tolerated me when she visited the meadow by herself. Lillie, as I could recall, had many friends and family members and was part of a thriving village in the forest, yet she still took the time to be with me.

That must be proof enough. Lillie would never waste her precious time on a boring, thoughtless person—if I was one.

I saw the familiar clearing, shaking off all the wild thoughts running through my mind, and angled my wings for descent. The meadow still had small patches of snow, but snowdrop flowers were evidently blooming. Although it was not yet time to meet with Lillie, I wanted to prepare the area for when the full moon came. I cleared away the fireplace and even entered the front of the forest line, gathering wood, and I realized that the looming forest no longer frightened me. I remembered Lillie telling me only dry wood would work for a successful fire, so I decided to bring home the sticks for the soggy wood to dry up before our first meeting. I did my best, gathering what I could find. Most of the sticks from the forest were damp and did not dry even after being placed in front of the eternal fire in my home.

I decided to then dismantle my strength training setup, ripping out the branches from the walls and breaking them across my thigh or against the stone floor. The branches had fulfilled their purpose, being utilized as methods of strength building. Now, they would provide efficient firewood after staying dry during the winter.

I visited the meadow, the riverbanks and the valleys as far as I could go in a day. I pushed boulders, threw stones well over my weight, and flew around carrying heavier rocks each time. The overexertion of activity made me hungrier. So, I looked for early signs of food. I knew the other animals would also be waking from hibernation and would also desire their first meals. It would become a scramble to find resources to satisfy the hunger pangs.

I traveled far up the river to find better fishing spots. I discovered mushrooms, ones that thrived during the cold seasons, as Lillie had taught me. I still had plenty of food in my storage, so I only ate what I needed during the day, utilizing my stocked food for evening meals.

Finally, the full moon arrived, and I returned to the area in which the mushrooms grew, and gathered enough to share with Lillie. Then, I filled my satchel with fish, and I embarked on the flight path to the meadow where I waited patiently for Lillie. I brought a large bundle of firewood and arranged it like Lillie and I had done before. I wrestled with the idea of starting the fire myself, but I was afraid it would burn too fast or would not be lit long enough after Lillie had arrived. I felt as if everything needed to be perfect before her arrival.

So, I decided to wait. I did not want the fire to burn while she was not present. I waited and tolerated the cold so that I could enjoy the warmth of a fire with the girl from the forest—the one I knew I loved. I felt antsy and anxious to see her. When I finished preparing the fire area, I started pacing around it and my apprehensive mind began to wander. What if she does not come? What if she forgets? What if Lillie found another male friend?

A male friend?

What are these thoughts? Lillie said she would see me again in the spring. Lillie always comes when she says she will. I have nothing to fear. She will come. And why would I be worried about another male in her life? I'm sure there are already plenty that she is around...

Lillie? Around other males?

Why does it matter?

Oh, it's that stupid upcoming mating-ritual.

I was beginning to understand the feelings of true anxiety and the pressure of other people's ideals set before me. I knew nothing of the mating-ritual, but I knew there was somewhat an expectation that all Teraganes would procreate, taking on the task of raising a youngling at some point in their lives. I didn't even remember my parent's ages. They did not seem significantly old. But they were also not particularly young like me. Or were they?

I had not seen either of my parents since I was in my early years of existence. Did they have more children? Were they expected to continue raising children, situating them on other mountain summits? It all seemed so foreign; my mind felt foggy, and the apprehension increased. Perhaps that is why the Sage informed me I would learn about this ritual before I'm fully-grown so that I would fully understand the traditions of procreating in our community. Then, they had said I would learn about pairing with a designated mate for procreation.

I thought about Kora and Deruk. Cami acted so disgruntled that I pointed out their obvious attraction. Yet he did not lecture them or reprimand their behavior. Maybe that was naturally how life would evolve.

I remembered stumbling into Polcha's enclave—the way she looked at me, the remark about my strength being useful for the future, and my instincts guiding me to avoid being particularly near her. Were the people in my colony supposed to eventually draw close together and then naturally pick out their mates?

Cami was training to become a Sage and was most likely without need for a mate—without companionship. Was that why he enjoyed my presence? Was he also lonely?

I thought about the others, wondering if they all were given the same instruction about the next phase in our life. Would Deruk and Kora be allowed to grow in their relationship? Would Polcha and Mika be paired? Or—

I gulped loudly, and looked up at the forest, wishing to see Lillie emerge to help calm my thoughts. Yet, she was not there, and my thoughts drifted, recalling the Sage informing me about the mating-ritual and the concept of a designated mate. I counted the members of the colony of Hira, realizing, without Cami, we were uneven as Teraganes.

Then—if I slipped away, all things would continue, and no one would notice, right?

But, was I ready to abandon the way of the Teragane?

I continued pacing around the meadow, kicking up small patches of snow as my wings rustled in the wind. I spent so much time focused only on building my own world that I could not comprehend how I could ever continue accepting the rituals of the Teragane culture.

I didn't want a chosen mate by the Sage.

I did not want to learn about it, nor did I desire to think about the obligations I was expected to fulfill. I did not want to be visited by a Sage informing me—no—demanding me to be with someone else and then procreate with them. I did not want to be like Cami, told to leave his home, say goodbye to his friends forever, and live by *their* standards. I did not want anyone else in my life to control me. I only wanted to be the master of my own life, and in that life I would choose for myself, and I would choose to be with Lillie. That was all I wanted.

I wanted to start a fire and begin cooking all the spring mushrooms and fish I had gathered that morning. I wanted to see Lillie again and hug her. I wanted to smell the earthy scent of her hair tickling the tip of my nose and to feel her warmth on my chest, and experience that comforting feeling within my body as her hands drifted around me.

I wanted to be with Lillie.

I wanted Lillie.

What if she doesn't want me?

I paused my pacing around the circle of stones filled with dry kindle-wood ready to be ignited. I clasped my hand against my chest and my wings twitched as a cold wind blew through the dark feathers.

What if she finds someone else? What if she already has?

I looked up at the red trees of the cedar forest. Would flying Lillie up into the trees be enough? I thought about her cloak that she stated needed to be replaced, or the shoes that often looked too small for her feet. Where could she get these items unless from her own people? Or—could she make them herself and I could help her gather the materials she needed? Perhaps she could continue to teach me her methods of survival, and I could make them for her as well.

Then again—what if someone else in her life could simply provide these things for her? Would living in the meadow bring her happiness when others could offer her more?

CHAPTER TWELVE
WHEN FANTASIES BECOME WORDS

L ike breaking free from the surface of water, breath filled my lungs as I gasped in utter relief after I detected Lillie's figure emerging from the forest. Overrun by impulsive desire, I ran towards her, skipping off the ground, and extended my wings, gliding halfway. She stretched her arms out, and I snatched her up, but, due to my rash choice of action, I lost my balance and faltered to the ground. Ignoring the sounds of her basket flying off to the side, I held Lillie tightly in my arms. I felt my feathers ruffle from the harsh landing, and my pride was a little broken from the fall, but I still held Lillie tight, even though she winced a bit. Her body wrapped up in my arms allowed the anxiety welling in my heart to dwindle, and the apprehension of uncertainty felt less intimidating—at least, for the moment.

"You're crushing your wings!" Lillie exclaimed, breaking my attention. As I realized I was lying on my back, I leaned forward and allowed my bent wings to move to the side, and I covered us for a moment, casting a shield of protection. I felt Lillie squirm within my grasp, but I nuzzled my face against her neck and tightened my hands against her sides.

"I don't care," I whispered as my nose gently caressed the curvature of her neck, and I inhaled deeply as I filled my senses with the herbal scents of her aroma, savoring every ounce of her presence now that we were finally reunited.

"Well, you're crushing me!" she shouted while bobbing back and forth, squirming like a trapped animal. "How are you so strong?!"

I released my grip, and she pushed off me, panting heavily and moving my wings aside as she escaped my hold. I only laughed; I was too busy thinking about how happy I felt seeing her again.

I adjusted myself to a sitting position and began brushing off the twigs and grass I had collected during my tumble. I noticed Lillie's items were completely dismantled as she picked off wet debris from her basket. I stood up and shyly helped adjust her things. She rearranged her brown scarf and green winter cloak that had been twisted around, and I noticed fresh dirt stains. I pulled out a few twigs from her white hair, and she helped remove some from my tangled hair. She then placed her hand on my shoulder, looking up at me, and our eyes met.

"It is good to see you again," Lillie said, then suddenly narrowed her eyes. "Even if you soiled my new cloak."

"Sorry," I said, even though I felt the opposite. My heart was too happy to feel ashamed. My hand drifted down to her cheek. Her skin had become dull and without a trace of the cool undertones of a stormy sky. Under her eyes were dark, and the rosy complexion of her cheeks and nose was weak; her hair was white as snow. Yet, I felt that she was still as beautiful as ever—like the icy mountain in the winter, only needing warmth and happiness to become fully appreciated in its greatest wonder.

"I'm so happy to see you," I said while stroking her cheek. It was surprisingly soft. Lillie's disgruntled demeanor diminished, and perhaps she forgot about the stain on her cloak caused by my impulsive behavior. She placed her hand on my wrist, gently caressing my skin as she maneuvered her thumb under the edge of the sleeve. As we stared at each other, I could barely breathe. The warmth of her hand felt like fire—a flame that passionately fueled my heart, and I looked at her lips. Again, I wanted them, as they looked so delicious and perfectly kissable.

Was this also part of my instincts?

Lillie abruptly let go and moved herself away from me, breaking the intense moment.

"So, let's make a fire," she said cheerfully. "It's cold and I'm hungry."

I helped her carry her items, and we walked to our designated spot. I proudly showed her the clean fireplace and the dry wood, and welcomed the idea that she could inspect my work accordingly.

"I'm proud of you," she said as she examined everything after setting her basket near the stones. "I taught you well. Didn't I?"

"You are my greatest teacher," I said with a nod, and my hands twitched at my side. She chuckled, then encouraged me to start the fire. Within a few moments, I procured the orange flames once described as uncontrollable and dangerous, but felt more familiar than that of the eternal-flame from the Sage. We unfolded the blanket together, laying it close to the fire, and, as usual, Lillie unpacked her basket, bringing out different types of food to eat. She unraveled brown bread, a few stalks of sweet grass, and potatoes. I showed her the mushrooms I had found earlier, and we roasted them over the fire along with the potatoes, which turned out to be exceptionally delicious after thoroughly cooking.

We ate together. We laughed. We enjoyed the long-awaited company of each other. And my heart finally settled with tranquility.

"It feels so good to be here right now," Lillie said after exhaling deeply. "Winter is always so harsh. I'm glad the sun has finally returned."

"Except, the sun never leaves, only hides behind the clouds," I said, causing Lillie to roll her eyes.

"You know what I mean," she retorted, and I smirked while nudging her arm close to mine. However, my grin faded as the brutal memories of my winter isolation encircled my mind. I thought about Cami's friendship, then his sudden departure, the visit by the Sage, and the upcoming mating-ritual. I shivered at the torture of being left alone for so many months, jumping around my home like a pent-up animal, and pushing my body to its limits just to avoid the unbearable loneliness.

I could feel my nerves becoming fully aware of my endeavor to talk to Lillie about a future together. All those months of fantasizing about a life with her—the joy and sense of tranquility I desired—seemed distant, particularly at that moment while I sat next to her. She seemed content and happy. What if she didn't want to leave her home behind?

Panic surged through my body. The idea of being rejected by Lillie became a very real possibility, and it scared me. What if she laughs at the idea? What if she doesn't love me? What if—

"Sable, you alright?" Lillie asked as I was staring deeply into the fire, lost in my stressful thoughts.

Why am I thinking about these things now?

"Yeah, I'm fine," I replied, feeling my wings twitch. I looked down at her hands picking up the empty napkins, intently observing the way that her fingers drifted across each crease. Normally, she never cared to line the edges, but today she carefully examined each corner as she meticulously creased the linen.

"You seem like you've got something on your mind. Want to talk about it?" Lillie shifted her sitting position, facing me, but still lining the napkins set upon her lap. I shifted my eyes up, meeting hers, and she tilted her head as the light of the fire danced in the reflection of her inquisitive eyes.

Well, I need to tell her at some point how I feel and what I want for her—for us.

Somehow, being the hero to save Lillie from her troubles in my mind seemed so much more valiant than how I felt in that moment. That sense of courage—the fuel of pride—dwindled away at the very idea that perhaps Lillie would not even want the same thing as me. She was obviously struggling with her home life, but what if she was okay with it? What if it was just part of her culture, her people's way of life, and me inviting her to leave it all behind would be detrimental for her future? What if she wanted a different future than what I had envisioned?

"I was just thinking about an idea I had," I finally said.

"An idea? Like what?" Lillie asked while leaning forward in anticipation of what words would soon come from my mouth. As I felt Lillie's eyes stare, I muscled up the courage to speak my mind. My throat felt dry and my face as if a fire burned within. I moved away from the roaring flames, shifting my position in hopes of finding a more comfortable sitting spot. Regardless of my efforts, I still felt very uncomfortable.

Why am I feeling this way? It's Lillie! It's all I've been thinking about for so many seasons!

"I thought a lot about what you said last year," I said, steadying my voice to hide my apprehension. "About wanting to live in the trees."

"Oh really? Ha!" Forced nervous laughter and the slapping of her thigh caused the heaviness to surge through my aching stomach. The abrupt vibration and volume triggered something even deeper within, especially as she shook her head and continued. "Oh, I was just being silly. I don't know why you would take me so seriously, especially after falling on you."

"Well, you seemed very determined. It sounded like that was what you wanted. You were very upset afterwards."

"I want a lot of things, but that doesn't mean I can always get them."

"But if you could have it?"

"Oh, it was just a silly thing."

"What if you could live in the trees?"

"I don't know. I don't see that ever being a possibility."

"What if it was?"

"I don't know! Why does it matter?" Lillie raised her voice at me. Her hands balled into fists, her cheeks became flushed, and she looked away from me. Her eyes did not look angry, but her tone of voice indicated otherwise. Why was she so conflicted? Did I say something wrong?

"I just wanted to know if you would choose that life for yourself if it was a possibility," I said and moved slightly away from Lillie, unnerved by her angered state of conflict. "If you could live in the trees—er, here, in the meadow—would you?"

"Listen," she said, and hung her head, sighing deeply, and her frustration slowly faded. "I'm sorry, I just—uh—don't have the luxury to think of such possibilities." Her answer took me by surprise. Lillie had always encouraged me to try new things and think of new possibilities. Now, she was stating that was a luxury—a privilege she could not allow herself?

"I do not understand how the idea could be considered a luxury," I replied. "Why not give yourself a better opportunity and a better life? You seem so miserable, anyway. Why not leave your life in the forest and live here?"

"Leave my life behind? You don't understand, nor can I even begin to try to explain to you why I cannot fathom such a future for myself."

"Try." I blinked steadily as I kept my eyes upon her. She raised her hands, flinging loose hairs in her efforts.

"Ha! You, the lone Teragane on the mountain—you could never understand."

"Why have so little faith in me?"

"Because you don't know what you're talking about."

"Yes, I know I am the isolated Teragane from the mountain, but have I not proven myself to be open-minded and capable of understanding new ways of life?"

"It's not that simple. Right now, you are encouraging me to think of the possibility of leaving behind my home, my friends, and my family! That alone proves to me that you do not understand the importance of my relationships. Yes, obviously you have observed that my life is filled with difficult aspects, whereas I come to the meadow to escape all of it, but only for a little while. That does not mean I can just abandon it because it is difficult for me."

There. Here is the truth—the truth I feared all this time.

The truth hit me like a tree branch bent too far, snapping back into place upon release. She didn't want the life I so often fantasized about. I could not be the hero, swooping her up into the trees and rescuing her from her hard life in the forest.

How could I be so stupid?

Silence overtook the scene with only the crackling fire looming next to us. My heart felt torn. My mind was racing. Was this how we would spend the rest of our lives—living separately, only spending time together once a full moon? Was it not possible to have more with Lillie? Were we obliged to live according to our predestined paths forced onto us by others? What happens when I start the mating-ritual? What will happen when Lillie also finds her own mate? Would we stop meeting together completely even as friends? Did I even want to stay friends with her after feeling so deeply about our affection?

"I'm sorry for even suggesting the idea," I mumbled, and I looked away, past the grassy meadow, and stared into the clear, blue sky.

From the corner of my eye, I shot a glance, noticing Lillie's expression of sadness. I hoped that she also felt conflicted and confused, and perhaps her heart also ached. I wanted her to feel crushed—like I felt at that moment.

"I'm sorry for yelling," Lillie said as she turned to stare at the fire. "I guess we both come from very different lives, different homes, and different expectations. Our meadow gives us great relief from those expectations, but our responsibilities are still lingering with us—no matter where we go. I know you probably think I'm miserable all the time, but I am making a good life for myself—finally."

"Perhaps, however," I paused, and stood up to overlook the great cedar forest, and then crossed my arms as I examined the vastness of the trees. I then turned and faced the cliffside. I took a few steps, but lingered close enough so that Lillie could still hear me. "However, the world is large, and there are many other ways of life and many possibilities. Regardless of our destined expectations from others, regardless of the life set before us, do you really want to live your life to fulfill other's wants and expectations? Maybe you are making a better life, but under what control do you still linger? You say you don't have the luxury of living apart from those who cause you pain." I glanced back at Lillie, slightly twisting my neck. She appeared paralyzed in her sitting position as her hands gripped at her skirt. But she was breathing deeply and seemingly listening to every word I said.

"The way I see it," I continued, "I now know that I am questioning this very idea. I am questioning the very concept of my existence. Should I continue living a life based on other's ideals, or do I not know what could be better for myself, or at least can I not learn such attributes for myself? Who is to say other people's ideas of life are better than the next person's? Who? Why? Can we not make a life good for ourselves based on what we love and desire? For, in the end, whose life are we responsible for anyway? Is it not our own? And why would we allow others to completely control us, especially if their ideas do not line with our own personal love and desires?"

I paused, nearly out of breath. I did not expect such words to vomit from my own mouth, yet there I was, standing as the wind blew my untamed hair around my face and my heart pounded with intensity. I may not have felt heroic, but I did feel bold and courageous. I felt relieved to finally express my internal conflict out loud to Lillie—out loud for my world to hear.

I looked behind me where Lillie sat quietly. Her hands were still tightly gripping her skirt, and tears were streaming down her face. I stayed in my place, and she did not move from her position. The sound of the howling wind filled the air. It was cold where I stood as the wind sent piercing sensations into my ears, but I felt too conflicted to return close to the fire again. My feet were cold, but my head and chest felt hot. My emotions were higher than ever and more complicated than I had ever experienced before. I did not know how to proceed.

So, I just stood in silence, looking away from Lillie, scanning the area, the vastness of the valley below, and the mountain range above. The landscape beyond was massive, yet so little in comparison to the world I could only assume expanded in the province. Why did I feel so limited? Did I even want to stay in the meadow, after all?

A new desire suddenly crept within my mind as I looked beyond the mountains in which the Sage patrolled, then I glanced at the cedar forest in which I understood to be the controllers of Lillie's life. Perhaps staying in the meadow wasn't what I really wanted after all. Maybe I wanted to escape and fly across the mountains and altogether make a whole new life—away from the expectations of either of our lives.

"Perhaps," Lillie said, breaking the silence. She sniffled, wiped her cheeks, and proceeded to choke up words. "Perhaps all you say is true. Perhaps ideals and expectations should be challenged, but..." Her voice faded.

I glanced back, and my heart ached for her. Her voice was soft, and all traces of anger had subsided. Her tone was purely unresolved. A desire to comfort Lillie persuaded me to return to her side. When I sat next to her, I waited as she struggled to find the ability to communicate what was deep in her heart.

"But maybe I am not ready to challenge these things," Lillie finally said. A sense of relief overcame my heart, and I reached out my hand to her, but she hesitated and kept her head low.

"There is no rush," I said while lowering my hand to the ground next to where she sat. "Take your time to find your strength." Lillie leaned her lowered head onto my chest. I wrapped my arm behind her, bringing her close to my side, and Lillie cried softly.

I sat in silence while holding her close. The warmth of her tears dampened my cloak, and the fire crackled and popped as its flames slowly died down into coals. My heart settled for a moment. Perhaps there was still hope for a future—a more distant future.

It was true; she had more expectations than I had. She needed to find her own strength and evaluate what type of relationships she wanted to keep or do without. Whatever she needed, I would support her. Even if it were true she was making a better life for herself, perhaps she still wanted me as a friend. Maybe there was still hope that we could be together.

"Lillie," I said after I noticed her crying had ceased. "I want to understand your life. I want to know more about the important relationships you have." Lillie sniffled while rubbing her nose with her green cloak.

"I know you do," she said. "It's just—" Her voice faded again.

"It's okay," I uttered softly. "You don't have to explain yourself today. I just want you to know that I care deeply about you and your life. I don't want you to make choices based on my desires, but I would like to know more about the struggle of why you cannot choose the luxury of being free from the expectations burdening your shoulders. You say you're making a better life, yet you cry as if my words cut like a deep wound within your heart...But, when you're ready to explain things or help me understand, I'll be here, waiting."

"Okay," Lillie said, and I felt her head nod on my chest. She wrapped her arm around my waist, and I adjusted my hand to the small of her back, pulling her up against my side, and she relaxed in my arms.

She did not speak, and I watched her rise and fall with my steady breathing. I kissed the top of her head and breathed in the scent of her hair when given the chance. I moved my wings to cover her, and she drifted off to sleep.

Lillie still cares about me. No need to worry. She just needs more time to evaluate what is most important and what is worth leaving behind.

Chapter Thirteen

WHEN THE TREE BRANCH SNAPS BACK

I had a new motive in life. I would wait for Lillie. I knew in my heart that she wanted the same as me—to be free, live happily, and do as we wished—but she was not ready to accept these terms of life, particularly the consequences of achieving such desires. She was not ready to leave her village, her family, and the only life she had ever known. Perchance, she had many other obstacles to overcome and other ties to cut before she could entertain the idea of starting a new life and accept a new concept of living. After all, our lives were different.

I had barely any ties to cut. If I disappeared one day, never to return to my mountain residence, I did not think anyone would come after me. Cami had left, and I acknowledged the fact that I would most likely never see him again. He moved on with his life as a Sage and he may never return to this area. The Sage came and went as they did according to methods never once explained to me, and I highly doubted my existence in their life was something beyond simply another Teragane they were subject to guiding through minimal efforts.

The others I lived next to, I rarely saw or interacted with, and they carried no special interest to me—well, except Polcha, but only as a potential mate for the future.

Another reason to leave.

Even in my absence, my colony would still be at balance, and I could easily slip away and live my own life.

There was not much enticing me to continue my solitary life on the mountain except the instincts and teachings of my kind. Now, I had begun my journey of questioning these ideals, contemplating the expectations and roles provided for me, and deciding whether I wanted to participate anymore. Lillie meant the world to me, and she gave me a happiness I never knew could exist. I doubted such happiness would evolve if I continued to live by the order of the Teragane colony. I was willing, at this point, to take the chance of leaving it all behind.

I desire nothing from the Teragane life...I want more.

As for Lillie, she obviously was not ready to make such drastic choices, and I accepted her decisions. She lived with her parents, and had numerous friends, neighbors, and an entire village. She had food to cook and gather, a job to attend, and many other activities that I did not completely understand. Her life was hard—yes—but full of action and interactions that were seemingly important. Perhaps her idea of living in the trees truly was what she had stated: a silly idea.

But a life of freedom together in the future? I believed it was not entirely impossible. She clearly wanted to be with me. She slept peacefully in my arms during our last visit. She had slept until the sun had nearly set. She was so relaxed, unthreatened by the world around us. She felt safe with me, and I knew that I wanted to protect her for the rest of my life.

If waiting for her to make her final decision to leave her life behind was all I had to do, then so be it. Even so, all she needed to do was open up more to me about her life. Maybe she didn't have to leave it behind. Maybe we could work out a new routine together. Perhaps we just needed to take small steps—small changes—for her to fully grasp the idea of change. Yes—perhaps that is all she needed to accept.

Maybe, then again...

What if she didn't want to leave it altogether? Perchance she only wanted our periodic visits to the meadow. Maybe she was happy with just being my friend—the lone Teragane destined for a life of isolation. I became anxious about these thoughts and the unknown future.

I knew that I loved Lillie, and I truly believed Lillie loved me. But I began to fear an unforeseeable prospect. I imagined a future together and hoped for a free life with Lillie. However, I feared for a different outcome. A future where we slowly drift apart—Lillie with her life in the forest, me slowly slipping into the mundane rituals of Teragane's idealism and isolation. The idea of learning about the Mating-Ritual caused me to shudder. I did not want to visualize myself with anyone else or accept that I would be forced into a situation where I had to procreate with another Teragane just for the sake of tradition.

No. Stop thinking about the unknown. Simply focus on what you can do right now...

111

I returned to the river every day and waited for the brown bears to arrive. During one breezy spring morning as I sat in a tree, I stared at my arms, noticing the definition of the curves of the muscles under my thin sleeves. I had sculpted myself into a magnificent creature, yet now my motivation was beginning to change. I started out hoping to be Lillie's strong hero, sweeping her off her feet and flying her into the distance, possibly leaving the area forever. Now, my thoughts were mainly of existential concepts on what it meant to live a life worth living. I knew I could only sit and wait for Lillie to accept me as I offered myself. I could only wait for Lillie to choose me—to choose me over everything else.

I must wait, like I wait for the bears to return or the full moon to arrive—why do I always have to wait for others?

The bears appeared, sluggishly wobbling their bodies out of the forest and into the river. They were thin, tired-looking, and ever-so-hungry while dragging their paws. The small family of bears were in poor spirits, obviously hungry from their long winter fast, and ready to part ways to establish their own lives. The fish were few, yet they gobbled up as much as they could, and I watched quietly from my tree perch on the other side of the riverbank.

They look so weak. I could probably take down the younger cubs before being torn to pieces by the mother.

Then again, how much longer until she would not care for their protection? Or would a mother always look after her children?

Watching the bears stumble around, snarl at each other, and sluggishly catch fish reminded me how even the mightiest of creatures had their weaknesses. Yet they were still feared and strong as a family unit, especially under the mother. A few more bears apart from the family joined the others in a weakened state, and I marveled at the concept of them all tolerating each other while desperate for breaking their fast.

I wondered if that was how Lillie felt about her own family. She often told me negative stories about her parents, yet she seemed loyal and devoted to them. Perhaps they stuck together because they were strongest when together, even if they were low on strength and exhausted from the harshness of life.

I hope Lillie can find the courage to explain to me her situation. One day I hope she can trust me enough to support and understand her. Maybe I just need to ask her more questions.

Perhaps I need to prove to her that I am interested in understanding her life—I really should have told her about my plan to fly her around wherever she wanted.

Maybe that would change her mind—sooner rather than later.

Further into spring, the snow had completely melted away. All the purple and white spring flowers were blooming, the bees were buzzing, and small critters were enjoying the pleasures of warmer weather after a cold winter. The air was fresh and humid, cleansed by the great slumber of winter, allowing me to soar around the valley with great exhilaration.

I anticipated the next full moon and decided to give less attention to an unattainable future with Lillie and focus instead on a more tangible present moment. I did not want to see Lillie cry; instead, I wanted to make her laugh, see her smile, and watch her cheeks and ears redden. During our previous meeting, she had fallen asleep after our emotional discussion. I wanted to avoid invoking further intense discourse and focus only on making Lillie happy. Although I did not mind her resting when needed, I hoped to be able to enjoy our time together, pushing aside emotional stress.

I caught some fish to share, packed firewood from the storage cache in my home, and carried it all wrapped in an animal pelt. I was stronger than ever before; perhaps I could just fly Lillie around for fun. I stopped fantasizing about an elusive future and instead focused on what *was* possible. I had an inevitable visit from the Sage in the coming spring I had yet to fully anticipate how to manage. At that present moment, I could just enjoy my current state of life in the meadow near Lillie's side. I would deal with the future when I was forced to face it.

When I arrived at the meadow, I cleaned up the fireplace and placed the logs accordingly. Again, I wanted to wait before starting the actual flames but preparing it for when Lillie arrived was enough motivation to have it perfectly set. I looked around, watching the butterflies bounce from the flowers and the grass dance in the cool breeze. I picked a few flowers according to their scents and physical beauty and placed them in a bunch, remembering to ask Lillie about the floral scents cast from her hair. I lifted each blossom to my nose, sniffing and determining if it were the same scent as the ones I detected from Lillie. I noticed the different colors ranging from deep purples to yellows, and the light green stems under the delicate petals, like the glistening shades of Lillie's eyes. The subject of my own eye color reminded me to ask Lillie—finally allowing myself the privilege of knowing something I always forgot to ask about.

As I gathered a bouquet of flowers, I thought about giving it to Lillie. She could make something of them—I was sure of it. I remembered when she once showed me how to make a flower crown, or another time she weaved a small basket of dried grass. My biggest hope was to make Lillie smile that day. Her happiness was my greatest joy. Her warmth was my greatest comfort.

Thoughts of her sleeping in my arms brought fuzzy feelings to my stomach. During the moment, I felt distraught for causing her stress to the point she slept most of the afternoon. But, as I thought more about the scene of her sleeping peacefully next to me, I enjoyed the sensations of being near her in such an intimate state. While she snoozed, I watched her rise and fall—I even let the ends of her hair tickle the edges of my fingers. I didn't mind if she wanted to sleep next to me again—I never slept near another person before, not even my own parents.

I glided around the meadow, picking flowers I thought Lillie would like, and smelled each one in case I could detect a familiar scent. I moved boulders, adjusting them near the fireplace for us to rest against. I stood on my hands, trying to do a cartwheel like Lillie did so often as a child, but I faltered in my attempts.

I'll ask Lillie to teach me to do a cartwheel. That could cheer her up!

I often glanced at the opening in the forest where Lillie always emerged. I waited patiently for her to show up. I lay on the ground, staring at the sky, counting clouds and flying ravens and the occasional eagle seeking a meal. I paced around the fireplace on the grass, watching grasshoppers flee on sight. I stared at the great forest, wondering how deep the roots of the giant cedar trees grew. I wondered greatly about my own future, about Cami, and where he was in his training and where he was sent off to. I recalled my promise to never forget him and decided to tell Lillie about him, especially how much he enjoyed her marmalade. For a moment, I thought about his request for me to comb my hair, and I began brushing my hands through the tangled strands, then got bored with the pointless grooming and I attempted to do a cartwheel again, but instead just balanced myself by doing a handstand. I did everything to keep my mind busy as I waited.

But Lillie never came.

The light of the full moon began to illuminate the area as the sun waned behind the mountains. I looked at the forest entrance, where I watched Lillie emerge hundreds of times.

This time, there was no Lillie. For the first time in all the years of diligently meeting, she did not come as usually expected. My heart began to race as my mind flooded with anxious thoughts.

Where could she be? Did she decide not to meet with me? Does she no longer want to see me? Perhaps she wants nothing to do with me anymore? Maybe she is angry? Or—

My heart felt as if it had dropped to my stomach, and fear overwhelmed my entire body.

What if something bad happened to her? What if she is in trouble?

I flew to the entrance of the forest, the spot where Lillie on numerous occasions emerged from. I stopped at the forest edge and stared into the darkness. The sun had nearly set, and the full moon was shining brightly from its reflection. Even so, the brightness of the moon was nothing compared to the darkness of the forest. It created a sense of mystery and fear. The sinking in my stomach and the aching of my heart nearly paralyzed me.

She's somewhere deep within this forest, possibly hurt—possibly in danger.

The image of Lillie screaming, crying, and bleeding came to mind. I saw the images of her scarred hands, the fading of her skin color, and her white hair wrapping around a terrified expression and her green eyes disappearing behind a great unknown. Whatever afflicted her with these things could have been the reason for her absence. Lillie never missed our visits to the meadow—never.

When we were children, she came every day. Then, as we grew older, it was every other day, then once a fortnight, and finally only on the days of the full moon. Regardless of the lessening of visitations, Lillie always came when she said she would. She had never missed our time together.

Something is holding her back...

At that moment, the courage and boldness of my heroic idealism came rushing throughout my body and mind. I knew at once I needed to find Lillie despite the unknown world lingering in the darkness. I did not care about anything else, only about Lillie's safety.

I spent the entire winter season without her and was facing the uncomfortable situation of doubts about having a future together. At that moment, I pushed aside the apprehension, focusing only on the present moment of Lillie's absence.

I puffed up my chest, breathing in as much courage as possible. I flew into the forest, not knowing if I was the most foolish Teragane in the province or the most absolute love-struck man willing to do whatever was necessary to protect his loved one. Regardless, I did not care, nor did I have the space to evaluate where my head was in such a moment. I flew into the forest with only one thing on my mind.

Find Lillie.

I entered the cedar forest determined to follow the path to Lillie's village. At least, I assumed it would lead directly there. I had not known this as a fact and only held onto my assumption to relieve the anxiety of the alternative, less desirable outcomes. I flew above ground, but as I ventured deeper, the trees became dense, the extensive branches blocking a clear flying-path, and the ground below was difficult to see. I landed on the mossy floor, examining the area around me. My desire to find Lillie gave me courage, but the fear of the darkness and the unknown forest area began to creep into my mind.

Just focus on following the trail. It's just a forest. Nothing to fear...

I focused merely on my logical thoughts rather than the fearful ideas of wandering alone in the forest without a guide. As I walked deeper, my eyes adjusted to the darkness of night while I carefully observed the trodden path that I could only hope would lead me to Lillie. At times, through the corner of my eye, I thought I saw movement. I felt the hairs on my arm stand up, my face cold, and my heart beat like the hum of a honey bee's wing—vigorous and fast. I looked forward, then down, watching where my feet landed.

The path was trodden and well established. It curved and maneuvered through the trees, noticeably different in width, according to how travelers had used it as a footpath. I could hear branches creaking as they swayed in the wind, and the hoot of an owl echoed periodically. The ferns and other foliage growing underneath the trees rustled in the wind, possibly from little critters scampering around through the night. The density of the canopy prohibited a lot of growth on the forest floor, or light from above.

I imagined that the forest held beautiful scenery under different circumstances. I envisioned Lillie pointing out to me the pleasantries of certain plants and different kinds of moss. Her keen interest in plants, her pleasant smile, and her kind voice comforted me in my imagination.

The rustling noise of something dashing behind me forced my thoughts to stop wondering about plants and their differences. I felt worried about my own safety as I turned around, scanning the area for lurking predators. As I continued down the path, scouring the area, my mind raced about what had kept Lillie from coming to the meadow.

I did my best to avoid thoughts about the worst scenarios, one consisting of her death and the other her utter apathy towards me. When such thoughts arose in my mind, I physically shook my head and imagined Lillie's smile, her silly remarks, and her obvious affection for me. Instead, I tried imagining her being caught up with work, but I did not know what type of work she would be caught up with. I thought about her needing to help her family. However, the idea of her parents punishing her due to unforeseen circumstances brought further apprehension in my chest.

Although the fearful scenarios caused my heart to flutter with anxiety, it kept my mind busy from being petrified of walking through the looming forest. Any other reason to enter the forest at night would have been fleeting, for I would have turned around and flown out as fast as possible.

What was that?

A sudden howl echoed deep within the trees. I stopped in my tracks, looking around for danger. I prepared myself to fly to safety up in the trees, if necessary, but nothing happened. No predator emerged from the darkness to attack me. So, I kept going, anticipating any danger lurking ahead.

I knew that wolves lived in forests in the province; their collective packs easily made them the most successful hunters and the most territorial. I had no desire to have my first encounter with wolves during the night in the middle of a strange location. I stopped many times to observe my surroundings after hearing noises. The simple hoot of an owl sent an alarm through my nerves. The creaking branches echoing above me caused me to stop and make sure nothing but the wind was causing them to move. Between the fear of the eerie forest and the distressing thoughts of Lillie's absence, I trudged through the forest, dread twisting my stomach in knots and fear of danger keeping me alert. I walked until I came upon the first light of a village.

This must be it! I made it!

Often, while flying over the cedar trees or sitting in the meadow with Lillie, I tried peering through the dense forest to see houses or a village, but never once could I detect anything beyond the blanket cover of the woodland. My eyesight was sharp and capable of detecting small details even from high above the ground like any avian. However, my vision was inferior to the impenetrable cover of timberland.

As I approached a new change of scenery, I found a small arch ahead made of the red wood of a cedar and twisting branches. Over-growing vines and ferns covered the curvature, partially blocking the entrance that I pushed aside to walk through. The feathery leaves of the ferns lightly brushed against my wings as I followed the low light cast from further away.

The giant cedar trees were still prevalent, but now I could see building structures at the base of the trees, stacking high into the overhead thicket. The further I entered the village, the buildings became denser, almost appearing as if the forest had disappeared altogether.

The path was no longer trodden dirt but instead made of flat stone. I stood near some buildings that looked unused and rotting away, and I gazed upward. The network of structures was built vertically on either side of the path, some connected overhead by wooden bridges staggering as it connected the vertical buildings, intertwining with the branch system of the cedar trees. Both tree, branch, bridge, and wooden structure interlocked in a web of design, making it difficult to recognize what was naturally grown and what was manufactured by artistic hands. I could not see the sky within the immense canopy; not a single beam of moonlight could break through the system above.

I looked onward. The path disappeared around a corner lined with increasing buildings that I could only assume were homes. There were so many windows, darkened due to the middle of the night, and small wooden doors with little stone stairs at the entrance, or others spiraling up to another level.

I had never seen such intricate buildings, let alone compactly built one on the other. All appeared to be uniquely designed and shaped, some unused and rotting, others well maintained. Small lanterns lined the stone path, allowing a flickering dim light to guide me through the maze of wood and stone. The village was quiet, although I noticed an indistinguishable hum filling the air. I turned the corner and realized the path split in three ways.

As realization that perhaps the staggering buildings was a single home for a villager, my heart began to pound within my chest as I realized the capacity of dwellers within the forest was not just as simple as I thought all these years.

The view from the ground significantly gave me a disadvantage. As an avian, I preferred to examine the surrounding area before embarking on a direction. I looked around, planning to find a higher advantage point, but hesitated at the narrowness of the area that could cause damage to my wings.

I noticed a low-hanging bridge and decided to aim for it. I angled myself so that my wings were parallel to the path, extending them partially, and I jumped, lifting myself high into the overhead area. Upon landing, I expected a sturdy footing, but the wooden bridge swayed and creaked. The sound alone caused fear of it breaking, and I jumped again to another bridge.

It also jarred upon my sudden impact, and I aimed next for a rooftop ledge. I had ascended above the buildings by now and could make out the top of a taller structure. Upon landing, the roof did not move; it only creaked, allowing me to adjust my footing and lower my wings, my breathing hardly stable.

These homes are built on each other, surely, they can hold my weight. I cannot be that heavy!

Feeling secure enough in my position as I angled my footing and the wooden roof stopped creaking, I took the opportunity to assess the surroundings. My heart sank once again as alarm ran through my nerves.

With one look around the area, the dim lights of the village exhibited an immense city of buildings woven through the trees. My sharp eyes struggled to comprehend the area with only the glow of the lanterns and piles of buildings stacked randomly, all covered by the immense canopy of the giant cedars overhead and throughout. Paths wove without patterns, and bridges connected the overhead structures like the web of a spider, which were high enough to access the taller buildings but low enough to cross under the branches of the trees. My eyes followed the curvature of the weaving area, but everything was straining my eyesight.

My nose picked up a vast number of new smells of unpleasant smoke, filth, and other alarming scents that caused me to scrunch my nose. Then, my ears heard faint sounds further ahead. A low hum, a rustling rhythm. There were sounds I had never experienced before, and the air was dense with a polluted draught.

I pushed my hair out of my face and felt sweat piling on my forehead. The stifling air was different from the open area I was accustomed to, causing my body unwanted perspiration. I had never imagined such a complex place could exist. My eyes hurt trying to find details and patterns in the city beyond. My nose tickled, but not with pleasantries, and my ears rang with irritating, rumbling noises, and my skin itched from the exasperating change of humidity.

Initially, I thought the giant forest was intimidating in itself. As I gazed upon the revelation of a hidden labyrinth, my mind raced with all the new information—new revelations of a world unforeseen. Row after row of buildings, streets, and stone steeples with puffs of black smoke, the whole area was distasteful to all my senses.

The dawn of realization only continued as I feared all the assumptions of Lillie's world were far from true.

How will I ever find Lillie?

CHAPTER FOURTEEN

WHEN A TASK IS HARDER THAN EXPECTED

A s the morning sun broke through slivers of the cedar thicket, the sound of the waking forest-dwellers became apparent. The quiet rumble from the night increased into a low roar with sharp clashing sounds and low murmurs. Black smoke rose from the chimneys, casting the smell of wood and charcoal throughout, intensifying the thick redolence. I sat perched on the roof, examining the buildings, the various colors of wood and stones, and I wondered how I would ever find Lillie's residence. I stayed in my position, patiently waiting for the city to wake up. But, in reality, I was too petrified to even move.

The initial shock of the mysterious city had decreased after observing it from above, but, still, my mind raced with anxious thoughts of how I would find Lillie. The city was too large for me to look in every building. Perhaps I would only need to find her neighborhood and could ask the local inhabitants about her whereabouts, in turn leading me directly to her or to others who were friends with her.

Talking to random strangers can't be that hard, right? Perhaps I will meet someone who knows Lillie—maybe a friend!

Lillie was friendly when I had first met her. Surely others would also show me kindness and display eagerness to help me, right?

As my eyes drifted down, I saw a group of people walking along the path underneath me. They looked similar to Lillie's kind—grayish skin, pointed ears, similar clothes, and they wore their long hair in braids.

I swooped down and landed in front of the group, bending my knees on impact. The sudden force shook the ground a little and I slowly rose, folding my wings behind me, and a dark shadow crossed over the locals whose mouths gaped wide with eyes to match.

"Greetings," I said. "I'm looking for a friend. Can you—"

"Get away, you freak!" one man yelled while grasping the other.

"A demon? Here?" another shrieked, and all horrified locals turned to run away while screaming, "I swear I paid my taxes!"

Well, I probably shouldn't do that again.

I scratched at the side of my neck, slightly grimacing as the little grey people turned around a corner, still shouting to each other about the dangers of demons and something else about *taxes*. A few faces peered around the building, then quickly dashed away, only indicating that I had made a blundering mistake in my method of approaching the forest-dwellers. Lillie had never been afraid of me—but, she did ask if I were a demon when we had first met.

Maybe these people believe that the Teraganes are dangerous demons—whatever that is.

I just need to be more approachable.

I saw a small child exit from a building, slamming the door behind him, and he wiped his face, smearing dirt across his cheeks. His skin was a stormy gray, similar to Lillie's when she was a young child. Although small in stature, the child displayed confidence as he skipped down the path, swinging his arms. He stopped at an open shelter filled with firewood and began picking up logs, placing each upon his thin but strong arms.

His resemblance to a younger version of Lillie drew me close, but I casually passed him by, allowing the child to notice me first. Perhaps he would also be curious, like Lillie was as a youngling. As my large shadow passed over the firewood storage, he twisted his head, and stared up at me with a curious grin. I darted my eyes and pretended to read some symbols next to the shelter, and stroked my chin while furrowing my brow. While feigning a puzzled contemplation, I mumbled, but, then, as I looked closer at the protruding sign with weird scribbles, I naturally became confused.

"Hey, mister!" he called out, and I felt a tug on my feathers. I turned to face the tiny child, and slowly crouched down to his level while his eyes gleamed with inquisitiveness and a sense of bravery.

"Hey there, little one," I said. He was holding several logs in one arm, and I noticed scratches upon his skin through the holes of his tattered clothing that seemed too filthy for a child to be wearing.

"What are you doing here?" he asked. "Why do you have wings? Are you a bird?" As he tilted his head, observing my wings, his little pointed ears perked with interest, and I smiled.

"No I am not a bird, but I was born with wings like one, I guess. I am looking for my friend. Do you know—"

"Can you really fly? Like a bird?"

"Yes, I can."

"Can you show me?"

"Unfortunately, this place is not suitable for flying conditions."

"Aw, why not?"

"Because, my wings are too large to fly around. It's better to be in an open space, like outside of the cedar forest. Anyway, do you know someone named Lillie?"

"The market is open. You can fly around there."

"Okay, but, please, do you know Lillie?"

"Who's Lillie?"

"Lillie—she is my friend. She is about my age, has long, white hair, and is probably this tall." I stood up and showed her height, pressing my hand against my chest near my shoulders, knowing that was where her head lay last when I had given her a hug. A sense of warmth overwhelmed my body with the memory, and I felt even more anxious to find her. "She likes to forage in the forest, bakes bread, cooks over a fire, and—uh, she lives somewhere in this city, but I don't know where."

"Hmmm." The young boy shifted the logs onto his other arm as he pondered out loud, then looked over his shoulder. "Does she like to play Pocket-Ball?"

"What? Uh—I don't know."

"How do you not know if your friend likes to play Pocket-Ball?" The child's eyes narrowed as his judgmental voice sent an unnerving sensation through my mind. I looked around, feeling uncomfortable, for, how does one respond to the criticism of a literal child?

"Some friend you are," he sneered, then shifted the logs in his arms again, then looked down the narrow street, and I followed his gaze.

"I guess I never thought to ask because I—" The door in which he first emerged swung open, and an older woman stepped in the doorway, holding a stick and wearing a rather ugly expression as she shouted with a screeching voice. The little boy's pointed ears narrowed, and he grumbled while pushing past me.

"Friends should know what kind of games their friends like," the young boy said with a final remark, then ran down the street, leaving me feeling bewildered at how a child could negatively affect me.

Stupid kid. Even if he's right. I should know what Lillie likes, shouldn't I?

I wandered the stone path through the narrow buildings as it curved, noticing doors open quickly, then slam shut. The city-dwellers quickly turned a corner when seeing me, making it rather difficult to approach anyone else. Yet, after taking another corner, the path opened up into a large square where people were crowded. I noticed a stone structure nearby where people were drawing water with buckets, and others were talking loudly, and some people appeared to be trading as they handed each other different materials. However, I noticed a man drop some shiny metal objects, then took a large sack from another. Then, a group of people were pushing carts fully loaded with large rocks. The longer I lingered with observation, the more complex it all appeared. Yet all of Lillie's stories—all of the things that never made sense began to connect within my mind as I watched her world unravel before me, despite not knowing what Pocket-Ball was.

Most of the people looked similar to Lillie. The older ones had dull gray skin, some stronger with undertones than others. All had pointed ears and heads full of hair in braids, men with beards and women with complex hairstyles. Most wore tanned hides as tunics, linen shirts in earthy tones, and many of the women wore skirts, and some men had aprons covered in dark substances, but I did not notice any colorful clothing items. It was as if the forest was alive, and the earth and trees were moving after their roots had turned into legs. However, unlike a forest, the noises were far from pleasant.

The area was loud with the rumble of people talking, squawking birds in metal cages, and there was constant movement of people and overbearing carts rolling across the stone ground. It was my first time seeing so many people gathered, although the space was rather large. My sharp eyes were struggling to make out what was a person, a stone, an animal, a moving cart, or a building. It became blurry the longer I attempted to observe each detail, and my inner ear began to ring. Beads of sweat dripped from my forehead, causing the discomfort from the environment to disrupt my entire body.

"Hey, watch it!" someone yelled next to me. I felt a powerful push at my legs, and I moved aside while looking around. A man was moving a cart full of dark rocks, and I continued to step aside from him, but then accidentally bumped into another person who tried pushing past me.

"Move it!" the man shouted after shoving me. He snarled and glared at me as he tried getting past others. I twisted around, realizing there were more heavily loaded carts coming, and I was in the middle of their pathway. The people directing their carts waved their hands, yelling angrily and flaring their nostrils. I stepped out of the way, only to get pushed by others.

Before, the people were avoiding me. Here, they didn't seem as motivated to get out of my way.

"Ode!" a woman screeched, then elbowed me in the stomach.

"Eek!" another shrieked, and I felt hands grip at my feathers. I began fumbling my way through the crowd, diving deeper into the dense area of people.

I was much bigger than them due to my height and wings, yet with their carts and other items, it was a game of push-and-shove. I could feel others being shoved away from me when I accidentally bumped into them. The people less fortunate of being forced into another direction by my faltering movements were feisty and quickly fought back, causing me to stumble onto others. It was a blur of chaos with apprehension of hurting others and trying to find a steady footing. I dared not use my wings for balance, afraid I could damage my feathers, especially after feeling people's fingers pass against them. I felt trapped in a back-and-forth motion, bouncing from one heavy shove to another. Regardless of my position, I felt no different than the helpless birds squawking in the metal cages.

"Hey!" I heard someone shout and consequently felt a sharp grip on my arm, and I was pulled through the crowd. Already disoriented and completely out of control, I allowed them to force me away, following their pull, not caring where I went. I only had a wishful hope that I could stop tumbling through the endless crowd.

The short person pulled me through the dense area and led me to a small spot where a few others were sitting near a cart and tables. They moved me to a safe place where I could finally stop moving and catch my breath.

"You alright?" a woman asked with a friendly tone. She still held onto my arm with a firm grip and patiently waited for me to breathe consistently again, casting cautious eyes upon me. Nearby, I noticed three other women observing. All were short in stature, and their faces looked old but kind, carefully examining me while lingering their working hands upon their laps.

"Yes, thank you," I said while looking at the woman who had just saved me from the crowd. I ruffled my wings, and looked over my shoulder, half expecting to see bent feathers, but thankful none were ripped out or broken.

"You can't let 'em push you around like that," the woman replied with a smile, and she released her hand from my arm. "Otherwise, they'll trample all over you. Not a cool way to go, if you ask me."

"Yes, I realized that too late."

"Never seen a Teragane brave Cedrus City before."

"Right now, I am regretting it." After I spoke, the four women laughed strangely at my remark. I looked around by tilting my neck up, noticing I was near the stone structure where I had seen people draw water from. The sound of water splashing echoed as people on the other side were lowering buckets, and I observed the carts near the group of women, noticing the textiles and objects that were inside. The women had tools in their hands, one was weaving a basket.

"Well, then what brought you here in the first place?" the woman who pulled me from the crowd asked.

"I'm looking for my friend, Lillie. Do you know her?" I questioned.

"Lillie?" the woman asked, and a surprised expression overshadowed her face. The other women looked at each other. At that moment, I realized how foolish I was to put myself in such a vulnerable position. They obviously knew of my people, possibly also called us demons. It was obvious that they acknowledged how rare it was for my kind to enter a dense area like this city. I was like a trapped bird, like the ones I saw in the cages.

"Yes, Lillie," I said, deciding to make the most of the situation. "She is seventeen, around your height, but has white hair; she likes to gather plants from the forest, and she loves to talk."

"Of course he would be looking for Lillie," the tallest woman said then rolled her eyes. "Who else would make friends with a Teragane?"

"Maybe they trade for medicine?" the basket weaving woman suggested.

"Then why'd she leave Jadis' shop and go looking for some Teragane? That doesn't make sense," sneered the tallest woman.

"Lillie used to bring me medicine when she trained with Jadis," the oldest of the women said while leaning over to another. "Now, I have to visit the apothecary on my own; stupid girl had to ruin such a good arrangement. I can barely afford to pay the taxes."

"Well, maybe you should work harder at your own trade," the tallest of the group sneered again. "Then you wouldn't have to rely on Lillie to help you. You know, she has no time for such things anymore. At least, that is what Marie says."

"She once brought us fish at random," said a woman who looked severely sleep-deprived. My brows raised at the subject of fish. "I was so grateful for her that day. Made such delicacies, but, alas, with five children, it did not last long."

"Oh, she gave me a fish too," the oldest woman said, then she began coughing.

"Where in the world would Lillie find—oh, never mind," the tallest of the group said quickly while shaking her head. "She was so pretty, but now her hair has gone white, and she looks terribly gaunt."

"Yes, Lillie, where can I find her?" I asked, interrupting the women's conversation, although I despised the last thing said. The woman who pulled me from the crowd examined me with a puzzled expression.

"And why are you looking for Lillie?" she asked. I noticed white powder on the tip of her nose, and she wore a beige covering over her clothes that was covered with specks of the white dust. I was curious if she worked with Lillie, for the scent of yeasty aromas of bread permeated from her clothes.

"Everyone seems to be looking for her these days," the tallest woman remarked loudly. "Poor Marie can't keep anyone from bothering her for something. It's the deer carcass all over again."

Deer carcass? Medicine? Oh, perhaps they think I'm here to trade—that's how this world works, right?

"I need to find her," I said directly to the helpful woman with specks of white powder upon her gray skin. "I have fish for her, and—uh, I have arranged to meet with Lillie, but I can't seem to find where she lives." Immediately, the other women leaned closer; their long, pointed ears perked in unison. I assumed the fish the women spoke of was the very fish I had given Lillie before winter. I had hoped that she would find a good use for the food I gave her, but a feeling of frustration festered, especially the tones in which the women used.

"Well, where did you plan to meet?" the woman asked, and a bead of sweat dripped down the side of my face.

"Her house, of course. But, I keep getting lost in—uh, Cedrus City. Can you help direct me?"

"Oh, that would make sense," the sleep-deprived woman said loudly. The tallest and oldest nodded and murmured in agreement, as if I needed a solid reason to seek out Lillie—perhaps she was someone of importance. A leader? An important trader providing the city with food from the forest?

"See, I told you it's the deer carcass all over again," the tallest woman sneered, her head bobbing. "Now, it's fish. Marie will not like this. They really need to open a market stall or something to control the demands. Poor foreigners getting lost in the Divcii district. Their little house is too small to run a business."

"At least it's food from the forest and not from the allotment," commented the sleep-deprived woman. The helpful woman glanced at the other talkative women, then looked at me. "And the taxes to run a business isn't worth the effort. Believe me. They're better off running things without the tax regime getting involved."

"All the more reason for the silly girl to stop this nonsense," the tallest woman scoffed. "She'll bring only trouble. Look what kind of attraction she has already procured." My eyes widened while sweat continued to drip down my skin, but the helpful woman suddenly grabbed my hand, and pulled me away.

"Come with me," she said. The other women's voices continued behind us as the woman with the powdered nose began weaving us through the crowded area. She was skilled at dodging overbearing carts and large items, and swiftly moved around people as needed, and she paved the way for me to follow directly behind her. As we wove through the density of people and market items, I realized how starkly different I appeared in the crowd of light gray-skinned people. I was taller than everyone; most came up to my chest, and some were even shorter. I felt like a giant amongst the forest people.

In contrast with their earthy tones of brown and green, my clothes were black and a dark gray. My black feathers cast a cryptic shadow behind me, causing me to feel like a looming, dark creature passing through the crowds of unsuspecting forest-dwellers born of roots and moss, warmed by the red hues of the cedar trees in which their homes and businesses rested within. They moved around me with alarmed faces; some even looked angry as they twisted their necks to gaze up at my formidable stature, and I distinctly heard some mumble the word *demon*.

The woman guided me to a different path on the other side of the dense area, and stopped at the start of a new street that was lined with buildings similar to the one I had walked through before.

"I couldn't stand to listen to them yap anymore," she said while looking behind us, and I nodded in agreement, ignoring the shiver running down my spine. "Anyway, follow this on the right side and past the blacksmith. Walk until you find The Crooked Bow—a sign with a bow and arrow—and two houses over will be Lillie's house."

"Thank you," I nearly gasped, feeling glad to be away from the crowd and group of women, but, more importantly, closer to finding Lillie.

"Listen," she said sternly and I looked intently at her. "I care about Lillie. Don't get her into any trouble, you hear? If you really are her friend, then you will do good by her, right? Her parents can be finicky, difficult to approve of their daughter's methods, but she deserves to achieve her goals."

"I agree," I reassured. The woman's hazel eyes narrowed, her thin brows furrowing, and she tapped the front of her covering, causing a puff of dusting to form. "I will always do good by Lillie."

"Alright. You better. Otherwise, you'll get a beatin' from me."

"Oh, okay," I said. Suddenly, a flood of memories of Lillie's stories of constantly fighting with others reminded me that these people are ones who easily defend themselves through physical aggression. I swallowed the discomfort piling in my throat, and held my head high as I nodded, hoping to hide my fear of this woman's threats. Despite her relatively short stature, her arms, however, appeared strong enough to follow through, and her wide stance easily capable of holding her own against me if she were to attack like a mother bear defending her cubs.

"Thank you for helping me," I said, and I walked away.

At least she cares about Lillie—enough to direct me towards her house—and threaten me.

She must be a good friend.

I trudged along the path, staying directly on the right side, following the woman's instructions. I felt lucky to be helped by someone who knew and cared about Lillie, regardless of the threats. As I walked, I began remembering the things the other women said about Lillie. It seemed odd that they would speak in such a way that felt condescending. And Lillie's mother? Well, I already knew that Lillie had a difficult relationship, but I did not realize how complex and involved others were. Why were these women speaking about it so openly? Why did it feel judgmental?

Did my mother ever speak to others about me that way?

What did my mother think of me? I didn't recall much of her nor anything negative about our relationship. Yet, I was only a child.

I thought of the little boy I had earlier seen. The woman calling for him could have been his mother. She appeared angry, demanding, and his little arms were strong, but thin—too thin. Was this the life of these children?

Was Lillie once also a little child with torn clothes and a screaming mother barking orders to gather firewood?

The overwhelming thoughts about all my interactions filled my mind as I walked down the path leading me closer to Lillie. I passed by many buildings and people who gave me glaring-looks, but I continued to ponder through the experiences. Yet, the unnerving sensation of the reality of this place overwhelmed me the most.

Why do I feel so weird right now?

CHAPTER FIFTEEN
WHEN SOMETHING FEELS FAMILIAR

I recounted that I had not slept nor eaten since the previous day, and even that wasn't enough, for I had waited all day in the meadow without eating any of the food I had intended to share with Lillie. Adrenaline was pumping through my blood and courage from my heart, but that alone proved to no longer hide my hunger and exhaustion. I was walking more than usual, and my feet hurt from the stone pathways. My soft and pliable leather boots were excellent for landing on different types of surfaces and keeping my balance. In contrast, the boots were not designed for treading for lengthy periods of time, especially on stones. The constant state of anxiety and discouragement from the negative responses from the people of the city also drained my disposition, causing me to slow down.

Just make it to the house and worry about sleep and food later.

I heard loud clanging noises that pierced the air as I passed by a spacious awning nestled between the towering buildings. Smoke and sparks caught my attention. A large, muscular man lifted his metal tool and swung it upon a metal surface, which created small sparks and clanking vibrations. After repeating the action, he then moved the metal into a fiery furnace, pulling a chain above that activated a mechanism I did not understand, only that the fire grew vibrant and smoke spewed intensely from the furnace.

The man was covered in soot; his sleeveless tunic exposed his gray, muscular arms, which were covered in scars. He then removed the now glowing object from the furnace, placed it on the metal surface, and began pounding it with a tool once again. He stopped and looked up at me, causing my neck to tense as his glare was one that could pierce through skin if he were to stare any longer. Fortunately, he resumed his work, directing his piercing gaze while swinging his powerful arm with the force of a bear.

"Hey, git!" someone yelled from behind me, and I jumped out of the way. A young man no older than Lillie approached next to me, pushing a wooden cart full of black rocks.

He sneered as he entered the workspace, attempting to imitate the muscular man's sharp glare, and I quickly resumed walking down the street, hoping to subdue the stabbing sensation pricking my neck.

The black soot covering him seemed oddly uncomfortable, but maybe that was the blacksmith. I wonder what he is making? Or what he uses with the rocks? Or—

Up ahead, I saw a wooden sign carved from the red wood of the cedar tree. There were jumbling lines under a curved stick with a string and another stick but with a feather on one end, a pointed object on the other. I recalled the woman's information about The Crooked Bow, and I curiously approached the small building and peered inside the dusty window. Animal pelts lined the walls, as did crates of supplies, and I recognized some metal traps I had once seen in the forests while in my early years of training. A small group of people gathered around a shopkeeper who was showcasing what looked like a weapon of some sort. The group of villagers were chatting, smiling, and observing the object. Another man was holding up a knife, inspecting its blade that looked oddly familiar to the one Lillie carried in her pocket.

This must be a hunting shop. Maybe this is where Lillie got her knife. She often talked about shops and markets...the trading system is so...complex, yet ingenious.

I counted two houses from the shop, then approached it cautiously. There was a side door with an awning above, and I knocked and then quietly waited. I heard a bustling sound of pots and pans, some shouting, and then a rustle of footsteps. The door opened and revealed an older woman who appeared rather disgruntled.

"What do you want?" she scowled. "I don't owe taxes for another week!"

"I'm looking for Lillie," I said. "I am a friend." The woman's face softened, but a slight change into deep concern flushed over her face.

"Lillie is the daughter of my friend's neighbor; she lives in the house above." The older woman pointed up, then suddenly slammed the door, startling me for a moment. I looked over and saw a small spiraling staircase leading towards the upper house, and I walked carefully up the narrow steps. It was made of cob, formed strategically to spiral up to the second level. Again, I feared my weight was not suitable for the infrastructure of the city. But, alas, nothing broke underneath my footing.

I entered a small, wooden balcony with a railing that overlooked the street below and was covered by the house from above. Two wooden stools stood on either side of the door.

A small wooden table had a clay pot that smelled strongly of herbs; a wooden tube with carved holes sat near the pot, stirring more curiosities within my mind.

I knocked on the door between the small cloudy glass windows. The wood was artistically carved, not of cedar but from a different type of tree that had long lost its scent. I noticed the variations in building materials, from the red cedar to the oak-like wood, the cob staircase, and the many different types of stones.

How interesting. Everything is made from different materials. There are so many details...so many—

"Who's there?" a muffled voice called as a shadowy figure emerged from behind the cloudy glass window.

"Greetings, my name is Sable," I called back. I bent over, leaning closer to the door. "I am a friend of Lillie."

"What do you want?" the feminine voice asked.

"I've come to see Lillie," I said.

A revelation suddenly popped into my head—I had no idea what Lillie's parents knew about me. Perhaps I needed to continue to lie about my purpose? Although I knew my reason was to see her and meet with her to affirm her wellbeing, I thought about the fish from my earlier encounter.

The door slowly opened up, revealing a woman cautiously looking up at me. Her face resembled that of an older Lillie, but perhaps more disgruntled.

This must be her mother, Marie.

"Friend of Lillie?" she said while opening the door wider.

"Yes, I am Sable. We are friends and I have some things to discuss with her," I said, hoping to build better trust in my purpose of visiting.

The woman was old, had deep-set wrinkles on her forehead, and had faded gray hair that was braided loosely. Her brows were thin, and her green eyes were hooded, almost engulfed by the dark circles underneath. She smiled with one feigning friendliness and rolled-up her sleeves, showcasing her aged skin even more.

"Welcome, Sable, please come in," she said and quickly stood aside to allow me within the house. "I'm Marie, Lillie's mother." I walked in, looking around cautiously. The ceiling was low, but not enough to bend my figure, only when walking through the doorway.

"You must have traveled a long way," she said. "Are you hungry?" My stomach growled instantly, and the aching shot a sharp pain through my abdomen. My eyes felt heavy, and my feet were weary from extensive walking, and I felt safe for a moment—at least safe enough to re-energize my body. I remembered Lillie specifying that there were no rivers in the forest, and the complexities of retrieving food too formidable for me to even attempt by myself.

"I am hungry," I said. "But I don't want to bother you."

"No bother at all. I was just preparing food for dinner, but you can have some leftover breakfast if you so desire." My stomach continued to make growling noises, as if the invitation was directed to my belly, and the smell of familiar aromas filled my nostrils. I recognized the scent of bread and potatoes. I could feel closer to Lillie already.

Marie beckoned me to follow her into the kitchen. We walked through a narrow hallway, passing by two doors, and entered a large, dim room that was rather stifling, but at least smelled wonderful. There was a small wooden table with three chairs in the corner, and, within the domed, clay fireplace, a pot steamed over the flames with delicious smells. Under the orange flames was a metal door, in which Marie leaned down to open, and pulled out a brown loaf of bread, and I recalled Lillie speaking about how often she had to clean the oven. There were giant pots on stones lining the walls, and dried plants hanging from a wooden beam across the ceiling. I noticed large legs of animals hanging as well, and recognized the crates filled with dirt-covered potatoes that I once helped Lillie clean during one of our cooking adventures.

Marie scooped with a wooden spoon in a pot, then poured the contents of mush into a small bowl, then moved it over to the wooden table. She gestured for me to sit, and I sat down and ate the soft mush. I began to feel even more ravenous, and Marie continued to bring bits of dried fruits, then nuts, and, soon, a slice of the freshly baked bread, which I shamelessly gobbled up every crumb placed before me.

"My, goodness, you are hungry," she said with a cackle. "I will need to cut more meat up for dinner—if you desire to stay, of course."

"Oh, please do not overwhelm yourself for my sake," I said as I lifted my head up, and placed the empty bowl down on the table. "I have just forgotten to eat anything today—or sleep." I didn't know the time of the day, for I normally would calculate by the position of the sun. However, in the forest, there was no sun—only a looming darkness from above.

"Gracious, you must be exhausted," she said while stirring the pot over the open fire. "Would you like to rest?"

Lillie. I must see Lillie.

"Please, I am looking for Lillie," I said desperately, and I tapped my finger against the table.

"Lillie is at work." The woman smiled reassuringly as she brought another bowl of mush and patted my shoulder. "You can see her tonight at dinner. What trading did you bring for her? That is why you are here, or?"

Trading? Oh, right. Yes, she must assume I'm here to trade with Lillie...

It was clear, by now, that Lillie was well known and often made trades, or connected with others—another thing to be hesitant about since it appeared that Marie was not supportive of her daughter's abilities, at least, on account of what the other women had said. However, it was all I had, and, perhaps to keep my position and earn the trust of this woman who was my closest connection to finding Lillie.

I thought about the fish again but realized I had not brought any. I needed something for that moment. I looked at my cloak, then at my satchel which I carried attached to my waist belt.

"A satchel," I lied. I untied the leather straps from my waist and placed the bag on the table. It was simple—the pouch made from linen and the straps of leather—given to me as a resource to gather my food. Marie walked over and picked up the satchel, observing it. She frowned, furrowing her brows. Then, in a flash, she switched her expression.

"It smells like fish," she said, her uncanny smile hiding her disgust. "We have plenty of bags. I'm afraid we have no use for this." She placed it on the table, then returned to stirring the pot over the fire. My heart began to beat fast, and panic surged through my body as I sensed a change of tone in Marie's voice. What if she turns me away before Lillie comes home?

Well, I could just wait outside until she arrives. Yet, what if her mother disapproves of me and unleashes wrath upon Lillie?

No. I needed to make a strong stance for myself with this woman if I was to prevent harm to Lillie—just like that woman said. I cannot cause my love any harm. I must do right by her.

"Yes, it's a satchel to carry fish," I continued. Marie's pointed ears perked up and she slowly twisted her neck, looking over her shoulder at me.

"Are you a fishmonger?" she asked.

"Yes," I stated, and Marie tapped the rim of the metal pot and walked over to my side again, holding the spoon over her hand as bits of broth dripped.

"Well, why didn't you say so?" she said, her smile beaming wide as her demeanor returned to one of friendliness. "Then, I would be happy to host you as you wait for Lillie to return. I'm sure the two of you have lots to arrange."

"Yes, we do," I replied, steadying my voice as my racing heart began to ease. Although I did not like lying to her, it gave me time and a place to rest while I waited for Lillie to return from work.

Marie's interest in me was based only on what I had to offer her daughter. Perhaps this was my chance to establish myself with Lillie's parents, including her father, whenever he would come. Hopefully, I could avoid disruption in Lillie's life, and gain her trust even more now that I was willing to enter this part of her life after she struggled to explain things to me she thought I was incapable of knowing.

"Is it still possible to rest while I wait?" I asked Marie while she continued to move about the kitchen, seemingly accepting me. The warm environment caused me to feel exhaustion overtake my senses, and I felt as if I would fall asleep sitting at the table.

"Of course," she said, then wiped her hands on the covering that was similar to the helpful woman in the city. "After you are finished eating, I will show you to a bed." I consumed the second bowl of mush, and Marie brought me another. She even offered a fourth, but I refused, feeling as if I would collapse as my stomach felt full, but my body ached for sleep.

Lillie's mother showed me to a different room. It was small, like the rest of the house, but filled with beautiful things and earthy scents that I instantly recognized. Dried flowers hung from the ceiling beams, and large paintings were pinned to the walls. Wooden beads, ribbons, and other sorts of strings sat idle on top of a wooden cabinet. Lillie's new deep green wool coat hung from a hook on the wall, and I noticed that the stain that I had caused from last month had been cleaned off. I recognized Lillie's basket sitting on the floor and the blanket lying on the foot of the bed. The smell of plants and dried grass reminded me of her earthy scent, bringing a sense of affinity. But, most importantly, I could smell the floral aroma I loved so much.

"I'm afraid I do not have a guest bedroom, but this is Lillie's room," the woman stated while smiling. "I'm sure she doesn't mind if you use it while you rest."

"Thank you," I said. "For the food and also for letting me wait for Lillie. Please wake me upon her arrival. We have much to discuss."

"Of course. Lillie's friends are very important to her, and I wouldn't want you to feel unwelcome. I look forward to hearing what the two of you arrange. I have many ideas on how to prepare fish." She beamed with an uncanny smile, slowly disappearing behind the closing door. The metal mechanism clicked, and I was alone, but ever so grateful.

I looked around again, allowing the familiar scents to fill my nostrils, making me feel less alone in this foreign city. I removed my boots, my belt and satchel, and my woolen cloak, and I laid the items on the floor. I stood under some hanging plants and drifted my hand into the stems, pressing against the small buds and brought some to my nose.

Ah—these little purple flowers are what she often smells like.

I picked a few more and placed the buds in my pocket, then I bent down and picked up the blanket I knew all too well. I brought it close to my nose and breathed in the familiar smells. The soft fibers felt comforting against my face. Then, I laid the blanket onto the bed, and crawled on top, allowing my wings to hang over on the side. I clutched the blanket and pulled it close to my nose, and the scents caused me to feel safe and closer to seeing Lillie again. I didn't know what to expect, nor could I imagine anything beyond the surprise Lillie would have upon seeing me in her house.

Yet, she had claimed I was the lone Teragane who could never understand her complex world.

So, hopefully, this would all prove how far I was willing to go for her, especially now that I was beginning to understand why she would not want to leave such an ingenious city that had more to offer than a simple life in the trees.

I slept for a while, and awoke to the floral scents against the blanket, but also the strong smells of the cooking stew from the fireplace. Familiar spices and unknown flavors wafted the room with their desirable scents, intermixing with Lillie's aroma. I sat up and stretched my shoulders. As my wings extended, a startling noise resounded, and I quickly caught a painting from the wall before it crashed onto the floor from my wings hitting it out of place.

While I folded my wings, I put the wooden frame onto the hook on the wall, straightening it as if it never fell in the first place. The bed was small—too small for my size. However, it was pleasant. Unlike my stone and animal pelt bed, it was soft, squishy, and smelled like Lillie. I cautiously moved around the room, looking for possible signs of her, hoping that she had returned.

Her basket sat idle in the corner, clothes scattered across the floor, glass items filled with plants, and odd trinkets made of wood sitting neatly on some furniture. There was an open basket with knitting supplies I had remembered her bringing often to the meadow, and a crimson material caught my eye. Then, my eyes noticed her brown scarf laying across the floor. I realized, nothing seemed different or changed than when I had first arrived.

I wonder if Lillie is even home yet. She will be so surprised to see me! I can't believe I slept in her house—on her bed.

A shiver ran down my spine, and a fuzzy feeling grew in my stomach as I eyed the bed still draped with the meadow blanket. An image of Lillie laying on top caused me to tremble for a moment. Would she be angry that I slept on her bed? Embarrassed? Excited?

Why do I feel so weird?

I put my boots on, and draped my cloak over my shoulders, allowing the split material to lay correctly between my wings and over my shoulders. After strapping my belt and satchel to my waist, I adjusted the loose ends of the cloak accordingly, yet the humid air felt stifling. I exited Lillie's room, following the delicious aromas coming from the kitchen. I easily navigated my way back to the cooking area, where Marie was stirring a pot set above the open fire and humming to herself.

"It smells delicious," I said, startling Marie for a moment, but she eased her alarm when she gazed upon me with her uncanny smile. Although it was obvious the women were related, Lillie's smile was more genuine, and her eyes intentional, even if a bit mysterious at times. Her mother? Also mysterious, but not in a pleasant way.

"Oh, you're awake," she said, her tone causing me to tense. "I hope you slept well. You were asleep all afternoon."

"Yeah, I am not used to walking so much," I said as I sat myself down at the table and I rustled my messy hair timidly. The chair obviously made for the smaller people of the forest creaked and I felt nervous that it could break, and my wings felt odd being separated by something against my back.

"Well, as a Teragane, I can't imagine you ever needing to."

"True, but it can be quite useful, especially in dense forests and cities."

"Of course. Do you often travel to Cedrus City to sell fish? Do you work for anyone in particular? Lords, families?"

Oh yeah. I'm a fishmonger...

"No," I said truthfully.

"Oh? Then, you are establishing yourself first as an individual?"

"Something like that."

"You're smart. Working for a master will only bring you hardship, unless, of course, you can move up in the classes. But I can hardly imagine someone like you able to do that." She eyed me with that unpleasant expression, and my eyes darted away. "And, you picked the right girl to establish your individual trade. Lillie is an excellent resource. She knows many people and can establish a good trading arrangement. Of course, she also demands a high price for such vendee purposes." Marie chuckled, obviously pleased with herself.

"And she deserves a reward for her extensive pursuit," I said, playing the part.

"Yes, she does. Not many traders have that same attitude. You can get trampled by greedy buyers if you're too generous. Being without a backer can also be troublesome."

"Of course."

"Huh, I've never met a Teragane merchant before. Life on the mountain isn't good enough anymore?"

"I uh—" I realized that I had no idea how much information Lillie's mother knew about me. I needed to keep Lillie safe but also protect my own kind. "I wouldn't say that. Lillie and I are old friends. We've traded in the past, and I—uh—decided to come see her here to—to establish my trade, of course."

"Ah, I see," Marie said. "Well, that is very kind of you. Except, I don't recall Lillie ever bringing home fish before..."

Oh, great...

I felt beads of sweat piling on my forehead, and the layers of wool material covering my body felt irritating in the heated cooking room. I had never lied before in my life—I never needed to—and I suddenly felt trapped in my efforts. My throat became dry, and my cheeks felt flushed. The stiff air from the lack of ventilation in the room caused me to choke, inducing a coughing fit.

"Oh, here, have some water," Marie said while pouring water from a pitcher into a wooden cup. I gulped it down, soothing my dry throat, but my fingers nervously tapped the surface of the table.

"Thank you," I said, my voice sounding raspy. She nodded, yet eyed me suspiciously as she awaited my reply. I quickly thought of other things Lillie often would bring home. I thought about her stories and her trading different plants and wild food with neighbors.

Berries, potatoes, plants, seeds, flowers—

"Trading fish is a new idea," I said. "We traded plants and berries in the past—uh, I showed her places to find these things outside of the city." I drank the rest of the water, hoping to hide my nervousness.

"I see," she replied while pursing her lips. "Well, I'm glad you can make some new arrangements. We could use some different meat sources."

"That's why I'm here."

"I may as well open up a hostel these days. And a trading shop. Everyone is always looking for Lillie and what new plants or creatures she finds in the forest."

"Yes, she has a true skill in finding plants and creating something from them."

"Of course she does; she learned from me. I taught her everything she knows."

"And you have done well." Marie looked at me and beamed with pride. It appeared she had finally accepted my story, and she happily stirred the pot of food. I let out a long exhale, wiping my forehead while her back was turned as she moved around the room.

I'm never lying again.

The sound of a door slamming resounded from the hallway, and I jolted my head up as I eyed the narrow walkway, feeling as if my heart would suddenly burst from within.

"Excuse me," Marie said as her smile disappeared, and she then exited the kitchen rather quickly. I stood up, patted down my clothes, and brushed down my wing feathers while my heart raced. There was a hanging steel pot where I noticed my reflection. I walked over and saw my face clearly for the first time. My hair was a black, tangled mess, in which I tried combing with my fingers, patting down the sides, but it was useless. My hair looked like a bird's nest after the eggs had hatched and learned to fly, leaving behind a disaster of upturned sticks. Then, I noticed my eye color for the very first time.

Red—crimson red, like the deep color of berries in the woods or that material I saw in Lillie's room—crimson red like fresh blood.

My eyebrows were thick but jagged, black as night, like my hair. I opened my mouth and noticed my sharp canine teeth. My jawline was angular and smooth, and my nose was narrow and straight.

I saw myself for the very first time and was not impressed, particularly how messy my hair looked—and my eyes. I stepped back, noticing how intimidatingly different I appeared in comparison to the earthy forest-dwellers with my dark presence and wings—my eyes the color of blood lingering after a fresh kill.

No wonder these forest people keep looking at me weird...

Low muffled sounds alerted me to the arrival of others, and I quickly spun around, no longer interested in my physical appearance as my heart raced to see Lillie again—but, alas, she was not there.

Only an older man with Marie entered the kitchen.

"Sable, this is my husband, Bene," Marie said while her expression had changed to one of distress.

"Hello, Sable," the older man said.

"Greetings, Bene," I replied with a slight bow.

"Do you smoke?" he asked, and Marie moved over to the pot and began scooping up the stew.

"I—uh—I'm afraid I do not understand," I replied, sensing the disapproval from the man as he scoffed, then sat down at the table while Marie placed three bowls onto the surface and then beckoned for me to sit down again. I obeyed, feeling nervous at making a decent impression, but I looked at the empty entrance, desperately hoping to see Lillie walk through. My stomach had grown hungry again, but discomfort still swirled through my mind. Yet, here I was, once again thinking how I could establish my place in Lillie's world while sitting with her parents.

Bene was a little taller than Marie, but much older. His face had deep-set wrinkles, and his skin was gray as stone. In the firelight, Marie's undertones were somewhat visible, but Bene had no hint of the vibrant undertones of the cool hues. His hands were rough and scarred, similar to Lillie's, but much worse. His hair was gray with dark undertones of brown and black. Similar to other men I saw before, it was braided, and pinned up, revealing his pointed ears. His full beard was thick and neatly trimmed along his square jawline, and it was dark brown with small patches of white. I easily recognized his loose brown shirt and leather trousers, remembering all the times Lillie used to mend clothes in the meadow.

Marie smiled sweetly at me, but I noticed a sense of discomfort, perhaps a dose of concern. Her clothes were similar to what Lillie would wear, but I did not see any wooden beads woven in her hair, and her green skirt looked relatively new—similar to Lillie's woolen cloak that she claimed was given to her by a friend. However, as my eyes noticed all the various difference between these caregivers, I grew rather uncomfortable being in their presence while Lillie had yet to arrive, and detested the sound of the wooden spoons scooping up the stew while her parents apathetically ate their meal.

"This is delicious," I said, breaking the silence. Marie smiled at me and nodded her head, but Bene's eyes did not move as he stoically stared at the table.

Why hadn't Lillie returned from work? Why are we eating without her?

I did not exactly understand the customs or rituals of these people, but I remembered many stories that Lillie talked about eating meals together as a family. Sitting in silence, eating their food, and not knowing anything about Lillie's whereabouts was slicing away at my heart. The intensity of the reticence pressed me to find the answer I so desperately sought for.

"So, why is Lillie not here for dinner?" I asked. "Does she usually arrive home well after the sun has set?" The older man paused his eating completely. He dropped his hand on the table with a loud thud. Suddenly, he stood up, pushing the table slightly, and glared at me.

"Marie, I need to talk to you in private," he announced, and she looked alarmed, her eyes widening, and they walked into the other room, closing a door behind them. I heard the muffled sound of intense conversation, eventually leading to yelling.

What could be wrong? Is it me? Are they hiding Lillie from me? But why feed and shelter me?

A whirlwind of questions and undesirable thoughts overwhelmed my mind as I tapped the table and bounced my foot. Did Lillie not want me around? Did something happen? Do they know about me and my suggestion for Lillie to leave this life behind?

My heart dropped as I halted my nervous tapping.

Over the years, Lillie spent less and less time with me due to her obligations. Was this the final act of cutting me out of her life?

No—she would have said goodbye, wouldn't she?

What is going on? Where is Lillie? If only I could just talk to her. Yes, if I could just talk with her and understand from her what she wants, then I would do as she pleases. If she wants me to leave and never see her again, then so be it. But what if she is in trouble?

"Young man," Bene said with a firm voice as he entered the kitchen again. I stood up, pushing the chair behind with my wings, and my figure towered over him, causing him to puff up his chest like an animal trying to intimidate a formidable opponent.

"We are grateful for the offer of arranging trade with Lillie, but we decided that our daughter needs to focus on her current work," he said. "You should not bother her at her home ever again. So, go back to where you came from. Cedrus City is no place for your kind."

"Bene, please," I said. "I am only concerned for her well-being. You see, we planned to meet yesterday, but she did not arrive, and that is not like her. I just want to know if she is well." Bene's gray eyes glared and a slight twitch appeared under one eye.

"I do not want you to ever meet with my daughter again. You are nothing but a distraction from her work. She is too old to be fluttering about with—well, people like you."

My eyes widened as my hands curled into fists at my side.

"Respectfully, I do not agree," I said calmly. "Lillie has always prioritized her life well. I see no reason for you to claim such an opinion."

"Shameful of you to speak so intimately of my daughter. How do you even know her? Did you attempt to pick her up as a meal? Teraganes don't belong here. You're nothing but savages of the mountains, feasting on the farm animals like demons in the night."

"I—I am not a savage. Please. I need to know where Lillie is and if she is well."

"I owe you nothing. My wife has already given you too much. Leave, now, before I call the enforcements to drag you out of the city."

His threats were obvious, his stubbornness and anger similar to Lillie's, but nothing of the sort of capable of reasoning with. I lowered my eyes, and slightly bowed.

"Your wife has been generous, and I would like to thank her for her kindness."

"She is a fool to show a savage any sort of kindness. Get out and never return."

I walked past the angry man, his eyes still glaring as my wings brushed against his broad figure. He followed me from a distance as I looked for Marie. I heard her exit the room across from Lillie's. She was wiping tears from her eyes, and she hobbled to the door. She looked at me with a grin, but a sense of fear emanated from her reddened eyes.

"Marie, thank you for your kindness and delicious food. Please tell me, where is Lillie?" I begged the woman. I could hear the man walking faster toward me as Marie's face sank into a shallow terror, and she lowered her gaze completely as I stepped closer to her.

"My daughter is making a great career for herself, and I'm afraid she has no time for trading with outsiders anymore," she said. "I'm glad you feel rested and filled, but we can unfortunately no longer host you." She bowed and opened the door for me, and a putrid city breeze pressed against my sweaty face. Her hands trembled, and she folded them behind her back, but she kept her head bowed, refusing to look at me.

"Leave, now, I will not ask another time," I heard Bene's voice come from behind me. I had a strong urge to attack him. I wanted so badly to turn and grab and push him into the wall, and demand to know where his daughter was, and my hands balled into fists as my muscles tightened.

I could easily overtake and threaten him. He is weakened by age. I could use my strength, size, and terrifying stature to interrogate him.

I could do it.

I turned around and looked straight into Bene's eyes. I felt raw strength, inspired by the power of the bears, gather in my arms and flex my fingers—a savagery sense flowing through my blood.

When I looked at him, I felt the intensity of both of our glaring eyes. Yet, for a moment, his eyes mirrored Lillie's. They were soft and caring—conflicted. As I stood face-to-face with Lillie's father, I saw the hurt in his eyes. I saw pain, and an unmistakable aura of terror. That man, angered in his face, a threat to my own pursuance of Lillie, was no more than just a terrified man who saw me as a threat—like a savage.

Was I?

I lowered my hands and relaxed my muscles, yet my wings still twitched.

No.

"Good evening," I said respectfully and exited the house, and the door slammed loudly behind me.

CHAPTER SIXTEEN

WHEN ANGUISH OVERTAKES THE BODY

Two Years Prior

I landed on the soft grass in the meadow, immediately folding my wings as I spotted Lillie laying on the blanket. I approached her quietly, realizing that she was asleep. Her chestnut brown hair was twirled around her face, and her eyelids slightly twitched as she breathed deeply. Beads of sweat formed on her gray skin, and I crouched near her head, blocking the sun from causing too much discomfort while Lillie slept. She appeared peaceful, and I observed her rise and fall with each breath, enjoying the moment while it lasted. Her shoes were still on, which was odd, and I had never seen her sleep before.

I hope she is feeling well.

After her eyes flickered open and she realized I was beside her, she rolled to her side, rubbing her eyes and stretching her legs, and I greeted her with a soft hello.

"I guess I am just extra tired today," she said while picking at the fibers of the blanket. "I had a rough couple of weeks."

"How so?" I asked while observing her hands move along the blanket. Then, I looked at her face, and realized that tears were forming.

"Oh," she replied and I watched as a tear streaked down his cheek and settled upon her chin. "My—my father found my books." She pushed herself into a sitting position and rubbed her chin with the back of her arm.

"He took my books away," she said with a trembling voice. "He told me that I can't visit Historia in the library anymore."

"Why?" I asked. "Why would your father take something away that you love?"

"He says he must toughen me up for the realities of life. I don't know. I think he means well, but I wonder why life has to be so tough? And, why can't I try to make it easier, you know? Why can't I still enjoy the things that make me happy?"

145

"I understand training your child to endure through the hardships that life holds, like the cold winters and natural ways of life and death. But I don't understand why your father would purposefully deplete the joys in your life." Lillie's sorrowful eyes cast upon me, causing a wave of grief to pierce my heart. Her rosy cheeks glowed, and the cool summer breeze twirled her hair around her face.

"I don't understand either. He doesn't explain himself well, but sometimes I see the hurt in his eyes. Maybe he is just trying to protect me by making me tough. Maybe he doesn't know any other way."

"Perhaps."

"Maybe it is his only knowledge of love. Maybe, because of the pain of his own life, he is just trying to protect me, you know?"

"But, does protection and love have to hurt like this?"

"I don't know. But it seems the only way he and my mother know."

"Maybe it doesn't have to hurt. Perhaps it hurts because it's not love nor protection."

"Then what could it be?"

As an old memory of Lillie's narrative of her parents flooded my mind, I felt paralyzed while standing outside of her house. During that interaction two summers ago, I experienced sympathy for my friend, but nothing as aggressively painful as the anger began to rise in my chest after officially meeting the caregivers of Lillie. I felt so disgusted with a man I had just met, yet knew from a distant narrative.

Launching myself from the wooden railing on the balcony, I jumped down to the lowest street. I landed with a firm thud, feeling numb and shocked by the irritating encounter, and I tightened my hands into fists at my side while anger suddenly shifted to fear.

How am I ever going to find Lillie if her own parents won't help me?

My mind processed my interactions with Marie and Bene. I heard many stories about them through Lillie, but they seemed so distant, like ambiguous characters in a legend unrelated to my world. After facing them, they were real people in the present moment. The many complicated and unfortunate events they put Lillie through all began to make sense. Marie was warm and welcoming at first, but changed immediately when things did not appease her. She seemed interested in me after I had won her approval, but her demeanor drastically changed upon Bene's arrival. Regardless of my useful resources, she betrayed me once Bene decided I was a distraction for Lillie—like the books he once tore away from her.

But why was Marie upset?

Bene seemed like a hard worker; age and time could be read from the lines on his forehead, the roughness on his hands, and the sternness in his voice. But he lacked consideration for Lillie's interest. At least, that is what I assumed from this interaction and previous narratives made by Lillie.

Perhaps he truly sees me as a threat, a distraction for Lillie, similar to books and other joys Lillie had. Maybe that is why she did not come to the meadow. Maybe her father told her not to visit me anymore. It was his fault!

My skin began to crawl, and my blood boiled. I felt angry—angry with the man I had just met. Regardless of her being his daughter, I couldn't understand how he could be so dismissive of me—he had no right to treat me that way, no right to assume such things about me!

Lillie was my best friend—my *greatest* of friends; I deserved to hear the truth from her, not an assumption from him. They assumed my only interest was in trading with Lillie, but was I so far into that lie that I could not recover any information? What if I returned and told them the truth? Would they even accept that their daughter is friends with me? Was it worth the risk? What if they don't know about the meadow? What if Lillie kept that secret from them, like she hid her books? Bene took Lillie's books away, and he told her she was not allowed to continue reading lessons from her friend.

Wait, that friend—Historia. What if I look for her?

No—Lillie was forbidden from seeing Historia. How would I even find her? I can't even find Lillie!

What if Lillie was also on the cusp of being forbidden from seeing me? But—why was Marie crying? Did Bene hurt her? Did something happen to Lillie?

Why didn't she come home like Marie said she would?

Memories of Lillie's stories flooded my mind. She talked a lot about her life, and I listened, but I rarely paid attention to the important details. That information could have easily given me clues to my particular situation, just like talking about fish since Lillie had given away her fish I had previously given her. I felt like a terrible friend to Lillie. She complained so many times, often annoying me, yet, here I was, enduring the very same behavior in which she lived with on a daily basis, and I selfishly did not pay closer attention.

A group of children suddenly rushed past me, sneering as they kicked a round object back and forth, and I looked around.

This was Lillie's neighborhood. All these houses were homes and shops of the people who knew her best.

Maybe I could ask them?

I began knocking on each door on the first level. If a door opened, it was quickly slammed shut. The city dwellers shrieked, they sneered, and their tones were of utter distress or disgust upon seeing me, but, peculiarly, they shouted about taxes and something about Den—things I did not understand as I feared they thought I was someone only a threat to their lives. I ventured to the second layer of buildings in the neighborhood, but, as the shouts from the frightened folks only continued to evoke apprehension of pleading my cause, the night had suddenly drawn to a close and windows and doors were being shut tight.

The fires of the blacksmith had gone out, and there were no more children running down the streets. People shouted from above, telling me to leave, and I called out for help. But, no one was willing. Young, old, little, and tall—no one gave me any positive responses. As the night drew on, there were fewer people in the public area. I was mentally exhausted from pushing my comfort limits. I felt distraught at how stubborn the people were when it came to disclosing any type of useful information.

Does no one care to help me find Lillie?

I trudged further through the buildings, looking for a place to rest as the city lanterns were beginning to dim and exhaustion was overcoming my body. I noticed a large opening with protruding broken glass from an overhead tower. I ascended above the ground, and carefully glided through the broken opening, and entered the obviously abandoned room. It was almost empty, except for a few crates and broken tools. There was a closed trap door on the wooden floor, and the surface was dirty, cobwebs hung from the corners, and it smelled murky with a hint of rusted iron.

Feeling hopeless, I began pacing around the small area. I placed my hands on my head and pushed hard against my temples. I could not believe such a place existed with so many unkind people. Lillie was so different from the people I had met. The way the other women in the busy square talked with judgment about Lillie—the look from Lillie's father and the anger in his voice. Marie being so kind—giving me heaps of food, letting me rest—then coldly casting me out of her house. The glaring eyes, the pointing fingers, the pushing around in the busy square, and the doors slamming in my face.

Calling me a savage—a demon.

Oh, Lillie, I'm so sorry. I had no idea this was your world.

Yet, I realized that Lillie did tell me about her life. She so often told me stories about her parents' treatment, the struggle of making trades with others, and trying to learn without her parents meddling with her affairs. She did tell me all these things, but I was so apathetic and so naive. I was selfish, only concerning myself with my own life and what I wanted. I was a terrible friend. I didn't even know anything about her job, where she worked, or how to find out. I did not even know if she played games, like the children running through the streets—was that Pocket-Ball?

You selfish fool!

Tears rolled down my face. I cried harder than I ever thought I was capable of. I was alone—truly alone—in a foreign place that terrified me. I was alone with my overwhelming thoughts and memories of Lillie's harsh life flooding my mind. The overshadowing trees and dense buildings, the glaring looks and spiteful treatment from the people—the unmistakable pit in my heart of true fear. I had never experienced this type of loneliness nor this type of angst. As memories of Lillie's life filled my mind, my past experiences enmeshed in my head.

I remembered the first time I learned to fly. I had to jump from my mountain home. I was terrified of falling, yet my mother and father were next to me, encouraging me to take that first jump. When I saw the bears for the first time with my father, fear struck my young heart as I watched their aggressive behavior. My father calmed me, teaching me how to stay safe in the trees. His presence and wisdom subsided my fears. I remembered my earliest tattoos. My mother let me sit close to her, holding my hand through the pain. I was only a youngling, yet with her presence, I knew that I was safe. Even the Sage performing the ritual was kind and soft-spoken. Then, despite the fear I felt upon entering the great cedar forest for the first time with Lillie, gathering firewood, Lillie was there, and she helped me overcome my worries.

When I faced terror and fearful situations, I was not alone. No—someone was always there with me, easing the pain, and reminding me that there was nothing to fear and I had the power to overcome any apprehension I faced. I lived my life with this confidence. I never feared being out of control of what I wanted. Even when faced with uncertain, unforeseeable future outcomes, I never felt incapable of overcoming them and finding solutions. I always found my strength, and I always found the courage to face adversity.

Why? Because I was trained to be self-sufficient as a survivalist. My entire life of training was to give me the strength and the courage to face anything and know that I would be capable of overcoming any obstacle. Deep within my heart, I knew fear was temporary, only an instinctual alarm to help me recognize the danger ahead and adjust my plan of action accordingly. I knew, no matter what, that I was capable of overcoming any hindrance that stood in my way. When given the time, I could think of ways, search my surroundings, and create a plan of action to get what I wanted. In every situation, I always conquered my apprehension. But at that present moment?

I looked around the dusty area. I could not think of anything. I looked outside through the dismantled opening; the sharp edges of broken glass glistened from the light of a city lantern. I did not feel courageous nor capable. I could not think of solutions, and I could not resolve to find answers. Everything I tried failed. Everyone was turning against me. Every time I tried thinking of new ways, a door would shut in my face. I needed guidance in the wake of this new world. All my years of training on how to survive suddenly vanished from my mind.

Is this why the Sage was to return to me for instructions in spring? Was my training as a Teragane only partially complete?

I was alone, crying in an abandoned tower in the middle of the night in a foreign city. I was in a city full of people who did not want to help. Who could I seek out for guidance here?

I did not know how to find Lillie. She was obviously well known, but no one thought to help me find her. Why? Why were these people so against helping me find Lillie? Why were they so apathetic? How could they not care about her friends?

None of my instinctual ideas were working. I did not know if I would ever see Lillie again. The buried worries of losing Lillie—the fear that her parents would keep her from me or, worse, she wanted to rid herself of me—came exploding from the depths of my troubled soul.

Fear—no—utter despair and anguish filled my heart. I was distraught, I was alone, I was terrified, and I was paralyzed by all these new revelations overtaking my mind and body.

Tears ran down my face, my sharp teeth clenched, and my hands gripped my hair. I stopped pacing and slumped to my knees, causing my stiff body to quiver. I pulled my hair in anguish, ignoring the sharp pain in my knees and scalp. My wings went limp, faltering onto the floor in a disoriented form.

What am I even doing? Who do I think I am? Nothing! I am only a thoughtless fool. A naive savage from the mountain who doesn't belong here.

I—I do not belong in Lillie's world, for I am nothing but the lone Teragane from the mountain.

My heart dropped. I gasped at this thought, my jaw unlocked, and my teeth unclenched. I grabbed my heart and gasped, hot hair escaping my trembling mouth. I fell forward, catching myself with one hand on the floor, the other still grasping at my heart. I panted heavily as the tears fell onto the dirty wooden floor. My hair dangled in front of me, and my eyes burned from the dusty air and salt of my unending tears.

*I—I do not belong **with** Lillie.*

My eyes widened, and the burning sensation grew stronger. I let go of my chest, both hands clamped on the ground. My hands balled into fists; a shockwave ran down my spine as the onset of torture ensued in my body. I let out a cry, a scream of despair, like a howling beast facing its inevitable fears of being abandoned from its kind.

I fell over onto my side, crushing my limp wing, and my body curled into a fetal position. My wings were disoriented, limp, and crushed from my apathetic faltering, but I continued to ignore all decency of concern for myself. I lay there, paralyzed, feeling empty and cold. The darkness of the night cast a cold air, but I was already numb from desolation and the unbearable, horrible thoughts encircling my mind.

All this time, all these seasons of feeling as if I belonged with someone came crashing down like a tree being struck by lightning, and a forest fire was beginning to consume everything beautiful in its destructive path.

Only smoldering ashes would be left in its wake.

The life of the forest forever changed.

CHAPTER SEVENTEEN

WHEN A STRANGER GIVES A HELPING HAND

I woke up to the sound of a loud crash from below the tower. Somewhere, people were shouting. I pulled myself up into a sitting position, distributing dirt as I moved my legs and wings. My bones ached, and my neck cracked as I adjusted it side to side. A sharp pain surged through my head, and I pressed my palm against my forehead while dust particles floated as the dim light beamed through the broken window. I had cried myself to sleep, not caring how I positioned myself for the night on the floor, and began to regret my negligence. Upon the realization of all the terror of being alone, I knew that I was the only one I could rely on—I couldn't fail myself now.

Why does it hurt so much?

I stood up in the small, abandoned area, afraid I would begin to cry again as my aching heart pounded within my chest, and I realized the pain was not just physical. I stretched my afflicted body by twisting my back and moving my neck around. I extended my wings, and a severe shock of pain went through my muscles, for I had slept with my wings sprawled out on the dirty floor. I shook them out, distributing massive amounts of dirt into the air, and pain continued to spike through my body. With trembling legs, I stepped over to the broken window and peered out. The city was bustling once again with crowds of moving residents pushing their carts and barking their orders, and the low rumble of the disturbances slightly shook the abandoned tower. I scanned the area, trying to notice anything that looked familiar, wondering how far I had ventured into the city.

Maybe if I could just find my way back to the forest entrance, I could—

The aching of my soul caused me to gasp as my thoughts of escape from the city began to formulate. How could I give up on finding Lillie now? Was I really that incapable? How could I resolve to leave without finding the truth about Lillie?

But how could I ever find the answer?

She could be anywhere! You're nothing but an outsider—the savage from the mountain who doesn't understand this world.

Perhaps she was busy with work or could have been avoiding her parents last night. Maybe she was with her friends—her real friends that understood her.

I'll just return to the meadow next full moon and wait. If she doesn't come—well...

Like a sinking rock cast into a lake, the cold depths like water overwhelmed my body, causing my stomach to ache and induce nausea. I knew that I was helpless and alone in the city. I could not trust anyone besides Lillie, and it was obvious that even the people who knew her—parents, those women at the market, the neighbors—had no intention of helping me find her. Yet, why would they? They didn't know me—it was obvious that Lillie kept me hidden.

Was it to preserve herself from the discrimination of others? Was it to keep me a secret out of shame or guilt? Did she see me as an escape from this city, living in her own fantasy world within the meadow?

As my heart plummeted further into the concepts of sinking within a mountain lake, I realized I also saw Lillie as the same. I allowed my fantasies to run wild, but kept her hidden from the world as a Teragane. I wasn't willing to tell the others—not even Cami. Was it out of shame? Fear?

It was reasonable; no one would ever accept an outsider in my—

Oh—of course. Lillie and I were the same. We have our reasons according to tradition and cultures. Fantasies were only for dreaming, not reality.

So. I really was a fool after all this time. A fool lost in a dream bound to wake up sooner rather than later.

I had no idea how hot a fire can burn when played with. That must be the reason a Sage was to return for further guidance, teaching me how to navigate through emotional turmoil. Cami was right all along about the dangers of orange fires and its uncontrollable flames.

I looked at my filthy clothes. My cloak in its various layers twisted around, and I straightened it, tucking the ends back into my belt. I did my best to brush off the dirt, and the air filled with dust again, inducing a coughing fit.

Accepting my state of uncleanliness, I disregarded any concern for my current physical state and instead scanned the outside area once again. Beyond the storage room tower, there were many bridges ahead, tree branches, and overbearing structures that made flying above risky. I could not see any clearing anywhere and did not want to risk crashing through anything lurking above. The streets that weaved through the labyrinth and led out of the towering buildings were my best option to leave.

Maybe if I get back to that market area, I can fly straight up and out of this city. Or perhaps I will locate a clear opening while I'm walking around. Or I can find my way back to the forest and return to the meadow, like how I came.

Somewhat satisfied with my half-baked plans, I exited the abandoned storage room, gliding down to the street. I walked along the paths, and, again, received the negative onlooker's disapproval of my presence. This time, I did not make myself more approachable nor friendly-looking. I resolved to only return the glaring looks with my own scowls. This helped ease my disposition, creating a sense of control over my hopeless situation. I felt less intimidated by the locals, allowing myself to be the one with the threatening aura.

These people think I'm a savage anyway. They are lucky I am not prone to violence.

At times, I glanced up ahead, looking for an opening. The narrow buildings and prevalent overhead bridges crossing from many different angles made it impossible to find a safe area to exit from above. The density of the city created too many risks of hurting my wings if I tried flying extensively. Just the day before, I felt curious to observe the looming structures. Now, I detested it all. The windows glowing with firelight caused me to hate the orange fire, missing the blue flames that existed in my home. How could I ever see a fire the same way?

"Hey, watch it!" a man shouted as my wing brushed against him as he pushed past me, and I simply grunted and narrowed my wings.

"Teraganes," the man snarled. "What does he think he's doing pushing around us Tamarines?"

"Go back to your mountains, ya savage," another hissed from behind.

Tamarine? I guess I never cared to know what these people were called. Why didn't Lillie ever tell me?

A new emotion evolved in my heart. My anger turned to hate. I began to hate those men snarling behind my back. I hated the way the women looked at me. I hated all these people, every last one of them.

The anger I felt when I faced Bene began to build up in my body. My muscles tensed, and a terrible feeling of wanting to hurt them overcame me. They were so cruel to me for no reason. I hated Marie for only caring about stupid fish. I hated Bene for calling me a distraction to Lillie. I hated them all—the women of the market, the sniveling children, the—

"Hey you—Teragane!" a woman called out behind me. I ignored her and kept walking, lowering my head as I had no desire to speak with anyone who would only slander or push me around. Yet, deep down, I was afraid of hurting someone out of pure animalistic instincts of lashing out like a wounded beast.

"Hey! You!" she cried again, her voice drawing near. A hand grabbed my arm, and I spun around with a snarling expression, and she stepped back after releasing her grip.

"Whoa there," she said, and I softened my eyes, recognizing her.

"You? I met you yesterday," I said. The rise of anger began to slowly subside, and my hands lowered to my side as her rounding cheeks glowed. Her skin was relatively clean, unlike the other day, and her front covering was slung over her shoulders.

"Hey, I didn't mean to startle you," she replied. "I just wanted to know if you got to see Lillie. You—you okay?"

Lillie—the reason I was in this horrible city in the first place. As if I were no longer a sinking rock but a fish rising to the surface to feel the warmth of the sun from above, hope began to fill my heart.

"No," I said, causing the woman's face to suddenly grow solemn, and a look of concern welled in her expression.

"Oh, don't tell me you went to the wrong house," she said jokingly. "I know the city is one easy to get lost in, especially for a newcomer. But, I was quite directive, yeah?"

"No, I met Bene and Marie. They told me that Lillie was at work, and I was not welcome."

"Oh." Her eyes widened as she spotted something behind me. "Hurry, come with me." She suddenly grabbed me, leading me to a nearby building, causing me to wonder why she was persistent on dragging me around. I looked past my shoulder and saw three large figures approaching. The woman pulled me under an awning, behind a giant pile of firewood.

"Get down," she whispered. The concern in her voice worried me, and I obeyed, lowering my figure behind the stack of firewood. She stayed standing, casually leaning against the wall as she watched the three large figures move past the area. I felt the ground vibrate as they stomped through the streets. As the woman's eyes followed the passing villagers, I stayed crouched, feeling curious, yet alarmed at the unknown reason why she was hiding me from the people walking by.

The woman was much older than Lillie, well into her adult years. Her undertones were noticeable under her gray skin, and her pointed ears were smooth and slightly pink at the tips. She had light brown hair that she styled in several braids that were twisted into a bun. Her earthy-tone blouse was relatively clean, as was the covering, and I wondered if she were heading to work like many of the others I could only assume as they pushed through the city. Yesterday, the people's clothing were filthy, covered in foreign substances. From the small bits of observation, the city people were rather clean in attire during the mornings.

"It's okay," she said as she cast her hazel eyes upon me. "You can get up." I stood up and peered down the street from behind the wall of firewood. The three large figures were beginning to turn a corner, but I saw their greenish-hued skin, massive bodies covered in spiked leather, and the formidable swaying wooden clubs at their sides.

"Who are they?" I asked, shocked at seeing such giant beings walking through the city.

"Those are Keepers," the woman said while casually picking at the bark of the logs. "They are nothing but trouble. You do not want to run into them." Loud noises came from the streets that the Keepers had turned into, and suddenly a crash of splintering wood echoed from the hidden area. Were these the men Bene threatened to force me out?

Good thing I didn't linger at the house.

"Anyway," the woman continued in a low voice. "They are the least of your worries right now. So, Bene and Marie. Did they say anything about Lillie?"

"Only that she was at work," I said. "But I don't know if that is entirely true."

"What makes you say that?"

"I—uh—I just felt like something was off. They were hostile towards me when I questioned where she was. I questioned her safety, causing Bene to become angry with me. They refused to tell me anything about her wellbeing, claiming I was a distraction and she had no time for me. Yet—Marie, she seemed distraught, was even crying. I—if I could just speak with Lillie, hear from her myself, then..." My voice trailed off, and the woman raised a thin brow, then turned to look down the street again, seemingly agitated as she picked aggressively at the wood.

"Did you say that they said Lillie was at work?" she asked with a low voice.

"Yes. Marie allowed me to wait for Lillie to return home from work, but when Bene arrived, she—she changed. Do you know where Lillie works? Where she is? Can I see her?"

"Look, stranger," she said while eying me. "Why is Lillie's wellbeing so concerning for ya? Huh? Who are you? I thought you were just some fishmonger here for trade. You seem a lot more friendly than that."

"My name is Sable von Hira, and I've known Lillie for many years. We are friends, often meeting together on a regular basis outside of the forest. Yesterday—no, the day before—we were supposed to meet. But she never showed up. That is unlike Lillie. After all these years, Lillie has never missed a reunion. I'm afraid..."

"Go on."

"I'm afraid something has happened." The woman looked around once again, and I also followed her gaze down the street. I did not see any alarming figures approaching—only some villagers passing by. I looked back at the woman; she bit her lip and then looked at me.

"Ok, *Sable von Hira*," she said while bobbing her head as she said my name. "I am also worried about Lillie."

Finally.

"Actually, my brother and Lillie work together," she continued. "I know sometimes the hours can be extended, so I just assumed that Jamie hadn't returned because of that. Or, the troublemaker scampered off like he does sometimes. But, yesterday, I saw Bene walking alone, and now I am feeling slightly anxious about the reason why Jamie, or Lillie, haven't returned home, especially after what you said."

"Do you think they ran into trouble at their work?"

"I don't know. But, maybe they..."

"Maybe? Maybe what?"

"Er! I don't know. Honestly, my brother tends to get himself into trouble. But it's not like Lillie to be missing for too long."

"What do you mean by *too long*?"

"I don't know. Sometimes she just disappears, especially on the full moon, usually in the forest or something. However, she should have returned from work yesterday. And Jamie normally smokes with Bene in the evenings. So, I thought for sure you'd run into both of them last night."

"I did not see anyone else at the house, only Bene and Marie."

As the woman began chewing on the tip of her thumbnail, she grumbled, speaking lowly, causing me to feel even more anxious to know about Lillie—especially now that someone else was concerned for her disappearance.

"This doesn't make any sense," she grumbled, then looked down the street. "Where are those two? Why now?" I shifted my position, feeling uneasy with what the woman was saying. I did not remember Lillie talking about Jamie nor his sister—who was this Jamie?

"Tell me where Lillie and your brother work," I said, feeling my eyes narrow at the thought some man was also missing—with her. "I will find out for myself where they are."

"I don't know. It's not proper to meddle with other people's affairs," she replied. "Lillie hates when I get all involved."

"What if she's in danger? I only care about finding Lillie. I don't mind participating in unacceptable behavior, as long as I can confirm her whereabouts, her safety. That is all I desire. I know that something isn't right."

"What if—oh, no he wouldn't do that. Oh, jeesh, if they're still at work then maybe it's just—Hey, Thabias!"

"What? Just what? Tell me where to go so I can find Lillie, please!" I looked over at a young boy approaching down the street, and the woman beckoned for him.

"You really do care about her, don't you?" she said while looking up at me with glimmering hazel eyes. "Alright, go find Lillie and make sure she's safe. And my brother, too, please. I worry about what trouble he's gotten himself into. Maybe he's the cause of all this, hopefully not. But—I'd rather he be the cause than—uh, something else."

"Yes, of course. Where should I go?" I asked, easing my voice, although unsure what to think about this brother described as a troublemaker—and involved with Lillie.

She stepped out from underneath the awning, meeting the young boy in the middle of the street and began speaking to him as she dragged him over by the firewood pile.

"I don't have time for—hey, ouch!" the boy jeered as the woman tightened her grip on his shoulder.

"You still don't know where Jamie or Lillie are?" she asked as she stared intensely at him, and he squirmed from under her death grip.

"Ouch, let go of me!" he exclaimed. "I already told you; I don't know! No one tells me anything."

"Then, please, take this man with you," she said, and the boy, Thabias, widened his eyes as I moved out from behind the wood pile. He gasped with an expression of one most displeased, turning his face again.

"Lara, are you crazy? Who is this guy?" he exclaimed. "Why do I—" The woman, who apparently was called Lara, leaned near his pointed ear and whispered something I could not hear. She tightened her grip on his shoulder, and he winced again.

"Okay, fine, but stop hurting me," Thabias said while shaking his arm away from her.

"Good," she said, then nodded, pleased with herself, then she turned to face me. "Follow Thabias. He'll lead you the way." Thabias had already started walking away, and I hurried after him.

"Thank you, Lara!" I shouted.

"Think nothing of it. Just find Lillie and Jamie. Don't take no for an answer, and, for goodness' sake, stay away from the Keepers!"

As my feet and heart skipped, I followed Thabias who refused to speak to me. He weaved around the city like Lara had once done in the market, successfully dodging others, and moving swiftly through the labyrinth with fluid experience.

I did not know what to expect, nor had I any idea what I was getting into. My perspective was hopeless not long ago, ready to leave the city and give up on finding Lillie. My mind had felt fuzzy, and I could not think of any real solution or plan. However, Lara gave me new hope. She gave me the confidence that there were still people who cared about helping. I was lucky once again to be sought out by Lara, a friend who actually cared about Lillie. Why was she seemingly more concerned about Lillie's wellbeing than her parents were? Was that the truth? Were Bene and Marie hiding something? If so, why? And why had she not returned from work? Did something happen? If so, what could I do? And why was she scared of these so-called Keepers? What kind of bullies were those guys?

Floods of thoughts overwhelmed my mind as I followed the young boy, and I began to ponder about Lara's description of her brother. Why was a troublemaker, as she so delicately explained, also missing? Were Lillie and Jamie missing together? Did something happen at work? Or, did Jamie pose a threat to Lillie's wellbeing?

The thought of a man bringing harm to Lillie once again caused anger to rise—an anger worthy of inflicting pain against anyone who would distress Lillie.

"This way," Thabias suddenly said as he took a sharp turn around a building, and I skipped to catch up. Lost in my thoughts, focused only on following his figure, I did not realize we had reached the end of the city and were facing the forest. Thabias walked through an archway that led into the forest, similar to the one I had found when I first entered Cedrus City. However, this exit from the forest led to a wide dirt path trodden heavily by many travelers. Dust of boots scattered around, and more workers began to emerge from the city from behind and ahead of us.

We were surrounded by the giant cedar trees, but, thankfully, there were no more buildings, only wandering men and women with dark circles under their eyes. The air was fresh, again, but the parade of quiet forest-dwellers caused an unnerving sensation as I crept closer to Thabias' side.

He carried a leather satchel strung over his shoulder, and I recognized his leather trousers as ones similarly worn by Lillie's father. His brown tunic had many mending patches, and his boots were large—too large for someone so young. I observed his brown hair, noticing the short length as his braids were only down to his shoulder. Then, I noticed a rather deep scar on his face, between his eye and ear, and wondered what pain this young man had suffered.

"What business do you have visiting Cedrus City?" Thabias asked. The forest trail rumbled with boots stomping upon the ground, and a few other people grumbled to each other. Surprisingly, no one seemed bothered by my presence. Maybe it was too early in the morning for them to realize I was even there.

"I came to trade fish and to meet up with Lillie," I replied, deciding to keep my story simple and believable. I dared not give details of the meadow or who I really was to Lillie.

"How do you even know Lillie?" he asked as his exhausted eyes darted up at me as I walked next to him.

"Forest friends, I guess."

"Figures. She's always making friends wherever she goes."

"Are you friends?"

"Pffff." Thabias huffed air from his mouth. "I've known her since we were kids, but I don't think of her as a friend. More like a nuisance for a neighbor."

"Oh! You live near her. So, you're from the same *neighborhood*." I felt excited to finally understand something about the strange world that Lillie once explained to me. However, I also remembered his name—and Lillie's disdain for him as a neighbor.

160

"Duh, that's what a neighbor means."

"Oh—yes. I thought it could also mean something else. Like someone who doesn't live exactly next to you, but just in proximity, like from the same area, the same neighborhood."

"Yeah, whatever."

"Just making sure I fully understand."

"Okay....whatever."

"So, you don't know anything about Lillie or Jamie going missing?"

"I already told Lara." He sneered under his breath while turning his face away, and his scarred face tensed. "I don't know anything. I work in a completely different area than Lillie or Jamie. If anyone would know, it would be Bene, you know, since he's like her dad."

"Yes. I already spoke with him. But he refused to tell me."

"Ah—so you're the mountain savage Bene spoke about last night."

"Last night? You spoke with Bene?" Thabias paused his footsteps and grabbed my arm as he nervously allowed some people to pass by us. He looked further down the winding forest trail, and I followed his gaze. All the people looked the same to me, at this point, but, for a moment, I thought I caught sight of Bene turning the corner of the forest trail.

"Look, I don't wanna get involved. I already have enough troubles as it is with my family. I can't lose my job, I literally just started. But—" Thabias paused, and another group of people passed by, some lifted their slouched heads for a moment, but walked by without further comment. He released his hand on my arm, and we began walking again.

"But?" I asked, feeling my heart race within my chest at the realization that this boy was with Bene after I had been thrown out.

"I don't want to admit this, but, Lillie has always been there for me and my family. I'd hate to see something happen to her."

"So, you also think there's something wrong?"

"I don't know. Just—Bene acted weird last night—thought it was just you disturbing his peace. But, it's not like Jamie to skip a smoke night. But, who knows, maybe those two scampered away together. I—I don't know."

"You think Jamie and Lillie ran off together?"

"Look, I said I don't wanna get involved and those two can do as they want." We turned around a corner and the sunlight beamed through the trees, allowing mist and particles to glisten in the rays. Yet, somehow, no light of the sun could warm my sinking heart. "However, Lillie is always disappearing. Who knows where that girl goes these days. Well, apparently far enough to make friends with people like you."

"So, why do you think Jamie is involved?"

"It's not usual for him to disappear, or for Bene to show fear. Nothing scares that guy."

"I see." As we trekked further into the woods and our conversation faded to the low rumbling of boots traversing, the unraveling of the mysteries only intensified, especially as I looked ahead, noticing a cave entrance that the people were filing through.

"A cave? You work in a cave?" I asked, and Thabias scoffed.

"No, stupid," Thabias grunted. "A mine."

A what?

CHAPTER EIGHTEEN

WHEN THE MYSTERIES KEEP UNFOLDING

Thabias and I walked along the forest trail towards the dark mine entrance. The opening was larger than I had expected, and the walls were precariously lined by wooden beams and thin stones. Lanterns hung from the ceiling, revealing a deep tunnel that curved further below. Workers were shuffling through, slowly disappearing as they descended into the depths. From afar it appeared like a natural cave, yet, upon closer inspection, it felt more like an ominous glowing mouth of a giant monster, steadily luring its prey into its belly.

"I must return to my work on my own; who knows what people would say if they see me next to you," Thabias said as he pulled out a metal object from his satchel, then strapped it upon his head, and the round glass reflected the low light. "Find Ezra. He can tell you where Lillie is—if she's still alive." The young boy suddenly sprinted and I needlessly reached my hand out.

"Hey! Wait! What do you mean?" I shouted in vain. "Who's Ezra? How do I—" As his small stature faded into the depths as if he was being swallowed up, a horrible paralyzing sensation crept over my body. I waited, hoping for Thabias to run back with a change of heart, and watched the lanterns swing ominously as a cold wind blew through the area.

"Still alive?" I said out loud, feeling a shiver run down my spine, and my wings jolted. Another group of workers passed by, ignoring me, yet, I couldn't find the courage to ask any of their passing figures for help.

As if my boots were filled with water, I dragged my feet along the dirt path and stepped inside the mouth of the cave.

Walking under the dark canopy of the giant cedar trees was initially my worst fear. I overcame such peril in small increments, encouraged by Lillie's presence. Entering a dense city within the forest was solely motivated by Lillie's absence. Precarious tunnels dug beneath the surface of the earth? Absolutely absurd. I am a creature of the sky; I do not belong underground.

But—Lillie. Something happened to her—something that causes fear for her parents and Thabias to suggest that she could be—

Sweat began to pile on my forehead at the thought. I tightened my hands into fists, and I felt a deep pressure in my chest. I looked behind me, observing the trail I had just traveled from. I observed the light of the sun beaming through breaks in the branches and the hazy lights from the city far away. I knew I had already come so far and done so much. I had overcome so many of my discomforts and fears; the anguish I experienced all night, the clear direction of hope that morning—I survived this far and was so close to finding Lillie.

I can't give up now.

I took one last breath of fresh air, my chest puffing up, and I proceeded into the mine. I accepted my resolve, and I acknowledged that there was no turning back. I would follow Lillie into the depths of the underground world, into the darkness, if it meant rescuing her—if it meant freeing her from the darkness of the world that controlled her.

I did not fully understand at that moment, but with my determination to enter the unknown for the sake of Lillie's wellbeing, a new level of comprehension began to evolve. Before, I had the privilege and luxury of ignorance. In order to fully understand the changes that threatened my world—compromising what bliss I anticipated creating with Lillie—I needed to drive away this ignorance. Lillie's confusing and formidable world was too complex for me to fully understand, yet my love for her drove me to move past such insecurities of comprehension. I knew that if I was to have any chance with any sort of future with Lillie, I needed to keep pushing through the web of confusion and surpass my personal fears and any obstacle standing in my way.

The air was stiff and heavy within my chest. The cold draft was different from my experience at the top of the mountains or in the stifling atmosphere of the city. This cold was depleted of life itself, filled with soil, and barren of positive energy.

I walked cautiously along the lantern-lit tunnel that gradually descended. The walls were carved and lined with wooden supports, steadily increasing in size. I heard noises further ahead—sounds of voices and heavy objects clanking together, like the pounding of the blacksmith. I was not sure what to expect as I approached the sounds, but what I saw was a sight to behold for an ignorant Teragane from the mountain.

A rush of stagnant heat filled the air as I entered a very large cavern, complete-ly lit by the orange glow of lanterns, furnaces, and luminous stones alike. Large stalactites covered the ceiling, some forming columns that looked as if they led to other tunnels, and crystalized stones shimmered within the walls and stalagmites. There were four-legged animals pulling carts, people moving around undisturbed, large structures, and machinery I had never witnessed before. I heard loud sounds of people calling out, minerals crashing together in metal containers, and wooden cranes maneuvering about. It was like a whole new city, but underground, completely running under the orange glow I had grown to detest. The sudden burst of energy emitted by another surprise hidden within the dark caused me to shudder.

So, this is a mine? This is where Lillie works?

No wonder she became so miserable.

My sharp eyes darted as I attempted to scan the area, finding it easier since it was openly displayed. I realized it was just like the city. The people were all working, moving about in their time and space. I had nothing to fear. Even though I was underground, entering a whole new area I was absolutely unfamiliar with, I made it this far. I already survived Cedrus City. What could go wrong in the mine of the Tamarine people?

Find Ezra, I remembered Thabias telling me. I could find my way to Ezra, who would help me locate Lillie. Once again, I was looking for help, but this time at least I had a better direction and a clue to this unraveling mystery I had found myself in.

I took a deep breath, then descended along the path, deeper into the large cav-ern. I remembered from before to avoid conflict by keeping out of the way of the busier-looking people. I stepped aside for the animal-driven carts, I kept my eyes away from the Tamarines carrying large buckets, and I did not bother those who looked overly burdened. Instead, I looked out for those who bore the same similarities to Lara. She had shown me kindness on two different occasions; both times, her eyes were filled with consideration. I directed my attention to seek out that same look of concern.

As I passed through the cavern, I saw expressions of confusion, apathy, and even disgust, but it took some time before I found the demeanor I was searching for. I passed by a group of workers who were arguing over something. They stood close to tables that were covered in shiny objects. Some had the same round glass objects as Thabias resting on their heads, and others wore a type of thin glass in front of their eyes. An older man, hunched over some minerals on the table, glanced up; his wide eyes behind the thick glass caught my attention. I walked towards him, and he straightened his back.

"What are you doing here?" he asked while pulling down his glasses. I steadied my voice, hoping to avoid conflict as the other men who were arguing eyed me with disgust.

"I am looking for Ezra," I said. "Can you tell me where I can find him?" The worker raised a jagged brow, then stroked his greying beard as he eyed my stature, then my wings. The others around the table began whispering, but I kept my eyes focused on my goal.

"You're a strange sight to behold," he chuckled as a smile crossed his aging face. "Are the Masters sending new recruits from the northern mountains? Or, are you a new messenger? Did Moritz kick the bucket?"

"What?" I muttered, feeling confused. "I'm looking for Ezra."

"Yeah, yeah. He's over there," the older man said, and he pointed to a wooden structure past the working table. The other whispering workers eyed me, and I turned my attention to the helpful man.

"Thank you," I said, and he simply nodded, then hunched back over his work. He focused on a black stone that had been broken into pieces, and a shimmering mineral caught my attention. I had never seen stones sparkle in such a way, but I returned my focus to my original reason for being in the underground.

I turned and walked towards the wooden structure. It was a small shelter, perhaps a meeting place with a square table with chipped edges and a few blackened chairs pushed aside. Three older Tamarines were talking over some parchment sprawled out on the table. As I approached, I could sense there was intensity in the conversation, perhaps a disagreement. The negativity felt repulsive, yet I continued forward, ignoring the heavy weight of anxiety increasing within my chest.

"Greetings," I said while approaching the three workers who suddenly creaked their necks to gaze upon me. "Pardon my interruption, but I'm looking for Ezra."

Their gruff voices had subsided as they stared. There were two men and one woman; all three appeared heavily aged by work and experience. Their eyes were deeply set and dark underneath, and their stagnant gray skin was rough, scarred, and similar to other older Tamarines I had seen. One man had a full-beard, while the other was completely shaven. The woman's gray eyes sparkled with curiosity as she gazed upon me. For a moment, the men looked surprised, perhaps a little frightened, but quickly resorted to puffing up their chests and extending their necks to increase their height.

"And why would a Teragane wander its way into our presence?" the bearded man asked with a scowl. The other man snickered, and the woman shook her head.

"Now, now, let's not be rude to our new arrival," the other man said while placing his hand on the bearded man's shoulder. "Now, dear winged-friend, who has sent you? You must be a new messenger, yes? Didn't realize Master Orvin caught himself a little birdie."

"Or, are you looking for a job?" the bearded man asked with a passive undertone. "If so, you're in the wrong place. Go back to the city. I could never use someone like you."

"Hey, a guy with wings could be useful," the woman said, and the two men grumbled for a moment. While they spoke, an intuitive sensation caused my muscles to tense, and my throat grew rather dry from an unknown fear. I was afraid of being mistaken, as well as involving others who perhaps had no desire to get caught up with whatever issue was happening. The fear displayed in both Thabias and Lara, even Lillie's parents, was enough indication that whatever was happening wasn't worth the effort to get involved.

"No one has sent me. I have come here on my own account," I said. "I am looking for Ezra."

"I'm a very busy man, but please tell me what good ol' Ezra can do for you," the clean-shaven man replied.

"You're Ezra?"

"That is correct, young man."

"Oh, good. I'm looking for my friend, Lillie. She hasn't been heard from for quite some time. It is unlike her, and I am concerned for her wellbeing. Last I heard, she was still at work, so I came here in hopes of finding her myself. I was also informed that another person—Jamie—has also gone missing. I came here to confirm that the wellbeing of both have not been compromised." Ezra's smile still beamed, but the bearded man and the woman looked at each other, causing my neck to tense even more.

"I have many workers who labor long hours, and sometimes the work demands more of their time. I'm sure she and the other fellow are fine and will return home soon," Ezra replied without any hesitation, but the woman suddenly scoffed, causing him to grunt loudly. "Nothing to worry about. If you're not here on orders, you are better off returning to the surface. Hey, I'll even have someone escort you. This is no place to be wandering about."

"I do not think you understand me. I will not leave until I see Lillie for myself and hear from her mouth that she is, in fact, well. I have been seeking for her and have been led

167

down to these depths on account of others being in fear of her unusual absence. I know that something is wrong. Do not push me aside after all I've gone through."

"You know nothing of this place," Ezra scoffed while he puffed out his broad chest once again, causing the front buttons to slightly creak. "You're just a mountain boy who knows nothing of life in the city. I think you do not understand me." Like the flash of lightning across the dark sky, the man's demeanor drastically changed as his smile lowered into a scowl and his eyes glared. He no longer feigned a welcoming tune now that he realized I was not connected with any leader—master, as he called. Yet, I did not allow his intimidation to push me aside, and I stared down the man as anger tensed my fingers into fists.

"I may not be familiar with the way of the Tamarine," I said with a low growl. "However, I know when a threat arises and how to fight for survival."

"Ohhh," Ezra jeered, and the bearded man grunted as he pressed his hands together and swayed side to side. The hatred I had for the cruel Tamarines of the city festered within my heart, and my lips snarled as my eyes darted from each man. I desperately wanted to scream at their careless behavior.

It was the same scene with Lillie's father: another careless man who did not value my concerns nor desire to confirm anything about Lillie's wellbeing. This time, I was willing to use force.

"Tell me where Lillie is now," I demanded. Before either man could interject or make a move, the woman finally stepped up by clearing her throat rather loudly.

"Do you really think you could take this guy down, you ol' geezer?" she sneered, and Ezra twisted his neck as he glared at the woman across the table. "You'd be better off taking down a Keeper. This kid is looking for his girl. Have any idea what kind of strength he's being fueled by? You'd win a fight against a stoked furnace with a bucket of water before you'd falter to him."

"Then, why don't you call someone to help me out, ye ol' hag?" Ezra demanded as his cruel smile returned, but the bearded man continued to crack his knuckles while glaring at me.

"I'd like to see someone put you in your place, any day, but, besides that, we have more pressing matters," she said as she tapped the parchment that lay upon the table. "Maybe the kid can help with the cave-in."

"That is no concern of this boy," Ezra said and he waved his hand at me. "He is no messenger or been sent by anyone. There is no need to inform him of anything. We have enough people on the job; we don't need some rugged mountaineer."

"What is a cave-in?" I asked while turning my eyes to the woman, seizing the opportunity to find answers after feeling settled I would, once again, have no need to use force against another. Her gray eyes met mine, and, finally, I saw the look of concern as sudden fear filled her eyes.

"Don't you dare," Ezra mumbled as his face reddened. She opened her mouth, and I was afraid he would attack her, but, instead, she continued with the determination I once witnessed in others from the city. A determination to help others, even if it could cause further problems for themselves.

"There was a cave-in three nights ago," she said. "We haven't been able to rescue the miners who were working in that area." Ezra's loud grunts increased, but the bearded man moved away from the callous man and closer to the woman. He looked at me, surprisingly with less apprehension.

"What do you mean?" I asked. "What is a cave-in?" The mine-workers slightly chuckled, but the woman waved her hand nonchalantly.

"A tunnel collapsed while our workers were excavating deep in the underground," she said, and the bearded man's eyes lowered as if grief finally struck his heart. "Lillie and Jamie are among the workers that are missing. That is why you haven't been able to find your girl, sweetheart."

CHAPTER NINETEEN
WHEN THE WORLD ONLY EXPANDS

During my training as a youngling, my parents taught me to listen to the distinct sounds of certain threats. The heavy thumping footsteps of a larger predator in the forest meant a quick escape into the trees. The cry of a dying animal could also indicate a predator or a hunter—a Tamarine who used weapons and traps—a savage resident of the forest to be avoided. The hints of an arriving storm could be sensed through the air currents and increase of moisture, providing adequate timing to take shelter before rain and lightning would cause the environment to be too hazardous to safely fly in. The sound of falling rocks after a disturbance in the terrain—this particular danger could damage even the strongest of Teraganes.

"Our homes in the mountains have been securely established by our ancestors," my father had told me. "But, like any rock of the ground, escape is crucial to avoid being crushed. A single boulder falling from the mountain side can crush the limb of any Teragane."

As I stood under the wooden shelter of the mine cavern, surrounded by arguing Tamarines, my heart raced as my mind flooded with images of falling rocks crushing Lillie. The distinct sounds I was once taught to flee upon the slightest disturbance suddenly exploded in my inner ear as my imagination began to run wild.

No. I cannot accept this fate—not yet.

"When a tunnel collapses during the excavation process," the woman explained. "It can cause a whole shit-show of rocks and problems."

"And bodies," the bearded man added, only increasing my worst fears of the situation.

"And—and this recent cave-in?" I asked, and swallowed the lumpy sensation in my throat. "W-what is being done to find the missing workers?" The two collaborating miners looked at Ezra, who quickly turned his back to them, crossing his arms, angrily sulking.

170

"I see no reason to let this boy know what's happening in our business," Ezra said while huffing heavily. "Maybe he is working for some lord and has been sent here to spy on us. Ever thought about that? Do you have any idea how many delays this is causing?"

"Ah, there you go again, all about the delays and job security, what about the people?" the woman exclaimed. "The good folk of the city deserve to know where their loved ones are, especially if they're dead already."

"We will privately inform them when we have a better idea of the situation," Ezra quietly said as he turned to face the woman again.

"We already know how critical it is!" The woman slammed the table with her fist and gritted her teeth. "There is no better knowledge of the situation. You're just looking out for your own goose-neck." Ezra rubbed his eyes with his thick fingers that were surprisingly clean in comparison to the woman and the other man. He sighed again while shaking his head.

"Taffy, you know the delicate position I'm in," Ezra said while he moved his hands away from his reddened eyes. "If—you know who—finds out about the delays." He hesitated and lowered his eyes. The bearded man grew solemn, yet the woman, Taffy, continued to fume with anger.

"So, that's how it'll always be with you, eh?" she scoffed. "Damn-you Ezra! This is why I feel like I am constantly fighting a lost cause! Nothing will ever change if it's only me looking out for others, especially when you geezers are only concerned about your own necks."

"Now, now," Ezra said quietly. "It's not about that—really."

"Really? 'Cause it sure as hell sounds like it!"

"Quiet, that's enough. We all know the risks that go with the territory."

"Only because we are forced to take risks and no one barks!"

"Taffy," the bearded man said. "You really should lower your voice."

"No," Taffy said; however, she did lower her volume, and her voice no longer echoed through the area. "We are forced to take risks, and people lose their lives too often." I looked over my shoulder and noticed other workers passing by, pausing in their steps as their pointed ears perked. Their soot covered faces sunk into the surrounding darkness, but their eyes spoke unsaid pain of fear of the environment. I didn't need to know the whole story, only that it was obvious that these people were put into danger every day just for the sake of providing for their families.

And Lillie has been here all along.

"Well, what am I supposed to do?" Ezra said while placing his hand on his chest and rolling his eyes.

"We have seven workers in danger," Taffy said and slammed her fist on the table once again. "It's been three days! We are running out of time!"

"I don't see you doing anything to rescue them," Ezra arrogantly chimed.

"That's what I'm doing right now, you bastard!"

"All you're doing is yelling at me and blabbing your mouth at some stranger who just happened to wander into the mine, possibly a spy for the lords."

"And more people will continue to flood in looking for their family and friends if we don't do something about this hell-hole!"

"You don't know if that would ever happen."

"Then how the hell did this guy get here?" The woman pointed at me, and a jolt of tension ran through my muscles and my wings twitched from behind.

This could last another three days—I need to do something!

"Where is the cave-in?" I asked, raising my voice in effort to be heard, and the three Tamarines looked at me while their varying tempers lingered.

"Ha! You think you could do better than our own rescue team?" Ezra sneered. He shook his head and laughed with a bellowing growl, like a wild boar—no, even worse than the vicious pigs of the forests.

"It's dangerous," Taffy said, her tone of voice changing as she relaxed her jaw. "But I'll take you if you think you can help. Hell—I'd even recruit witches at this point, for hell hath no fury when innocent lives are suffering in the flames."

"What good would it do to take a Teragane to the cave-in?" the bearded man snarled, like a younger boar pig imitating its father.

"He's the only one who seems motivated enough to actually get shit done around here," Taffy said, causing the two pig-like men to snort. Her gray eyes glistened in the reflection of a lantern, and a smile began to cross her round face.

"So, what? He has delicate wings," the bearded man said while his sunken eyes gazed upon me. "He knows nothing of working in a mine. Look at the guy. He's a delicate boy who has never done a hard day's work. His hands are softer than a baby's bum." I avoided looking down as I crossed my hands behind my back. Flashes of Lillie's scarred hands

172

caused guilt to overrun my mind, yet, their sneering attitude in light of danger brought more hatred towards the cruel, careless men I deemed even less than the pigs of the forest.

"He obviously came this far, and he may not have an ounce of hardship laden upon his skin," Taffy said while shooting a glare at the bearded man. "He obviously knows how to track down his friends. His determination may be the vital key our missing people need."

"Please, I mean no offense," I pleaded. "I only want to help, whatever that looks like. I'm strong, I can move rocks easily, and can carry people if needed. Lillie—she means so much to me and I only want to find her. I will even help free the other trapped workers."

As a flood of emotions caused sweat to pile on my forehead, the thin air made my unsteady breathing even more difficult. The heavy weight of guilt and fear surged through my muscles, and I was so terrified that my strength would not be enough—whatever threat was holding my Lillie trapped.

Oh, Lillie. Please still be alive.

"As long as you can accept that there are many dangers upon entering deeper into the mine," Taffy said while she rolled up the parchment on the table. "If you're willing to risk your safety, I will take you." She then stuffed the parchment into a round holder upon her waist belt.

"I'm willing to risk everything for Lillie," I said. Taffy's eyes softened as her dirty cheeks rounded, and she looked over at Ezra who had stayed rather apathetic to involving me now that I was willing to take a risk he was not.

"I'm taking the kid—he's willing to do what all of us cannot," she said. "Plus, dare I mention, it's better than us just yelling at each other while those poor folk suffer a slow and painful death—if they haven't already. Then, you can tell your masters we've got a special force on the team if they ask about their delayed exports. If this is affecting Teraganes to come wandering into the city—higher ups will be forced to reevaluate their lack of safety precaution, especially if the desert bastards come next."

"What?" the bearded man suddenly said with a jolt of his neck. "You don't think—"

"Oh, that'll be the day," Taffy said with a laugh as she continued to gather items, placing each into the leather pouches attached to her stout waist. "Just imagine the next to be a Teshamen looking for his Tamarine lover. Ah, then we'd for sure lose those export trades if we upset those guys."

"Fine," Ezra said, suddenly flinging his clean hands into the air, and he began moving aside. "If that day comes, we'd all lose our jobs, for the desert bastards haven't stepped foot in Ciimera since the beginning of the war. Oh, and make sure no Keeper finds out about this. If I lose my job, it's on your head." He pointed menacingly at Taffy, then turned his back and walked out from under the wooden shelter. His clean boots stomped away, and he barked orders for the massive crowd of workers to return to their stations, and they all scampered away, causing a loud murmur as people shot glances at me.

"What a chicken," Taffy chuckled, and she stood by my side. "Glad to see at least there are still good folk out there—even if you're a little young to risk your life."

"It's bad luck, if you ask me," the bearded man said as he stood by my other side. "Take care not to damage those pretty wings." The bearded man huffed while rolling his eyes and then walked away.

"Follow me, yeah, sweetheart?" Taffy said as she stepped out from under the shelter, and she waved her hand. As my heart raced, a sense of hope rose, regardless of the circumstances and I hurried after the helpful Tamarine woman.

We walked past many workers, machinery, and large areas where rocks were being examined and resting in metal containers. I did not understand what type of minerals, rocks, or ores they were examining, for it all looked the same to me. Dark, dirty, and grossly unentertaining. Only the shimmering stones from earlier seemed interesting, but those seemed to be far from the normal rocks being transported. The tools looked dangerous, the air was stiff, and the people working looked exhausted. Many wore simple clothes that were covered in dark substances. They wore round glasses to protect their eyes, and some even wore scarves around their mouths. The loud sound of metal tools crashing onto rocks echoed through the cavern as we moved deeper within.

"What is your name?" Taffy asked as she pulled out a brass object from her waist belt pouch.

"Sable," I replied while observing the object that opened up, revealing markings and a thin needle in the middle that spun. "And yours is Taffy?"

"Yup, that's me. Taffy Mari Ki."

"It is very nice to meet you. Thank you for being so helpful and allowing me to seek Lillie."

"Likewise. It's about damn time someone has the determination like a fire—like you!"

"What is the purpose of this mine?" I looked around the area, and my mind wondered about the specific people Taffy was referring to that caused the other men to cower—like a chicken.

"We excavate mainly iron, copper, tin, coal, but we find other minerals like gold or silver, other gemstones—anything that is deemed useful and desirable by others. Amethysts are a big hit with the elites. Black onyx, interestingly, is heavily sought out for too."

"What do you mean by useful?"

"Well, some ores are useful for blacksmiths who create iron works. Like this—" She reached out and grabbed a pointed tool from a miner.

"Hey!" the unsuspecting worker exclaimed, and they twisted their blackened face, but their eyes were one of a young child, causing my heart to ache.

"Hey, sorry, just one moment—this is a pickaxe," Taffy explained while moving the tool over for me to look at for a moment. Then, she swung it back to the young Tamarine who took it while grumbling. "It's dirty work, but after the ores are sold, some artisans can make some pretty amazing stuff. I've heard stories about what they make up in the north, specifically in Larcosia. Pretty immaculate jewelry. And we mine the gemstones fit for noblemen and kings! But, yeah, those desert bastards mainly need the exports for weapons for their endless wars. Good thing they just fight each other. Good business for us—not so great for those dying by the weapons we make."

I frowned, feeling even more confused by the world I was utterly ignorant of, and began to wonder why the Sage kept the Teraganes isolated from such an expansive world. Yet, as we passed by the workers, young and old, and exhibiting a weariness from the life they were born into, I began to theorize that my ancestors kept us apart to avoid ever being subject to such a cruel life.

"It sounds like you like this job," I replied as my eyes wandered, observing all the tools the Tamarine miners were using. As cruel as it all was, I had never seen so many forms of rock, nor ever thought something elaborate could be made from the earth.

"Oh, don't mistake me, I don't like it. Mmm—no, not even a bit," Taffy said while giving a disdainful chuckle. "But I can at least be proud of some of the work since it is what I've fallen into."

"Why don't you like it?"

"Well, for one thing, it's dangerous and dark—my eyes used to be blue, did you know that? Hey, yours are rather intriguing. Never met someone with red eyes before. Then again, never met a Teragane, although I remember hearing lots of stories, especially from my father about his hunting trips. Oh, that reminds me, my brother once was approached by one. He said it scared the piss out of him! Some winged-kid came from behind and attacked him."

"Oh, I—that's unusual."

"Yeah, your folk seem to be just as weird as us Tamarines. Ha, anyway, I can appreciate what we do here, but I do not like the fact that we are often forced to take risks and not everyone is willing to follow safety protocols."

"Why? Who is forcing you?"

"The Masters, of course!"

Masters? Keepers? Lords? Desert bastards?

What more lurking predators are there?

"But, hey! I'm doing everything I can to get some better safety measures," Taffy continued. "At least those pesky Keepers stay out of the mines. At least I can have some control over the area."

"Who are the Masters?"

"Oh, just a bunch of rich snobs, if you ask me," she said and stepped aside for a worker to pass. I followed her movement, and while we paused our walking, Taffy looked up at me. I had furrowed my brows, and she continued explaining. "They run this mine, basically. Owners, investors, noblemen, yaddy yaddy. Higher ups of the capitalistic system of Cedrus City. You'd need a whole week to get the history. Even that may not be long enough. No, better yet, go to a tavern and listen to the workers talk after a couple pints."

"Oh, I thought Ezra led the mine," I said, and we continued walking through the working area.

"Well, kind of. Ezra manages this place. For, why would those pretty people wanna get their hands dirty? Ha. Yeah, us brave folk work here. Hey, Teraganes probably don't have hierarchies, do they? Hmmm."

"No. Only spiritual and parental guides."

"Ah, that sounds way nicer. The higher ups been running the city for a while, since the dawn of its first establishment. Historically, this area was founded on the mine work after the discovery of its rich sediment. Wars in the desert brought more exports, need for weapons, tools, blah blah, and the Masters began benefitting from partaking in the politics, yeah. Life evolved over decades, but things weren't bad until they brought the Keepers from the west to enforce their every little whim. Then it became brutal and more problems entered the depths."

"Those big green men?" I recalled the three large figures I briefly saw when I was with Lara.

"Yeah, those guys. Those bastards are mean. They do—how can I say this—the dirty work of the Masters. Anyway, they made life a little harder to fight back when the Masters became more demanding. Just made politics more complicated. No one could just do their honest work without prying hands and eyes."

"Okay..."

"But, yeah, that's old news. I got them out of the mine after extensive measures. Couldn't get work done when they kept banging up our machines. Now, I only have to deal with Ezra, and the constant pressure of heavy demands from the upper snobs who are too greedy to understand the ways of common folk and honest work. Anyway, let's focus on the task at hand, shall we, sweetheart?"

"Yes."

"We can push for safety measures once we get our people out, yeah?"

"Yes, of course."

While I appreciated Taffy's extensive explanations, it was difficult for me to wrap my ignorant mind about the world surrounding it all. I could not fully comprehend other people coming into a new city and claiming ownership over other people's work. Is this why Lillie did not explain things to me? Did she even understand how the city functioned? Or was she too busy trying to survive under the boots of bigger oppressors?

I continued to follow Taffy through the extensive mine. We passed by workstations manned by several people at a time. I recognized the sound of tools clashing with fired metal—hammers, Taffy explained. Sparks flew as several blacksmiths smashed their hammers with powerful swings. Furnaces twice as big as the city-blacksmith pumped heat and smoke into the air.

"Those are smelting furnaces," Taffy explained while pointing to the circular stones where puffs of smoke escaped. Large carts of ore were pushed towards the area, and workers shoveled rocks into piles near the furnaces. On the other side of where we passed, small donkeys brayed as they pulled two-wheeled carts, led by very young workers. Along the ground, metal tracks led in different directions. I watched as a four-wheeled cart appeared from a tunnel to my right, swiftly moving down an incline, and Taffy and I stepped out of the way as it rolled past us directly on the metal track. I twisted my neck as I watched the cart move to another workstation. A group of workers examined the newly unearthed material. One took a slab of rock to a different area, where a man with thick glasses carefully examined it.

"Keep up!" I heard Taffy call. I had slowed my pace to watch the action, but I hurried after her, lowering my gaze. The mine was becoming less frightening and more intriguing to watch.

However, my mind returned to thoughts about Lillie's wellbeing. I thought about the others, the young workers—were they actually children? The idea of being forced into an exhausting and dangerous work environment sent chills down my spine. I knew that Lillie did not want to work, yet she was forced to do so by her father. How many other people were also forced to be here?

I could only imagine the feelings of working daily in an unsafe environment and how it impacted the people. I thought about Lillie and her rough hands and how there were always new cuts and deep scars upon her once smooth skin. The image of Lillie sifting through sharp rocks, cutting her up, wafts of dirt filling the air around her began to make sense in light of her changes over the years: her fading hair color, the dimming of her stormy cool undertones, and the dark circles under her eyes. If Taffy's eyes faded, would Lillie's glistening green eyes also disappear into a lifeless gray?

The surrounding rumbling of crashing rocks alerted my survival instincts, and I jolted my neck. Suddenly, my mind envisioned Lillie buried underneath heavy, sharp rocks, her scarred hands and legs exposed, crushed, and lifeless.

No, I cannot accept that this is her fate. Lillie, hold on a little longer! I'm going to find you, no matter what.

Taffy kept talking about different aspects and changes she could implement to make the mine a safer environment. I didn't understand, nor did I care at that moment while Lillie's lifeless body haunted my mind. Earlier, the shock of the cave-in had not impaled me as I logically assessed the situation. But as I walked deeper into the depths, I was afraid of the possible scenes of horror and tragedy. Fear of the situation, fear of the unknown, and fear of losing Lillie now began to overcome my mind, shaking my body to its core. As Taffy mused her ideas out loud, I felt numb, cold, and terrified. I blindly followed her, and I only felt the cold embrace of dread and the air thin as we descended deeper into the mine.

"Sable, sweetheart?" Taffy said, breaking my transfixion. "You okay?" She stopped walking and looked at me with concern while we stood at the front of a tunnel entrance.

"Yeah, I'm just really worried about Lillie," I said while looking behind at the large cavern we would soon leave. The rumbling, the orange glow, the sunken faces—I hated what it represented, beyond the intriguing aspects, but felt even more fearful of what would come next.

"I bet you are. Don't lose hope yet, okay?" she remarked while grabbing my hand with a squeeze. It felt warm, but her skin was rough, and I became very aware of the smoothness of my skin. "I think you can be very helpful in a rescue effort."

I moved my eyes to meet hers. She seemed more excited than before. Her pointed ears perked up, and her cheeks rounded. The protective lenses resting on top of her graying hair reflected glimmers of light from overhead lanterns. Her hand tensed as she released me and crossed her stocky, but strong arms at his wide hips. The dark leather trousers held up by thick straps over her shoulders were torn in places, and she was obviously in need of mending as her green blouse had several tears on the rolled-up sleeves.

"How can I help?" I asked, really clueless beyond the ability to lift rocks or carry someone. Yet, staring at her stocky figure, I could only assume she was just as capable.

"Oh, I think you have some useful assets," she said, then looked at my wings. "This way." She moved through the entrance of the tunnel that was lined with support beams and glowing lanterns. Her boots stepped along the metal track leading along the decline of the tunnel, and I followed from behind, feeling the dramatic change of air now that we had left the cavern filled with furnaces. While Taffy seemed optimistic, I could only hope that I truly could find Lillie and the others even if I felt the least adequate while stepping deeper into the belly of the monster.

Chapter Twenty

When a map leads the way

M y eyes widened as we continued walking through the tunnel system. It had many different directions, splitting and stopping in some places. Many areas were lined with support beams; other tunnels were in the process of building the support. It felt terrifying at times as the dangerous sounds of moving earth alerted my inner senses. Although the workers passed through and Taffy spoke with an air of familiarity, it was hard to imagine anyone could adapt to the weaving tunnels of shifting rocks being forcefully manipulated by their tools and hands. We had to step aside whenever a miner pushed a cart full of rocks, and the overhead beams seemed to creak the loudest whenever the carts rolled across the metal tracks. It was all—claustrophobic.

How could Lillie's parents force her to work here?

"So, here's the thing," Taffy said. "We don't exactly know where the survivors are."

"What do you mean?" I asked, my breath shallow from the thin air. Small amounts of dirt fell onto my shoulder, and I brushed it off with a few flicks of my hand. I looked up, feeling terrified of rocks suddenly collapsing from overhead as the beams creaked and the earth rumbled.

"Well, in cases of collapsed tunnels, we can just dig through the new settled sediment, usually uncovering those trapped underneath, sometimes behind," Taffy explained.

"Okay."

"Well, three days ago, in this particular tunnel, excavators were worried that the floor was unstable. Some felt there could be a chance that the tunnel was excavated over a cavern—open space underneath, maybe something similar to the main hall where we met. Actually, it was Lillie who had informed me about these concerns. Come to think of it, the team skipped the inspection pre-excavation. This is a problem with cuttin' corners—something I can't seem to drill through these leader's thick skulls to never skip."

180

"Okay..." Taffy pulled out the roll of parchment from her belt. She unraveled it, revealing a map of the mine, so she explained, as well as pointing out that the main cavern was marked with a large circular shape. Along the edges, many different squiggly lines spread throughout. Some were hard lines, perhaps indicating a functioning tunnel. Other lines were faded while other lines had crosses marked over in red ink. As a Tergane, I never had the use for a map, nor remembered anything like the object within Cami's collection of books from the Sage. Yet, my inner sense of direction allowed me to create an instinctual flight pattern of the terrain I often visited. I began to wonder if this was how Tamarines were able to manage finding their homes and different places, or if they also had instincts to guide them.

They moved around the city with ease...

"Yeah, so, basically, they were right. We don't exactly know the extent of the cavern or where the workers fell. The entire tunnel floor gave way. Our rescue efforts have been precarious due to the fact that some sections of the original tunnel have been blocked by a collapsed ceiling, while other sections have had the whole floor open up completely. And the cavern below is also uncharted. We would need extensive teams to evaluate the extent of the cavern and recent tunnels, which take weeks, if not months, to map and discover."

"The workers can't survive that long," I said, ever so aware of the dryness in my mouth.

"I know. That is the problem with the situation and why time is not our friend at the moment." Taffy pointed at a drawn line on the map, and we turned into a tunnel to our left. I followed close behind, looking over her shoulder as she directed us according to the map. She followed the line with her finger, leading it to another area with freshly drawn ink, and I saw a large red X drawn over the end of the line.

"We haven't experienced something as extreme as this in a while, normally only small cave-ins," Taffy continued. "It's why Ezra is unable to make any real efforts because he knows the perilous situation and has given up hope of recovering the workers since it takes weeks to make extensive surveys. It delays the work progress, which is not in the favor of the greedy Masters. Although they don't appreciate losing workers, they also don't like delaying their exports." Taffy chuckled, causing my heart to continue to race within my chest and my throat felt far worse than before.

How can she laugh at something like this?

"But!" Taffy continued, and adjusted the straps over her broad shoulders. "I have not given up hope, especially since you showed up. Perhaps you can uncover the survivors all in one piece."

"How can I find the workers?" I asked.

"You, my friend." Taffy turned and smiled at me, her gray eyes glistening under a lantern light. "You can fly."

"We are in a mine, underground; how could I ever fly?"

"If you remember what I just said, the tunnel collapsed over a cavern." My mind began to make the connection. Although I preferred flying in the open space of the sky and above trees, I thought of the possibility of flying overhead in a large cavern. Yet, still, it sounded like a horrible idea—at this point, everything was wretched, no matter the positive light intended to be used in terms of lifting spirits.

"I think I understand," I said, and a shiver ran down my spine. My stomach lurched with pain, and I realized that I hadn't eaten anything that day, yet, how could I even think of food at a time like this?

"Good," Taffy said. "My rescue team has been using a pulley system to access the cavern, but it takes a lot of time-consuming work that is dangerous and a very slow process—at least, for us wingless folk. We gotta use ropes and pulleys, and climb every rock in our way. You, kiddo, can easily fly around and find the missing workers."

"I'm not sure how easy it would be."

"It's better than what we've got going. How long does it usually take for you to fly across the forest?"

"Uh—not very long."

"Where do you live?"

"The summit of Mt. Hira."

"How long does it take for you to fly down to Cedrus City to see your girlfriend?" My cheeks flushed with warmth, and I looked down at the metal tracks along the tunnel ground.

"Not very long."

"Like half a day?"

"Oh, no. I can fly from Hira to the cedar forest long before the sun has passed above the summits opposite of mine."

"So. That settles it, sweetheart. Which is good, 'cause I don't think anyone can survive much longer.

"Of course. I'm willing to do anything I can."

"Good, 'cause we are here." Taffy rolled up her map, securing it back into her belt. We entered an area that had several wooden fences blocking the tunnel. A young man stood by the blockade, but, upon seeing Taffy, he approached us.

"How's it?" Taffy asked cheerfully while tipping her head as a greeting.

"Slow going," the man said as his eyes darted toward me, then he pointed with his thumb while mumbling. "Who's this?"

"New rescue team member," she replied. "Move the fence, won't ya?" He nodded suspiciously, but he obeyed the woman, and he opened up the blockade, and we walked into the tunnel.

Further ahead, lanterns flickered along jagged rocks and precarious stone walls, illuminating a new scenery that had a new redolence drifting through the stifling atmosphere. A large wooden structure lured over a dark hole; the ground was scattered with loose rocks, large and small, making it difficult for me to step through without feeling the discomfort in my ankles. As rubble shifted underneath, the sound of tumbling stones joined the beating of my heart and the shallow breaths escaping my mouth.

"Watch where ya steppin'," Taffy said casually as she skillfully trudged along the unstable ground. We carefully crept towards the pulley system, where a few workers stood managing it. I saw a thick three-cord rope leading down into the hole. It was tense and stiff from holding a hidden weight.

As we got closer, my view of the hole widened. Although the wall of the tunnel held intact, the ground beneath it had completely disappeared into the depths. Piles of rocks on one side created a landslide, but I could not determine if it continued or was held by a floor below. As I stepped closer to see where the rope led, a worker stretched his arm against my stomach.

"Hey! Step back," he called, causing his voice to echo throughout, and a disturbing rumble followed.

"What's a kid doing here? Get him outta here," another worker announced quietly.

"It's okay, guys—the kid's with me," Taffy declared, causing the others to shift in place. She walked up to the workers, and they began to converse in low voices. Their faces were barely visible by the dim light of the lanterns, but there was no mistake of the exhaustion bearing down upon their shoulders.

I peered over at the pit again, now that the team accepted my presence under Taffy's declaration. There was a glow of light far below, but nothing strong enough to expel the surrounding darkness. Only the sharp rocks of the walls around were visible. It was like the gaping mouth of a monster filled with a thousand teeth, waiting to consume unlucky prey. It was as if there was a stream of monsters lurking the deeper I traversed into Lillie's world. First the cedar forest, then the mine, now an unchartered cavern that had swallowed up my love.

Would this be the last gaping mouth I must enter? Would there be more monsters lurking? Did it matter?

"Okay, sweetheart," Taffy said, and I looked over at her and the group of workers. "We're gonna bring up Stew who's already been down there for quite some time. When we get him up, you're next. He can tell you where they've been searching."

"Okay," I said. It was all I could say. My head spun, and I stopped looking below. I felt paralyzed once again by sheer terror as I looked at the gaping mouth of the abyss.

Am I really capable of doing this?

While the current rescue team sent a message through a flare down below to Stew, I sat and waited nearby. I felt sick and uneasy, but a rush of adrenaline began to spike. This could be Lillie's only chance of survival. I had to at least try to find her. I had to swallow my fear and trust my strength and stamina. After all, it was Lillie's security that motivated my strength training—although I would have never thought it would bring me here.

I thought back to the previous year, all those days spent building my strength, gaining muscle and weight, and motivating myself to be the man to save Lillie from her depressing life. I thought it would be impressive to fly her around, through the trees, above and below, wherever she wished. I thought I would give her the gift of freedom by offering to live with her in the meadow, to abandon our lives and live together, free and happy.

Yet, here I was—sitting in the rubble of a collapsed tunnel—perhaps the very rubble crushing her lifeless body.

How could it have come to this?

I thought so simply. I thought all she needed was someone to be her wings. This, all of this, was more than just needing freedom. How could I ever be a hero in a world far from simplicity? Regardless of my two days of learning more and more, it was beyond my complete comprehension. That fateful day in the meadow when I had asked if she would choose to live in the trees began to make sense. Her shrill laugh had pierced my heart. Yet, how foolish did I sound to her?

How could I ever face her again? How will life be after all of this? How could I ever return to my normal life? Could I live here in the city with Lillie? Would the Tamarines accept me? They had called me demeaning names—savage—kid—demon. How could I live among a group of people who would only continue to mistreat me?

But what if I can't save Lillie? What if it's too late?

The stifling air caused me to slightly wheeze through my clenched teeth, and I stared at the pulley system as I waited for the next step in my quest to find Lillie. Yet, the overwhelming emotions filling my mind caused a sense of numbness to set in. The only thing I could feel was the pain in my stomach as it growled for sustenance.

"Hey, Sable," Taffy called out to me. "Let's get you ready." I shook off the uneasy feeling and walked up to the group. Taffy motioned for me to remove my personal items that she insisted would only get in my way. I took off my cloak and satchel, then handed them to one of the workers. Taffy pulled out the map of the mine and a wooden marking tool. Near the large red X, she drew a circle.

"Here is the cavern below this opening," she said while pointing to the newly drawn circle and then at the dark hole. She traced a line up to the red X. "And this is where the workers *most likely* fell after the cave-in." She tapped the map, then pointed to the rock blockade next to us. "The cavern is massive, and we theorized that the workers fell somewhere north from where we are standing. Due to the blockade, we must enter through the cavern. There are many tunnel systems that are possible where they fell. I think if you head north after descending into the cavern, you might find where they fell. Also, don't be loud or make unnecessary noises. We wouldn't want any more cave-ins, ya know? We will use the pulley rope to place a marker for you to return to when needed. Use this compass and twine to help guide your direction and way back."

"Compass?" I asked while narrowing my eyes.

"Yeah, it points in different directions, like so." Taffy handed me a small metal orb, the one I had seen her use before. "It's a special compass, actually, one specifically for underground work. It's how we make maps and not get lost. Just make sure you're heading in the direction where the needle points N. Then, use the twine to mark your trail for a safe return."

"How?" I asked while holding out both my hands, and she placed a spool of vibrant yellow twine in the palm of my hand. Taffy grabbed a leather belt with various hooks and pouches. She wrapped it around my waist and strapped it securely. The spool of twine had a special hook that she fastened onto my new belt.

"Tie it to the pulley rope, and let it loosely unravel as you move further into the area," she said. "This method will reassure you that you can find your way back to this exit. Think of it as a life-saving trail—like the trail of a snail. You don't wanna get lost down there, not while you're our last hope."

"Okay." The longer I spent time with the people of the forest, I realized how wrong the Teraganes were with their understanding of the complex Tamarines living in the forests. These people were far from primitive folk—they were ingenious, creative, and innovative in their endeavors.

As the other workers approached me carrying more items, I felt ever so grateful for this particular group and their determination to also save the others from the perilous situation.

Like Lillie, I suppose there can be others who show kindness, especially to someone like me.

"When you find the survivors, they'll be thirsty, hungry, and most likely injured," Taffy continued her instruction. While Taffy verbally prepared me for the potential outcomes, the other workers began strapping items in pouches around the waist belt. "In here, there are medical supplies."

"This is water enough for each individual to share, but don't let it go to waste on one person," one of the workers said as she strapped a canteen onto my belt. "Encourage them that they'll receive more later."

"This lantern can last for a couple hours, but there is more oil in this bag," a worker said while pointing to the pouch. "It can also be strapped to your belt like this." He snapped the lantern onto the belt. It was small, but it gave off adequate light to see around me.

"You look strong, but don't overexert yourself, and, for goodness' sake, don't move anything," Taffy said. "You can disrupt the surface, cause another cave-in, or worse."

"Stew's here," someone announced, and they all moved to the pulley and began turning the device, which lifted the rope from below. It took some time before Stew came to the surface. He removed his protective lenses, revealing a sweaty and dirt-covered face of a rather exhausted young Tamarine man on the brink of faltering from fatigue. Taffy quickly explained the situation to Stew, who looked relieved, although still weary.

"The cavern is massive, but there are so many pockets and chambers towards the surface," Stew claimed. "They could be anywhere up there, or down there. I don't know how anyone can look at all the possible locations. It—it may be too late after so long." He then turned and pointed to the map, reiterating to me to go looking for the survivors to the north, explaining that they climbed pretty high, but still couldn't find any evidence of survivors. Tears began to form, and he rubbed his eyes with a filthy rag, smearing dirty tears around.

"You've done your best," Taffy reassured while patting the defeated man's back. "That is all we can ask." She beckoned one of the workers to take care of Stew, who led him out of the area. Taffy then turned her attention to me, and a shiver ran down my spine as my eyes darted over to the hole in the ground.

"Any questions?" Taffy asked while her eyes of courage glistened in the low glow of the lantern light. "Need anything else?"

"No," I said while I patted the belt upon my waist.

"You're gonna do awesome, kid. I believe you will find the lost miners." Her pointed ears perked up, and a hint of redness appeared on her nose and cheeks. "You're gonna find your girl."

"Okay."

"And don't get lost. Don't get hurt, and, for all good things in this world, come back in one piece."

"Okay, I will." I turned around and faced the jaggedly lined hole. I patted my new belt again, checking that all the new supplies were securely attached.

Satisfied with my preparations, I allowed my wings to narrowly open. Taffy and the other workers gasped as they all stepped back, causing a shuffle of rocks to shift. The opening was large enough for my wings to be partially extended, enough to easily glide down. I planned out my strategy of descent in my mind. I knew I could easily slide down—I was, after all, a Teragane built for falling from high places without causing harm.

I took a deep breath and exhaled slowly, allowing my determined heroism to push back all the apprehension lingering within my mind. With a courageous jump, I once again began my descent into the monster's mouth.

Hopefully, it was the last one before finding Lillie.

Chapter Twenty-One
When There Is Only Darkness

Many times before, I had skillfully descended great heights with a simple glide. In fact, I could adjust my wings to catch the air currents and effortlessly skim through the sky. I knew exactly how to feel *free as a bird*.

In stark contrast, the freedom of descending into the deep abyss with effortless gliding was far from that elevated sensation of control. There was only the dim light of my little lantern to guide me, and the darkness that surrounded me hid any obstacles that could be potentially dangerous to my safety. I could not afford to drift at ease. There were no air currents. There was no broad view of my surroundings. There was only darkness.

As I glided directly below into the abyss, my eyes began to adjust. After first entering the hole, it was narrow, but it expanded greatly to a massive cavern, bigger than I could detect in its fullest expansion. My ears picked up the sound of water rustling below. The further I plunged into the cavern, the more eerie it became. I could hear the sound of water dripping from stalactites, disrupting small pools of water on the floor. The small lantern gave off enough light for me to notice the bottom of the pit, and I landed on solid ground. It felt firm, slightly damp, and not a threat to my safety—much different than the rest of the underground.

Looking above, I could only see the small haze of a glowing light, and I listened for the distinct sound of the mechanism of the pulley system. Taffy had informed me that they would lower it, and that I should wait so I can attach the twine to the platform. As I waited, my eyes scanned the dark outlines of the eerie cavern. It was different from what I had seen before.

This cavern was carved by natural forces, unlike the mined tunnels formed by the pickaxes of the Tamarines. The natural glisten of unscathed glistening stones in the rocks reflected my lantern light. As the wooden platform from the pulley system began to descend, it ignited more light within the area as it slowly unveiled a partial view of the various columns of stone and glistening rocks within the walls. I glanced at my compass, and my eyes looked north, but I could scarcely make out anything other than the dark shadows ahead.

"That could be where the possible tunnels are," I said out loud, and my voice carried throughout the spacious cavern. I imagined the hand-drawn map Taffy had shown me, creating a map within my own head as I moved the compass around. When the lantern-filled platform finished its descent, I moved over to it. I tied the end of the yellow twine to the rope, and then I began to make my way north towards the suspected area where the miners could be trapped.

I cautiously walked north, allowing my lantern light to guide me. I did not feel comfortable enough to fly the entire time as I traversed through the unknown area by foot. The cavern was expansive in size but filled with rock columns and formations that were difficult to see until the light cast upon their true forms. I maneuvered my way around the pillars, occasionally needing to fly over rock platforms that blocked my desired path. I scanned the ground, hopeful to find the missing workers wandering about or waiting to be rescued, but, alas, turn of events were never that easy.

I continued glancing at the compass, allowing it to guide me north. My pacing was slow as I traversed through the ominous cavern, occasionally calling out for Lillie or for any signs of survivors within the cavern. I listened for any noises that could give me clues, but I only heard the sound of dripping water and the echoing noises of my footsteps. I expected to hear scattering sounds of insects or hidden cave dwellers of small forms, but there was no indication of life within the depths—not even in the slightest.

Up ahead, I noticed the northern wall, and dark outlines appeared.

"Those must be the tunnels," I said while examining the area further ahead. "No wonder it was taking so long. How could they even get up there?"

I should focus on the caves closest to the ceiling. That is where the survivors could have fallen from the surface above, since they aren't here in the cavern.

Satisfied with my plan of action, I scanned the area. Only a few columns obstructed my path, but I decided to begin my ascent, and I carefully maneuvered through the columns. As I ascended higher, the outline of more openings became apparent. Some water dripped on my face, and I looked directly up, then dodged to the side as I nearly ran into a thin stalactite.

I felt my heart race as the shock of nearly piercing my eye buzzed through my body, and I noticed that as I flew upwards, more stalactites were revealed by the lantern light. I had to weave through the draping rock formations as I ascended further, and the actual understanding of the area began to confuse my flight path instincts. I glanced down at the compass, and breathed a sigh of relief as I was still following the right course of direction, even if my natural sense of direction felt disoriented.

Then, suddenly, I saw something new glisten in the darkness near the wall of hazy outlines, and I flew straight to it, landing on the flat surface of the cave. I found a metal tool and a rope attached to the stone wall. I examined it, allowing the strong rope to shake from far below, and I guessed that it was left behind by the previous rescuer-team members.

"Lillie!" I called out, causing a rumbling vibration of my voice, and my eyes darted around as I feared causing a disturbance in the earth.

But there was only silence.

The cave was nothing but a naturally forming inlet, so I ascended to another opening. I looked around, walked deeper into the cave, but found nothing. I looked for clues—anything that indicated that another person had been here.

I continued flying around, entering caves, and looking for signs of survivors, only to find secured ropes left behind by the previous rescuers and plenty of empty inlets. Some openings were wide, others deeper within, but all ended without any indication of hope. As I ascended higher, I noticed there were no longer ropes left behind, but there were still caves, many caves—so many caves.

"Lillie!" I cried. I called out her name periodically and would wait for an answer. But I heard no reply, only a short echo, and the deafening silence that followed. Nevertheless, I kept searching each cave, jumping from one to the next, over and over, ascending more and more in my pursuits.

Until, I found an opening, but it appeared different. As I drew closer, I noticed it was completely round in structure, unlike the others I had searched before.

"Lillie!" I cried once again. This time, the echo repeated itself from a further distance. *A tunnel.*

I entered the cave entrance, which I had hoped was a passage—one that could lead further north where the survivors could have fallen. It was only a theory, but the Tamarine miners were already well established with their ability to chart through the darkness.

I trusted Taffy and her team—I followed their guidance, for their desire to help was genuine.

The light of the lantern guided me through the entrance. It was different from the tunnels of the mine. The mines were hand-manipulated, supported by wooden beams. The cavern caves were jagged and naturally occurring.

This tunnel had rippled but smooth rock formations. It felt stable yet, for some reason, more terrifying. It did not make eerie noises of ready-to-collapse rocks, but my mind began to wonder about the formations.

What made these tunnels?

The hairs on the back of my neck stood on end, and an uncanny feeling overcame me, and I darted my eyes away from the walls of the curving tunnel. I pressed on, forcing myself to not run away with my imagination.

Just focus on finding Lillie.

I followed the eerie path as it curved but stayed horizontally the same. It was large in size, yet not enough for me to use my wings to their full extent. Perhaps partial, for simple gliding, but not enough to fly through.

There was no rumbling like in the mine, the air felt different, and I eventually came to a large opening. As I entered the open area, the tunnel split into several other tunnels. An overwhelming feeling of disappointment overshadowed me as my eyes scanned the ominous area.

I tugged on the yellow twine. It was loose, but it was starting to run out of material. How much further could I go? What happens if I run out and still haven't found the others?

"Great," I said. "Now what?" I slumped onto my knees on the cold stone surface. It was smooth—much smoother than I expected. As a surge of pain from my empty stomach caused me to cramp, a brutal reminder that I hadn't eaten since I was with Lillie's parents. Even though I ate heaps of food with them, I was accustomed to eating many times a day, fueling my exertion of constant activity. The memory of eating at Lillie's house also caused pain—one of guilt and a cruel awakening of meeting the people who I would have considered her protectors.

I didn't even know how much time had passed since I first woke up that morning. It could be the middle of the day or the night—how could I know? How could anyone know what day it was in the depths? The shadow of doubt, uncertainty, and hopelessness crept over me as my stomach growled from neglect. I hung my head and clutched my aching side. My hair dangled in front of my face, and sweat dripped from the jagged tips. Again, I looked down at my hands, feeling shame of the smoothness of my dark skin, and lack of scars in comparison to these hard-working people risking their lives everyday just to survive.

This pain in my stomach is nothing compared to theirs. How can I be so selfish?

I stood up, pushing the damp strands of hair out of my eyes. Yes—I was hungry—but my hunger pains were irrelevant compared to the survivors stuck in their current situation. I knew I had a safe way out, but Lillie was trapped. Her safety was all that mattered at that moment, for I was her only hope—as long as it wasn't too late.

I decided to just start with the tunnel on the right. I would follow it and hope for the best. However, I quickly discovered that it led to nothing but a dead end, and I returned to the large opening. I gathered the twine as I retraced my steps, winding it back onto its spool.

Then, I entered the next tunnel. As I walked, guided by the light of my lantern, I noticed dark shadows on the ground, and I picked up my pace. The scene was clear upon closer inspection, and I saw a large pile of rocks and looked around, noticing the tunnel walls and ceiling had collapsed, dismantling the circular passage.

A cave-in!

"Lillie!" I shouted, sending alarm to the unstable walls and causing bits of sediment to fall from above, but I clambered over the pile of rocks. Then, I jumped over, partially gliding to the other side, and I continued through the dismantled passage. It led to a dead end, but the area was heavily disrupted. As I twisted, I felt a tug of the twine at the belt, and fear began to surge.

Oh, great. That's the end.

I retraced my steps while winding up the twine that had collected dirt and debris as it dragged loosely behind me. It caught on several rocks, and I tugged at it, nearly snapping it.

Thankfully, the twine was still in one piece despite my abrasive tugging, and I exited out of the tunnel and back into the opening, and I stepped in front of the next passage. An eerie feeling overcame me once again as a warm, foul smell came drifting from the area. My throat felt dry, and my heart beat fast, but my adrenaline spiked once again.

I allowed my safety-twine to drop, and I trekked forward. I came upon more signs of a cave-in sooner than the other tunnel. I could sense I was getting closer to something. This time, I examined the rocks, checking for limbs—just in case. I dreaded the thought of finding a lifeless body, but my instincts told me I had to check.

A sudden, clear awareness of the situation came to my mind. I was looking for a group of people who had fallen into the depths. I had pushed myself to look for Lillie and was dragged into searching for others. The very horrible image of multiple lifeless bodies overwhelmed my mind. No amount of training or guidance from my past could have ever prepared me for that moment. Was I really capable of handling the situation?

I had seen blood and dead animals before. I had often witnessed the destructive behavior of bears violently ripping apart their prey, but never had I ever faced such emotional ties to death. I truly did not have any idea how I could face the very real potential of witnessing something horrific—the death of someone I loved.

Yet—if I did not continue, who else would find the lost people? Who else would rescue Lillie? Who else would return to the surface to inform the others who cared about her what happened?

No. I couldn't let her just fade away! Lillie deserves a better life. She deserves to be known for who she really is—even if I didn't know her completely.

I pushed my thoughts aside, accepting that I was Lillie's last hope—I was the group of survivors' last hope. I ignored the fear of finding her dead for the sake of my draining spirit, allowing the catalyst of hope to guide me instead.

The light of my lantern flickered along the path, guiding me onward. The passage was heavily damaged, and I had to climb over more rocks, carefully examining each new disruption. The air felt warm and smelled weird. Again, I hit a dead end, this time clearly made by a cave-in that ended the tunnel.

"Lillie!" I yelled at the rocks that ended the path. My ears perked as I listened for any sounds besides the low rumbling. I was tempted to push the rocks and try to move the blockade, but Taffy's voice echoed in my head. She explicitly told me not to move anything.

"Lillie, are you there?" I called out again.

I waited for the echoes to stop.

Silence.

I turned back, grabbing the twine as I returned to the open area. There were three more tunnels to explore. I entered the next opening; that time, the air was instantly warm, and the weird smell turned foul and rotten—like rotten eggs from an abandoned bird's nest. The eerie feeling became stronger, and my head spun from the uncertainty and all my instincts were running rampant. As a Teragane, I should have long escaped from the situation. I had never pushed myself beyond the initial alarms of instincts. This was all new territory, and the old teachings were betraying my new ambitions.

Further in, caved-in rocks completely blocked the passage, but there was a small opening that I noticed near the ceiling. I climbed the pile of rocks, and I squeezed my body through, careful not to tear myself up. I could barely see down from the pile I had just clambered through. Some rocks fell, and it sounded like a faraway distance from below. I slowly climbed down, wanting to fly, but my footing was precarious, and I was afraid of getting hurt. The floor had been extensively broken through, and the tunnel did not appear like its normal smooth way. The foul smell filled the air, and I covered my nose for a moment.

Snap!

The sound startled me, causing me to lose my footing on the uneven ground, and I fell to my knees, feeling a drastic cut rip through my leg.

"Raaahhhh!" I screamed, unable to hold back as excruciating pain in my leg shot throughout my body, and I grabbed my limb and seethed through clenched teeth. The sound of disturbed rocks echoed around the area again, and I looked down at the spool of twine on my belt.

The end of it was frayed, clearly broken.

I looked back and saw the other end of the twine trapped between the rocks I had just climbed over.

"No!" Pain and anger overwhelmed my mind. I heard unsettling noises as my scream echoed around the unstable area, vibrating throughout. I imagined the rocks falling from the ceiling, crushing me like I had been told would happen if I were to linger near the sounds.

Was I too late? Was this the end of my story? After all my training of survival, had I betrayed myself to my very own demise? Me? A strong, mighty Teragane built for the skies—was I to die down here, crushed by the very rocks shifted by the vibrations of my voice?

I breathed heavily as the intensity of the pain began to subside, and the unsettling noises of shifting rocks stopped. Fear of being crushed to death abated, for the time, and I leaned down to examine my wounded leg. I removed my hand from where I was gripping, noticing blood oozing from the tear in my trousers. My hand was covered in dirt and blood, no longer noticeably smooth and causing guilt.

The foul smell permeating the area filled my nostrils, and my stomach ached with nausea. Sweat dripped from my forehead down into my eyes, and I rubbed my face with my sleeve, smearing debris and sweat. My eyes stung, and I winced, feeling almost depleted of motivation.

"I must be crazy," I said out loud to myself as an unusual moment of humor rose in my chest. What would the Teraganes of the mountain think if they saw me right now? My parents would scold me for disregarding my instincts and following my emotions. The Sage would remind me, again, that I was in need of further guidance because I wasn't grown enough to make my own life choices.

What would Cami think? I started to laugh at the idea of Cami lecturing me.

"You might as well dig your own grave down there," he would sneer. "Only a fool would go to the depths for *some* girl."

Yeah, that girl made the delicious marmalade you enjoyed so much.

I coughed through the laughter of a crazed man, but the dryness in my throat grew worse, and the sweat and blood dripping from my body felt disgusting, and the queasiness in my stomach perpetuated. I pushed my hair aside, smearing blood on my forehead. I didn't care if the others on the mountain would call me crazy. I shook my head at the thought. I knew Lillie was not just *some* girl.

Let me die down here if it means that I was Lillie's last hope. If I am to die, what an honorable death! To die for the girl I love—yes, I could die with ease knowing I tried my best, for she was worth every effort I have made to come this far.

Then, ever so quietly, I heard something.

I steadied my breathing, narrowing my eyes and ears. I heard the faint sound of muffled noises. I stood up straight and walked further into the darkness. Again, I heard it.

The quiet, muffled noise of voices.

CHAPTER TWENTY-TWO
WHEN HOPE RETURNS WITH LIGHT

I stumbled further into the tunnel, ignoring the numbness that overtook my senses as I only focused on finding the source of the noise I had just heard. By the orange light of the lantern, I could observe that the area no longer resembled a tunnel but rather an uncanny, large opening. I could not make out a ceiling or any distinct walls—just a wide, ominous uncharted space. The floor was covered in rocks that shifted when I walked, causing the moving rubble to echo with each step. The air was incredibly foul, but I did not care what was creating the putrid smell; only that, as it grew stronger, the muffled sound of voices also became apparent.

"Lillie! Are you there?" I finally cried out. The vibrations resounded off the unstable area, and I regretted yelling for a moment.

"Hello?" I heard a weakened voice call out.

"Yes, hello," I answered, this time quieter.

"Is someone there?" a young voice called again. I followed its traces, stumbling through the loose stones, and the sound of disrupted rocks overhead became concerning once again.

No! I'm so close. I can't be crushed! I can't die now!

I followed the putrid scent instead of calling out. As it grew stronger, the ground became more uneven. My foot slipped into a hole, shooting pain up my injured leg, and I scanned the uneven floor, noticing all the dark outlines that were potentially deeper than expected.

Could they be inside a hole?

"Call to me," I pleaded, desperate to find the source of the voices.

"Help!" the weakened voice cried out. "We are stuck down here!" The young voice sounded close, but, like I feared, it came from below the uneven ground. I walked carefully, using the light to guide my feet. There was a large hole in front of me where the ground had sunk beneath itself. I peered below, but it was too deep to see anything. Yet, it was the foul stench that wafted from the pit that fluttered my heart.

"Over here!" the voice cried from deep within. Without hesitation, I jumped into the hole and glided down. It was not too far, and, when I landed on a jagged surface, my legs bent on impact, but I ignored the pain shooting up my injured leg. My light lit up the area, revealing the dirty faces of Tamarines sitting around, resting against the wall that was obviously too tall and smooth for anyone to climb. I stepped closer to see their faces, scanning each one to find the only one I was truly seeking for.

"What the hell?" an older woman cried.

"The demons of death have finally come for us!" an older man screeched as he covered his head in fear.

"No, look, he's from the mine!" a young boy exclaimed while pointing at my supply belt.

"Sable?"

My eyes widened as I peered at the young girl sitting against the wall, seeing past the layers of dirt upon her skin or the dustiness of her unusually white hair.

Lillie.

"There you are," I gasped, and quickly crouched down before her, ignoring the others arguing whether or not I was here to end their lives or save them. A sleeping man lay next to her, and Lillie tried moving, but her weakened state prevented her from making more than a simple adjustment in her sitting position. I placed my hand on her cheek that was dangerously cold.

"How?" she weakly uttered, and her green eyes were noticeably faded.

"Shh," I said, and I unbuckled the water canteen and brought it to her lips. She gulped while I held her trembling hand. For a selfish moment, I ignored the others while I allowed her to drink as much as she wanted.

I found you. I really found you.

She pushed the canteen aside while still blinking past her dumbfounded demeanor, and I looked over at the others who stared with similar expressions of disbelief now that they seemingly accepted that I was no threat to their lives.

"I have water for everyone to share," I said, and the other two survivors moved closer to me. The older man reached for the canteen, but I held onto it to keep him from drinking too much as he smacked his parched lips a little too greedily. The older woman gladly allowed me to give her water, and the young boy next to Lillie anticipated his turn. Then, I looked down at the man sleeping next to Lillie.

"Allow me," she offered with a weak voice. I handed her the container, and she carefully let water run into his mouth. He was lethargic as his eyes flickered while Lillie whispered to him, but he drank enough to cause him to gasp.

"I also have medical supplies," I said. "Tell me, what do you all need? I heard there were seven missing workers—I only see five. Where are the others?"

"David and Mira didn't survive the fall," Lillie said as she seemed to regain her senses, and sat more upright. "I think they were instantly crushed after the collapse of the tunnel. I can't see well, but I'm too afraid to examine their bodies."

That was the foul smell—the smell of rotting bodies under piles of rocks.

"Jamie's leg is badly damaged," she said while pointing to the lethargic man. A sense of conflicted relief passed over my mind as I remembered Lara asking me to also find her brother—his injury was problematic, but at least he was alive. I instantly opened the satchel with the medical supplies and found some cloth material. I wrapped Jamie's leg in the cloth, covering his open wound. It smelled infected and was noticeably broken.

Lillie, leaning over him, spoke softly as she stroked his forehead. He winced and took short breaths, but stayed still through the process. His sluggish demeanor and fevering body meant he did not have much time left. Yet, as I lifted my eyes, observing Lillie's affectionate hand upon the man's sweaty forehead, a sudden pang of jealousy rose as I remembered Lara speaking about the concern of Jamie being a troublemaker.

"I'm fine," said the young boy while crouching next to Lillie, and I shook my untimely thoughts aside.

"Yes, Peak is fine," Lillie chuckled. She leaned closer to me and whispered, "I hope Aro and Tim will also be okay, now that they've had some water. They haven't spoken much since the cave-in."

"I'm going to get everyone out," I said, and I handed out small portions of dried meat to the survivors. Everyone ate slowly but eagerly, and I could sense hope had returned. They moved easier and were antsy to be officially rescued.

"I will even bring the bodies of the dead for their families to properly bury," I said heroically. I had not thought about it, but at that moment, I knew I wanted to complete the rescue mission. I found the missing group—and Lillie—and my fear of facing the undesirable outcomes subsided. I felt competent enough to handle the horrific situation now that I knew where the survivors were and how to get out.

"Oh, Sable," Lillie quietly whimpered, a tone I had never heard. "I don't know how you ever came here to begin with. How is this even possible? Am I dreaming? Am I dead?"

"You are very much alive," I said while smiling at her. "It's a long story—one I will enjoy telling you when we are all in a safer place." I placed the lantern in the middle of the area. The survivors huddled close to the light, seeking warmth and comfort. Their faces were sunken, covered in layers of dirt, blood, and sweat. Yet they possessed hopeful eyes as they stared at me, anticipating my direction, and I gave everyone one more round of water, but the food had been depleted.

I sat next to Lillie and held her hand, rubbing her thumb gently with mine. Her skin was rough and sullied, but, for the first time, so was mine. I finally found her and wanted to savor the moment to the best of my ability. My sheer determination to find her led me to this dark hole, deep within the underground world—through the series of monsters. My surroundings were nauseating; the smell of rotting flesh, infections, and excrement filled the air. Sunken faces, depleted of life, sat staring at me. They were waiting for me to be their final act of hope, and they saw me as a savior in their bleak circumstances. Hope had returned to them, but it brought doubts about my own capabilities. I wanted to be Lillie's hero. Now, I needed to be a savior to others.

How am I going to bring all these people back?

I knew that I could go back the way I came, however, my greatest concern was the perilous journey I had just made by myself. These people had been trapped underground for days. They were weak and could possibly not survive the journey. The rock blockade where my twine had broke and where I had cut my leg was most concerning. I could carry them all individually, but at that point, they would need to climb through the small opening. I could try with Lillie first or Peak—he seemed the least affected by the circumstances. That could determine if it was suitable enough for the rest of the survivors. My other option could consist of finding a way out of the ceiling where they first fell. Perhaps there was a way out from straight above. Maybe Taffy and other rescuers could dig away from the collapsed tunnel and make a safe exit.

I looked above me. It was pitch black. There were no signs of a ceiling or any safe openings. Then, I remembered Taffy's map. No—this was the problem in the first place. The original ceiling of the tunnel collapsed, and the floor opened up, dismantling everything they had mapped. There wasn't a way to enter the collapsed area above the surface. It was too dangerous for further excavation, risking even more weakening of the unstable rocks, possibly causing further obstruction.

No—my fastest option was from how I entered and through the stable tunnels and established cavern. I would need to focus on getting everyone through safely. I would take it one step at a time—one body at a time.

"The way here was long, but manageable," I said out loud as I stared at the tips of my filthy boots stretched out before me. "There is only a small rock blockade that needs to be climbed. Then another series of tunnels to travel through, eventually a cavern. But I will fly each person to safety where a rescue team awaits at the surface."

No one spoke—only a cough from Tim and shifting positions as the survivors listened to my words.

"I will carry each one for as long as necessary," I said, and gazed at Lillie's trembling hand in mine. "I'm strong and can help."

"Sable," Lillie said quietly. "You don't have to do this on your own. You can return to the surface; tell the others where we are."

"Yes, but the others can't help you like I can," I replied. "That's why they haven't come yet. They've been looking for you this entire time, but they never could make it far enough to find you."

"You've done so much already. I don't know how you can keep this up."

"There is no other way. I'm the only one capable."

"I know you're capable, but you may not be strong enough. Bringing us supplies and waiting for more help may be the safer way."

"I cannot leave you—any of you—to wait for help." I turned my head, facing Lillie, and her eyes darted down. "Please let me help in the way I know is best. Allow me to do this in the way that I know assures *your* safety."

She was scared, obviously, perhaps she had already accepted death. But, if I knew anything about Lillie, it was that she could never allow others to come in harm's way because of her.

Perhaps she was feeling guilty of my rescue mission and expected to simply fade away from her disappearance.

Yeah—I'm not letting that happen.

"Let me carry you to the surface," I said and stood up while still holding her hand, and I gently pulled her up into a standing position.

"No," she said rather harshly, and removed her hand from mine. "Take Peak first. He is the strongest. I'll stay here with the others."

Of course you'd say that.

However, I agreed that taking Peak was a good option, and I pushed my fears aside. I looked at the young Tamarine who was listening with perked ears, and his blue eyes widened. His golden hair was covered in filth, and his undertones were still visible, although difficult to observe in the low light. He appeared young—too young to be facing death.

"Peak," I said as I adjusted my belt. "Ready to return to the surface?"

"You betcha I am," he said and pounced to his feet with childish energy.

"Unfortunately, I need my light," I said while grabbing the lantern, and I connected it to my belt. "But I will return. Just keep holding onto hope and the knowledge that you will all be safe soon. Be ready for my return." Lillie moved close to me, and I looked at her face, our eyes meeting. I finally found her, and could hardly believe I was leaving her behind. I hadn't anticipated her refusing to let me take her first, but, knowing Lillie, she had the determined mind of a raging storm that no one could control.

As the young boy stood closer to me and Lillie feigned a smile, I grabbed her waist, and pulled her close to me.

"I'll be back," I whispered in her long, pointed ear, allowing my nose to touch her skin, cherishing the intimate moment as it encouraged my mind, but internally, I was screaming, especially as her tone of desperation increased.

"Please," she uttered. "Return to me." I pressed my lips against her cheek, kissing her gently. Her warmth had begun to return, and there was still a hint of the purple flower emitted from her soiled hair. Yet, the other unpleasant smells reeked; I was also filthy, and my lips tasted salty and gross. The smell of fresh blood permeated my body, but I held fast to the hope that soon we'd be able to clean up and embrace once again—maybe I'd even get a chance to kiss her lips and finally have an intimate moment to confess my ardent love for her.

I grabbed Peak, held him close to my chest, and then, with a powerful jump, I flew out of the hole. He was lightweight, and I easily ascended back into the uncertain cavern ahead. I placed him on the ground as we neared the blockade. The light of the lantern faithfully showed us the path and we carefully walked toward the wall of stone. I spotted the twine wedged between the rocks above where it had snapped.

"See, there?" I asked, and I pointed toward the gap between the rock blockade and the ceiling. Peak nodded. "I'm going to fly you up, but you'll have to climb through." He nodded again in response, and I grabbed him. I flew up as close to the hole as I could, and landed Peak near the cramped entrance. He clambered through the gap with ease. He was small and agile, even after being trapped in the depths for days.

"Well done," I called out, "now, carefully descend; I'm coming through." I could hear him scaling the rocks, and I climbed through the gap after him. I heard rocks continue to fall on either side, and Peak gave out a small shriek as he slid down.

"Careful!" I shouted, and I suddenly lost my grip and also slid down the cascading stones. Peak tried moving out of the way, but I fell on top of him. The clanging noises of rocks hitting the lantern echoed through the area.

"Are you alright?" I asked while quickly lifting myself off the young boy. He grunted as he dusted off his arms, ignoring my question, but then pointed to the lantern as we both stood up.

"Light's gettin' low," Peak said. "Do you have oil?"

"Oh, yes," I said, and I pulled out the canister of oil Taffy had given me.

"I'll do it," Peak said. He grabbed the canister and filled the lantern with fresh oil, and the light became brighter as he adjusted it. "There, that's better."

"Thanks," I said while brushing off my tunic, and I saw tears in my sleeves and the bloody cut through my torn trousers. Ignoring my state of filth, I led Peak through the rocks until the tunnel floor became sturdy again. Eventually, it opened up where the twine lay motionless, leading the way down to the next tunnel. Peak was capable of walking on his own allowing me to not worry about his ability to move freely. It was obvious that he felt safe with me, perhaps also allocating a new found strength after his time in the underground. We followed the tunnel in silence until we came to the end, where it dropped off into the great cavern.

"The yellow twine is our path out," I said after needlessly pointing. It was loosely hanging in the air, running deep within the cavern, disappearing behind the dark shadows lurking below. "Let's go."

Grabbing Peak once again, I glided down to a safe distance where I could fly with ease but also follow the twine. I was grateful for its yellow color, as it reflected the orange, glowing light. With the help of the twine and my previous travels through the cavern, I felt confident enough to fly through. I maneuvered past the stalactites, swaying back and forth as they appeared before me.

It was my first time carrying someone while flying—too bad it wasn't Lillie. All my training to strengthen my wings was evidently effective. Peak gripped my arms tightly as we flew through the darkness, but his short legs dangled underneath my figure. As we flew steadily, my eyes darted around, watching out for danger. The twine went between two large columns, too narrow for me to fly through, so I went around, losing sight of the twine for a few moments.

"Ah! Watch it!" Peak squealed while squirming in my arms. A massive rock formation came into view, and I bolted straight up. Peak bent his legs, barely avoiding the rocks as we passed over. The young boy tensed, pinching my arms with his fingers as he held me tight, causing me to wince, but I continued until I spotted the twine again, and returned to its guidance.

That was close. I need a better method to carry people. Peak is shorter than the others, but his legs are still in danger.

I followed the yellow twine further into the darkness, swaying past the dangerous rocks. Then, finally up ahead, I saw the pulley that held the platform with lanterns. I felt a sense of relief as I realized we had made it back.

"Time to go up," I said loudly to Peak and he grunted in response. Regardless of his small stature, my arms began to grow tired. I was exhausted from my rescue search, and I was becoming weary. My wings pushed me towards the surface, bending strongly as we elevated, and Peak's body shifted parallel to mine as we ascended. The glow of the surface light became clearer as we approached. I heard voices calling out, and blurry figures gathered around the glowing light. I ascended to the surface, exiting the original opening where Taffy and her crew waited. I felt relieved to set Peak down on the ground, away from the gaping hole of the cavern below. He was instantly recovered by the workers standing by. They began to rejoice, cry out for others to see, and congratulate me on a successful rescue. But my heart sank, for I still had more bodies to carry.

This was far from over.

"Damn you, brilliant kid," Taffy chimed as she patted my shoulder. "You made it! And you found Peak."

"Please," I said while heavily breathing. "I need more water and food to give to the other survivors."

"Oh, you found the others?" Taffy asked, but turned to inform the others to retrieve my requested items. "Hey, there, Peak!" She slapped his back and he gave a weak smile in response. "Good to see you alive. So, who else is there besides Peak?"

"David and Mira are gone," Peak said solemnly.

"Aw, that's a shame; they were good people," Taffy said.

"But Lillie, Jamie, Aro, Tim, and me's survived," Peak said. "And this guy is gonna bring us all out!"

"Ah, of course he is," Taffy said, still grinning largely. "But, first, let's get you out of here. You've been in the caves long enough, sweetheart." Taffy ruffled Peak's dirty golden hair, casting sediment along his shoulders, and he continued to grin. She beckoned another worker to escort Peak away. He waved at me, then walked away with the obvious joy that he was going to see the light again. As Taffy continued to congratulate me, I explained further to Taffy of my journey.

"They're barely alive, and they need their strength for the return journey," I explained.

"You're a true hero," Taffy said to me in a quiet tone. "That little guy just survived hell and he's smiling like a little trooper."

"Well, not everyone is smiling," I said while pushing the hair out of my face, feeling unnerved of an early celebration.

"Hey, look kiddo," she said. "You saved his life, and that matters. Gotta celebrate the small wins, alright? Don't want you runnin' out of courage. You'll get the rest of the folks. I know you will."

I was not ready to celebrate. I knew she spoke with encouragement to keep my motivation strong, but my chest felt ridden with guilt as Lillie was still trapped deep in the belly of the monster.

"I will. I will not stop until every-body has been brought to the surface."

"Yes, but first" —Taffy looked down at my leg— "let's get that wrapped up."

CHAPTER TWENTY-THREE
WHEN AN EERIE FEELING LINGERS BEHIND

I winced as a worker poured water over my wound. Blood and water trickled onto the rocks as it dripped down my leg. The man cleaned the wound, wrapped a cloth around it, and then gently pulled down the torn pants over the bandage.

"That should stop the bleeding," he said while looking up at me. "You should see a doctor when this is over. Wouldn't want you to lose your leg." I shook my head and he grinned, showcasing several missing teeth. He patted my knee, then grunted as he stood up while wiping his hands with a clean cloth.

"Kid needs to eat," Taffy said as she trudged over with a wooden bowl in her hands. "Get your hands washed up." The helpful man allowed water to pour over my hands, and gave me the cloth to wipe away the dirt and blood before Taffy gave me sustenance. I chewed the dried meat, and devoured the stale bread, but my aching stomach exceeded the flavorless meal.

"I'm not a kid, by the way," I said as I picked at the small crumbs on the bottom of the bowl.

"Ah, well, you're a kid to me—how old are ya?" she asked after a low chuckle.

"I just entered my seventeenth year," I replied, and then handed the empty bowl to Taffy.

"That's a funny way to say your age, but, hey, you're right. You're obviously not a kid. It's just—so many young ones come here—they all grow up too fast. So, I try to remind them that they're still young. Like Peak. Even Lillie—damn she's smart for her age. After all is said and done, I'm gonna make sure she works directly under me. Could use her sharp mind and writing skills. Tell her that, won't you? Might give her hope for a better future."

A better future, here?

Is that what will happen?

As a group of workers handed over to me the new supplies of a water canteen and another sack of dried meat, they also filled the lantern oil, and even provided a second so that I could leave it for the survivors. While I readied myself to return to my mission, I saw the rescue workers admire me with their hopeful expressions. Although I still carried guilt, fear of the future, and apprehension of the perilous task still at hand, a small glimmer of pride began to rise in my heart. I positioned myself near the gaping hole once again, and took another glance at the Tamarine workers.

"Good luck," Taffy said with a wave that she extended from her forehead. A murmur followed from the other workers, and one even bowed their head. I descended once again into the dark abyss, this time knowing exactly which way I wanted to go. I instantly saw the yellow twine and flew above it, following its slow ascent towards the tunnels in the north. With two lanterns, I saw further around and could safely guide my way through. The glistening of gemstones in the cavern became more impressive to me. I felt more at ease, finally knowing that I was returning to Lillie and she was, in fact, going to live.

I'm coming back, Lillie. I'll free you from this pit of gloom once and for all.

I was worried about what Taffy said, particularly about Lillie returning to the mines for work, but shook away the future aspect as I maneuvered past the columns, and steadily flew above the rock formations. It was easier without holding someone, and the second lantern allowed me to easily see obstacles ahead. As I followed the twine upwards, I saw the outline of the tunnel and quickened my pace.

I entered the tunnel where the twine led and walked along it. My leg felt better now that it was covered, but small amounts of pain still lingered with each step although the man had said the cut was not too deep. He told me that the bandage was to prevent further damage to my leg, but also protect me while reentering the depths. Still, I could feel the sharp pain at each step of my foot.

Despite the injury, I kept a steady pace as I walked along the tunnel. It was too narrow to fly through without risking damaging my wings, but I did not need to. The less energy I exerted, the more strength I had to carry the other survivors back. Peak was in good health, considering the circumstances. The others would possibly need to be carried. Jamie was unable to walk, and perhaps the older man and woman needed to be supported. Lillie—well, I didn't mind carrying her.

The thought of her returning to work in the mine lingered in the back of my mind, and I wondered what would follow as I had planned to bring Lillie all the way back to her home. I anticipated the look on her parents' faces and the pride that would well in my heart as I proved myself worthy of being part of Lillie's world.

Those cowards didn't have the audacity to look for their missing daughter. And Lara will be happy to see Lillie safe—and her brother. Safe because of me! The whole city will know who I am and how I saved Lillie and the others from this wretched pit of despair! Yes! I will be the legendary hero they will talk about. They will think twice before frowning upon a Teragane in their presence—I'm no savage from the mountain.

As I entered the opening where the tunnel separated into many directions, I continued to follow the yellow twine towards the next tunnel opening. Suddenly, that same eerie feeling crept over me and I paused my steps. The hairs on my arm stood up, and my neck tensed.

Slowly, I turned around and my eyes scanned the other two tunnels that I did not explore. As my alarm instincts rushed through my body, I slowly walked towards the unexplored tunnels, feeling drawn by some mysterious force. The uncanny affect was heightened as I stared deeply for a few moments, confused about what was influencing the eerie sensation.

Why do I feel this way in this area?

A slight breeze exhaled from the tunnel permeating with an odd warmth that stunk of rotting eggs.

Rotting eggs? It cannot be an abandoned bird's nest.

Isn't that what sulfur smells like?

A chill ran down my spine, and I stepped away, remembering the teachings of my parents instructing me to use my strong sense of smell to determine if a cave was filled with certain scents that could potentially be dangerous or deadly. I was taught that sulfur smelled like rotting eggs and could be problematic if its presence was too overwhelming in the depths of natural caves.

"It could cause you to suffocate," they had warned.

I shook my head and covered my nose, then turned towards the entrance with the twine. A shiver ran down my spine as I felt grateful to not have gone too deep in the other tunnels, although the sulfur stench lingered around the walls.

As I came to the rock blockade, I jumped to the opening and squeezed through, taking greater precaution as the two lanterns clinked as the glass scraped across the uneven stones. The objects were sturdy, obviously built to withstand the work of a mine, but, still, without the orange light, I could fail my mission. There was no more twine to follow after the blockade, but the nauseating smell guided me to the sunken ground where Lillie and the others waited.

"I'm back," I called softly from above.

"He's back!" someone shouted. A loud crash of falling rocks came from further within the dismantled area and echoed throughout.

"Shhhh," voices mumbled, and I jumped into the hole, gliding cautiously down. Instantly, I scanned for Lillie, who was sitting near Jamie, but she stood up with a new strength—with hope of survival.

"Sable, you're alright," she said as she drew closer, and I wrapped my arms around her, hugging tightly and nudged my nose against her ear.

"Of course," I whispered, and I felt her hands drift around my back. I could feel our hearts both racing, and I was ready to just jump out with her still in my arms. Alas, the others needed my help, and I disbanded our embrace.

As the others slightly grimaced at our affection, I handed out the canteen of water to the older man and woman, this time, allowing them to take what they wanted from the water and food. I placed the second lantern on the ground near the surviving group, and looked over at Lillie as she quietly munched on a stick of dried meat.

"Ready to go?" I asked Lillie.

"No, you must take Jamie first," Lillie demanded. "He is weak and needs to see a doctor." I looked down at the resting man. His fever had grown worse, and his breathing was dangerously shallow. A sense of guilt overwhelmed me as I thought about Lara and her concern for her brother. But my eyes darted over to Lillie wondering how many others she would put before herself before accepting my help.

"I don't know how to get him through the gap," I said. "He will need to pull himself through."

"I can help with that. I will climb over, then help him through the other side if you can help with lifting him."

"I can't carry both of you down the cavern. I can only take one person at a time."

"That's okay; I can wait for you to return."

Another clash of rocks colliding suddenly echoed, sounding dangerously close. I stretched my neck and sniffed the air.

Sulfur.

The instinctual alerting sensation indicated that something was different—danger was near.

"Hey," Lillie said while grabbing my arm. "It's not safe here. There's something out there."

"You can sense it, too?" I whispered as I leaned my head closer to hers.

"Yes. I don't know what, but the collapse of the tunnel—" She hesitated, but pulled on my arm as she stood on her tiptoes, and her nose touched against my jawline. I could feel the fearful tone as she lowered her voice, and a trickle of sweat dripped down the side of my face.

"The ground caved in a very unnatural way—this wasn't a typical cave-in," she continued, and I lifted my eyes, noticing the man Tim and woman Aro observing us with suspicious eyes. "I think something made it collapse, and I think it's still out there."

"Okay," I said, then swallowed, noticing the dryness of my throat. "Then, maybe I can move all of you out of this pit—away from what danger lurks."

"If you can. I have felt so weak, but since you came, I have felt my strength of mind return, and can now think clearly about the situation. I did not want to bring fear to others, especially if I'm wrong, but I'm afraid whatever is out there is drawing near." We both looked toward the corner where the decaying bodies lay.

"We must leave them behind," Lillie pleaded. "If possible, we can retrieve them later, when the living are safe. For now, we must leave this death pit."

"Help me prepare the others for escape," I said, and Lillie nodded as she released her hand from my arm. She then walked over to the other two, explained we would all be leaving, one at a time, and then she moved over to Jamie. As she crouched down next to him, she wiped his forehead with a dirty sleeve, speaking intimately.

"Hey Jamie," she whispered. "Sable is going to carry you out of this hole. Then we are going to finally have that tea-party." She chuckled to herself as the man only slightly mumbled, and I raised a brow, but the others began to rise to their feet as Lillie looked up at me again.

"Take them first while I prepare Jamie," Lillie said to me, and I nodded, then my eyes directed at Aro. She pointed to herself, and I beckoned for her to come to me. As I wrapped my arms around her waist, she latched onto my limbs, and I flew her out of the hole. I moved towards the rock blockade, then placed her on the ground, directing her to stay put, even in the dark.

I went back for Tim, who seemed hesitant at first, possibly afraid to fly with me. However, I didn't have the privilege to hesitate while potential danger lurked in the darkness, and I quickly grabbed him, and flew him out of the hole. I placed him with Aro, and he jolted away from my grip, grumbling to himself with obvious disdain.

Even when facing death, the man cannot escape his partiality.

When I returned for Jamie, Lillie had him sitting up, and his eyes were flickering. I put his arm over my shoulder and carried him horizontally in my arms. His body felt sweltering hot; the mixture of sweat, dirt, and infection permeated his body. I took off once again, flying directly to where the others waited.

"Hold onto him," I said as I brought Jamie to them. "Here, take this too." I unfastened the second lantern and left it with Aro.

Now, back for Lillie.

A loud crash and movement of rocks came suddenly close to the hole. I quickly dove in, following my instincts to move fast and efficiently. Lillie was waiting, lantern in hand, and I scooped her up into my arms and flew her back to the others. I carried her similarly to Jamie across my arms, and, as we were airborne, she tightened her grip around my neck and shoulders. I was finally flying with Lillie.

Too bad it wasn't more romantic.

The loud sounds of falling rocks came crashing behind us, causing me to refocus my attention on getting everyone to safety. When I settled Lillie onto the ground, she became cheerful and encouraging to the others, ignoring the danger behind us.

"Okay, we are out of the hellish pit. Let's now go through the tunnel," Lillie said, then she looked at me, her green eyes sparkling in the lantern light. "Can you carry Jamie?"

"Of course," I said, and I picked him up once again and led the way to the rock blockade. He mumbled about a tea-party, asking for something called a strawberry, but his body began to limp as his limbs swayed. Lillie walked beside me, holding out the lantern for guidance, and Aro held out the other lantern. It was easier to see now with the lanterns spread out, and we came to the blockade after a few moments. The sound of crashing rocks still echoed from behind us, but no one dared look back.

"There—see the yellow twine?" I said while I pointed, to the best of my ability, to the elevated points where the broken twine sat wedged between the rocks where the gap was, and Lillie nodded.

"Okay," she said. "I'll go first, then you hand me Jamie and I'll drag—"

"No, let me; I'm stronger than you," Tim suddenly announced as he puffed out his chest. He sneered as Lillie hesitated to respond, but he then quickly turned to climb the rocks. Surprisingly, Aro, without a word, followed him. Even though they had been trapped underground for three days, adrenaline spiked their energy levels. Was it a final act of desperation to be the first to leave while the scent of sulfur rose and colliding rocks echoed behind us?

Small rocks and rubble slid down at their desperate efforts, and Lillie and I gave each other nervous glances, especially as the older Tamarines grunted as they neared the top. Jamie mumbled again, and Lillie whispered for him to stay alive, and I watched as Tim disappeared through the gap, followed by Aro handing him the lantern, then moving through.

"You ready?" Lillie asked, and I nodded. I flew toward the gap with the feverish man, lethargically speaking about foods I had never heard of, and Tim and Aro were waiting for me on the other side of the small opening.

"Head first, yeah?" Tim suggested.

"Yeah, be careful; he's very lethargic," I said while positioning Jamie's head first. His neck bent, but Tim stretched his thick arms as he grabbed Jamie's tangled hair, and steadied his head as he pulled the man through. Slowly, we worked together to maneuver the Tamarine man through the gap, and his braided golden hair dragged through the rocks. After Tim pulled the mumbling man through, I turned around and spotted Lillie waiting for me while she held the lantern. My heart skipped a beat as she gazed at me, and I jumped down from the rock blockade and landed next to her.

"Your turn," I said, and her eyes were filled with a new expression—perhaps it was trust.

I picked her up in my arms again, and, with a powerful jump, I flew up to the gap and positioned us at the confined entrance. A few rocks slipped from under her footing, but I held her waist as I directed her to climb through.

Then, there was another loud noise of rumbling rocks, and both Lillie and I finally looked back to where the survivors had been trapped for days. Within the darkness, a glowing red light appeared from where the noise was coming from.

And it was moving.

Lillie gasped, then scrambled through the gap. I watched the mysterious glowing light move slowly in the distance. That eerie feeling overcame me once again, sending chilling coldness throughout my body. I heard a strange sound of crackling and massive amounts of rocks were moving as if something was slithering about, and the smell of sulfur and smoke overwhelmed my senses.

"Sable, hurry!" Lillie called out from the other side, and I jolted through the small gap. I tried calming my nerves, but the sound of moving rocks and the crackling, mysterious unknown moving around caused me to push myself too much. I felt the scraping of sharp rocks against one of my wings, and I winced at the pain. Horrifying images of being crushed caused my heart to race, and I frantically exited the hole and rushed to glide down the other side.

As I bent over, hyperventilating, I rested my hands upon my thighs, and sweat dripped from the tip of my nose. Then, I felt a hand upon my shoulder, and saw Lillie stand by me, still holding the lantern.

"You really are the bravest man I know," she said, and I looked up through the tangled hair covering my eyes, and Lillie moved her fingers through the damp strands. I felt my breathing steady as I straightened up, and Lillie continued to move her hand around by brushing through the disrupted feathers of my wings.

"Thanks," I finally said. "That means a lot."

"I know," she said with a sly smirk. "That's why I said it." I placed my hand on her cheek, but my eyes lifted at the other three survivors who waited in the middle of the tunnel. The older man Tim grimaced, but Aro's eyes were soft with admiration. Jamie, well, he was twitching while lying on the ground.

"Let's continue," I said as I moved my hand away from Lillie's cheek and walked over to the lethargic man. I picked him, causing his eyes to flicker, and the stench of his leg was strongly noticeable now that we had left the other area of foul scents.

"Now," I continued. "We follow the yellow twine."

CHAPTER TWENTY-FOUR

WHEN A FACE LIGHTENS THE SITUATION

"**H**old on, Jamie," Lillie said as she applied water to his lips after I had crouched down for her to reach. The water ran down his colorless face and she used her sleeve to wipe the excess. She then applied her damp sleeve to his forehead, hoping to cool him from his feverish state. She unraveled strands of tangled golden hair, moving it away from his sweaty forehead. His fever had grown dangerously high, and his breathing was becoming even more shallow.

"We need to keep moving," I said while standing up again. Lillie nodded and walked next to me as we traversed through the passage, following the twine. Tim and Aro walked ahead, guiding the way with the light of a lantern. My heart was beating heavily as I thought about the moving and glowing light I had seen and all the terrifying noises it was producing.

"Lillie," I whispered. "What was that thing back there? The glowing red light?" Lillie's long, pointed ears narrowed, and she glanced over her shoulder.

"I don't know," she apprehensively replied, but did not continue, not even with a single theory. Occasionally, Lillie would adjust Jamie's faltering head upon my chest, smiling whenever he mumbled something, which, if it were not for the perilous situation, would have been rather amusing since it was often simple nonsense. For a moment, I wanted to ask her about him, specifically who he was to her, but as fear of a thousand other threats lingered in my mind, he was hardly someone I needed to worry about as death lingered closer to him than anyone else.

The thin air was void of the putrid smells from the pit in which Lillie and the others were trapped, save for Jamie's infected leg, but the hints of sulfur still drifted through the passageway. I looked at the walls of the tunnel once again, noticing the smooth-looking rocks with overlapping wedges. Nothing appeared jagged, like the other natural caves, but the perfectly round formation caused me to wonder what had created the tunnel in the first place.

"When I first found these passageways," I said, breaking the silence. "I had a weird feeling and thought: *what made these tunnels*?" Lillie looked around, examining the walls with the lantern. Then, she placed her hand on the wall, gently feeling the grooves as she walked along.

"The rocks are volcanic," she said. "*Pāhoehoe*, I've heard others call it. Formed by lava."

"So, lava made these tunnels?"

"Yes, possibly."

"Why possibly?"

"Well." She hesitated as she inched closer to me, then lowered her voice. "There is a chance these tunnels are ancient relics of lava flows from an extinct volcano. However, the tunnels themselves do not look ancient."

"They were formed recently?"

"I don't know for sure, but it would make sense in light of other factors."

"Like what?"

"Uh, it's hard to explain."

"Just do your best." Lillie looked up at me, her green eyes glistening, but she wedged her hand under my bicep, gripping tightly near where Jamie's head rested.

"Something feels different—a change," she started. "It's been hard to notice since I often numb myself to the deafening dangers of the underground, but recently, as we pursued a new excavation tunnel, I felt a change while noticing unusual things. I can't explain, only how I felt. Like a deep cry of thunder underground and an uncomfortable feeling of a shift in the earth—but not like with the excavation of our pickaxes. Jamie noticed the volcanic rocks, and we began discussing it with our superiors, but they didn't listen. Safety was far from their mind, I guess, especially as we continued to find more valuable minerals. Jamie predicted the empty space beneath us, but still, no one felt concerned. Well, until a few days ago, I went further into finding a better solution." She paused and quickly looked over her shoulder again, slightly pressing her fingers against my arm. As my wings twitched from behind, I peered over, but saw nothing but the lingering darkness.

"It's okay," I said. "Nothing is there. Please, continue."

"After I returned to evacuate the team, the ground gave in. I don't know what happened on the surface, but the darkness engulfed me and the others. It was horrible. I thought for sure I had died. For hours, rocks moved, crashing around. It was torture. I thought for sure I would be crushed. The terrible sounds above were so horrible—something I've never experienced or heard before. Eventually, the rumbling faded away. Who knows how long or when it was? I don't even know what day it is."

"Supposedly, you've been underground for three days. Maybe more, now." Jamie suddenly grunted, jerking his neck, and Lillie helped maneuver his head onto my chest again. His eyes flickered as he groaned, this time, he distinctly whispered Lillie's name.

"Three days? No wonder I feel like death," she said, unmoved by the man's suffering, and she tucked her hand under my arm again.

"All of this sounds like a bad dream," I grumbled.

"Yet—you are here. A bad dream, yes, but an unforeseeable twist of fate. How is that even possible?"

"When you did not emerge from the forest on the day of the full moon, I became worried. I waited until nightfall, yet you did not appear. So, I set out to find you."

"Oh, that's right. I never work on a full-moon."

"Why did your superiors keep forcing you to dig deeper into the mine? Why didn't they value your safety after you spoke of your concerns?"

"Huh? Probably because they are selfish, greedy, and egocentric; they only care about money, not the lives of the people who bring them resources. The deeper we went, the shinier the stones became. It's not like this doesn't happen—I mean, this particular event was worse, but there are a lot of cave-ins within the mines."

I felt my lips snarl as a low growl escaped my mouth. Just the thought of Ezra and the bearded man filled my mind with hatred towards the apathy of Tamarines looking only to serve themselves. I thought about all the things Taffy told me about the Masters and Keepers who were in control of the environment. My eyes darted from Lillie, then ahead at the others carrying the lantern, then down to the fevering man who I was afraid would stop breathing.

All this pain and suffering because of stupid, shiny rocks.

"Well, after we all get to safety, I think there are some major changes that need to happen," I declared.

215

"I hope so," Lillie replied. "Unfortunately, I don't know if anything will change. People go missing in the mines. Lots of illnesses take their lives too. This place has always been dangerous. Everything in life is like this, to be honest."

"Well, I will force a change. I will stop the Masters from forcing the people of Cedrus City to live miserable and dangerous lives."

"How do you know—"

"I've picked up a lot of information since I've been looking for you. See, I can learn and understand your world after all."

"Then, you will also realize that not a single person can make such drastic changes." Lillie's tone changed as her eyes focused on the path ahead. "The Masters and Keepers have extensive control, especially over the mine."

"Well, someone should stop them."

"Oh? Someone like you? And how would you go about doing that?" Lillie raised her eyebrows and my mind went blank. I had no idea how to stop the elusive Masters who made this world—Lillie's world—so miserable. I was prideful in my rescue efforts, but at that moment my pride was blinding my logical reasoning.

"I, uh—I don't know yet," I said. "But I will find a way to stop them."

"And why? Who are you to enter a world different from your own and claim the right to overthrow their power?"

"Huh? Don't you want me to stop them?"

"Ideally, yeah." Lillie sighed, then looked up at me. "I want you to bravely overthrow the group of Tamarines who make Cedrus City miserable. However, how could you possibly ever come to this? It's not that simple. And why would I ever expect you to do so? No—Sable. I'd rather you forget the idea altogether."

"But what about the mine? What about you? Taffy said you should return to work with her. But—what—how can I help you? How can I do what is right? That's why I'm here in the first place."

"You are not here because it is what is right. You are here because you chose to follow your heart, and you've made your way here—a journey I've yet to hear or can even comprehend at the moment."

"So, what are you saying?"

"I'm just trying to be realistic about the situation. This is why it was difficult for me to explain to you about not just abandoning my life because it is hard. We cannot always make our ideas of life work for others. Sometimes, we have to survive among the selfish beings of the world. We can still make the most of it by doing what we believe is good and trying to make the world a better place for others and ourselves."

"That is exactly what I want."

"Then don't get carried away with the idea that you can overthrow the Masters, especially with a system that's been established for quite some time. If it were that easy, I would have already done so myself." Lillie grinned, causing her cheeks to round, but I still felt uneasy with the way she spoke about the powerful oppressors causing so much pain.

"I only meant that to assure you that this will never happen again."

"And how can you be sure of that? No one can. We can only *hope* to make changes that avoid such problems. We cannot force anything or predict a perfect outcome. We can only do what we think is best."

"No, but I can try to help in making a better life for others."

"And if no one listens? What if no one in power makes a difference?"

"I'll keep trying."

Lillie was right, to some degree. How could I make any major changes for the honest folk of the mines? I was nothing to them, only a day-hero who sacrificed his safety to rescue someone he loved and those she was around.

She was right. If it weren't for her absence, I would never have entered the underground. I would not be holding Jamie's limp body. I would have never met Lara, who helped direct me to the mine, not only for Lillie but for the sake of her brother. What did I know of these people's true problems in life? Who was I to demand changes in a world I knew so little about?

But she was also wrong.

I possibly could not bring about major changes—like changing everything about the work environment—but I could at least spark a chain of events to help inspire others, especially those in power, to make a change. I thought of Taffy and her authentic desire to rescue the survivors. My presence alone seemed to inspire her and give her hope. I would also do everything I could to keep Lillie safe. If she wanted to return, then that was her choice. But, after I returned her to the surface, I would make sure to help provide her with a better way of life.

"Hope is powerful," I said. "Maybe change doesn't happen with one person—with me—but it's still worth trying to find new ways to make life a better place."

"The cavern!" I heard Tim shout from ahead, and we all approached the end of the tunnel that opened up into the massive cavern. The group peered over the edge and then backed away, their darkened eyes gazing upon me as they waited for my lead.

"I'll fly Jamie to safety, then come back for the next person," I said while adjusting the fevering man in my arms. Lillie grabbed my belt and moved close to me while she attached the lantern back to my waist. She gently caressed my left arm, her eyes transfixed on the torn areas showcasing the triangle tattoos on my arm.

"I only say these things so that you do not carry the burden to change an entire system that has functioned this way for who knows how long," she said. "I am so thankful for you being here, and none of us will ever forget the sacrifice you have made for us. I hope that your bravery will spark change and provide a safer environment. I do have hope, especially in you."

"Thanks," I said, then leaned over to nudge the top of her head with my nose. That lovely hint of flowers drifted around, and I pressed my lips ever so gently, kissing her head. She let go of my arm, and I, once again, took off into the abyss, and I followed the twine back to the pulley rope. Holding Jamie in my arms made it much easier to maneuver through the hazardous cavern, and I decided to carry the others in the same position. I approached the pulley rope, spotting the lanterns from further away, but the lanterns were dimly glowing, and two had already been extinguished.

Those need a refill.

I ascended to the surface, following the rope straight up. Once again, my appearance through the opening was greeted with grateful workers, including Taffy. As I landed upon the jagged rocks, they all swarmed around me, and I folded my wings.

"He needs a doctor," I said while handing Jamie over to aid workers who readily received him with open arms. I didn't know what a doctor was, but that is what Lillie had originally stated. "And quick, death lingers too close for this man. Someone, please, give word to his sister Lara that he has been found. Please make sure she knows of his wellbeing."

"You betcha kid—I mean, grown-ass man," Taffy said, and she began directing a new group of workers to come help. I noticed an increase in enthusiasm, and more Tamarines had arrived since the last time I had come with Peak. Hope had returned, and the rescue team was prepared.

Despite the influx of anticipation, my rescue exertion was wearing me down. My breathing was heavy, and I was growing tired, but I still had more lives to bring to safety. I had no time to think about my approaching fatigue; I needed to allow my survival instincts to keep me moving.

"I brought the others out of the original tunnels where the floor collapsed," I informed Taffy. "But only as far as I could to the larger cavern. I will need to fly them individually now."

"Well done," she applauded. "Your quick thinking is admirable—you really are a smart man."

"There's something dangerous, though."

"Oh?"

"I don't know what, but something is moving around in the depths, possibly the origin of the collapsed tunnels." Taffy handed me a water canteen and her gray eyes widened with concern. "Lillie can explain more, but I saw something. A glowing red light; it was moving rocks as it made a horrible crackling sound and filled the air with sulfur." I paused to drink the stagnant water, making loud gulps, and Taffy pondered, staring into the abyss below. She stood with her one hand on her wide hip, the other scratching the top of her head underneath her safety glasses.

"Then you must hurry and bring back the others," she said while keeping her gaze on the pit. "Whatever creature of the depths is down there—it is most likely one best left undisturbed. Don't get curious."

"The lanterns need more fuel, too." She nodded, and directed the workers to replenish the lanterns. I poured water over my face, and rubbed the trickling water across my forehead, and I rested, but only for a moment while the lanterns on the pulley platform were refueled. I looked down at my sleeves that were permeated with blood, sweat, and infection from Jamie's injury. I untied the cord, removed the sullied sleeves, and threw them on the ground. I also examined my tunic and trousers, wondering how I was to ever fix the tears or clean the deep stains of dirt and blood.

Perhaps Lillie can help me.

I smiled, thinking happily of life after I would bring Lillie to safety, allowing the thoughts to energize my mind as I reentered the cavern and flew back to the survivors, following the guided path of the yellow twine. I wanted to fly Lillie back next, but she refused, causing me to only slightly resent her selflessness. I knew that there was no use arguing, yet that heavy weight of guilt returned to my chest.

"Stay here," I said to her before leaving with Aro, who, on the other hand, happily volunteered to leave next.

"Of course," Lillie said, her voice changing. "Where else would I go?" She wrinkled her nose and displayed a witty smirk. After all that had happened, I was happy to see that her sense of humor had refused to fade. Even though her eyes were darkened, her face was covered in dirt, and her white hair was filthy and tangled, I thought her to be stunning, her very presence tantalizing, and I wanted more than ever to wrap my arms around her and kiss her lips.

As Aro tugged at my arm, Lillie's eyes glistened as she examined my bare, muscular arms, and she bit her lower lip.

"Let's go, please," Aro begged. "You can flirt with your girlfriend another time."

I took one last glance at Lillie's teasing behavior, savoring her admiration but also my strong attraction towards her. After all she had gone through, perhaps she really did love me and this was my final proof that I would do anything to be with her.

I then picked up Aro into my arms who wrapped hers around me, and I set off into the cavern, flying fast and efficiently, anticipating the final stretch of my rescue efforts. I felt at ease flying through the cavern as my keen sense of intuitive direction set my path in motion. Similar to how I flew my familiar flight paths from my mountain home, a subconscious compass led me directly where I needed to go. I remembered the columns to move around, the rock formations, and the stalactites to avoid.

"So, how did you actually meet Lillie?" Aro asked as she raised a curious brow. "I always knew that she was different. Didn't realize how strange she really was."

"Lillie isn't strange," I remarked, and stayed quiet as the woman scoffed. For a moment, I regretted saving someone who Lillie was willing to put before herself, only to be sneered at from a distance.

"Well, still, how does a low-life like her meet a strong, handsome guy like you? You got any older brothers? A single daddy?"

She continued to ask me insensitive questions, and I breathed a sigh of relief as I saw the refueled lanterns brightly illuminate the other side of the cavern, guiding me to the surface. I placed Aro in the safe environment provided by the surrounding workers, and ignored her last request of being *hooked up* with an older Teragane, and I immediately returned to the cavern.

Perhaps Lillie will let me take her next—who knows what Tim will say to me while she waits. Even so, I'm almost done. Two more trips, and Lillie will be safe. Everyone will be safe at last.

I followed the twine, guiding my path through the darkness. To help ease the insensitive remarks from Aro, I thought about Lillie's admiration and sarcasm. I enjoyed the flirtatious behavior, and couldn't wait to tell her officially how I felt about her—maybe she will also tell me about her true feelings.

Although my eyes diligently followed the line of the yellow twine, I did not feel the need to fully depend on it anymore; I only followed it to continue establishing the familiarity of the path. Soon, I could fly without even looking at it. A few more trips, and I would establish this path forever in my mind.

And only in time to never come here again!

Then, like a dropped stone plummeting into the murky waters of a lake, it vanished.

I halted my flight path, pausing in mid-air, and my eyes scanned the abyss below.

The twine! Where did it go?

I looked ahead. I could barely make out the shapes of the tunnels. My heart began to beat fast, and panic overwhelmed my body. I breathed heavily while glancing around, trying to calm the fear overtaking my body.

Just follow your instincts.

I pulled out the compass and pointed it north. I directed my flight, intuitively picking up on the correct path again. The fear of losing the twine dissipated as I allowed my instincts to guide me, but new thoughts overwhelmed my mind.

Did the twine break again? Maybe by accident? Did it get moved from the rocks?

Yes—maybe Tim or Lillie tugged on it, and it came loose from its perch between the rocks where it had originally broke.

Everything is fine. I've done this flight path so many times now. I can easily just follow my instincts. Everything will continue to go as planned.

I'm almost done.

I ascended toward the tunnel, steadying my breathing as I drew near. My heart wanted to see Lillie's face again. I wanted to hear her make another sarcastic comment. I wanted to banter back or nudge my face near her ear. My mind wanted to truly believe I was almost done.

I expected to see the light of the lantern and two figures waiting for me.

But I did not.

I landed inside the round tunnel. It was empty.

That eerie feeling returned.

The air was warm and permeated with sulfur.

Terror and fear reentered my body as I once again stood alone.

Where is Lillie?

CHAPTER TWENTY-FIVE

WHEN A BAD DREAM CAME TO EXISTENCE

I wanted to shout, scream, or call out for Lillie and Tim. But my instincts said otherwise.

Something was not right. Something happened while I was gone, something terrible enough to cause them to leave. I looked down the steep drop off. I did not want to believe that they both fell, so I decided to search the tunnel first. Maybe they went back for something?

I walked into the passage I knew all too well. As fearful outcomes surged through my mind, the hairs on the back of my neck rose, and my heart raced within my chest. I had hoped I would simply stumble upon the missing Tamarines lingering somewhere in the tunnel—maybe Lillie got curious, maybe they needed to relieve themselves—anything but the reality I was afraid to find. I was sick of the nightmare; I wanted it to end.

I wanted to be free from it all—the gloom, the constant fear of losing Lillie—I wanted to wake up from the bad dream.

I am so close. We are almost out of this darkness. When will it be over?

I heard the dreaded sound of rocks being unearthed. The walls of the tunnel began to vibrate. A scream. More collapsing rocks.

So, I ran.

I ran with great strides, lowering my upper body and wings to increase my speed. The sounds ahead echoed through the shaking tunnel, blurring my vision for a moment. The smell of sulfur and freshly unearthed rocks saturated the air. A loud final crash, then silence.

I ran until I saw the glow of the second lantern, but no one was near it, so I jumped over as it lay cracked and flickering.

I stepped into the large opening before the tunnels, pausing as I gasped.

It looked completely different. It was covered in disheveled rubble. The tunnels were indistinguishable, and different piles of collapsed rocks filled the area, except for one tunnel—a new one.

It glowed a fiery red radiance, and the entire area smelled strongly of sulfur, smoke, and burning flesh. The air was also permeated with ash and dirt, making it difficult to breathe. Rubble fell from above, creating a terrible scene before my eyes.

I looked around; sweat dripped from my forehead, and I pushed my hand through my dirty, tangled hair.

"Lillie!" I finally cried out. Rubble shifted on the west side of the area as a body emerged from underneath a pile of small rocks.

"Lillie!" I ran toward her. She was covered in ash and dirt as she pushed the rocks off herself.

"It killed Tim!" she cried upon seeing me. "It killed him!" I moved her tangled hair from her eyes, revealing cuts dripping with blood and tears. I shushed softly as she whimpered while grabbing my arms and digging her nails in a tight grip.

"He's gone!" she cried. Her eyes looked hazy in the low light of my lantern. "I couldn't stop him!" Before I could answer, the ground began to shake. I turned and looked at the newly formed tunnel.

Deep within, that mysterious red light glowed, and it grew stronger by each passing moment, and smoke began to disperse from the opening of the tunnel.

"We need to go," I said, and I grabbed Lillie. I pulled her up, removing her completely from the rubble. I ran, holding Lillie in my arms, and her hands clutched me tight. I jumped over the broken lantern, running faster than ever before.

I focused on the path in front of me, refusing to glance back as the sound of crashing rocks came from behind. The air became thicker with sulfur and smoke. An extraordinary increase in heat on my back and wings informed me that the creature, the terrible nightmare, was fast approaching.

"There it is!" Lillie screamed near my ear, yet that was the least of my worries. I increased my speed by flapping my wings dangerously low to the ground. The outline of the end of the tunnel came into view. The horrible crackling sound from the creature was close, and a terrible new sound erupted.

"It's lava!" Lillie cried. The sound of spewing lava behind us drove a new level of fear into my heart. I could feel the ends of my wings singe, and my legs ached with each stride. One wrong step, and we would burn to death.

"Hold on!" I yelled. I jumped out of the tunnel, soaring into the cavern. Instantly, the heat subsided.

We made it out. I flew further, believing we were at a safe distance, then turned around to view the nightmare chasing me.

Smoke and lava poured from the tunnel, and a grotesque creature emerged from the entrance. It was made of molten lava and rocks, and it spewed lava from its awful mouth. Smoke rose from its flaming figure. Its eyes were made of a hollow red light, set deep beneath its horrible face, and it had a mouth large enough to engulf a person.

Its limbs of boulders, with joints of lava, emerged from the opening, and it began grabbing at the wall directly underneath it. Its body emerged completely from the tunnel, showcasing its enormous size—the size of the tunnels it had been making all along.

Then, its glowing eyes shifted up.

"Sable!" Lillie screamed.

The creature lunged into the air with a terrifying roar and immense power.

I spun around and flapped my wings vigorously.

I felt the scorching heat on my back again.

I kept flying forward, fueled entirely by survival instincts.

I saw stalactites, and dodged them, and Lillie's screaming pierced my inner ear as her nails dug into my skin.

Then, the heat directly behind me subsided.

An excruciating sound came from below. The cavern echoed with a deafening crash, and the entire area trembled. I dared not look back or below, as a terrible vibration ran through my body, and my face dripped with sweat. Lillie screamed and sheltered her face against my neck, and her nails dug deeper into my skin, drawing blood at this point.

The stalactites started falling from the ceiling. The air became thick with ash and smoke, burning my eyes.

I flew from side to side as the falling rocks came from above.

I had no time to think; I could only act instinctively in my final effort of survival.

My sharp eyes focused only on clearing the falling rubble and moving forward, regardless of the burning sensation and Lillie's gripping nails puncturing my skin.

Small pieces of rock scraped my wings and back.

The large columns I had easily maneuvered around before were falling onto its sides, breaking on impact, and rocks flew in all directions.

I kept going forward. I dared not slow my speed. I allowed my instincts and familiar flight patterns to guide me through the chaotic area that was only partially visible by the lantern strapped to my waist, but even that was hardly adequate. Adrenaline pumped through my blood, fueled by pure survival instincts. Salty tears ran from my eyes as they burned from the smoke, blurring my vision.

Keep going.

The terrible sounds began to subside as rocks and large stalactites stopped falling from above. The vibration in the area slowed down. I no longer felt any heat on my back. Still, I kept flying forward through the darkness illuminated by the glowing light of magma below. I felt Lillie's grip loosen, and she raised her head again. We still heard the sounds of moving rocks and that horrible crackling sound.

"Where is it?" she whispered.

"Somewhere below," I said with short breaths. "I don't want to look." I slowed my flying speed to a glide, allowing my wings to rest for the moment, but fear still lingered as Lillie moved her head around. I didn't know if we were safe yet. I could only fly forward, following my intuitive direction.

"There," Lillie said. "I see it. It's at the bottom of the cavern." My heart beat fast, my throat felt dry, and my eyes burned, but Lillie's presence in my arms reminded me that we had come so far.

"It's okay," she said. "I think we are safe from it. It's quite far below." I carefully kept my flying speed, but allowed myself to take a peek. When I looked down, I saw the creature.

The creature of natural elements was moving across the cavern floor with a disturbing crawl, destroying everything in its path. It spewed lava from its grotesque mouth while pieces of rubble flew from its backside, and smoke and ash rose from its magma. Behind its wake of destruction, a molten trail of lava hardened into solid rock—pāhoehoe. Fumes of sulfuric gas and ash rose from its body, filling the air with its putrid smell. Enough of its gases could suffocate one to death. Its red eyes darted back and forth as it writhed along the cavern floor almost as if it were looking for its next prey.

So. There was another monster after all.

"Is it looking for us?" Lillie asked.

"It can't get us from up here," I said, hopeful. It crashed through a pile of rocks, sending rubble flying once again, but I easily moved out of the way. I shifted my position, moving far behind it. We watched the lava creature descend further into the cavern, knocking over columns and causing only pure destruction. I steadied my flight path and maneuvered out of the way each time. The monster looked back and forth, groaned its terrible crackling sound, and continued its search—or whatever such a monster does.

"Are you following it?" Lillie asked.

"It's safer, I think. It can't see us from behind, and I can see where it flings the rocks," I said. "And, it doesn't seem too intelligent. Only destructive."

"What if it finds the mine?"

"Then everyone will be in danger."

"We have to warn everyone."

"We will, as soon as we return." The creature felt less intimidating now that I could fully see it, especially as I flew high above its destructive path. It was terrible—the worst thing I had ever seen in my life. But, with Lillie in my arms and us flying above and far behind, I felt safe for the moment. I did not know how long that feeling would last, especially when we brought the news to the other mine workers. Another wave of fear settled into my mind.

How long would it take for it to reach the people in the mine? What other tunnels will it create, causing more cave-ins?

Up ahead, I saw the light of the lanterns on the pulley platform. My heart fluttered and a sigh of relief escaped my mouth. The creature was slowly moving through the cavern, but I picked up my speed, and my wings flapped harder, pushing myself to ascend faster.

"We are here," I said to Lillie. She had gone quite cold, shocked by it all, but held me tighter as I ascended towards the hole above. I did not know what to expect as I entered the mine, but this time I had Lillie in my arms and I was never going to return to the pits of hell. Tim had died, the others were gone—there was no other reason to return.

"Lillie!" Taffy gasped, "You're here, safe, and covered in—"

"There is a lava monster down below!" Lillie cried. She let go of me, and I settled her on the ground. "It killed Tim and possibly devoured David and Mira! The creature is the cause of all this destruction. It caused the cave-ins—it—it's caused—"

Lillie slightly faltered, and I braced her with my hand on her waist. She looked frantically around, as if she didn't know who she was speaking to, waving a hand and I wondered if her vision had been impaired. The blood from the wounds on her head had mixed with her sweat, and tears streaked down her face.

"You're safe now," Taffy assured Lillie as she beckoned for other workers to come and help.

"No! It's right below us!" Lillie shouted, her voice trembling. "No one is safe! It will only continue if we do not evacuate the mine."

"She is right," I chimed while standing behind her. "No one is safe. Everyone must evacuate the area." Taffy stared at us as her usual enthusiasm began to wane.

"Just look for yourself," I said while pointing to the abyss below. "It wanders the cavern, looking for more souls to devour."

Taffy and several others walked towards the edge of the hole and looked deep within. I did not need another inspection. I never wanted to see that lava creature again. I did not want to believe that thing even existed in the first place.

Lillie and I stood in our place, but I felt her tormented figure begin to tremble even more. I slipped my hand into hers and still held her by the waist while standing behind her, but she felt cold. Her strength began to falter, and I knew that it was time to remove her completely from the mine.

A sudden vibration shook the ground, and the Tamarine onlookers gasped, and I could only assume that the creature had reached a wall in the cavern and was already creating another tunnel. I didn't know if they would enact a full-wide evacuation, or would inform others to flee while they had the chance, but I knew that Lillie was in no condition to linger. She was sacrificial for the others—it was her turn to be guided to safety.

"I'm taking Lillie home," I said out loud, and Taffy looked back at me.

"Well done, Sable," she said. "And thank you for everything you've done today. We've got it from here." I nodded in response, then whispered to Lillie.

"Let me take you home," I said while wrapping my arms around her waist. As I lifted her again, she sluggishly melted into my embrace, burying her head while the rumbling of the earth continued, and the rescue-aid workers began to scramble around.

With aching muscles, I pushed past the pain and began walking out of the dangerous mining area. I did not care for anyone's opinion; I did not want to fight anymore or solve the problem of the giant lava creature creating havoc. I did not want to think about the problem of it climbing out of the massive cavern or causing more cave-ins, wrecking further destruction, death, and decay amongst the miners.

I decided that it was beyond my capabilities or my desire to find the right choice of actions. I was reminded by Lillie's words from earlier when she had told me to forget the concepts of changing the ways of the city. She had told me to forget the idea altogether, and, at that moment, I did. Lillie's distraught demeanor and safety were all I cared about. At that moment, she trembled in my arms, covered in bleeding wounds that could easily be infected.

This mine has brought the cursed creature upon itself. May they deal with it on their own terms.

I walked along the incline of the curved tunnels, passing other pathways, following the steep trails where I knew it would lead me back to the main hub. The large cavern was busy, as usual. No one stopped; no one came up to me with concern. I heard the murmur of whispers, saw the quick turn of inquisitive glances, but I ignored it all as I moved through the hustle of the workplace.

I was shocked at first, because everything was as it was when I had first entered. The furnaces still blazed, the hammering chimed, and the carts rolled. The tragedy happening beneath did not stop the working Tamarines. The future tragedy awaiting all these people did not stop the noise. I did not understand how the very concept of life and death had no impact on the work environment. I knew what I had done was necessary. The rest was up to those in charge and those with the knowledge we brought from the depths.

So, be the outcome of what is right or what is wrong. I have no part to take anymore. I did what I thought was best.

Perhaps I understand Lillie a little better now. How can one change a system when a threat of a monster isn't enough to cause the people to flee?

Lillie's body stopped trembling, but her hands upon my chest gripped my tunic tighter. Her eyes were closed, and I could feel her warmth returning. My arms were exhausted and my legs felt like they were about to collapse, but I still marched forward.

My heart hoped that Taffy and others would do what was necessary to protect the people and to fight against the Masters who forced the workers to put their lives in danger. At the moment, I had no energy to observe such actions. I thought only to get Lillie to the forest, or at the very least the surface above this death zone. I wanted to be far from the lava creature—far from its destructive path. I just wanted to know that Lillie was officially safe from the depths and all its dangerous creatures.

CHAPTER TWENTY-SIX

WHEN THERE IS BLOOD IN THE WATER

I carried Lillie out of the mine, through the forest trail, and entered Cedrus City, officially escaping the looming underground. She directed me towards her home in a sluggish manner, but well enough for me to understand the direct path as I took each turn through the labyrinth. Everything was dark, and the streets were nearly empty, and I only heard the low hum of the city—a sound more appealing than the rumble of the underground.

My entire body ached with fatigue, but I still found the strength, wondering how much longer I could last until my body would give up. I walked through the narrow streets between the tall buildings, weaving through the vast labyrinth of the city, and I noticed the glow of the orange light in the lanterns and different windows. I no longer detested the orange flame, and I felt grateful to overcome the hatred I had once felt for it after it being a vital tool in finding Lillie.

After I carried Lillie up the narrow cob stairs, I arrived at the front door of her house and kicked it with my boot. Lillie grunted in my arms, but her head slumped against my neck. I cooed softly and kicked the door again, and noises of shuffling from inside finally erupted.

A blur of motion followed as the initial opening of the door was met with aggression, but soon turned to utter shock as both Marie and Bene exclaimed at my presence. I moved inside, following Marie, who quickly guided me to the kitchen and asked a million questions. Bene joined the interrogation with an aggressive tone, but his attitude was quickly changed as I laid Lillie upon the table and it was clear she had gone unconscious.

"You saved our daughter," Marie cried as she stroked Lillie's bloodied face. "Oh, Sable! How can we—"

"You're welcome," I quickly replied, and gazed over at her father who stood in the doorway, stiffer than a tree. The pain in his eyes was obvious, but his pride overshadowed his gratitude. Nevertheless, he nodded and grunted again while glancing down at the ground. He and Marie were wearing thin, long tunics, and I could only assume that their disgruntled attitude was on account of being disrupted in the middle of the night.

"Lillie needs a healer," I said. "She was cut by falling rocks, maybe has worse injuries that need immediate attention." Without hesitation, Bene left the room, and I heard him scramble as he left the house. It was late in the night, but I was thankful the man would seek out a healer, regardless of the time. Marie immediately began preparing a fire, claiming that she would begin boiling water. As I stood over Lillie's limp body on the table, I watched as Marie grabbed a few dark brown bottles and walked over to her daughter's side.

"Let's get her cleaned up," Marie said while rolling up her sleeves.

It took several days for Lillie to recover from her injuries. Initially, the healer and Marie took care of her wounds, cleaned her sullied body and hair, and eventually settled her in bed while I watched with a careful eye. I had no intention of leaving while she was in a lethargic state, and took care of carrying her when needed.

The healer, whom I learned was called a doctor, also examined my own injuries: the deep cut in my leg, a wound on my wing, and several cuts from sharp rocks. He treated my injuries and gave me a small bottle of medicinal herbs to help fight any infections. I asked about Jamie and the other survivors, in which the doctor claimed that he did not know anything, but would ask around and give me more information when he would return to check up on Lillie. After the man left, I felt grateful for finally understanding what exactly a doctor was in the Tamarine world.

I knew that the Sage of my own culture partook in healing abilities, although I never witnessed—or needed—such healing care from the Sage. I only knew of their existence as a precaution if anything dangerous happened or if I was struck by illness.

The doctor visited a few times as promised, and told me that Jamie would make a full recovery after finding out his family doctor was able to save his leg. Eventually, a Tamarine woman named Jadis came, claiming that she was a herbalist—a previous mentor of Lillie. She provided tinctures made with herbs, and I finally learned why Lillie had so many wonderful floral smells within her hair, including the small purple flower that was apparently called lavender.

Yet, once again, I found Lillie's world bigger than I had anticipated, fully understanding why she never could imagine leaving it all behind. No wonder she seemed conflicted.

I did not leave Lillie's side throughout her recovery. I did not care if her parents approved or not, nor did I ask for permission. I slept on the floor in her room at night, and stayed close to her by day. Eventually, Marie brought some blankets for me to sleep on, and always provided food for me to eat and help serve to Lillie while she was awake.

But both Bene and Marie kept their distance from me. Perhaps they felt indebted since I saved their daughter from the depths of the mine. I assumed that Bene knew of the cave-in—how could he not? Perhaps, on the day I first came to their house, he had accepted the loss of his daughter. Perhaps he had felt powerless to save her, but now that she was alive and recovering, he felt conflicted, unable to show his gratitude towards me—a savage of the mountain. The only thing I could grow to accept is that he did not threaten me ever again, and he even brought my items I had left in the mine—my satchel, sleeves, and cloak—stating that Taffy demanded for my items to be returned.

Marie was the opposite in demeanor. Once Lillie had been taken care of and the doctor had left, she drew a bath for me, asking me to thoroughly wash my dirty body and hair. I had cleaned myself with the warm, soapy water, feeling refreshed and rid of the nightmare of the depths. The bath water was murky with dirt and blood, reminding me of the horrors I had witnessed. Marie had offered to wash my clothes, giving me clean items to wear while doing so. The leather trousers were too large for my waist, but I used my belt to keep them up, but the loose shirt was problematic due to my wing blades.

"Hmm, maybe I can cut a hole in the back," Marie had suggested while I stood in the kitchen, wearing only the oversized trousers.

"I can go without," I had suggested, not wanting to ruin one of Bene's tunics, but the older Tamarine woman eyed me while her cheeks grew flushed, and she insisted that she would make a suitable tunic for me to wear while my clothes dried over the fire.

I didn't really care, nor did I mind dumping out the small tub of sullied water outside the house. There was a back storage room with a small window that opened up where water could be dumped. I watched the murky water fall to the ground, splashing below the small patches of moss that grew at the foot of the tree. I nearly forgot about the cedar trees, but looking behind the house, I remembered how intricate the forest city truly was. After I took the tub back and placed it in the corner of the kitchen, Marie announced that she had successfully altered the loose shirt and helped me slip it on. She had cut the back completely, but sewed ties so that I could overlap the material and loosely secure it accordingly.

Marie eventually repaired my woolen trousers, but she informed me that the detachable sleeves were torn beyond repair. However, she offered to make new ones so that I could feel comfortable in my personal attire. I alternated between my clothes, enjoying the new concept of wearing varying items untypical of my culture's rigid aspects. I had never experienced wearing anything other than what was given to me by the Sage, which was always exactly the same, all my life. The form of the loose linen shirt felt odd, yet, I enjoyed the aspect of having something different for a change.

I continued to stay by Lillie's side, often only leaving to retrieve food or stretch my wings. I sat on the floor near her bed, and listened to her breathing as she slept most of the time. Occasionally, I would stroke her cheek, or twirl the ends of her hair, and I waited for her to overcome her lethargic state of post-traumatic affairs.

After the excitement of the initial events settled, Marie's helpfulness subsided. She began keeping her distance from me and even Lillie. She left us alone, happily accepting my quick update on Lillie's wellbeing, then quickly moved along with her life.

It seemed weird to me at first, but after a while, I stopped caring and accepted the strange behavior. Even as her friends came to visit and I heard their low mumbles of obvious disdain for my presence, I ignored it all, knowing that my only desire was to be near Lillie. Her parents easily moved on with their daily lives, as if they accepted Lillie's condition and my sudden existence. Bene continued his work routine, returning to the mine every morning and arriving home before dinner. Marie's day consisted of hundreds of chores, occasional visits from gossiping Tamarine women, but then she would leave, and I would be left alone in the small house.

I could barely comprehend that the mine still functioned while an actual threat existed within its environment. I did not learn how they managed the situation or if anything else detrimental had happened. There was no conversation about it. No one came to question Lillie, nor ask about the lava monster. It was as if it had never happened.

Or, as if the life-altering events were simply forgettable.

The way Bene casually came to and from his work bothered me tremendously. He would work during the day, then return home to eat, and then smoke his pipe on the balcony. Even the neighbor Thabias would join him as if nothing had changed. Lillie's parents avoided any conversation about the mines—at least anything negative. I did not understand how something so threatening and terrifying could be simply ignored, especially after it took lives, almost Lillie's.

As confused as I was, I shifted my entire attention to helping Lillie recover. She slept most days and cried often during her waking hours. Actually, she cried a lot, but I did not mind. She did not always elaborate on why she cried, but I did need to know exactly why. I let her cry, I let her hold tight to my hand, and I wiped her tears with a clean cloth. She would often wake in the middle of the night, tossing in a frantic fit. I would then help calm her down and remind her that she was safe. All I knew was that she was safe with me to express her pain, her sorrow, and all that plagued her mind. I would listen, care, wipe her tears, and bring her food. I realized the shock of her experience was the reason for it all, and that the balance of life and death haunted her. But slowly, she recovered, and I was there for her—every step of the way.

———◆○◆———

"A monster? A creature made of lava?" Lara exclaimed one afternoon after I had just described the creature that Lillie and I witnessed.

"From what I understand," I said. "But I'm no monster expert—or rock, er, lava."

"Still, what a sight to behold," Lara said. "And you saved Lillie from it, and my brother. Jeesh, what would have happened if you hadn't arrived that day in the city?"

"I try not to think of that," I replied as I looked over at Lillie sleeping on her bed. I wiped the corner of my mouth, savoring the flaky bread that Lara had brought to share with me. She had come to visit, bringing a plethora of gifts, including bread, meat, and a bouquet of sweet smelling flowers that she had placed on a wooden cabinet in Lillie's room, claiming that she hoped it would give Lillie a faster recovery. But, since Lillie was sleeping, I invited Lara to sit on the floor with me, and I told her the details of my perilous journey.

"You really are an amazing hero," Lara declared while also looking at Lillie. I grinned, but slightly scoffed, and she narrowed her hazel eyes. "I'm serious! Not many people are willing to risk their lives for others. People are lost in dangerous environments all the time here."

"Why?" I asked as I slowly leaned the side of my arm against the wooden bed frame, and my wings folded awkwardly, but I had grown accustomed to being in smaller spaces by now.

"Huh?" Lara pondered as she looked over at the open door. "Isn't that an excellent question."

"Why don't the people take better care of each other or themselves? Why does it feel like people don't care about each other out here?"

"I don't think it's because people don't care. I think, er, well. I think there are a lot of pressures and problems around here that not everyone has the strength or power to face, you know?"

"The Masters."

"Yeah, but they are just part of the problem—it's hard to explain. A lot happens here, and there are always problems to overcome. You kinda just numb yourself to it all."

"Like what? I truly just want to understand more about how this place functions."

"Yeah, I see that. Hmm, well, I guess one example is the fight to bring food home every day. There are always problems in the fields or with food allowances, job scarcity as well. It's a daily struggle for everyone, mostly. Except maybe for the Masters or Keepers, or wealthier families."

"Why does that matter? Why are some people allowed to struggle less than others? Why isn't it equal?"

"Isn't that a fond idea."

"Why?"

"Oh, I really don't have the heart to talk about such politics. Maybe Lillie can tell you more when she feels strong enough. For now, I must return to my work." Lara stood up, then bent over and kissed Lillie's forehead. "Please tell Lillie I wish her a swift recovery and will visit again when I have time. You both are welcome to visit me and Jamie back home, too. You can also visit my uncle's bakery, and I'll give you fresh bread."

"Okay." I stood up and followed her out of the house. I could sense a shift in discomfort from Lara. Perhaps she did need to leave, or perhaps she felt uncomfortable discussing the subject of inequality. As I followed her out of Lillie's room and onto the balcony, I thanked her for the visit and the food that she had brought to share.

"Thanks for talking," I said as I wished her goodbye. "Thank you for being kind to me. I wish Jamie a swift recovery."

"Yeah, no problem. He's recovering well, although very troublesome with his constant demands," she said with a laugh. "Darn brothers, but, hey, at least he's alive. It's a cruel world out here, but it's nice to meet people who care. Thanks for rescuing my brother.

And thanks for caring so much for Lillie. Don't ever stop. You have a big heart. Lillie deserves your kindness—she deserves someone like you. So, you know, keep it up. I always wondered if she had a secret sweetheart."

With a nudge to my arm with her elbow, the sweet Tamarine woman bid me farewell, and I watched her descend down the cob stairs, disappearing into the dense city below. My heart felt heavy, yet a sense of relief overcame me. I sighed deeply as I scanned over the area. I felt determined to keep learning about Lillie's world. I wanted to continue to care about Lillie, meeting those in her life, and understanding what ties she had created after all this time.

Her world felt oppressed and full of mystery. But the people, even the ruthless ones, were carrying heavy burdens that I did not completely comprehend. Perhaps if I could understand their deepest pains, then I could feel more compassion for them and less frustration and confusion.

I entered Lillie's room again, and the smell of the flowers permeated the room. She slept soundly, rising and falling with steady breathing, and I sat down on my knees next to her bed, overlooking her. I lifted my hand to her face, gently caressing her forehead with the back of my fingers.

You deserve so much, Lillie, and I will make sure that you are always taken care of.

After some days—or more, who knows, I did not keep track nor cared to pay attention to the time passing—Lillie stayed awake longer through the day, and, soon, she wanted to walk through the forest. We left her house, and she showed me a trail outside of the city limits. We started taking this trail every day to help build her strength. We gathered spring berries and mushrooms to bring home for meals. The stronger Lillie became, the further we went. She cried less, and I noticed that her warm aura returned a little more each day.

I grew more comfortable in the city; however, I still craved the open air. In the early mornings or late evenings, I would maneuver myself to the canopy of the cedar trees directly above Lillie's house. I began breaking off branches of the overbearing cedar trees, and I created a small opening for me to exit through whenever I desired. It gave me a chance to leave swiftly and return after I had stretched my wings and exerted my pent-up energy. Although I had exhausted myself during my rescue efforts, my own strength returned, and I still desired to continue strength training. However, as time passed, Lillie's parents became restless with the situation of me staying in their house, and Marie began demanding we bring more food, stating that I alone would completely deplete their food storage by the end of the month. So, naturally, I offered to return to my fishing grounds and bring fish for all of us to eat.

"I can fly you to the river if you want," I said one morning after we ate our breakfast together in Lillie's room. She mentioned that she wanted to visit Jamie and Lara, then go gather extra food.

"Really?" she said with a smile, her tone of voice changing. "Are you sure you're not tired from carrying me around?"

"I would fly you across the greatest of forests, through the deepest of valleys, and above the highest mountain peaks."

The crimson red on her cheeks and ears grew vibrant. Her stormy undertones were slowly returning underneath her gray skin. Her green eyes sparkled as she twirled her hair. Although I knew that she was being sarcastic, my heart felt too happy to banter with humor. I was too enamored with the idea of flying Lillie across the valley, essentially entering my world.

"Okay," she said, and threw her loose hair across her shoulders. "Let's visit my friends, then go fishing."

We packed our items, changed into clean clothes, and then left the house. She directed us to another part of the neighborhood where her friends lived. We visited Jamie in his house, who was still recovering from his own injuries. The two joked and made sarcastic comments, yet I felt intrigued by their interaction. I hadn't had the courage to ask about their connection, but from the slight interactions, it was obvious that they were just friends, and any sense of jealousy dissipated.

After we left, we visited Lara at the bakery where she worked. Lillie asked to borrow a large sack for our fishing trip, and Lara obliged, with the demand for fish for herself as payment. As Lillie interacted with her friend, I found it all curious and interesting to observe. I had never seen Lillie happy with others. With her work-mates, she was distraught due to the situation. With her parents, she acted defensively and struggled with their never-ending disapproval, even after her near-death experience. With Jamie and Lara, she seemed happy, sarcastic, and definitely more amused by their remarks.

Yet these friends were people I did not expect Lillie to choose. They were twice as sarcastic and dramatic as Lillie, often exaggerating scenes and stories. Yet, was Lillie just like them? Did she also display such an inflated form of story-telling and excitement? Did I really know who the real Lillie was?

Chapter Twenty-Seven
When responsibility beckons

"I was so scared walking through these woods alone," I said as we moved along the trail through the forest leading to the meadow.

"Yeah?" Lillie said nonchalantly while she walked next to me. "Tell me the full story of how you came to find me in the depths of the mine. I'm dying to know." I grinned, then began to tell her the excruciating details of my perilous journey. She listened, nodded her head at intervals, then, finally, as I finished my tale, she tucked her hair behind her long, pointed ear, seemingly bashful.

"You really are so brave," she said, then quietly, "I would have never expected this from you."

"There is a lot more to me than you know," I replied as I looked over at her. "You are worth my bravery." Her green eyes lifted, and I smiled for a moment. But, then, she turned her face, looking forward, and she pointed to the end of the trail.

When we exited the forest and stepped into the open area of the meadow, a strong sense of tranquility filled my heart. The purple and white spring flowers were in full bloom, the bees buzzed, and the winds blew a warm breeze through the grass. I felt a sense of hope and peace upon returning to the meadow, this time, from Lillie's path.

"Feels good to be here again, especially with you," I said as I inhaled a long, drawn-out breath. My eyes scanned the area, feeling enlightened from entering the clearing from the forest—never a feat I had endured.

"Yeah, it does," Lillie replied as her eyes also darted around. It had been so many years of us meeting in the meadow, always arriving from our perspective locations. This occasion—this arrival—was momentous, and my heart could hardly contain its excitement as it pounded within my chest.

"Ready?" I asked, and I held my palm out to Lillie.

"You bet I am," she said, and grabbed my hand, our fingers intertwining, and we headed to the edge of the meadow, both skipping with excitement. The cliff was steep, dropping into the valley below that swept into vast forests. As Lillie looked over the edge, a wind blew her loose hair around, and she grinned while her eyes filled with excitement.

"Let's go," I said, and I moved my hand behind her waist and hoisted her up, grabbing her legs with my other arm. She wrapped her arm around my neck and placed her hand on my chest with a warm embrace. As she faced me, her green eyes glistened, and her smile exhibited one full of anticipation. My heart beat fast, and chills ran down my spine. Her face was so close to mine, and I savored the moment, especially as my eyes darted down to lips that had curled into a smile.

I slowly bent my knees, drawing out the intensity of the moment as I only desired to fill every waking moment of Lillie's life with extraordinary experiences and utter desire to be with me. I extended my wings to their fullest width. I could feel the warmth of the sun kiss my wings, and the breeze rustled my spreading feathers. The shadow of their massive size cast over Lillie's face, and her smile of excitement changed to a look of awe. I held my breath, savoring every sensation running through my body.

Finally, I can fully prove myself to her.

My legs pushed off from the ground with a powerful jump, and my wings guided us across the air currents. With each downward stroke, a power of precision displaced the air with a *whoosh*. Upward, my wings moved with equal deliberateness. I glided with ease, adjusting subtly through the air with minimal resistance. As the air rustled through Lillie's loose, white hair, her face of pure delight shone brightly against the sun's light.

"Try this," I said to her, but her face jolted, and her eyes widened.

"What?" she shouted, looking excited but nervous.

"Trust me," I said. "Remove your arm from my neck." She nodded and moved her arm away. I released her legs, and she swung beneath me, giving a little shriek. She gripped my hands as I pivoted her directly in front of my body, holding her close and her head next to mine. I angled my positioning into a slight decline, allowing the air pressure to keep her straight and flat against mine.

"Spread your arms!" I cheered. "Be free as you should always be!"

Like a small chick first learning of its freedom of flight, Lillie hesitantly extended out her arms. As her limbs shook, she suddenly shouted, and I could sense our connection of utter trust and love—something I absolutely adored as I drew closer to her.

"This is amazing!!"

Yes, be free, Lillie! Coast along the currents, and let me be your wings!

As we glided over the valley and forests, I directed us to the river I so often visited by myself. I was thrilled to finally take her with me. My heart beat steadily, but happily, as my dreams and fantasies were increasingly becoming real. I landed us on the riverbank, instructing Lillie to stay at that spot while I fished upstream. I left her behind, taking the linen sack from the bakery, and glided over the river, catching fish with my bare hands.

When the bread-smelling cloth sack was full of wiggling river fish, I returned to where I had started. Lillie splashed around in the river with the enthusiasm of a youngling finding the waters after a long day in the sun. Her stormy gray skin glistened as the midday sun shone brightly above. It was a warm spring day, and the cold water felt enticing. She danced around in a shallow area, twirling her green skirt.

The scene reminded me of the times I played in the river as a child and, once again, when I brought my friends. For a moment, those memories felt bittersweet. Those moments of happiness were fleeting, soon evolving into the inevitable outcome of disappointment of expected isolation destined by the traditions of old. As my world of rituals and obligations overshadowed my life, moments of happiness were hard to make on my own. However, as I watched Lillie move freely, and laugh at her playing efforts, I knew that moment would not end in disappointment—not while I stood resolved to be the master of my life.

"Dance with me!" she called with a beckoning hand and a pause in her step. I stood watching from the riverbank, still holding the sack of fish that eventually stopped wiggling.

"Come on, Sable!" she called as she twirled again. I dropped the sack of fish, securing it on the ground near Lillie's shoes. I pulled off my leather boots and rolled up my woolen trousers. I smiled when I saw my clover tattoo on my ankle, thinking fondly of the inspiration behind its occurrence. I was wearing my new shirt, but I decided to also remove it, remembering the last time I played in water I soaked through all my clothes. The warm spring sun hit my bare skin, filling my body with a pleasant sensation. Then, I flew towards Lillie, and landed near her to create a giant splash.

"Hey!" she cried while closing her eyes, and she shielded her face with her hands. I laughed as she threw water back at me. Her fiery spirit brought me joy as she came after me with vigorous splashing. The cold water hit my warm body, but I savored the happy moment.

I grabbed Lillie's hands, stopping her from gathering any more water. She tried pulling away, but I held her tight. She stopped resisting, obviously intrigued by our playful banter, and spun me around while our movements kicked up water. My heart felt so happy as our fingers intertwined while we circled together in the cold, refreshing water. My feet became numb, but my heart felt overwhelmed as we played together with pure happiness deep in our souls.

"Ah, my feet are totally numb now," Lillie said while heavily breathing. "I can scarcely move my toes."

"Me too," I replied while grinning, and nudged my nose against her forehead. She giggled, again, but then whispered that she felt tired, and I led her back to the grassy riverbank. We sat close to our items, spreading our feet out in the warm rays of the sun. Lillie's clothes were quite damp, but she smiled while hanging her head backwards, absorbing the warmth of the sun.

"I wish to live my days like this forever," Lillie said as she tilted her chin up while we sat on the riverbank.

"You can, with me," I said while looking at her. My heart began to beat fast, and that awful feeling of anxiety rose in my chest. I shifted my position, feeling nervous. I knew that whenever Lillie spoke like that, it often led to her quickly dismissing any happy or realistic ideas.

I realized, after watching her interact with the people in the city and her friends, that I did not truly know Lillie outside of my own expectations and limited understanding. I was afraid to allow hope to rise, but I was curious—after all we went through, perhaps this time would end differently.

"Yeah?" she simply replied.

"Yes, of course," I said. "Why not?"

"Hmph." Lillie grunted. "That is a good question." I waited for her to answer, allowing her time to think of her reasons and to come to her own conclusions. I looked at the river and focused on the rushing water. It was shimmering in the light, moving swiftly downstream. It was mesmerizing to watch as I waited for Lillie to find her words. Yet, my eyes darted over to her hand resting on the grass, and mine smoothly moved over and rested on top of hers.

"Remember when I told you that I did not have the luxury to think of my life as my own?" she finally said while removing her hand from mine. She folded her knees and held her legs with both arms.

"Vividly," I replied, and the abandoned affection left my lingering hand to fold into a tight fist. The memory of our previous conversation sent a shiver down my spine, and my neck stiffened. I shifted my position, leaning forward, and I continued to stare at the river.

"My whole life has been doing things for others," she started. "In light of recent events, I guess I realized that if it wasn't for you, I would not be here right now."

"Mmhmm," I grunted, my throat becoming dry.

"I guess it feels like my life isn't my own, you know?"

"Yeah."

"Today, for once, it feels like my life is my own." Lillie rested her head on her knees, her face angled toward me. I slightly twisted my neck, and looked at her. She began grabbing grass, ripping it from the earth, and clenched her fists.

"I'm being summoned to return to the mine," she said while clutching the tufts of grass.

"What?" My heart pounded, remembering Taffy's declaration of Lillie working with her. Yet, the very idea of Lillie returning to the pits of hell caused me to jolt my head up.

"I—uh."

"You can't go back!" I raised my voice while leaning closer to her. I didn't want to control her—no, that was never my intention, but I also could not idly stand by her side as others around ignored the horrors forced onto her innocent soul.

"I don't want to!" she shouted while lifting her head, her eyes welling with tears.

"You can't! It's too dangerous and—well, life threatening. It only brings you misery. You're worth more than that place. You can live a better life—a life with me." I wanted to reach for her, but I resisted my urge, but, suddenly, she moved towards me, grabbing the back of my neck, and she pulled herself close. "You don't have to go back. Not while I'm here. You never have to return to that death trap. Ever."

"I think you're right," she said as she slid her other arm over my shoulder. Her hand on my neck tugged at my hair. I wrapped my arm behind her and grabbed her waist, pulling her directly onto me as I leaned backwards. Her chest came to mine, and I could feel her heart beat fast. I savored the moment, breathing heavily as I allowed her warmth to overwhelm my nervous system. Her arms around my neck felt tantalizing, and her eyes staring into mine were invigorating.

"Stay with me," I said with a shallow voice. "I will do whatever it takes."

"Well then," she said while moving closer. The vibrations of her voice sent shivers down my spine. My heart continued to beat like the hum of a honey bee's wing, and I held my breath. While her fingers twisted my hair, I felt paralyzed as her entire body rested upon mine. Then, as if my mind couldn't take another moment of her proximity, she nudged her nose against my ear, whispering softly. "I guess we have some things to talk about if you're gonna stick around."

"G-go on," I said with a shaky voice. Lillie leaned her head back, and her eyes darted while her finger still twisted my hair. She looked at my eyes, then at my lips, teasing me like a warm sun before a winter storm. She continued to play with my hair as her eyes darted as if she were truly subjecting me to utter submission. I raised my eyebrows, and the rest of my body froze in anticipation. Then, a mischievous smile crossed her face.

"Let's start a fire," Lillie stated. "I'm pretty hungry."

After a final tug of my hair, paralyzing me to a stupor, she pushed herself away from me, releasing my hair, and stood up to gather the needed supplies for the fire. The sensation of her closeness numbed my body for a moment. My neck quivered as I stared at her, feeling utterly tantalized. My bare chest heavily rose as I gave a deep sigh as I gathered my breath.

What a tease! Yet, she seems to finally accept my love—ah, Lillie. I cannot bear another day without you.

As we gathered wood, we played and teased each other. I felt so liberated, and Lillie openly expressed her joy once again. Perhaps she finally felt the wonderful sense of being free. Maybe she felt reciprocated love and kindness for the first time.

I was ready to hear her heart, her thoughts, and all the mystery of what was keeping her from accepting my love completely. I was ready to understand her and know Lillie better than anyone else. I was ready to tell Lillie exactly how I felt. I was ready to create a life with her. Her smile and laughter told me that she was also ready.

The tantalizing feeling of her on top of my chest overwhelmed my heart. My neck tingled with excitement as I savored the feeling of her hands playing with my hair, and I excitedly thought about exploring such feelings once again after our bellies were full of cooked fish and after we thoroughly discussed what a future together would look like.

Finally, we can be happy together...forever.

When the fire had been started and the fish were cooking, Lillie and I sat together along the riverbank. She plopped herself next to me, and I immediately grabbed her hand. I no longer felt her cold rejection as she worried about life; a sense of acceptance was noticeable with her change of demeanor.

Yes, we would finally be happy together.

Yet, in that moment, the hairs against my neck rose, and I lifted my head, feeling suddenly alarmed. I sensed a disquieting presence, and realized that I was in the valley of my territory with Lillie—another realm of threats. Was it bears? Wolves, boars—Teraganes?

I tried shaking it off, but the fear of the something threatening made me jolt up, and, this time, I released Lillie's hand.

"Everything okay?" Lillie asked, her voice sounding concerned.

"Yeah, I think so," I said. "I want to check the area. I want to make sure we are safe."

"Safe? From what?"

"Maybe bears." I looked down at her still sitting near the fire cooking our afternoon meal, and I patted the top of her head. "Nothing to worry about. I just want to look around. Stay here."

I moved away from Lillie and the fire, scanning the area as I trudged along the grass with my bare feet, following the curve of the river. My sharp eyes shifted as I continued searching for the source of my discomfort. While in the open valleys of the Teragane territories, I knew my chances of being spotted by another were high, indicating that my instincts were never wrong, and my heart rate quickened as I anticipated what I would find.

A shiver ran down my spine. Not from the cold—not from the lack of clothes—but from something I saw.

Across the river, I spotted the source of my instinctual alarm.

A cryptic figure lurked within the shadows of the forest beyond the shimmering waters.

The face of an owl mask.

And they were watching me.

www.ingramcontent.com/pod-product-compliance
Lightning Source LLC
Chambersburg PA
CBHW020619110726
47899CB00002B/574